Praise for F

"Rosanne Bittner proves time and time again that she is a master at her craft! Highest praise should go to Rosanne Bittner for creating characters that are unforgettable!"

—*Literary Times*

"Rosanne Bittner's stories are powerful because she creates memorable characters who enlighten readers as they rekindle the magical spark that belonged to the first people to love this land."

—*RT Book Reviews*

"There's danger at every turn in Bittner's exciting tale of romance in the Old West, and readers will find themselves wrapped up in the adventure."

—*Booklist Online* on *Paradise Valley*

"One of the most powerful voices in Western romance returns with a gritty, earthly, moving love story that captures the true spirit of the West. Bittner sweeps readers away with a powerful tale."

—*RT Book Reviews* on *Paradise Valley*

"Excell[...] racters
to capt[...] on that
special [...]ed."

Hearts

To my three grandsons, Brennan, Connor, and Blake, for bringing me so much joy and because they like "shoot 'em up" Westerns as much as I do!

One

July 1866

ELIZABETH CLASPED HER GLOVED HANDS IN HER LAP, irritated by the way the two men riding with her in the stagecoach kept staring. The train she rode as far as Chicago had boarded several other female passengers, most of them respectable wives or teachers. From there on, her means of transportation was stagecoach, and as she traveled farther west, the number of women passengers dropped off dramatically until finally, upon leaving Virginia City and heading north into Alder, Montana, she was the only one left. She was now left with two bearded, tobacco-chewing men who she guessed were prospectors headed for the same gold town. It was no wonder no women were left. Why would any decent woman want to come into such rugged, desolate country?

To get away from something worse back home and never be found.

She had no experience being completely on her own, and she was scared to death, but she was determined to show confidence and not let anyone know she had no idea what she was going to do next—or that she was terrified of this wild country. Leaving what little civilization Virginia City had to offer and heading alone to an unsettled, remote gold town made her wonder if she'd lost her sanity, and others would probably wonder the same. She told herself not to appear too jittery. Such behavior only brought suspicion. Was that why the two men kept eyeing her? She dared to meet their gaze and took a deep breath for courage. "I will thank the two of you to stop staring at me," she said.

The coach lurched over a rock, then swayed side to side as the team pulling it made its way around a corner. Elizabeth clung to a hand strap hanging from above and prayed she wouldn't vomit from the constant sway, or fall right into the laps of the men opposite her. The bustle at the back of her dress made it impossible to sit fully back into the seat, and she was tempted to find a way to rip the annoying bunched material completely off at the next stop.

The coach finally steadied and Elizabeth pulled aside a canvas shade covering the window and swallowed in terror at how close they were to the edge of the rugged mountain road. She couldn't even guess how deep the canyon that yawned just a few feet away might be.

One of the men tipped his hat. "Ma'am, you have to excuse us," he told her, "but there ain't anyplace else to look in here except across to you, and I have to say, you're a right pleasant sight. You ain't dressed like no kind of woman who'd be out in places like this, and a woman young and pretty as you is gonna get stared at plenty, 'specially when you reach Alder."

Elizabeth looked away from the terrifying depths just beyond her window, deciding it was better not to watch. She raised her chin and eyed the men boldly. "Thank you for the compliment," she answered, not wanting to appear totally rude.

"Where are you from?" the second man asked.

Elizabeth hesitated. "St. Louis," she lied. She offered no further explanation as she brushed dust from the overskirt of her blue polonaise silk dress. She had only three other dresses with her, having packed quickly to make her hasty exit from New York City. To preserve what little she had to wear, she'd worn this dress for days now and couldn't wait to take a bath and change clothes once she reached her destination. The ruffles at the hem were already looking frayed from brushing against nothing but dirt and gravel in this forsaken land. The dress's short train was completely tattered, and from what she'd seen women wearing out here, nothing she'd brought with her was suitable for life on the Western frontier. No wonder people stared. She hated being conspicuous. That was the last thing she wanted.

The first man who'd spoken began coughing in an ugly wheeze that ended with him leaning out the window and spitting. Elizabeth struggled not to make a face at the crude act. He leaned back inside, folding his arms. "Well, ma'am, there is pretty much only two kind of single women who go to a mining town like Alder. Either they are lookin' to find a husband…or, uh…they are the kind who don't want no husband…the kind that goes to a place like Alder to get rich by makin' a *lot* of men right happy, if you know what I mean."

Elizabeth thought a moment, then gasped, her eyes widening in horror and her cheeks turning crimson. "I am not going to Alder for *either* reason! My personal choices are my business, and I am *not* a…a…lady of the evening. How dare you even suggest such a thing!" The remark made her so angry she fought tears.

"Well, ma'am, you can't blame a man for askin'. I mean, you're right damn pretty, with that dark hair and them green eyes and your youth and all."

The second man nodded. "You're gonna have a time of it when men see you step off this coach in Alder."

Elizabeth straightened. "I can handle myself. I'll be just fine. I…I plan to teach," she lied, remembering the schoolteacher with whom she'd ridden to Virginia City.

The two men looked at each other and rolled their eyes. "Teacher or not, a woman like you is takin' a big chance in a place like Alder. You'd best buy yourself a gun, ma'am, or somethin' else for protection. Fact is, you should have stayed in Virginia City. It's still pretty rough there, bein' a gold town and all, but it's a lot bigger and more civilized than Alder."

Elizabeth realized they were probably right. "Thank you, sir. I'll consider that."

The man chuckled. "Ain't been called sir in my whole life," he joked. "Most call me Spittin' Joe, and this other man here is Whiskers."

Spittin' Joe and Whiskers! Elizabeth nodded to them. Surely in Alder there were a few decent women, and hopefully men with a bit of education who dressed respectably and kept themselves shaved. She felt a renewed anger and deep sorrow over what had happened to her mother, and hatred for the person who'd terrified her, forcing her to make the decision to run off to a place like this. If she didn't have to find a good place to hide, she never would have considered such a destination. Alan Radcliffe would surely never dream of looking for her in a remote gold town deep in the mountains of Montana. A new life...a new name. In spite of how lawless a place like Alder might be, her situation there would be better than what she'd left behind.

Her thoughts were interrupted when she heard a bang in the distance and something pinged against the side of the coach. The driver yelled out, "Hah! Hah!" and the horses took off at full speed. Elizabeth grasped the hand strap again to steady herself and held on to her lace bonnet with her other hand. "What's happening?"

"Goddamn robbers!" Whiskers answered. "You'd best get down, lady!"

More shots rang out, and before Elizabeth could duck to the floor, the coach careened one way and then another so that she instead simply had to hang on for dear life. She heard gunfire from up top and realized it must be the second man riding there. They'd called him the shotgun, and now she knew why. His job was to shoot back if they were attacked. She peeked outside again and was relieved to see they were now in open country and not about to go flying off the edge of the road into a canyon. She heard shouts and whoops behind them. More shooting!

"It sounds like Indians!" she wailed.

Spittin' Joe took a handgun from where it was stuck into the waist of his pants. "No, ma'am, it's outlaws.

I think this coach might be carryin' a payload for the bank in Alder."

Dear Lord! Elizabeth wondered if she would die right here before ever reaching her destination. Spittin' Joe leaned out and fired a couple of shots, then cried out. His body jerked back inside at the next veer of the coach. Elizabeth screamed at the sight of a bloody hole in his head. He slumped to the floor. In spite of his unkempt condition and crude habits, Elizabeth couldn't help feeling sorry for him.

"God, save us!" she wept, sure she'd die today after all.

"Hell, I don't even have a gun," Whiskers complained as he leaned over Spittin' Joe and ducked down. "I think Joe dropped his outside the window when he was shot."

The coach swayed and tipped, and Whiskers fell against Elizabeth's shins. There wasn't even room for her now on the floor of the coach. She cringed as far into a corner as she could as more bullets hit the vehicle. She heard cries from up front and realized either one or both men in the driver's seat had been shot.

The coach careened in the other direction then. Dust rolled, and the approaching men shouted more war whoops and continued firing their guns. Then there came a cracking sound. Elizabeth hung on for dear life when the coach tipped completely to the right and crashed to the ground, sliding on its side for several feet. Elizabeth tumbled forward, then sideways, hitting her left shoulder on something. The blow sent an excruciating pain through her shoulder and arm, and she cried out as the coach finally came to a halt.

Elizabeth momentarily choked on the dust that filled the interior of the coach. When things cleared, she found herself lying on top of Spittin' Joe and Whiskers. She raised up slightly to see that Whiskers's head hung grotesquely crooked, his neck obviously broken. The sight brought back an ugly memory. *Mama!*

What was happening? What should she do? She put a hand to her breast, where her secret and most valuable possession was hidden in her bodice.

Voices! Men's voices—all around the coach. Laughter! Curses!

"Find the money box!" someone yelled. "And see who's inside. Maybe they have money on them."

The pain in Elizabeth's shoulder was so intense she thought she might pass out. She struggled to keep her wits and her consciousness. She gasped when someone flung open the door above her. A man looked down at her, then grinned and shouted, "*Yahoo!* Look what I found!" He grabbed her right wrist and yanked her up and out of the coach. Elizabeth screamed from the pain, then fell to the ground. She rolled onto her back and looked up at the five men who'd gathered in a circle around her.

"Whaddya think, fellas?" one of them asked. "Should we search her?"

All five men were unkempt and scruffy, with scraggly hair protruding from under filthy, worn hats and soiled clothing. All were well armed. When they grinned, they showed yellow teeth, and some no teeth at all.

"I reckon we'd better," one of them answered. He was fatter than the others, and his belly wiggled when he laughed. "Women tend to hide their valuables down inside their…uh…*valuables*…if you know what I mean."

They all roared with laughter, and the fat one reached down to grasp the front of Elizabeth's dress.

The necklace! No, it was hers! She couldn't let them take the necklace! She kicked the man in the groin, and he let out a yowl. The others laughed more, and one of them made ready to finish what the first man started. A terrified but furious Elizabeth folded her arms tightly over her chest and scooted away.

"Get away from me you stinking, ugly, hideous rabble!" She felt faint from the pain in her shoulder.

All five men just laughed and hooted, one of them holding his privates.

"She's a fighter," another remarked. "This is gonna be fun!"

Just then, a shot rang out. "Step away from the woman or die!" a deep voice ordered.

All five men looked in the direction of the voice.

"Jesus Christ," one of them muttered. "It's Mitch Brady."

"Sonofabitch!" another cursed.

Elizabeth managed to quickly sit up. She looked in the direction of the outlaws' stares and saw a big man on a big horse. He slowly rode closer, and Elizabeth could see he wore two bandoliers crisscrossed over his chest, one six-gun in a holster at his side, and another in his hand, pointed at the outlaws. Two rifles were secured on either side of his saddle, as though he was prepared for war. He was so dangerous looking that Elizabeth had to wonder if he was just another outlaw

come to shoot these men so he could have the loot…
and her…for himself. Maybe he was the leader of
these outlaws.

"There's five of us, Brady," one of the outlaws
reminded him.

"Do you really think that concerns me?" the
man answered.

"Hell, it should." One of the men pulled a gun
and Mitch shot him down just as a second man fired.
Elizabeth watched in shock as the second man's bullet
grazed his side. Mitch barely flinched and immediately
shot down the second man. The man Elizabeth had
kicked ran off, but before he could get far, Mitch shot
him in the back.

The remaining two men stood frozen.

"You'd best drop your weapons," Mitch told them.
Dear God, who are you? Elizabeth wondered.

Mitch glanced at her, and against a very tanned face
his eyes looked as blue as the Montana sky behind
him. That one look felt almost physical in its force,
and it left Elizabeth breathless.

"Welcome to Montana, ma'am," he told her in a
deep voice. "You'll be fine now."

Elizabeth couldn't find her voice. She grasped her
shoulder and looked down at the bloodstained skirt of
her dress, feeling faint. She leaned against the roof of
the overturned coach, wondering if this was all just a
bad dream.

Two

MITCH BRADY ORDERED THE TWO REMAINING OUT-
laws to strip to their drawers.

"You bastard!" one of the men growled as he began
undressing. "You just murdered Cal!"

"And either he or one of you murdered Billy
and Juno, caused this accident, and meant to put the
woman there through hell and maybe kill her too.
Now, get your clothes off!"

"Whaddya gonna do, Mitch?" the second man
grumbled. "Hang us right here? Lord knows, you and
them vigilantes you run with wouldn't think nothin'
of it."

Mitch grinned. "Be glad there is a woman along.
I won't hang you in front of her." He waved his six-
gun at the men. "That doesn't mean I won't shoot
you if you don't hurry up getting those clothes off.
You aimed to humiliate her. Now you can suffer
some of the same by stripping in front of her. Besides,
a man in his underwear and no boots has a hard time
of running off to hide, in this country. I'm going to
have to leave you here for a while, so I'm not taking

any chances, even though I intend to truss you to that stagecoach till someone comes for you." He walked closer, carrying handcuffs.

"Leavin' us here in the hot afternoon sun—chained like animals?" the first man asked. "You gonna leave us some water?"

"Be glad you're alive, boys, water or no water. Billy and Juno would love to be sitting here chained to a wagon wheel rather than lying over there dead!"

The men hurriedly finished undressing and sat down. Mitch cautiously approached, holding his six-gun in one hand, the cuffs in the other. He warned both men that if they tried anything, they knew damn good and well they would die. Elizabeth could tell the men knew it. They could have tried attacking Mitch, but they sat still while he cuffed them to a wagon wheel. Profanities spewed from their mouths.

Mitch stepped back and holstered his gun. "You're just describing yourselves, boys." He walked over to Elizabeth. "You injured? You look like you're in a lot of pain."

Elizabeth managed to find her voice. "My left shoulder. I think it's broken or something."

Mitch leaned down and grasped her good arm, helping her to her feet. He turned her around and plied her shoulder. Elizabeth screamed from the pain. "Please don't touch it!"

He turned her back around, his blue eyes holding her gaze intently. "It's dislocated. I can fix that for you. It'll hurt bad when I do it but will feel a lot better afterward."

Elizabeth backed away slightly. "How would you

know that's what's wrong? I'm not sure what you are, mister, but I know you're no doctor!"

He grinned again, his teeth surprisingly straight and white. "Ma'am, out here you soon learn to do your own doctoring. Real doctors aren't much handy, and if I can do something to help your pain right now, why wait? The pain will only get worse."

Elizabeth started to object, but he suddenly grabbed her left wrist and gave her arm a jerk. The surprising move brought a choking gasp and shocking pain that nearly caused Elizabeth to pass out. She bent over from the pain and Mitch grabbed her around the waist to support her.

"Why did you do that?" Angry tears came to Elizabeth's eyes. "I never said you could."

"Needed doing, that's all. If I'd warned you, you would have kept resisting. It's easier to set a bone or a bad sprain when the person is completely relaxed and unprepared."

"Well, right now I'm agreeing with some of the names those men called you," Elizabeth fumed, fighting more tears.

"Call me what you want. You'll soon learn that things out here are a lot different than where you came from. I don't know exactly where that is, but it sure as hell isn't any place west of the Missouri River." He led Elizabeth to the shade of a tall pine. "Sit down here. You're bruised up pretty bad—could be hurt in other ways I don't know of. I'll take you to the doctor in Alder."

Elizabeth sat down on a flat rock, appreciating the shade. She hated to admit it, but her shoulder truly did feel a bit better. She met Mitch Brady's eyes and looked him over. He was indeed tall, with shoulder-length sandy hair and a square jawline. His blue checkered shirt looked decently clean under the leather vest he wore over it, with the crossed cartridge belts over that. He was the picture of danger and had an air of outlaw about him, even though he'd just saved her from the same kind of men. "I know your name is Mitch Brady, but what are you doing here? Are you an outlaw, too?"

Mitch removed his hat and ran a hand through his thick hair. "Some say I'm no better than one, and I guess I came close to that side of the road at one time, but the thought of jail or hanging at the end of a rope just doesn't set well with me." He nodded to her and grinned again. "I'm the local law in Alder."

"We told you he's a damn vigilante!" one of the outlaws yelled out. "And he's right—he ain't any better than us. You saw him shoot our friend in the back! If you weren't here, lady, we'd be hanging from the nearest tree already! Don't trust that sonofabitch! Vigilantes is the lowest form of Montana justice, and more ruthless than any outlaw ever thought of bein'!"

"My brothers will come after you for this, Mitch Brady!" the other warned. "You'll regret this!"

"You just remember what happened to Henry Plummer and his bunch because of their underhanded robberies. You know what happens when you try to rob a stagecoach and kill men doing it."

"Someday *you* will be the one at the end of a rope!" one of them answered.

Elizabeth cringed, totally confused about this man who apparently meant to help her.

"Don't listen to those two," Mitch told her. "They are Hugh Wiley and Jake Snyder—troublemakers who just went over the line. They'll pay for it."

Elizabeth frowned. "What do we do now?" she asked. "Will you help me get to Alder?"

Mitch crouched in front of her. "'Course I will. I have a couple of things to take care of here first, but I'll get you there." He squinted, studying her in a way that made her feel uncomfortable. "And you know my name, but I don't know yours. What the heck is a beautiful young woman like you doing, headed for a hellhole like Alder? You aren't much more than a kid."

Elizabeth looked away. If this man truly was the law and apparently showed no mercy, she certainly didn't want him knowing the truth about what brought her here. "My name is…" *Emma…* "Elizabeth…Elizabeth Wainright," she answered, "and my reason for coming here is nobody's business, including yours."

"Makes no difference to me." Mitch rose, grimacing.

Elizabeth noticed a growing bloodstain on his lower left side. "I'm so sorry! You've been shot! I've been so wrapped up in what just happened, I didn't realize you could be badly wounded yourself. Can I do something?"

He waved her off. "I'll be all right. It's just a flesh wound. You stay here and rest a minute." He walked into the distance to bring back the team of horses that had broken loose from the stagecoach. They were still hitched together, and he tied the four of them to a wagon wheel. Elizabeth watched as with great effort he picked up the driver and shotgun one by one and slung their bodies over the backs of two horses. He rummaged around behind the driver's seat then, finally pulling out a metal box. He held it up.

"I reckon this is what you fellas were after," he shouted to the outlaws. "This money is badly needed at the bank in Alder, and a lot of people there need it to keep their businesses going and food in their bellies."

Amid more curses and name-calling from the outlaws, Mitch tied the metal box to his horse. He returned to the coach and did some more searching, coming up with a leather mailbag and a gunnysack. He tied the mailbag to the stage team, and amid more curses he took another pair of handcuffs from his saddlebag and walked over to where the outlaws sat. He knelt down and added to their misery by cuffing their ankles to each other, then picked up their clothes and shoved them into the gunnysack. "Just making sure you two stay in your drawers," he told them. He proceeded to add the gunnysack to the items tied to the team of horses.

"You know who's going to be the angriest about you two trying to steal that money?" he asked as he worked.

The one called Hugh spit at him.

Mitch rose. "All the men who visit the saloons, and that's most of the town," he continued. "How mad do you think those men will be, knowing you tried to steal the money saloon keepers need to buy more whiskey?" He shook his head "Hell, I can't think of a better reason to hang a man. The crime of withholding whiskey money is worse than jumping a claim or stealing a horse."

Elizabeth could only wonder at the remark. What

a strange way of thinking men had out here. They hanged a man for stealing whiskey money? She watched as Mitch gathered his own horse and one of the outlaw's horses. The others had run off. He brought the two horses over to Elizabeth.

"Can you ride?"

Elizabeth nodded. "Only sidesaddle."

He towered over her, handing her the reins to one of the horses. "Well, out here you'll have to learn to straddle a horse like a man." Before she could take hold of the reins, he stepped back a little, looking her over again. "I have to say, ma'am, you're the prettiest woman I've seen around these parts in a long time. Something about you just doesn't fit out here, but I have to ask—might you be a, uh, lady of the evening, so to speak?"

Elizabeth's eyes widened in dismay. Was that all the men out here thought about? "Certainly not! And I am already getting tired of answering that question."

He pushed his hat back. "Lady, you're going to get asked again once you reach Alder, I guarantee it. You'd better be prepared for it." He shook his head. "I have to say it's a disappointment finding out you're not here for that. I would have been your first customer, you can bet on that."

Elizabeth stomped away, her anger giving her strength. She used her right hand to untie and pull her bags from the top of the stage, now on its side. "I'd like to take my things with us," she demanded, fighting tears of anger, pain, and plain old fear. She still wasn't so sure she could trust Mitch Brady, whose size reminded her of another man, a brute and a murderer who would love to find her and take her back with him…or maybe kill her.

Mitch walked up to her and took the bags. "Yes, ma'am." He carried the three bags, one small and two larger carpetbags, to the stage horses. Elizabeth tried to untie a small trunk she'd also brought with her, but the pain in her shoulder made her step away. Mitch came back to where she stood. "I'll have that trunk brought to you when I send men back out here to get those two no-goods," he told her. "I can't tie anything more onto the horses." Elizabeth noticed him cringe again, and when he turned away he stumbled slightly.

"That's it!" she told him, leaning down to pull up her dress slightly. With great difficulty thanks to the pain in her shoulder, she ripped away some of ruffles from her petticoats. "I'm tying something around that wound before you bleed to death. All I need is for you to pass out and leave me here lost in no-man's-land." Ruffles in hand, she walked closer. "Raise your arms," she ordered. "This won't be easy, with all these gun belts and weapons in the way."

"Yes, ma'am," Mitch answered with a slight grin. "And if I should pass out, all you have to do is keep following this road north and you can't help but get to Alder. There's no other way in or out."

Elizabeth worked the cloth under the cartridge belts and wrapped his middle tightly. "I prefer not to finish this trip alone, after what happened here, although I'm not so sure I'll be any safer with you."

Mitch grunted. "Hey, leave me some room to breathe."

Still angry, Elizabeth gave the cloth an extra yank, which caused her to gasp from her own pain. Ignoring

Mitch's soft chuckle, she tied off the strips. "There. I hope that will do until we get to Alder." She looked up at him, suddenly self-conscious about how she must look, bruised and filthy, her hair coming undone, her dress torn and covered with blood from Spittin' Joe, her hat gone. It seemed almost comical to realize she was still wearing gloves.

The man who returned her gaze was disturbingly handsome, and she couldn't quite read the look in his eyes—part humor, part concern, part admiration, and a hint of danger. How safe was she truly with a man who was so disappointed she wasn't a whore? He'd shot down three men with no reservation, and the remaining two seemed to truly think he might hang them on the spot. She stepped back. "I'd like to get to Alder now and find a room and take a bath and feel human again," she told him.

"I wouldn't mind the same for myself," Mitch answered. He led her beside one of the horses. "You'd better let me help you up," he told her. "You can't pull yourself up with that bad shoulder. You'll mess it up all over again."

Elizabeth put a foot in the stirrup and reached up with her right hand to grasp the saddle horn. It was too high for her, so Mitch grasped her about the waist, grunting as he lifted her into the saddle. Elizabeth was surprised at the strength she felt in the lift in spite of his injury. "It's the same for you," she said with true concern as she settled into the saddle and pulled her skirts down over her legs as best she could. "Helping me up here could have made you bleed even worse."

"I'll make it," he told her, looking a bit pale.

"Mitch Brady, you dirty, low-down bastard!" Jake cursed. "You leavin' us here all night? You'll never get to Alder and back before dark! What if wolves come? Or a grizzly?"

"You two should have thought of that before you tried to rob this stage," Mitch told them. He managed to get on his own horse, then bent over and groaned. He straightened then and looked over at the cuffed outlaws. "If a grizzly comes and makes a meal out of you, it will just save us a hanging. Right now the best I can do is send some men back here soon as we get to Alder. I'll be sure to send some of the town's most avid whiskey drinkers. I just hope they save your hanging for a town picnic and don't decide to do it right here. A hanging makes for right good entertainment."

"You'll die for this, Brady!" Hugh growled.

Mitch just shook his head and rode over to the stagecoach horses, taking up the lead reins. "Follow me, Miss Wainright." He turned to look her over again. "Please at least tell me it is *Miss* and not *Mrs.*"

Elizabeth raised her chin. "It's *Miss*," she answered. "And what about the two passengers? Are you going to leave their bodies here?"

"Have to for now. The drivers were good friends and have family in Alder, so I'm obliged to take them with us. Even so, we'll be lucky to get even these two back without the horses getting skittery. I'll send men back with a wagon for the rest."

So matter-of-fact about death, Elizabeth thought.

"How the hell old are you?" Mitch asked then.

"You're built like a woman, but I see a kid in those pretty green eyes."

Elizabeth swallowed. "I'm twenty-two," she answered firmly.

Mitch grinned and shook his head. "Yeah, and I'm eighty." His horse stepped sideways nervously, already catching the scent of dead bodies. "See what I mean about the horses?" Mitch clucked his tongue, then talked softly to the animal. "Keep lying, Miss Wainright," he added to her, "if that's even your name. Just about everybody in Alder lies about their past, their age, and their name."

Elizabeth wanted to hit him. "Do *you* lie about such things?"

"Lady, I never lie. I'm twenty-five, I'm a worthless, no-good, murdering vigilante, and I'm real disappointed you're a proper lady." He met her gaze and grinned. "See? No lies."

Elizabeth rubbed at her aching head. "Please just get me to Alder before dark, if possible. I don't want to spend the night alone with a complete stranger."

"Hell, I just saved you from a fate worse than death. Why on earth do you think I'd bring you any harm?"

"Because you're a man, plain and simple."

"And I'm about to fall off this horse. I sure as hell don't have the energy or strength to mess with a feisty thing like you, but I wouldn't even if I could. I don't make a habit of hurting women."

Elizabeth caught a hint of anger in his words. "I'm sorry," she told him. "I just hurt everywhere and want to get someplace where I can rest and get some help."

Mitch nodded. "Well, I need the same, so let's

get ourselves to Alder." He headed north on the narrow, rutted road, leading the stage horses with two dead men, Elizabeth's bags, mail, a metal box full of money, and the outlaws' clothes. Behind them lay five other dead bodies near two cuffed outlaws still cursing Mitch.

Elizabeth followed, wondering what on earth she'd gotten herself into. It was becoming more and more clear that Alder, Montana, was not an inviting place for a proper young woman alone, especially one who was only eighteen. Still, it was better than what she'd left behind...but she couldn't imagine that something as ugly as a hanging could actually be considered reason for a picnic!

Three

By the time they reached Alder, Elizabeth's shoulder ached fiercely, and she could see Mitch wavering in his saddle as though he was about to fall off. People gathered in the streets to stare, mostly men who gawked at Elizabeth. She had no doubt what some of them were wondering about her, and she felt conspicuous in her torn, bloodstained dress, her hair fallen from its pins, and some of her lower legs showing from riding astride her horse rather than sidesaddle.

She noticed one woman among the men who was dressed just like them, wearing denim pants that were too big for her and were gathered at the waist with a big belt. Was she a prospector also? Did women actually come out here for such things? Despite her reservations, Elizabeth couldn't help thinking how much more practical pants would be in a place like this.

Mitch straightened more when men began hooting and whistling at Elizabeth.

"Hey, Mitch, whatcha got there?" an old-timer asked.

"A respectable woman who needs a doctor," Mitch answered. "Is Doc Wilson in?"

A couple of men walked up to take the reins of Elizabeth's horse, while another took Mitch's. "He was there last I knew," one of them told Mitch. "Tendin' to Henry Fillmore. His horse kicked him."

Some of the men gathered around the team of horses Mitch led, lifting the heads of the dead bodies to see who they were.

"It's Billy Polk!" one yelled.

"And Juno Martin!" another shouted.

"Hey, Mitch, what happened?"

"Stagecoach got robbed," Mitch answered as more men led their horses down the street. "Two other passengers were killed. The woman here says they called themselves Spittin' Joe and Whiskers. That's all I know about them."

Elizabeth gawked at a town that was a startling contrast to New York City. Everything looked hastily built, and practically every establishment was a tavern. In the mix was a livery, a dry-goods store, an office with a lawyer sign hanging out front, what looked like some kind of excuse for a hotel, a feed store, a mining supply store, a bank, a jailhouse, more saloons, and finally the log building with a doctor sign out front.

Several women gathered on the balcony of an adjoining saloon, all wearing dresses that revealed far too much bosom, a couple of them wearing just pantaloons and corsets.

"Hey, Mitch," one of them called down. "Need somebody to nurse you tonight?"

Mitch looked up and grinned, tipping his hat. "Right now I'm too weak for your kind of nursing, Hildy."

The women screeched with laughter. Elizabeth

looked away, embarrassed. Secretly she felt a bit terrified of what life was going to be like here for her. This place was unlike anything she'd ever witnessed. She wondered if there was one man in town who actually wore a proper suit, if there was a decent woman around she could befriend, and if the doctor was even a real doctor. It dawned on her then that if this doctor was going to look at her shoulder, he might ask her to remove the bodice of her dress.

The necklace! She had to find a way to hide it someplace else without anyone knowing. Men tied the horses to hitching posts in front of the doctor's office, and too many hands reached up to help Elizabeth off her horse. She heard Mitch answering a barrage of questions.

"…left Hugh Wiley and Jake Snyder chained to an overturned stagecoach about ninety minutes south of here. I shot and killed three other men with them. One was Henry Wiley, Hugh's brother. Don't know who the other two were."

The crowd broke into a din of questions, and it was obvious they all knew the two men Mitch mentioned.

"Hugh and Henry have more brothers, Mitch. They'll be comin' after you."

"Let them come."

"Why in hell did you leave Wiley and Snyder out there?" another man asked, seeming angry. "Hugh is my good friend."

"Bobby, he turned out to be a goddamn killer and thief," Mitch answered. "He and his brother and the rest of them attacked the stage for the bank money it was carrying. Killed Billy and Juno outright and caused the stage to overturn. This woman says that's what killed Whiskers. The other passenger was shot in the head, and the lady here is hurt."

The crowd broke into shouts, fists raised, some men spouting their disbelief that Hugh and Jake would do such a thing, all angry that it had happened. Mitch walked over to Elizabeth, taking her arm. He looked pale and weak, yet Elizabeth felt comforted by the surprising strength in his grip.

"This lady is hurt and I've been shot," he shouted. "Anybody wants to be angry that I left Hugh and Jake out there, know that it's because I didn't have much choice. I had to get help for both me and this lady. I wasn't in any shape to tangle with those two killers all the way back to Alder. They're handcuffed to a wagon wheel. Some of you can go out there and get them and bring them in along with the other bodies. Throw Hugh and Jake into jail till we can have a trial!"

Now the crowd was in an uproar. Some of the men ran to get horses. They rode off shouting and whooping in excitement. Others were actually celebrating the fact that there would be a trial and probably a hanging. Men continued to stare at Elizabeth, several mentioning she was the "prettiest woman ever to step foot in Alder."

"Hope you're lookin' for a husband!" one man told her with a toothless grin.

"Hell, I'd rather she came out here to join up with Hildy and the girls!" another whooped.

There followed laughs and whistles.

"Leave her be!" Mitch ordered.

Most of them sobered somewhat and backed away. Mitch ordered the only decently clean man she'd seen among them to grab the money box and make sure it got to the bank. Mitch called the man Randy, and Elizabeth noticed he wore a gun belt. He looked younger than Mitch, and Elizabeth could see by the way he looked at Mitch that he totally respected the man and was eager to obey.

"Yes, sir!" he answered, tipping his hat to Elizabeth before hurrying away to untie the cash box. Elizabeth wondered if he was some kind of deputy.

Other men were untying and lifting down the bodies of the two drivers. Everything was chaos and commotion, and Elizabeth was grateful for Mitch's presence. He ordered men out of the way as he led Elizabeth up a couple of sagging wooden steps to a small front porch on the front of the log cabin.

"You men keep away from this woman."

"She a prostitute?" one man asked.

Elizabeth cringed. Was that all these men thought about?

"No!" Mitch turned and shouted at the crowd. "Everybody quiet down!" He looked down at Elizabeth, and she was surprised at the wisp of kindness she saw in his startling blue eyes. "Go on inside. Doc Wilson will help you."

Elizabeth blindly obeyed, hearing Mitch giving orders for someone to leave her bags on the doorstep and go see if Ma Kelly had a room for her. Inside the doctor's office she was met by a bearded man with shaggy, graying hair who introduced himself as Doc Wilson. Nearby a man lay asleep on a cot, an ugly bruise on the side of his face. Elizabeth realized it must be the man who'd been kicked by his horse.

Mitch came in behind her and closed the door, then walked over to sink into a rocker, wincing with pain as he did so. "I'm shot, Doc. Just a flesh wound, but I've lost a lot of blood."

"Get over to that other cot and lie down," the doctor answered. He was a short man, his brown eyes kind. "Ma'am, you look pale and hurt."

"I'm in better shape than Mr. Brady. Tend to him first. I'm mostly tired and shaken and in bad need of some sleep."

"Well, you sit down there in that rocker, then, and I'll tend to Mitch," the man answered.

Mitch got up and walked over to a second cot, where he all but collapsed, still wearing his boots and guns. Elizabeth took his place in the rocker.

"Get these weapons off," the doctor ordered Mitch, helping him unbuckle the gun belt at his waist and the bandoliers across his chest. "You wear enough weapons to fight an Indian war." He dropped Mitch's gear to the floor and helped Mitch get off his vest and shirt. Elizabeth quickly looked away, flustered by Mitch's muscles, broad shoulders, and hard-looking stomach. She felt uncomfortable seeing a near stranger with his shirt off. When she wrapped his wound, she'd done it all with his shirt still on.

Mitch vented a string of cuss words when the doctor dashed his wound with whiskey. "I'll have to take a few stitches," he told Mitch. "It's not going to be fun for you."

"I've been through it more than once," Mitch answered.

Doc Wilson reached over to a table and grasped a

small brown bottle, handing it to Mitch. "Here. Drink some laudanum and it will lessen the pain and help you sleep afterward. And watch your cussing around the lady."

Elizabeth stared at the blood on her dress while Mitch growled and grimaced as the doctor cleaned his wound more, then pulled catgut through the ugly rip in his side to close it up. She grimaced, feeling sorry for how much the stitches must hurt. She wondered at the kind of life Mitch Brady led.

She remembered the necklace then. Ignoring the pain it brought her, she reached inside the bosom of her dress and camisole while the doctor kept his attention on stitching up his patient. Making sure no one was looking, and glancing over to see that the other patient appeared to still be asleep, she pulled out the necklace. On the trip here she'd insisted on keeping her drawstring handbag with her because it contained most of the money she had. Quickly she pulled open the handbag and slipped the necklace inside.

She clung to the bag then, part of her terrified and wanting to cry, part of her glad she'd made it here, surviving a long, lonely journey all on her own, surviving an outlaw attack, and holding herself proudly against the prying eyes of the men outside. She could still hear shouts, as well as piano music coming from the nearby saloon, along with laughter and a couple of gunshots.

She watched Mitch Brady slug down more laudanum. Rough and rugged and ruthless as he was, he was apparently, for the time being, her only friend and protector…maybe. She'd know more when he was back to one hundred percent health. Realizing that the only person she could rely on for now was a triple-gun-toting lawman who shot men in the back and thought nothing of hangings was not terribly comforting.

So...this was Alder, Montana. The ad she'd read in a newspaper back East gave no clue as to what this place was really like, but she was here now, and somehow she'd find a way to stay without losing her sanity...or her dignity.

Four

Doc Wilson pulled a blanket over Mitch, leaving his bare arms and shoulders exposed. "Too hot to cover him all the way up, but I expect you don't want to be looking at a man's half-naked body," he remarked. He bent down and retrieved the bloody pieces of what once was part of Elizabeth's petticoat, then turned to face her. "I'll have to throw these out."

Elizabeth nodded. "That's fine. What would I do with them now?"

The doctor looked her over curiously.

Elizabeth sighed. "To answer your question, no, I'm not a prostitute, and I'm not here to marry anyone."

The doctor grinned and nodded. "I'll tend to you in just a minute." He picked up a bowl of bloody water. "Got to get rid of this stuff." He started out, then hesitated. "By the way, thanks for wrapping that wound. Mitch might have bled to death if you hadn't, not that there aren't a few men on the wrong side of the tracks who would celebrate. But most of us do care about that big lug. He keeps some sense of law around here."

Doc Wilson went out the back door, and Elizabeth stared at Mitch, wondering if he was sleeping or simply passed out. She supposed he could even still die, maybe of infection. What if he did? How strange it was that she cared…that she felt as long as Mitch Brady was around, she'd be okay. She glanced at the other patient, also still asleep, or then again, maybe just passed out from too much laudanum.

She closed her eyes and took a moment to enjoy the sudden quiet after the rough, rocking trip topped off with shooting and murder and mayhem. She ached from the long ride astride a big horse, let alone her injuries. She was glad to be in here, away from prying eyes and too many questions, shouts, and laughter and whoops and men riding off to the scene of the robbery to retrieve dead bodies and two outlaws stripped to their underwear and chained to a wagon wheel.

Doc Wilson came back inside. Elizabeth realized then that he was the first man she'd seen who wore a suit, although it looked as though it had been worn too long without a cleaning. His brown eyes looked very tired, but at least they showed kindness, and there was an air about him that made Elizabeth suspect he really was an intelligent man who truly did know what he was doing. From what she'd observed so far, one had to wonder about the truth behind every person here. *Just as they should all wonder about me.*

Doc Wilson came closer and pulled up a chair in front of her. "Now, tell me about your injuries. Is there anything I can do besides just give you something for pain? Any bleeding, broken bones that you think you might have? You look pretty bruised up."

Elizabeth shook her head. "I think I just need a bath and some sleep. Mitch set my shoulder—said it was out of place. I don't know if he knew what he was talking about."

"Mind if I feel around it?"

"Go ahead."

The doctor plied her shoulder and she winced, but it did feel better than when Mitch first touched it after the accident.

"Feels like it's in place, but once you have an injury like this, it's going to feel like someone stuck a hot iron into your shoulder joint off and on for a while. I certainly wouldn't sleep on that side." He felt down her arms. "How about the ribs?"

"It's just the shoulder and bruises." Elizabeth almost felt like crying at the doctor's kind touch and concern. She wondered what in the world brought him to a place like Alder, Montana. "Where should I go now?" she asked. "I need a place to stay."

Doc Wilson rose and walked over to a table to pick up a bottle of whiskey. He poured himself a shot. "I have a spare room with no patients in it for now. I'd like you to stay one night so I can keep an eye on you—make sure there isn't something wrong you haven't noticed yet. That happens sometimes after an accident. You wake up with a foot you didn't even know was broken, internal injuries you didn't realize you had, things like that. I just want to be sure." He drank down the shot. "Besides, with two injured men here, I can't accompany you to the boardinghouse and help you get settled. You sure don't want to be wandering alone out there amid that bunch of woman-hungry no-goods. A woman like you needs someone to accompany her at first in a place like this, and I suspect Mitch is the one who'll be doing it. I heard him telling those clowns out there to back away and leave you be."

Elizabeth shook her head. "He certainly is an unusual man. He killed three men back there as though they were nothing but target practice, yet then he was very kind to me. He was so ruthless at first that I thought he was an outlaw, too."

Doc Wilson grinned. "Some say he's no better than one, but he has his reasons for his behavior." He nodded toward the door. "Most of the men out there are basically good, too, miss. They just get a little eager when they see a beautiful woman come to town. Most of them are pretty lonely…prospectors who spend weeks up in the mountains looking for treasure. Some even have families back East somewhere." He sighed and poured himself one more shot of whiskey. "I'll have Lee Wong and his family bring over a tin tub and some buckets of hot water and you can take a bath and get some sleep."

"Lee Wong?"

The man slugged down the second shot. "Chinese family. They own the town laundry and bathhouse. His wife speaks very little English, but she's kind and accommodating. She'll help you out. She's the kind who doesn't need to understand English to know what you need." He held up the whiskey bottle. "Might you be needing a drink?"

"No, thank you, not unless you have hot water and tea and a strainer."

The doctor chuckled. "No, but I can send for that, too. There is a restaurant two doors down. Some folks figure it's a dare to eat there. They swear the steaks are made from horse meat, but I figure you can't go wrong with tea. And they do make good biscuits. I think you ought to have a couple with some jam or something—get something into your stomach."

"That would be very welcome."

The doctor frowned. "I don't recollect you or Mitch telling me your name."

"Elizabeth Wainright."

Doc Wilson nodded. "Well, Miss Wainright, you seem like an educated lady who surely came from better places than Alder. I know good breeding when I see it, and that dress you're wearing speaks of a fancy store or dressmaker back East; but then, I've learned it's best not to pry into other people's business. A lot of men here, as well as the, uh, women who live above the saloons, have unknown backgrounds and nobody cares. You're probably wondering what I'm doing here."

Elizabeth pushed a piece of hair behind her ear. "It's like you said—it's not my business."

"Well, to reassure you, I really am a doctor. Went to school at the University of Michigan and got my degree. Did pretty well till…" He looked away and poured yet another shot of whiskey. "Till I couldn't save my little girl after she was run over by a wagon. And just months later my wife and son died of cholera and I couldn't save them either." He slugged down the third shot, then held up the shot glass. "I took solace in this stuff for a while, until I woke up in an alley beat up and my money gone. I decided then that I had to just get away from all things familiar. I didn't even do any doctoring for a while, but then I guess it's in my blood, so I came to a place where most folks don't care all that much about each other. Figure if I lose a patient here it won't hurt quite so much. Know what I mean?"

Elizabeth saw the tragedy in his eyes. "Actually I do, Dr. Wilson. I've had some personal sorrow of my own that made me want to get away. I'm sorry for your loss."

He nodded. "I can see you are. Thank you."

Mitch stirred and moaned, and Elizabeth glanced at him. Even lying on a cot he looked huge, muscled shoulders and arms exposed, his still-booted feet hanging off the end of the cot. "What do you know about Mitch Brady?" she asked.

The doctor laughed and shook his head. "Only thing I know about Mitch is like I said—he has a good heart, but on the outside he's a grizzly. He's from back East, grew up in New York City."

Elizabeth's heart quickened at the remark. How odd that Mitch Brady was from the same city she grew up in. She didn't dare show her surprise.

"According to what I've learned, he left New York years ago, only twelve years old or so. The rest is for him to tell if he wants. He's bent on keeping the law around here, and most men know better than to mess with him. He's good with fists and guns, and from what I can tell he knows no fear. He came to town one day as a prospector, but that didn't work out. Then one night a man beat on one of the town prostitutes pretty bad. Mitch kind of went berserk and beat the man half to death. Once everybody saw how Mitch can handle himself in a fight…well…" He chuckled. "After that, men grew to respect him, and we had a big town meeting and decided to officially make him our sheriff. Since then he's also joined the vigilantes and roams the road coming into town from Virginia City when he knows there is money on the stage. Lucky for you that's what he did today, or your ending might have been a lot different."

Elizabeth's curiosity over Mitch was growing. "Yes, I suppose it would have." She glanced at the whiskey bottle. The doctor noticed her concern and set it aside.

"You don't have to worry about my drinking, Miss Wainright. I no longer drink until I end up in an alley. I know when to quit." He pointed to a doorway at the back of the room. "That's the only extra room in this poor excuse for a hospital. Go on inside and rest, and I'll get your tea and have Lee Wong come over here so you can clean up. I'll sleep out here on that extra cot in the corner. Tomorrow I'll take you over to Ma Kelly's boardinghouse. It's nothing fancy. I suspect it's a far cry from the hotels where you came from. Ma will put you up until you decide what you're going to do here, or if you even intend to stay." He looked her over. "I would buy myself a gun, Miss Wainright, and learn how to use it. Mitch can help you there. Most men around here hold a lot of respect for a proper lady, but the fact remains, there are bound to be others out there who will have a hard time looking at you without an ache in all the wrong places and no self-control."

Elizabeth reddened. "I will keep that in mind."

He walked to the door. "Knowing Mitch, he'll keep an eye out for you once he's up and around. He obviously already has." He opened the door. "Oh, and be prepared for a big ruckus tonight and into tomorrow. That posse will be back in a while with those two outlaws, and there will likely be a trial and a hanging. Out here such things happen fast—no formalities. It doesn't take long for men around here to make up their minds when someone tries to steal their whiskey money and kills their friends doing it. Ole Billy and Juno were well liked."

Elizabeth nodded. "I felt sorry for what happened to them." She shivered at the memory of the two dead men in the stage with her, one with his neck broken, the other with an ugly hole in his head. "And for the men who were riding in the stage with me."

The doctor went out, and Elizabeth winced when she rose to go into the spare room. She passed Mitch's cot, stopped, and stared at him for a moment. *Don't you die on me,* she thought. For the life of her she couldn't figure out why she cared. He looked so peaceful lying there asleep, such a contrast to the man who'd shot down three outlaws earlier in the day. What made him so ruthless?

She walked into the spare room and sat down on a cot, then realized she still clung to her handbag. She was alone now. She opened the handbag to reach inside, taking out the magnificently jeweled necklace she was determined to keep and protect forever. She studied the exquisite perfection of the design and the glittering jewels. "Oh, Mother, was I crazy to come here? What am I going to do with my life now? I feel so alone."

She put the necklace back into her handbag and brushed away tears. Outside, the streets remained alive with shouts and piano music…women laughing, and horses and wagons clattering back and forth… all strangers who knew little about each other. She thought about her grandmother, who came to America from England so many years ago, scared and alone. It must have been like this for her, everything strange and frightening, but she was strong and she'd survived. *I can do the same.*

After all, she might have led a pampered life the last few years, but it wasn't always that way. She darn well knew how to live the life of a working woman if necessary, thanks to her mother. And she was well educated. Perhaps, just as she'd told those miners on the stagecoach, she really could get some kind of teaching job here in Alder…if indeed there were any small children about. She realized that wasn't too likely, but she would inquire. If she couldn't teach, she'd find something else to do…certainly something that did not require wearing skimpy clothing and cavorting with men! Her horrifying experience with just one man back in New York had convinced her none of them could be trusted, and she damn well wasn't about to let any man touch her…ever again.

Five

ALAN RADCLIFFE PACED THE POLISHED OAK FLOOR OF his smoking room, his mansion of a home seeming much too empty now that his wife was dead and his stepdaughter gone. He lit yet another cigar, angry that it was taking his good friend Prosecutor Gerald Hayes so long to get here. He had to act quickly, make sure no one knew the truth about his wife's death. He wished he knew exactly what Emma had planned, where she'd gone.

He should have acted sooner, gotten Emma thrown in prison before she had a chance to leave. If only he could have learned from her or her mother where the damn necklace was, a lot of his headaches would have been avoided. Now he was left looking for a way to keep his name clear and still find Emma. Once he did, there would be ways to make her talk. Maybe she would tell him where the necklace was if he could promise to keep her from spending the rest of her life in prison, although she damn well deserved it!

He walked over to a large mirror hanging on one wall between two potted palms. Leaning closer, he adjusted his tie and smoothed back his thick, dark hair, thinking how distinguished he looked with a touch of white at the temples. The women thought him quite handsome, and he was proud of the fact that age had seemed only to improve his looks. He admired his tall and still well-built physique. He smoothed his velvet lounge jacket, glad he didn't have the potbelly most older men developed. It seemed that older, handsome, well-dressed men with money were always attractive to women, even younger ones.

"Except for Emma...the little bitch," he grumbled, turning away. If things had worked out differently, he could have made a wonderful life for her.

Finally someone thumped the heavy knocker at the front door.

"It's about time." He took a deep breath against a bit of nervousness, then walked around to sit down behind his grand mahogany desk, waiting for the maid to answer the door. He set the cigar into an ashtray, listening to the distant voices and footsteps. In a twenty-room mansion it took a while for a visitor to make it to one of the back rooms. He thought about how all the bedrooms upstairs were empty now, except his own. He couldn't bring another woman into the house until he waited a proper time after his wife's death. It irked him that he had to wait, and he decided he would find a way to sneak some young wench into his bedroom without anyone knowing. There were plenty of women who would accept pay for giving him pleasure.

The huge oak door opened, and his maid ushered Gerald Hayes inside.

"Mr. Hayes to see you, Mr. Radcliffe," she said with a slight nod.

"Thank you, Bess."

The young woman quickly left the room and closed the door behind her.

"Gerald!" Alan rose and walked around his desk, towering over Hayes as he reached out to shake the man's hand. "Glad you finally got here. I was afraid perhaps you'd forgotten our appointment."

Gerald removed his hat and shook Alan's hand. "Sorry about that, Alan. A court case I had today took much longer than I thought it would. And since I haven't seen you since your wife's death, I'd like to take this moment to extend my sympathy—also my wife's— over your loss. Sounds like it was a terrible accident."

"Thank you for your sympathy." Alan turned and walked back behind his desk, asking Gerald to have a seat opposite him. "But that is why I called you here, Gerald. It wasn't exactly an accident. Some things have been going on here that no one knew about, mainly because I didn't want to sully my stepdaughter's reputation. But things have gone too far, and now that Emma's mother is dead and Emma has run off—"

"Run off?"

Alan nodded. "I feel it's time you knew the truth. I need your help."

Gerald frowned, his bushy gray eyebrows nearly covering his eyelids when he did so. His matching gray mustache moved into a crooked dip as he pursed his lips in concern. He settled into a plush red leather chair and tossed his hat onto the seat of the chair beside him. "What on earth are you talking about?"

Deep concern and feigned sorrow moved into Alan's dark eyes. He leaned forward, resting his elbows on the desk, and looked steadily into Gerald's eyes, determined to be as persuasive as possible, giving a deep sigh before continuing.

"It was more of a murder, Gerald."

Gerald's eyebrows shot up in the other direction this time. "*More* of a murder?" He let out a gasp of exasperation. "Alan, murder is murder. There is no more or less about it!"

"Well, let's just say second-degree murder, somewhat intended but only at the last minute, not planned."

Gerald leaned back, shaking his head. "I'm afraid you'd better explain yourself, Alan. Are you saying you—"

"No!" Alan interrupted. "Not me! It was Emma."

Gerald straightened again. "*Emma!*" He rose, walking around behind the chair. "Alan, get to the heart of the story!"

Alan leaned back, rubbing his forehead. "Emma's gone, Gerald. She ran away to escape the truth before I had her arrested."

Color came into the prosecutor's cheeks. "For killing her own mother?"

Alan closed his eyes. "I know it sounds impossible, but it's true. Like I said, things have been going on here that no one knew about, Gerald. I've fought coming out with this story, wanting to protect Emma while at the same time wanting to see her put away for what she did. I loved her mother, very much, and I always loved Emma as any man would love his daughter… Stepdaughter in this case, but still like a daughter to me. She was, after all, my brother's offspring, and when he died I hoped to take his place in her life when I married her mother."

Alan turned his chair around so that Gerald could not see his face as he continued his story. "But when Emma turned sixteen two years ago, she began having...womanly feelings toward me. I assure you, Gerald, that I did nothing to entice her. My God, she was my daughter. I never told her mother about any of it...the times when Emma would deliberately put her hand on my knee...or sinfully flirt with me when her mother wasn't around. Once she came and sat on my lap in the library...and once she even..." He let out a long sigh. "She even came into my bedroom one night when her mother took that little trip to New England."

Gerald moved back around the chair to sit down as Radcliffe finally turned to face him again. "It kills me to have to tell you these things, Gerald, but I can't live with it any longer. The night Mary died...she didn't just trip and fall down those stairs. Emma pushed her."

Gerald closed his eyes and shook his head. "I find that hard to believe, Alan."

"Believe it. She was jealous of Mary...wanted me for herself. She'd come to me more than once asking me to divorce her mother so we could be together. She's still just a child, Gerald, who fell foolishly in love with her stepfather. You know how some young people can be about crushes. She wasn't thinking straight, and she was upset at the fact that I constantly turned her away. In her mind it was only because of my loyalty to her mother, and I'm sure she thought that with her mother out of the way, she could have me."

"Alan, I find this all so hard to fathom."

"A lot of families keep terrible secrets, Gerald. Mine was one of them. I didn't want others to know any of this because of the way they would think about young Emma. I didn't want that for her. I thought she would eventually meet some young man her own age and fall in love and that would be the end of it. But the night of her mother's death...she'd decided to tell Mary that she was in love with me. She lied and said I loved her, too, and we wanted to be together and that Mary should divorce me. A terrible argument ensued at the top of the stairs. I was in my bedroom changing at the time. I came out just in time to see Emma in a rage. She screamed, 'Why don't you just leave him and let me have him? I hate you!' She pushed at Mary, and Mary tripped and fell down the stairs."

"My God!"

Alan hung his head. "The worst part was when Emma ran down the stairs to find her mother's neck was broken. At first she said, 'Mama, I'm sorry.' Then she looked up at me—no tears—and said that now we could finally be together. She left her mother and came back up the stairs, pleading with me to tell others it was just an accident and not to say anything about the argument. I've wrestled with the truth ever since, and now that Emma has run off, I just can't handle it any longer."

Gerald kept shaking his head. "Emma? She and her mother seemed so close. Mary has only been in her grave a month or so."

"All the more proof of Emma's guilt. She's been gone since two days after Mary's death. I was hoping she would return, which is why I waited to tell you, but it's obvious she's not coming back. Why would she have run off if she didn't have something to hide? What more proof do you need that she committed a crime and is afraid of going to prison?"

"Indeed." Gerald scrutinized Alan with piercing eyes. "I hope you're being honest with me, Alan. This is serious."

"Why would I be anything *but* honest?"

Gerald sighed. "Because sometimes you try to get favors out of people who owe you gambling money— favors instead of the money. You did it to me just a year or so ago, when you asked me to arrest a man who owed you money and threaten him with prison if he didn't pay you off. You even threatened once that if I didn't pay you off, you'd make sure the whole city knew I had a gambling problem."

"This is different."

"Is it? I owe you nearly a thousand dollars, Alan. And I know you and your wife were having problems over your drinking and gambling. How did Mary *really* die?"

Alan's gaze darkened. "It was just as I told you. Yes, Emma and her mother were very close at one time, when Emma was little. But maturing into a woman did something to her, and her childish love for me turned into something more."

Alan stood up and walked to a window. "I sometimes wonder if it really was love, or if it was a desperate attempt to make sure she held on to the way of life she'd come to enjoy." He turned. "After all, Gerald, her mother was once nothing more than a servant to my family, and a bastard child to boot. My parents accepted her marriage to my brother, and eventually she came to be accepted into society's higher circles; but there was always that underlying gossip that she'd hoodwinked my brother into marriage so she could live like those for whom she'd worked for so many years. Having a daughter that bore our name just sealed her and Emma's place in the family."

Gerald's eyebrows moved upward. "I'm sorry to say my wife and I have thought the same thing at times, but we came to really like Mary and feel she genuinely loved your brother. But I have to say that when she married you, it raised even more questions. After all, your parents could have taken everything from her but the bare minimum for a decent life, although because Emma was their granddaughter, I doubt they would have done that. They were nice people. Of course, now they are both dead and gone, I'm sorry to say, so that gave Mary even more reason to be married to you."

Alan nodded. "Is it making sense now? Emma might have been thinking the same thing. What would happen to her once her mother was gone? Marrying me would have secured her future. With her mother out of the picture, she could make it all happen—at least that's what *she* thought."

"But surely she knew you *couldn't* have married her. It's incest!"

"For heaven's sake, Gerald, I wouldn't have married her! I'm not an animal! I'm just telling you how *she* was thinking because of her foolish youth and her determination to have me." Alan rubbed his head in a display of irritation. "She got anxious to make things happen sooner rather than later. She tried to break us up, and then…the accident. When she realized I truly would never marry her or return her affections, she got scared I would tell the truth about what happened, so she ran off." He shook his head. "I tried to reason with her and told her that I would say it was more accident than deliberate."

Gerald rose. "Well, accident or not, she probably *would* go to prison, at least for a few months if nothing more. Of course, it would still be quite a disgrace, and she'd lose her inheritance." He sighed. "Are you asking me to arrest her?"

Alan rubbed at the back of his neck as though regretting his decision. "I hate doing that to Mary's daughter, but yes, I think she should be arrested. If you can serve up a warrant, I'll take care of the rest. I am going to find her for you, Gerald. I have a few ideas about where she might be—maybe at her mother's friend's place in New England, maybe at our Florida estate, maybe in some other city. I had a considerable amount of money in one of my drawers. She took it—stole from me—and that must be what she's living on."

And she's got the damn necklace, I'm sure of it, he thought. *That alone would keep her just fine for a long, long time*. He was not about to tell Gerald about the necklace he'd coveted ever since marrying Mary. He'd never been able to get her to tell him where it was, but Emma damn well knew, he was sure of it. She'd taken it and fled his clutches.

"Well, this is quite some bit of news, Alan." Gerald

picked up his hat. "I can have my own investigators go looking for Emma."

"No. I don't want this known to anyone but you and me and whatever judge issues the warrant. Make sure he knows that. I want this kept quiet for as long as possible. I'll take care of the search. You have enough on your hands, keeping the law in a city the size of New York. Just bring me an extra copy of the warrant so I can have it with me if and when I find her, so I can show it to the law enforcement there and bring her back here with me. I don't want this to hit the papers until you and I and Emma talk about what should be done about this." He walked closer. "Do me that favor, will you? After all, you owe me quite a gambling debt, remember?"

Gerald grinned in spite of his concern. "I was wondering when you were going to get around to that."

Alan smiled sadly. "I'll consider you keeping quiet about this as your payment. I hate to collect this way...hate doing this to Emma...but she's out there alone somewhere, and I can't quite forgive her for taking Mary from me in such a violent way. The fact remains that out of jealousy she killed her own mother, intended or unintended. She's got to be found and made to own up to what she's done."

"I agree on that one." Gerald put his hat on. "Did any of the maids see what happened?"

Alan shook his head. "No. And I don't want them questioned, at least not until it's absolutely necessary."

"Very well." He reached out and shook Alan's hand again. "I'll get the warrant and bring it to you. I'll leave the rest up to you. I hope you can find her, Alan."

Alan squeezed the man's hand, wishing it were Emma's neck. "I'll find her, Gerald. You can be sure of that."

Gerald turned and walked to the door. "I'll let myself out. And I think I'll go have a drink somewhere. This is indeed shocking news." He shook his head. "Shocking." He left, and Alan walked back to look out the window again at his well-manicured garden behind the mansion.

"Shocking indeed," he muttered. *And little Miss Emma will be shocked when I find her and show her the warrant for her arrest. If that doesn't scare her into telling me where the necklace is, I guess I'll just have to let her go to prison, or arrange for her untimely death.*

Having that necklace would have gone a long way toward relieving some of his gambling debts. Even the wealthiest man could end up a pauper when he couldn't control his gambling. It was an addiction he'd fought most of his adult life, and a battle he endlessly lost. It irked him that not being able to have the necklace, which was rightfully his, had meant cutting back on his gambling to make sure he didn't go bankrupt. Right now he was faced with selling some of his real estate. He'd be fine for a while yet, if he could keep himself from gambling, and if he could find Emma and get his hands on that necklace!

❧

Gerald Hayes nodded to Bess as she led him to the front door. He stopped there and looked down at the young waif Alan Radcliffe had hired out of his own garment factory. The man had a habit of doing that and then letting young maids go after a while. He always claimed he found better jobs for them, but Hayes always wondered if there was more to it than that. He'd run in the man's gambling circles, knew him well enough to see something in those dark eyes of his, something seedy and evil. He'd never liked Alan Radcliffe, but he'd also never been able to find any proof that the man was anything but a wealthy, philanthropic citizen of New York City. Men like Alan were difficult to catch doing anything wrong.

"Bess," he said quietly. "Were you here the night Mr. Radcliffe's wife fell down the stairs?"

A quick look of fear flashed in her eyes. "N-no, sir. I mean…I was way upstairs in my attic room, asleep."

Gerald studied her intently. "Bess, I know when someone is lying to me, and you're lying."

She looked around like a panicked, caged animal, glancing toward the hallway that led to Alan Radcliffe's office. Gerald put a hand on her arm, feeling sorry for the thin, pale, quiet Bess, who'd probably never known a decent life.

"Bess, I don't want you to be afraid to tell the truth. Alan claims Emma killed her own mother, that she was in love with him and wanted him for herself, that she pushed her mother down those stairs. I don't believe any of it, but I need proof of what really happened, and now Emma has run off, so I can't question her. You liked Emma, didn't you?"

Bess blinked back tears. "Yes, sir."

"Then tell me what really happened. You witnessed it, didn't you?"

She backed away. "No! It's just like I said, sir. I was asleep in my room."

Gerald sighed. "Did you ever see Emma flirting with Alan, trying to seduce him? Did she ever tell you she was in love with her own stepfather and wanted to marry him? Surely you heard or saw *something*!"

"I...yes, she did those things. She wasn't as nice as you think she was."

Gerald frowned. "You're afraid of Alan Radcliffe, aren't you?"

"Please go, Mr. Hayes. I have no power, no say, no family, no anything. Men like you and Mr. Radcliffe can make life good for me or destroy me. I just do my job and nothing more. Please go!"

Gerald shook his head. "It doesn't have to be that way. Help me, Bess, and I'll help you. You needn't fear me, I promise."

"Please go! He'll come out of his office any minute and know we've been talking!"

Gerald nodded. "You remember what I just told you." He walked out the door and Bess quietly closed it, squeezing her eyes against tears. She felt sorry for Emma, understood why she'd fled. She knew the ways Alan Radcliffe had of making life miserable for those beneath him.

The man didn't know she'd witnessed what happened the night his wife died, what had really happened to Mary Radcliffe, what he'd done to Emma. She'd stayed in the shadows and seen all of it, but she knew Alan Radcliffe, knew she didn't dare tell the truth. He'd told her more than once that if she ever betrayed him in any way, he'd accuse her of theft and prostitution and have her thrown into prison. He'd said no one would believe a poor orphaned girl off the streets, and he was right.

He was Alan Radcliffe, businessman, philanthropist, respected gentleman. She had no hope of winning a battle of right and wrong against him, and she needed this job…needed the extra money he'd bribed her with, to take care of her grandmother so the poor old woman didn't end up starving in the streets. She couldn't tell the truth. She just couldn't. She would continue putting up with the man coming to her bed at his whim and keep her mouth shut, hoping poor Emma had escaped someplace where Radcliffe would never find her.

"Bess!"

She jumped when Alan spoke her name from the hallway.

"Yes, sir?"

"Why are you still standing there at the door?"

"Oh, I noticed the doorknob needs polishing. It's getting tarnished."

"Then polish it, but get me some tea and a newspaper first."

"Yes, sir."

He walked back down the hallway, and Bess breathed a sigh of relief. Thank God he'd not seen her talking to Prosecutor Hayes.

Six

MEN'S SHOUTS WOKE ELIZABETH. SHE PEEKED OUT A window, and by the light of a just-rising sun she saw that the two outlaws Mitch had left behind were now being herded down the street, still in their long underwear and nothing more. They looked haggard and terrified.

"Let's hang them right now!" some of the men were yelling. "We already know what happened!"

"We are going to do this legally!" came a shouted reply. The voice sounded familiar, and Elizabeth glanced over at a saloon just two doors down and across the street to see none other than Mitch Brady standing there trying to keep order.

"What on earth!"

How could the man already be up and dressed and outside trying to handle a hanging mob? He should still be resting! Elizabeth turned away from the window to retrieve a watch from a front pocket on the dress she'd worn yesterday. It was just a little after seven o'clock in the morning. After a wonderfully warm and sudsy bath, thanks to Lee Wong and his wife, she'd drunk some tea and slept much more soundly than she'd thought possible for a stranger in a wild town, surrounded by danger. She supposed it was from pure exhaustion.

She went to the door to peek into the outer room to see that the other patient who'd been there yesterday was also gone. Doc Wilson sat bent over his desk writing something. Elizabeth called out to him. He straightened his shoulders and turned to look at her.

"Well! You're awake! How do you feel?"

Elizabeth noticed he wore the same faded, wrinkled suit he'd been wearing yesterday. He'd likely slept in it. She kept the door to her room just slightly ajar so the doctor couldn't see her in her nightgown. "I feel much better so far. What is going on outside?"

"Oh, there will be a trial, of course. They'll turn the Antelope Saloon into a temporary courtroom and make sure the hanging is done legally. Mitch will see to that."

"Shouldn't Mitch still be resting?"

The doctor grinned and leaned back in his chair. "You don't keep Mitch Brady down for long. He was up and dressed and out of here about six this morning—wanted to make sure that bunch out there didn't hang those two without a trial. I tried to keep him down, but he wouldn't have it. He said to tell you to get dressed as soon as you were up in case you have to testify to anything. He'll try to keep you from having to go through something like that. At any rate, I'll bring you some fresh-heated water for the wash-bowl in there and some soda to scrub your teeth with." He rose. "You strike me as the type who doesn't go out unless she's properly clean and has every hair in place. Will you need help? Lee Wong's wife is good at pinning up a woman's hair and such things. She can even heat a round iron on the stove to curl your hair more, if you need to freshen up those pretty locks."

Elizabeth put a hand to her hair, realizing it must be a tumbled mess. Last night she'd noticed a bruise on her right cheek. She wondered if it was any worse. "I...no, I'll manage."

She closed the door and walked over to her biggest carpetbag, pulling out a dark green dress that would be considered quite fashionable back East. She wondered if it was possible to find anything like it here in Alder, where everything was so uncivilized. She would have to ask the woman who ran the boardinghouse. *Ma Kelly*. Even the women here were referred to with nicknames. What was her first name? Should she be called Mrs. Kelly?

Whoever she was, Elizabeth hoped the woman could help her find a seamstress to make more dresses for her. She'd left home in a hurry, forced to sneak away with as little baggage as possible, which left her with only four day dresses, one fancier evening dress, a nightgown, and a robe, and two sets of petticoats, one of which had been thrown out after she ripped it up to bandage Mitch Brady. She had a couple pairs of stockings, two pairs of shoes—one pair for day and one fancy pair—a handful of jewelry, and a couple of hats. She was in sore need of expanding her wardrobe, although she could already see that being properly dressed probably meant little to the rowdy mob of miners gathered just outside her window.

She hoped she could avoid getting involved with the melee in the street. All she wanted now was to get a room of her own where she could gather her thoughts and plan what she would do next. One day of peace and quiet would be so welcome. The journey here had been a nightmare of fear and noise and filth…a loud, smoky train part of the way, followed by a riverboat ride, then the bouncing, dusty stagecoach and the accident and the attack, and now this—a lynch mob in the street, some members of which might insist she step forth and identify the two men outside.

She shuddered at how horrible a hanging must be, yet the men outside seemed excited about it. She remembered Mitch saying something about a hanging being a reason for a picnic, of all things! His attitude about it left her wondering just how "good" Mitch Brady really was. Did the man have any true feelings for anything, or did he just go around shooting lawbreakers and drinking in saloons and visiting the whores? He'd been disappointed to learn she wasn't a prostitute, and the painted women who'd greeted them yesterday obviously knew Mitch well.

Perhaps she should have stayed in Virginia City. It was nothing like New York, but it was certainly much bigger and more civilized than any other town she'd seen west of Chicago, with more of the amenities a woman needed. Still, she had to find a place where she was absolutely unlikely to ever be found by Alan Radcliffe. From what she'd seen of Alder, Montana, so far, it certainly fit the bill.

She hurriedly dressed, missing the help of a maid and wincing with the deep pain lingering in her shoulder. She'd have to learn to stiffen her resolve and do a lot of things on her own now, ignoring pain and other difficulties. She carried her grandmother's blood and her mother's blood, and both women were strong and resilient. One thing was sure, from what she'd seen of others in Alder, no one would much care if she wasn't properly dressed or coiffed. She leaned into the rather faded mirror and removed what was left of the combs in her hair. Piling it on top of her head would be impossible without help, so she brushed it out, then pulled back the sides with combs and let the rest hang down her back. Her face and body were clean from last night's bath. She pinched her cheeks a little, sat down to pull on shoes and button them. Just as she finished with that she heard someone come into the outer office.

"Is Miss Wainright up and dressed?"

She recognized Mitch Brady's voice.

"I'll see," the doctor answered.

There came a knock at her door, and Elizabeth opened it to see Mitch standing behind the doctor, still wearing the bloody shirt from yesterday. Right now he wore only one gun belt, slung low on his hips but holding two pistols. Mitch looked her over, a bit of surprise in his blue eyes as he removed his hat.

"You look even more beautiful with your hair down like that."

"I agree," Doc Wilson chimed in, smiling. "You look well rested, Miss Wainright." He frowned then and leaned a little closer to study the bruise on her cheek. "Too bad about that bruise. How do you feel?"

Elizabeth flushed with embarrassment. "Right now

I feel fine. My ribs are sore and of course my shoulder hurts, but I'll live."

"I for one am damn glad of that," Mitch told her with a handsome grin. He looked down at himself. "I apologize for the way I look, but I haven't had time to clean up."

"You shouldn't be up at all," she told him. "I hope you can go home soon, wherever that is, and get more sleep."

Mitch frowned. "Right now I just want you to step outside for a minute and tell that bunch out there that the men they brought in are the ones who attacked the coach and killed the drivers and passengers. I won't make you go over to the saloon. A proper lady like you doesn't belong in a place like that. I promise this will only take a minute. Once we herd the men over to the saloon and get things over with, I'll jail them and I'll come back here and take you to Ma Kelly's."

Elizabeth took a deep breath for courage. "I…I don't have a hat on."

Mitch chuckled. "Nobody out there cares about that."

I'm sure they don't, Elizabeth thought. "Very well." She walked past the doctor and Mitch to the front door, then stood aside, waiting for Mitch to open it. "You'll stay right beside me, right?"

"Of course I will." Mitch gently took her arm and opened the door, leading her out onto the stoop. Men cheered and whistled, and Mitch put up his hand and yelled for them to quiet down. The two prisoners glared at her, both looking haggard as well as terrified. Elizabeth wondered how the men got them here so early in the morning and realized that after she and Mitch arrived in town yesterday, the posse that quickly formed must have ridden hard to get to the site of the disaster before dark fell and left before daylight to get back to Alder. Such was their desire for retribution and, she suspected, for excitement.

"I only brought this woman out here to make a quick identification," Mitch shouted. "I don't want my word to be the only testimony to what these men did. Those of you who went to pick them up saw the wreckage and the other dead bodies. Late yesterday some others of you buried Billy and Juno. I caught these two in the act of dragging this woman out of the coach and trying to rob her. She was wounded and helpless."

Mitch turned to a man wearing a black top hat, a silk morning coat, and a buttoned paisley vest underneath. When he moved his arm to write something on a tablet, Elizabeth noticed a gold chain pinned to his vest. The end of it was tucked into a small pocket, and she had no doubt it held a gold watch.

"Take your notes, Jackson," Mitch told him. "I want it known there was more than one witness to this, and that I allowed these men proper representation."

The man he called Jackson was of average height, with dark hair and eyes and mustache, a decent-looking man who was the best-dressed Elizabeth had seen so far. He glanced at her and smiled kindly as he nodded his acknowledgment. He held a small tablet and a quill pen. Another man with him who looked to be just another miner held out a bottle of ink, and Jackson dipped his pen into it.

"I'll have this woman state her name," Mitch

shouted to the others. He looked down at Elizabeth. "Go ahead."

Elizabeth swallowed. "Elizabeth Wainright," she said louder than her usual voice but not shouted. Again she felt guilty for lying about her name.

Jackson scribbled her name on the tablet.

"And are these the two men who were part of the gang that dragged you out of the overturned stagecoach yesterday?" Mitch asked.

Elizabeth nodded. "Yes." In spite of what they'd done, part of her didn't like having to testify against two men who would soon be hanged.

"And did you fear for your person and your life?" Mitch asked.

Elizabeth scanned the crowd. "Yes. The stagecoach drivers were shot and killed, as well as one of the passengers inside the coach. The other passenger died when the coach overturned."

"Let it be known that Miss Elizabeth Wainright here has identified Hugh Wiley and Jake Snyder as part of the gang that tried to rob the Virginia City stagecoach yesterday of money meant for the bank here in Alder. These same men shot Billy Polk and Juno Martin and passenger Spittin' Joe. They also caused the death of a passenger named Whiskers and caused Miss Wainright here to suffer a dislocated shoulder and great humiliation."

Fists went into the air, and the outlaws hung their heads.

Jackson kept writing. "Where are you from, Miss Wainright?" he asked as he wrote.

Immediately Elizabeth was afraid. She didn't like all

this attention. For someone hiding and trying to keep a low profile, this was the last thing she wanted. "I'm from…St. Louis." *Another lie.*

"And what brings you to a place like Alder, Miss Wainright? It *is* Miss, right?"

Elizabeth looked up at Mitch. "What does that have to do with what happened?"

"Nothing." Mitch answered. He turned to Jackson. "This woman's background and reason for coming here makes no difference in what these men did," he told Jackson. "Suffice it to say, she has identified them as being part of the gang that attacked the stagecoach yesterday, killed three men, caused the death of a fourth man, and intended to rob and shame Miss Wainright, perhaps kill her, too. That's all that matters."

Jackson nodded. "All right, then." He glanced at Elizabeth, looking her over curiously. "Sorry to offend, ma'am. Name's Carl Jackson…*Attorney* Carl Jackson, if you should ever have need of my services. And I can assure you that this town is proud to have such a lovely lady as yourself grace our presence, whatever your reason for being here."

"You'll die for this, Mitch Brady!" someone yelled before Elizabeth could answer.

The words came from a man about Mitch's age. "You're bound to hang my brother vigilante-style, and I can't let that go. And don't forget that Hugh has friends. You'd better watch your back!"

"If you want to defend a murderer and robber, that's your right," Mitch shouted back. "But I'd think twice before I'd go threatening people, Sam. If you defend your brother by trying to murder me, you'll hang, too."

Sam fingered his sidearm nervously and then backed away. "We'll see about that," he said before turning to put a hand on the shoulder of one of the outlaws. He walked away then, and men jeered at him.

Mitch turned and led a grateful Elizabeth back inside the doctor's office and closed the door. Elizabeth wilted a little, glad to be away from prying eyes. "Thank you," she told Mitch.

"Wait here, and when this is over, I'll come get you and take you to Ma's place."

Elizabeth sat down in a wooden rocker. "You don't need to keep escorting me everywhere," she told Mitch.

"Yes, I do," Mitch answered. "You don't know your way around town yet, and there are plenty of men out there still too curious about why you're here. I have to admit I'm one of them." He looked her over with a mixture of wonder and irritation in his eyes. "You've got to be more forthcoming, Miss Wainright. Even though we've all got our secrets, leaving people completely in the dark only makes them pay more attention to you, and I have a feeling attention is the last thing you want."

Mitch went back outside, and Elizabeth looked up at Doc Wilson.

"He's right, you know," Doc told her.

Elizabeth decided she'd better get to work on a credible story. Outside, the crowd broke into another uproar, and their shouts began to fade as the two outlaws were dragged to a saloon down the street.

"That man called Jackson. Is he a lawyer?" she asked Doc.

"Yes, but lawyer or not, his background is as much a mystery as most others around here."

"What happens now, Dr. Wilson?"

Doc grinned ruefully. "A trial, if you want to call it that, will take place over at the saloon and the men will be taken to jail to await a hanging. That probably won't take place until tomorrow or the next day. That gives people time to prepare the scaffold."

Elizabeth shook her head. "I've never seen a hanging, and I don't think I want to see this one."

"Your choice. They aren't pretty, that's certain. By tomorrow you will have a room of your own and you can stay there during the hanging if you choose."

Elizabeth leaned back in the rocker. "I think I will do just that." She wondered at Mitch's ability to be up and about already and at his strange sense of doing the right thing, combined with a seeming unconcern for the fact that he was sending two men to the gallows. "Who was that man who tried to defend that one outlaw?"

"That was Hugh Wiley's brother, Sam."

"Will he really try to get some kind of revenge against Mr. Brady?" she asked.

The doctor shrugged. "It's a possibility. They're all a bad bunch, but some men have a way of blustering bravery and vengeance when they really don't intend to do a damn thing. I can't think of one man in Alder who'd willingly go up against Mitch Brady." He frowned and looked at her teasingly. "Are you worried about Mitch? Maybe you care a little too much?"

Elizabeth rose. "I only care because the man helped me. It's nothing more than that." She walked into the room where she'd spent the night and closed the door. She sat down on the cot and put her head in her hands. What had she gotten herself into? The last thing she wanted was this much attention. Worse, being around Mitch Brady created disturbing emotions. She worried that she was starting to care about the man, which went against every vow she'd made to herself upon leaving New York.

Seven

THE SO-CALLED TRIAL TOOK HARDLY ANY LONGER THAN it took Elizabeth to repack what little she'd used overnight and twist her hair into a bun at the back of her head. By the time she'd secured the bun and attached a small hat to her head with a couple of large hat pins, Mitch was at the door again. "See if Miss Wainright is ready to leave," he was telling Doc Wilson.

Elizabeth opened the door and faced Mitch. "I'm ready. And you can call me Elizabeth…both of you. I think the experiences of the last couple of days call for first names, since I intend to stay here in Alder for some time to come."

Both men nodded.

"Actually, nobody calls me by my first name," he told her. "It's just Doc."

Elizabeth nodded and glanced at Mitch, thinking how the man seemed to fill every inch of the room, not just because of his size but also because of the impact of his demeanor and attitude. "Can I call you Mitch, then, or do you prefer Sheriff Brady—or is it Marshal Brady?"

"It's Sheriff, but call me Mitch."

Elizabeth felt a bit too warm at the way his blue eyes scanned her. She hardly knew this man, and it irked her that she enjoyed the feeling of safety she experienced when he was near. "What about my things?" she asked.

Mitch approached, and she stepped aside as he went into the room and picked up one of her bags. "I'll come back for the other two and that trunk," he told her.

"You should send someone else after the other bags," Elizabeth suggested. "You need to get cleaned up and get some more rest, and although you are obviously a very strong man, you are in no condition right now to be lugging the biggest, heaviest bag all the way to the boardinghouse, whether it's six blocks away or one. Surely there is someone you can send to get them for me. After all, you know everyone in town."

Mitch pushed his hat back slightly. "Much as I hate to admit it, I do need more rest. Let's get you to Ma Kelly's." He carried the lighter bag and Elizabeth followed him to the door, turning to thank the doctor for boarding her overnight.

Doc Wilson smiled. "Ma'am, having you here has been a pure delight."

Elizabeth couldn't help but smile as she left. Men like the doctor and Mitch Brady were a far cry from big-city men back in New York, and certainly vastly different from the one man she hoped to never see again. Men like Mitch and the doctor had an honesty about them, a warmth to their eyes—even Mitch, who, as she'd seen firsthand, could be completely ruthless. The only man she'd known well back in New York was also ruthless, even to the very good.

Mitch walked on the street side of the boardwalk, as though to shelter her from the activity beyond that point.

"Is the trial over?" Elizabeth asked him.

"Didn't take more than a few minutes," he answered as they walked. "Everybody knew they were guilty. The hanging will be in two days. If we didn't need to build a gallows, it would be sooner."

Elizabeth shivered. "Sounds gruesome."

Mitch shrugged. "Not to this bunch. It's the way things are done, ma'am…or I guess I should call you Elizabeth. Feels a little too familiar right now."

"I assure you, it's all right to use my first name."

They came to two steps down and Mitch took hold of her elbow to descend the steps, cross an alley, and climb back onto the boardwalk. Men gawked and moved aside as they walked. Elizabeth suspected they kept their comments to themselves because Mitch Brady was with her.

"What will happen the day of the hanging?" she asked.

"Oh, there will be quite a crowd. Some workers will even come in from the mines, take a day off. The few wives who are here will prepare picnic baskets, and the few children around will be told they have to watch in order to learn a lesson about good and bad and that if they don't walk the straight and narrow, they could also end up at the end of a noose."

Elizabeth drew in her breath and stopped, looking up at him. "Children watch?"

Mitch grinned wryly. "Yup. Teaches them a lesson about obeying the law. Afterward there will be

picnicking, and the whores will be kept busy, what
with so many men in town. Pardon my bluntness,
but you might as well know what life is like here and
make sure you really want to make this your home
for a while."

He took her arm and they started walking again,
past three saloons, a supply store, and a barber shop.
Some of the buildings were obviously hastily built of
raw wood, and most were no more than tents with
stovepipes sticking through the tops. Piano music
filtered outside, combined with men's shouts and
women's laughter.

And will you visit the whores, too? she wondered. She
couldn't help remembering how disappointed he'd
been to find out she wasn't a lady of the evening. Two
gaudily dressed women with painted faces approached
them, one giving Mitch a sly grin and a wink.

"Got a new girl, Mitch?" she asked.

"Hildy, this is Elizabeth Wainright, and she's a
proper lady," Mitch answered.

Hildy, who Elizabeth guessed to be perhaps twenty,
pursed her lips. "How boring!"

Both women giggled and nodded to Elizabeth.
"Welcome to Alder, honey," the other woman told
her. She was much heavier than Hildy, her bosom
billowing above her low-cut dress.

Hildy looked up at Mitch. "See you later, Mitch?"

"No." Mitch kept hold of Elizabeth's arm and led
her past the women. "Sorry about that."

"You don't need to be sorry for anything. It's not
my business. They were friendly enough."

"Oh, they're friendly, all right."

Elizabeth felt Mitch's uneasiness as he led her down a couple more steps and turned to cross the street. "Watch out for horse dung," he warned. They quickly walked across the churned-up dirt street and climbed up some steps in front of yet another saloon.

"The boardinghouse is just two doors down. And speaking of why you came here…" He paused, stopping to face her. "Why *are* you here? A lady like you alone in Alder just doesn't make any sense. Are you married? Did you leave a husband behind?"

Elizabeth pulled away. "I thought you understood that I prefer to keep my reasons for being here to myself."

Mitch set the bag down and folded his arms. Elizabeth couldn't help noticing the muscles outlined under his shirtsleeves. "I know that, but you have to admit, someone like you doesn't belong here. I'm sorry, but a woman pretty as you coming here alone and unattached is going to stir up curiosity…and trouble, which makes my job harder. I need to know what to tell people, because they'll be asking."

Elizabeth held his gaze, surprised at the concern in his amazingly blue eyes. "Tell them whatever you want. I'll be fine. And to answer one question…no, I am not married and never have been. And I am here because I lost my mother and I needed to get away from things too familiar and from…from a rather bad situation I prefer not to discuss."

"You could have gone to another city, a place more civilized. You could even have stayed in Virginia City."

Elizabeth turned. "Enough questions."

Mitch sighed and picked up her bag, and Elizabeth

noticed him wince slightly. Perspiration dampened his forehead. "Mitch, you don't look well. You got up and around much too soon."

He led her to the front door of the boardinghouse, which was the only two-story building in town. "I'll be all right."

In spite of being two stories, the house didn't look very big. Elizabeth guessed there couldn't be more than four rooms for boarding. "Are you sure there will be a room for me here?"

"I already arranged it." He stopped at the entrance before going inside. "Got any idea what you will do once you're settled?"

Elizabeth was both irritated and touched that he seemed to care what would happen to her. "I would like to teach. Are there any children in this town?"

"A few. Most live out of town, closer to the placer mines where their fathers work along the creek. It would be hard to get them all together in one place every day. I'm guessing there are no more than three or four kids, plus a few here in town. Life in a place like this isn't very well suited to normal family life. It's also not well suited for a young, pretty, well-bred woman alone. You should get yourself a gun and learn to use it. I can help you there."

"Doc Wilson and Spittin' Joe told me the same thing." Elizabeth rubbed her forehead. "I need to think about all of that. You are throwing a lot at me all at once, and you really have no right to tell me what to do. I just got here and I barely know you, Mr. Brady. Please go home, wherever that is, and clean up and get some rest. I'll be fine."

"I have a right to tell you what to do because I'm the law here, and if you don't watch out, you'll cause more trouble for me than I can handle. At least lay low until after the hanging. After that I'll take you to buy a gun and we'll go outside of town and I'll teach you to shoot."

Elizabeth frowned. "Is that really necessary?"

A stern look came into his eyes. "Yes," he answered.

Elizabeth was too tired and confused to argue. "Come see me the day after the hanging and we'll talk about it."

Mitch adjusted his hat again and opened the door to Ma Kelly's place. He picked up Elizabeth's bag and followed her inside. They entered a small parlor, and Elizabeth was pleasantly surprised at how tidy it was. Lace doilies decorated a coffee table and two smaller tables that held flowered oil lamps. Two rockers sat in front of a stone fireplace, and Elizabeth smelled fresh-baked bread.

A slender woman who looked old enough to be Elizabeth's mother came down a hallway to greet them, her brown eyes sparkling at the sight of Mitch. "Well, you big lug, it's about time you brought this young lady to a decent place where she can have her own room." She turned to Elizabeth, pushing a strand of gray hair behind her ear. "And you must be Miss Wainright. I'm so sorry for what you went through getting here. Most of the men in this town are good-hearted and decent, but they're a rough lot with no manners and no understanding of the word *bath*. I assure you that the kind who attacked your coach are not the norm here, but it's still not a real safe place for a decent young lady alone."

Elizabeth was getting irritated with the constant reminders about "a woman alone," but she didn't want to be rude to Ma Kelly.

"You're safe here, honey," the woman added. "Nobody will bother you." An honest warmth filled the woman's eyes, and she grasped Elizabeth's hands as she talked. "I'm Ma Kelly. I hear you don't want to be questioned about why you're here, and that's fine. Nobody knows why I'm here either, so we have a lot in common." The woman winked. "I just made some fresh bread. Would you like some bread and butter with some tea?"

Elizabeth sighed with relief at finding a clean, decent, caring woman. "That sounds wonderful! I wasn't hungry until I smelled that bread."

Ma Kelly chuckled. "Come on. I'll show you to your room, and Mitch can find somebody to bring over the rest of your things." She turned to Mitch. "And you, young man, as soon as you arrange for this young lady's belongings, you come back here and go to your room and get some sleep."

Go to your room? "You live here?" Elizabeth asked Mitch.

Mitch grinned. "Don't worry. I'm gone much more than I'm here. I do have a room here, but I sleep at the jail a lot and I'm often out on the road patrolling, when I know gold shipments or payroll shipments are coming and going. Sometimes I'm gone a week or more at a time." He set down her bag. "Does it bother you that I live here, too?"

Elizabeth felt herself blushing. "I'm just surprised, that's all."

"Mitch keeps to himself," Ma Kelly told her. "And he's right—he's gone more than he's here. Be glad he lives here, because him being around means you and I are doggone safe. Mitch's room is down the hall there. Yours is upstairs. Come with me. You can unload your bags and your hat and gloves and come down to the kitchen for that bread and tea."

"Thank you." Elizabeth looked up at Mitch, not sure she liked the idea of his sleeping in the same house. Was that why he'd brought her here? That part of her that held no trust for men was battling with the fact that she liked the thought of his being close. She'd been determined to remain completely to herself and make friends with no one, especially a lawman who apparently saw everything in black and white. If a man did something wrong, he was hanged for it, and that didn't bother Mitch Brady one bit.

"I'll go get the rest of your bags," Mitch told her.

Elizabeth noticed he looked a little pale. She felt a deep concern that surprised her. She looked down, picking up her bag. "You needn't go out of your way for me," she told Mitch, meeting his gaze again. "Heaven knows you have enough on your hands, keeping order among that bunch outside." She frowned. "And for heaven's sake, please clean up and get some rest. You can't handle people like that Sam Wiley when you're still weak from loss of blood." She turned to Ma Kelly. "I'll see my room now, if you don't mind."

More anxious to put some distance between her and Mitch Brady than she cared to admit, Elizabeth followed Ma Kelly down the hall. It was then that they

both heard a crashing sound. They looked back to see
Mitch on his knees, a small table overturned. He'd
apparently grabbed it to keep from falling, and both
man and table went down together.

"Mitch!" Ma Kelly ran to him and Elizabeth
followed after quickly setting down her bag. Both
women tried to help him up.

"I knew it!" Elizabeth exclaimed. "He never should
have gotten out of bed so soon! He's lost a lot of blood."

"Come on, Mitch. Let's get you to your bed."

"I'll be all right," he objected, his voice weak.

"No, you won't! Come on, now, let's get you to
your room."

Mitch leaned on both women as they led him to
a room at the end of the hall. Mitch fell into the bed
and rolled onto his back. Elizabeth noticed fresh blood
on his shirt.

"My God, he's bleeding again! Go get Doc
Wilson, Ma."

"Of course." Ma left but came right back with
some towels. "Press these against the wound till Doc
gets here." She hurried out again, and Elizabeth leaned
over Mitch, pulling his shirt out from the waist of his
pants to expose the wound. She pressed the towels
against it, glad that at least today he wasn't wearing so
many cartridge belts she couldn't get to the wound.

"You don't...need to—"

"Yes, I do. You saved me from a fate worse than
death yesterday. The least I can do is try to stop this
bleeding till Doc gets here." Elizabeth saw a strange
look in his eyes, something bright and difficult to read.

"You're a sweet young lady," he told her, grasping

her arm gently. "I won't let anything happen to you." He held her gaze, and Elizabeth felt a splendid warmth, a feeling of total safety. She felt like crying. Somehow, she believed him…and it had been such a long time since she'd felt safe.

Eight

ELIZABETH LISTENED TO THE WIND HOWL AROUND THE boardinghouse as it whistled through cracks in the wood and swished sand against the window of Mitch's bedroom. Overnight a hot wind had come charging through Alder, making signs squeak as they blew back and forth on their hinges, sending weeds and no small amount of trash sailing down the street, and drowning out the normal sounds of the restless gold town. It seemed just another demonstration of how wild and untamed this town was, just like the man who lay groaning in his bed, a high fever requiring the constant application of a cool cloth to his face and neck.

Doc Wilson had asked her if she could do the job. He had two other new patients to tend to, and Ma Kelly was busy with cleaning and cooking and tending to her other tenants. Three different prostitutes had shown up at Ma's door, offering to help out with Mitch, but Ma told them Miss Wainright was taking care of him, and with her being so new in town, maybe it was best she not be surrounded right away by ladies of the evening. "Besides, I've got two other men staying here. Makes things a bit uneasy, if you know what I mean, girls," Ma told them.

Even though the women were not exactly the kind of company Elizabeth would have wanted, she hoped they weren't angry about being turned away.

"They understand," Ma told her. "I know them well and they know I don't mean insult. Some of them are a lot nicer than you'd think. I just thought it best they stay away."

"How did they even know Mitch was passed out in here?"

"Oh, news travels fast in this town, dear."

Elizabeth was grateful for Ma's thoughtfulness, but she was so tired that she had to admit she wouldn't have minded the help, prostitutes or not.

She glanced at a mantel clock on Mitch's dresser—2:00 a.m. Her back hurt from being in a sitting position for so long. Her shoulder ached. Her ribs hurt. Her head swam with all the events that had accompanied her journey to Alder, especially since the stage robbery. None of it seemed real. What in God's name was she doing, sitting here in a strange man's room nursing him, seeing him lie there with his shirt off again while she sponged his fevered body? She should find his big, powerful frame revolting, after what she'd been through.

What was it about this particular man that made her feel as if she'd always known him? Why had she felt oddly stirred by the way he'd touched her arm earlier, the way he'd looked at her as though she were made of delicate crystal? And why did a man of his size and his violent nature make her feel safe? She told herself to be more wary, more alert, and to remember that right now Mitch Brady was not at full strength. Under normal circumstances, he was likely not to be trusted any further than any other man.

Once in his delirium he had thrashed about so wildly that she backed away for a moment. "Get away from her! Get away from her!" he'd groaned before finally slipping back into a restless sleep.

Doc Wilson had been compelled to re-stitch the wound, and this time the bandages around Mitch's middle showed no bloodstains. Elizabeth dared to pull back the covers, revealing his bare torso again so she could check once more. The bandages were still clean. When she put the covers back up over most of his chest, she caught him looking at her.

"Well, you're awake." She touched his forehead with the back of her hand. "And cooler. How do you feel, Mitch?"

He just studied her a moment. "I don't know yet. What time is it?"

"Two a.m."

"What?" He turned his head to glance at the clock. "For Christ's sake, have I been lying here since early yesterday?"

"Yes. I *told* you that you got up too soon. You passed out on us and Doc came over. He had to put more stitches in that wound to close it up better, and you came down with a fever. Doc had other patients to tend to and Ma is busy, so I volunteered to nurse you through the night."

He rubbed at his eyes. "You shouldn't have had

to do this. There is a whole town full of whores who would have been willing—"

"They volunteered, but Ma didn't want them here overnight because of other male guests, and out of respect for me—not that you would have considered that."

He studied her, frowning. "I'm not an inconsiderate brute, if that's what you think. And I agree with Ma. It probably wouldn't have been right letting one of the girls sit in my room all night." He looked around the room, then tried to sit up. "I have to get out of here. There's a lot going on in town and I should be out there."

Elizabeth pushed at him. "You stay right there, at least until daylight. There are still a couple of disgruntled men out there who would like to shoot you for hauling in those two stage robbers. You're in no condition to fight. And for heaven's sake, give that wound time to heal."

He settled back against the pillows. "Why are you doing this? You must be so tired that you hurt all over."

Elizabeth dipped the cloth into the pan of cool water again and wrung it out. "I am, but somebody had to tend to you, and in spite of everything, the fact remains that you helped me out of a bad situation and saw me safely to Alder. I owe you."

She leaned over him to apply the cloth to his forehead and he grasped her wrist. "You don't owe me a thing. I was just doing my job—and believe me, just being able to look at you is payment enough."

Elizabeth felt herself blushing. She laid the cloth over his forehead, just then aware of how close that brought them. Someone else's face sheared through her thoughts, and she stiffened and pulled her wrist from his grasp. She warned herself how dangerous it was to get too close to any man. This one was weak and healing right now, but even in this condition, he could likely still throw her across the room…or onto his bed. She was a new young woman in town who'd literally spent the night in this man's room! It only hit her then how that must look.

"I… Those women who came here… If they tell the whole town who's taking care of you, it's going to look bad." She suddenly felt terribly uncomfortable. "You said yourself I'd have a hard time proving I'm respectable here. What will those men out there think of this? I guess I shouldn't—"

He grasped her hand before she could get completely away. "Elizabeth, don't worry about it. When I'm up and around later, I'll make sure no rumors get started." He squeezed her hand. "I don't know why in hell you're here, but you remember you can come to me if you need help, understand?"

She looked down at the big hand clasped around her own, felt the strength there. How could the strength of one man be so terrifying, while the strength of another could be so comforting? She met his eyes. "You're telling me to come to a worthless, no-good, murdering vigilante for help? That *is* how you described yourself to me."

He grinned. "I guess I did, didn't I? Well, it's true, but women don't need to be afraid of me, especially pretty, respectable ones who I have a feeling are scared to death and running from something."

Elizabeth pulled away again. "You seem to be

much better, and I am so tired, I'm about to pass out. I'm going to my room now. Promise me you'll stay right here and sleep a little longer than usual in the morning. Don't make all these hours I've spent with you be for nothing."

He looked her over in a way that made her feel both warm and embarrassed. "They won't be for nothing," he told her. "Go get some rest. And thank you for sitting with me. You don't even know me, and you're hurting, too."

She rose. "I just did what needed doing," she answered.

"Elizabeth."

She turned.

"I meant what I said about coming to me for help. You don't fool me one bit about coming here to teach or whatever other reason you claim for being here. And the best way I can help you is to know the truth."

Elizabeth hesitated. She longed to tell him just that—the truth—but he was a lawman, and a ruthless one at that. "Why do you care?"

"Because I hate to see a woman feel helpless and alone."

Elizabeth frowned, meeting his gaze. "Why?"

He put an arm over his eyes. "Long story."

Elizabeth just stared at him a moment longer. "Have you ever been married Mitch?"

"Hell, no. Go on now. Get some rest. You sure as hell deserve it."

For some strange reason, Elizabeth wanted to stay with him, but it was too ridiculous and embarrassing to admit. She left the room, wondering about his restless tossing earlier, and the words he'd mumbled: "Get away from her!"

You accuse me of keeping secrets, Mitch Brady, but you apparently have some of your own.

Nine

"I CAN'T BELIEVE HOW LONG I SLEPT," ELIZABETH TOLD Ma Kelly. She sat in the woman's small kitchen eating a fresh biscuit and an egg Ma had prepared for her. "I should be eating lunch, not breakfast."

Ma Kelly carried over two cups of coffee and sat down across from her. "Well, you needed the rest, after what you went through," she answered, "and then sitting up most of the night with Mitch. Sometimes things like that catch up to you later. Having your own room where you can truly relax also helps. Any time you want to take a bath, I'll bring in the tin tub and heat some water for you."

"Having a room on the second floor at the back of the house helps. There isn't so much street noise."

Ma Kelly re-pinned a strand of gray hair that had come loose. "Lord knows the nights around here are just as noisy as the days. How is your shoulder?"

"Doc Wilson told me it would give me stabbing pain at times if I moved it the wrong way. He was right. Getting dressed and pinning up my hair is the hardest."

"Well, you do a good job of it, but you seem like a young lady who usually has help with such things."

Elizabeth lost her smile. "I did once...in another life. I left that life back in New—in St. Louis."

Ma Kelly nodded. "Must have been something very wrong with that life to bring a lady like you to a place like this. I hope you find the peace you're looking for."

The woman's keen insight, combined with what seemed like genuine concern, soothed Elizabeth's loneliness. "It's strange that a wild town like Alder can actually make someone feel more at peace. I have to say, though, that I don't look forward to the noise and activity that will take place tomorrow at the hanging. I intend to stay in my room and not watch."

Ma Kelly chuckled. "Honey, if you live here long enough, you'll find that a person jumps at the chance to turn just about anything into entertainment and a chance to get together with others socially."

Elizabeth sipped her coffee. "I find that hard to believe, but I guess you would know." She finished her biscuit, hearing heavy footsteps in the hallway. To her surprise, Mitch walked into the kitchen wearing guns on both hips.

"Well, good morning," Ma Kelly greeted him. "You sure you should be up?"

Mitch sat down at the table, glancing at Elizabeth. "I should have been up a long time ago, but Miss Wainright here advised me to sleep as long as I could, and I decided to take her advice." He nodded to Elizabeth. "Thanks again for sitting up with me. I'm embarrassed you had to do that. I don't generally find myself at someone else's mercy. It's usually the other way around."

Elizabeth looked at her coffee cup. "That I do not doubt." She felt irritatingly flustered at the sight of him. Cleaned up and wearing a blue shirt and leather vest, his sandy hair clean and combed, Mitch looked disturbingly handsome, yet intimidating. His tall, broad presence seemed to completely fill the little kitchen. "I'm glad you listened to me," she added, meeting his gaze again. "There is nothing wrong with admitting you need a little extra rest once in a while. Ma Kelly and I were just talking about how an experience like yesterday's can catch up with you. I slept far too many hours myself. I have to get out of here and find work of some sort."

Mitch frowned as Ma Kelly set a mug of coffee in front of him. "You should wait until I can escort you," he told Elizabeth. "Or until I help you pick out a gun you can carry in your purse."

Elizabeth shook her head. "Is that all you think about? Shooting people?"

Mitch scowled, picking up the cup. "Just the ones who deserve it, and there are plenty of those around here." He drank down some coffee.

Elizabeth felt an odd uneasiness at how close she felt to this man she still hardly knew. It irked her a bit that she was sharing the same house with him. Something about it seemed too intimate. "Be that as it may, I don't need you following me around like a bodyguard. I chose to come here, Mitch, and I will find a way to survive."

He studied her with eyes that seemed to know everything she was thinking. "And I still can't figure out why in hell you're here."

Elizabeth stiffened. "I thought it was agreed that was no one's business, just like it's not my business why you chose to come here and make yourself the law of the land—why you hunt down the bad element and shoot or hang men with no qualms."

Their gazes held for a moment, and Elizabeth could have sworn she saw a hint of hurt in the man's eyes. "All right," he said, leaning back. "Go ahead on out there and make your own way. I have better things to do than follow you around like a bodyguard, as you put it. I have to make sure a gallows gets built. After what those men did yesterday, you're right. I won't have any pity over them getting what's coming to them. I'll watch them hang with no qualms." He drank down some coffee and rose. "I've got a lot to do, Ma. I won't be home till supper, if then."

"Mitch, you need to eat."

"I'll stop by the diner when I get time." He headed for the back door, grabbing his hat from a hook nearby and glancing back at Elizabeth. "Have a pleasant day, ma'am," he said with a strong hint of sarcasm.

"Mitch—"

He stopped, his hand resting on the doorknob.

"I truly am grateful for what you did for me yesterday. Please don't think I'm not."

He nodded and went out without looking back.

Elizabeth turned her attention to Ma Kelly. "I hurt his feelings."

"Mitch's?" Ma Kelly chuckled. "That's a pretty hard thing to do, with a man like that." She sat back down across from Elizabeth. "I have to say, though, that I see something between you two. Mitch pretty much doesn't care what anybody thinks of him, but I suspect he *does* care what *you* think of him." She winked. "And here you two have only known each other for two days." She leaned closer. "Could it be that the man made quite an impression on you when that stagecoach was robbed?"

Elizabeth scowled. "Not in a good way, I assure you. I'm not accustomed to seeing someone open a hole in a man's back, shoot two other men, and then chain up another two like animals. At first I wondered if he was one of them, intending to have me and whatever he could steal all to himself."

Ma Kelly nodded. "Well with some men the line between good and bad is pretty thin. I suspect at some point in his life, Mitch could have gone either way, but that something happened to make him choose the law instead of being an outlaw. I don't know much about his past, but I do know when a man has a hankering for a particular woman, and that man's got one for you. Can't say as I blame him. He's young and alone, and you're the first really pretty, respectable, available woman who's come to Alder in a long time."

Elizabeth waved her off. "How on earth can you think that so soon?"

"I've been around a lot of years, Miss Elizabeth— long enough to know when the feelings are mutual."

Elizabeth rose. "Well, you're completely wrong, Ma. For reasons I won't explain, the last thing I want is a man in my life." She smiled. "Thank you for the breakfast, or lunch, or whatever you want to call it. I am going upstairs to make myself proper for stepping out and looking for work. I intend to spread it

around town that I am willing to teach for a small fee.
I happen to be quite good at reading and writing."

"Well, most folks around here are only interested
in working the placer mines, not learning their ABC's.
And if you're going to teach, you'd have to go out
to the mines all along the gulch where there are a
few wives and kids. 'Course, it's dangerous out to
the mines, too. Men try to steal claims, steal food,
sometimes steal some other man's wife for a night.
Wherever you go here, Elizabeth, you'll find danger.
Mitch was right that you should carry a gun if you're
going to be out and about a lot, especially at first,
when nobody knows anything about you and most
men will think you're here either as a mail-order bride
or…something else."

Elizabeth lifted her chin. "They will soon learn I
am a respectable woman here to…well, here to live
my life the way I choose and to teach children who
otherwise would not have the opportunity to learn.
Maybe I will even get some of those men out there
to build a cabin I can use as a little school, somewhere between town and the mines, close enough
for some of those miners' children to come a day or
two a week."

Ma Kelly rose and picked up their coffee cups.
"Things are very different out here than back East,
Elizabeth. You watch yourself."

Elizabeth shook her head and headed into the
hallway and up the stairs to her room, not wanting
Ma Kelly to see how truly nervous and afraid she was.
She was not about to let anyone know it. She went to
a window and looked out into the alley below, where

two men shoved each other around in an argument over a bottle of whiskey. The language they used made her wince.

She turned away, taking a deep breath. Going to a mirror, she checked to be sure her hair was in a proper bun, then donned a small straw hat and a dark blue cape that accented her lighter blue dress. She realized she would have to find a seamstress who could make her some plainer dresses. Hers were too fancy for a town like Alder. It made her stand out a bit too much. She would have to ask Ma Kelly about a seamstress so she'd know where to look. She pulled on some gloves, wondering when the pain in her shoulder would subside.

Hoping the necklace she'd hidden in the lining of her trunk would be safe, she walked out the door. It was time to get used to life in Alder.

Ten

ELIZABETH MADE HER WAY THROUGH THE TOWN, determined not to allow anything or anyone to stop or intimidate her, including Sheriff Mitch Brady. He had no right ordering her around. After all, she'd made the decision to come here and she'd learn to survive here on her own.

Barreling straight ahead, she ignored the stares as best she could, shutting out some of the remarks and not answering questions about whether or not she would attend the hanging tomorrow. She headed for a fairly large tent Ma Kelly told her was just a few buildings down from the boardinghouse, where a sign hung that read Sarah's.

"Be aware that Sarah has other ways of making money besides sewing," Ma Kelly had told Elizabeth. "But if you need more dresses, she's all you've got."

Elizabeth decided she would just have to get used to the kind of people who lived here and not judge them. If living among them meant never being found and starting a whole new life, then so be it. Many of the people here had some reason for accepting this kind of life, other than gold. Some intended to get rich by supplying the miners…or in the case of women like Hildy and Sarah, servicing the miners in other ways. Surely there was a host of other ways to make a living. The miners needed food, clothing, tools, and horses and mules, which in turn needed shoes and feed and grooming. They needed legal help in filing claims, plus they needed lumber, lamps and the oil to light those lamps, utensils, pots and pans and dishes, soap, candles, towels, boots, and shoes. They needed barbers and bathhouses, loved their liquor, and their children needed teaching. Maybe some of the miners themselves needed help in that area, perhaps in reading contracts and claim forms. From what she'd seen so far, a lot of men in this town were poorly educated.

The street was alive with the sounds of men sawing through wood, hammers pounding nails, and horse-and-wagon traffic in the street hauling lumber and supplies for a town straining to change from a tent city to one of real wood buildings. Elizabeth remembered reading somewhere that out West, gold towns sprang up like mushrooms and sometimes died as fast as they grew. She supposed Alder would last as long as the gold in the hills lasted, and she wondered what it was like to pan for gold. Living out in the mountains and along cold streams had to be difficult, especially for any woman who'd come along to be with her husband while he searched.

Perhaps life here wouldn't be so bad after all, when one considered all the needs a growing town presented. It offered options to anyone with a decent education to make a living without trudging into the distant hills to look for gold. Perhaps she could write a town newsletter, or even start a newspaper. People here seemed to hunger for any kind of entertainment. That was obvious from the fact that a good many of them actually looked forward to a gruesome hanging. Her head swam with all the possibilities, including her first choice—teaching—but she reminded herself she'd need to be very careful not to do something that might draw too much attention outside of Alder.

By the time she reached Sarah's, she noticed a throng of men were following behind her. She was beginning to understand why Mitch said she should have an escort, but she was determined to prove to him and to herself that she could do this on her own.

"You goin' to see Sarah about maybe workin' for her over at the Saddleback Saloon?" some man behind her asked.

"Whooee!" another shouted. "There's gonna be some good fights over who gets to be your first customer, lady!"

Elizabeth abruptly walked into Sarah's tent and closed the flap, standing stiff as she looked around inside. Half-finished clothes and stacks of material lined the walls, leaving just enough room in the center for the table where a middle-aged woman was cutting some material. She looked up, her eyebrows arching in surprise.

"Are you Sarah?" Elizabeth asked, holding her chin high.

The woman nodded. "I am. Name's Sarah Cooper."

Elizabeth thought she looked very tired, her red hair pinned into a clumsy bun at the back of her neck, circles under her brown eyes. She was of medium build, her blue dress well fitted.

"And my name is Elizabeth Wainright. I came here—"

"I know who you are and how you got here, honey. What do you need?"

It was a bit unnerving to realize that on only her third day here, the whole town knew who she was and about her involvement in the stagecoach disaster. Elizabeth wondered if it was all the talk clear out in the mountain mining camps already. "Well, Ma Kelly told me you're pretty much the only seamstress in town," she told Sarah. "I can sew a little, but mostly I knit and crochet and embroider. I came here with only four dresses, and they are all a bit too fancy to wear here. I need some more practical dresses, and I was hoping you could make some for me. I can pay you."

"I wouldn't make them for any other reason," Sarah smirked, looking Elizabeth over. "So—you're the one those men attacked."

"Yes."

Sarah picked up a cup of coffee and sipped some of it. "You seem to be handling it well. I heard you were hurt, and all that violence and shooting must have been quite a shock."

Elizabeth ached to spill out her terror to someone, anyone, especially a woman. Oh, how she missed her mother! "I'll be fine, thank you," she answered, feeling defensive of her own feelings. How could she confide in this total stranger, who according to Ma Kelly was more than just a seamstress?

"Well, be careful. The aftereffects of something like

that can sneak up on you at unexpected times. I know. I've had a few bad experiences of my own."

Elizabeth wasn't sure what to say. "I...I'm fine for now."

Sarah smoothed her dress and nodded. "I hear Mitch Brady has an eye for you."

The remark embarrassed Elizabeth. How on earth had such news, which was not even necessarily true, traveled so fast? Had Mitch already been to see the woman since he left this morning? And if so, what on earth had he told her? "I wouldn't know about that," she answered. "I've known the man all of three days. He simply stopped what was happening and brought me here afterward. That's all there is to it."

Sarah chuckled. "Honey, I've seen Mitch Brady in action, and with him, nothing is that simple. Considering what must have happened out there, surely you had to be impressed. One of Mitch's specialties is rescuing women, even the whores, if some man decides to use one of us to vent his anger with fists or a knife."

One of us. The woman used the expression as though there was nothing unusual about it. Elizabeth forced back a need to shudder. "I don't know much about the man and I don't particularly care," she answered. "Can you make the dresses?"

Sarah shrugged. "Sure. Look around at the bolts of cloth here and pick some out. You're about the size of another woman I make dresses for. I shouldn't need to do much measuring, except that you're a bit taller than average." She set the coffee aside and rose, putting her hands on her hips. "How did something as young and pretty as you get through that mob of no-goods out there?"

Elizabeth walked over to a wood table where bolts of cloth lay in piles. "I just looked straight ahead and ignored their stares and their filthy talk."

Sarah chuckled. "Well then, I admire your courage, honey." She fell silent then as Elizabeth sorted through the material, but Elizabeth could feel the woman watching her. By the time she chose three samples, Sarah was sitting at a sewing machine, which whirred quietly as the woman used her feet to pump the machine's pedal, which in turn forced a needle up and down through the seam of what looked like a man's shirt. Elizabeth thought it odd that a woman of the evening actually had domestic talents, but then Sarah was, after all, a woman like any other. "Where did you learn to do that?"

"Oh, my mother taught me from a very young age."

Her mother. The words reminded Elizabeth of her own mother and how much she missed her. She felt a sudden urge to cry. "Where is your mother now?"

"She died a long time ago," Sarah answered. "Like her, I made my living sewing. Then I got married and my husband decided to come West and make his fortune. That was in '56. That didn't work out and he ended up dying in a mine collapse in California. I started back East but realized I had nothing to go back home to, so I stayed on...ended up in Colorado. I found out that you can't always survive just by making shirts for men, and then one came along who decided to force me to learn a better way to make money."

Elizabeth shivered, not really wanting to hear such a

horror story. It only reminded her of her own experience, which had made her fled New York. Would she end up like this, cooking and doing laundry for others by day and sleeping with men for money by night? "I…I'm sorry." She wasn't sure what else to say.

"Oh, I should have realized it could happen at any time." Sarah kept sewing as she talked, not looking at Elizabeth. "By the time he got done with me, I decided to stab him to death one night when he was passed out drunk. I fled Colorado and worked my way through various mining camps over the years, and now I'm here in Alder. I'm getting too old to make a lot of money at…well…" She sighed. "So I've turned back to sewing to make ends meet."

Elizabeth felt like crying. "I…I was hoping I could make my way by teaching, perhaps starting a newspaper, things like that."

Sarah shrugged. "You might be able to." She finally met Elizabeth's gaze. "Do what you can to avoid the ultimate way most women out here make their living."

They shared a look of understanding. Elizabeth knew from experience how one bad experience could steal away a woman's pride. She wished she knew this woman well enough to talk to her about her own experience with Alan Radcliffe. "I have every intention of avoiding such a life," she answered.

Sarah smiled. "Young lady, I can tell you right now, Mitch Brady would never allow it anyway. And God help the man who tries to force anything on you. He'll have to answer to Mitch, and you don't want to know what Mitch can do to a man."

"I've already seen what he can do."

"Not to a man who'd abuse a woman, even the whores."

Elizabeth was stunned at the woman's frank attitude toward such a reprehensible practice, although part of her understood and sympathized with what had happened to her. "Why do you think that is?"

Sarah shrugged. "That's for Mitch to explain, if he chooses."

Elizabeth nodded. "Well, I hope you are able to make your living as only a seamstress eventually," she told Sarah, "if that's what you want. I would think that there are plenty of men here who need shirts and pants and such, and the women…no matter what their occupation…all need dresses."

"Oh, a lot of clothing is shipped here from Virginia City. But there is always a need for more, and in winter we sometimes get snowed in and supplies can't get through. There aren't enough wives here to make clothes for their men, so I'm busier in winter." Sarah stopped her work at the sewing machine and leaned back. "So, show me the material you want me to use and tell me if you want any special design."

Elizabeth laid three different bolts of cloth on a nearby table, one a blue gingham material, one an array of tiny flowers with a pale green background, and one a medium brown color with tiny yellow flowers in the print. "Nothing special. Just simple dresses with a slightly scooped neckline because of the heat, and a simple button-down front." She folded her arms. "I wonder if you could tell me how to go about letting people know I can teach."

Sarah looked her over again. "Well, I have to say you could get very rich very fast at the other profession we discussed, but I can see you aren't cut out for that. As far as teaching, I would simply get paper and pen and post some notices around town letting people know where they can reach you."

Elizabeth nodded. "Yes, that's a good idea. Thank you. Where would I find some paper and such?"

Sarah shrugged. "I'd try Carl Jackson's place—little log building across the street and down a ways. He brings in a lot of that kind of thing for all his paperwork. Calls himself an attorney, but a lot of men call themselves a lot of things out here. No way to prove it, although he seems to do a decent job and knows what he's doing."

"Yes, I met him the day of the trial, if you can call it a trial."

Sarah laughed. "Vigilante law is nothing like the law back East, is it?" She shook her head. "Watch Jackson, though. He's a smooth talker and I suspect a bit of a shyster. He seems to end up with shares in a lot of the mines he helps men lay claim to."

Elizabeth rolled her eyes. "Is there anyone in this town who *can* be trusted?"

"Sure." Sarah smiled. "Me, Ma Kelly, and Mitch Brady. I'll bet he told you to get yourself a gun, didn't he?"

"Yes, but I don't like the idea."

"Well, he's right. Get one. Most of the women around here carry one. I've already used mine, and I'm not even young and pretty like you. Of course if word gets around you're Mitch's girl, you'll be pretty safe."

"Oh, for heaven's sake, I'm not *anyone's* girl and I don't *want* to be."

"I didn't say you had to be, but if those men believe you belong to Mitch, even if it's not true, let them believe it. It will help you."

Elizabeth wondered if there was anyone in town whose life wasn't affected in some way by Mitch Brady. "I'll keep that in mind. How long before you can have a dress ready?"

"Oh, give me three or four days for the first one. I work pretty fast. I'll need about ten or twelve days for all three dresses. I charge two dollars a dress plus the cost of the material, usually about fifty cents."

"That's fine." Elizabeth turned and opened the door. "Shall I come back here on a certain day?"

"No. I'll bring them to you. It's best you stay off the streets as much as you can, and coming here too often is a bad idea. Men will get to thinking we're discussing something other than these dresses."

Elizabeth felt embarrassed. "Fine. I'm staying at Ma Kelly's."

"I know where you're staying."

Elizabeth let out an exasperated sigh. "It seems everyone in this town knows all about me."

"News travels fast in places like this. People are hungry for something to talk about, and the arrival of a young, pretty, unattached woman who's a lady to boot is food for all kinds of gossip. You be careful out there now."

Elizabeth nodded. "Thank you. I will."

She stepped outside to see most of her following had dispersed, to her great relief. She headed out and across the street to Carl Jackson's little log office, but as she passed a saloon on the way, someone reached out and grabbed her arm, dragging her into a room full of smoke, piano music, laughter, and bearded men who surrounded her.

Eleven

STRONG ARMS BEGAN WHIRLING ELIZABETH AROUND A straw-and-peanut-shell-covered dirt floor to a fast-strutting tune coming from a piano and a fiddle.

"Don't worry, honey," assured the short, bearded man who'd grabbed her. "We all think you're quite the beautiful, respectable lady. We just want a dance, that's all."

Elizabeth was so startled she hardly knew what to say or do. Would they be insulted and get rowdier if she fought this?

"Least you can do is be a hurdy-gurdy gal," her partner told her before another man shoved him off and started dancing with her. This one was taller and darker and smellier. Elizabeth heard women laughing in the background. Were they laughing at her? "Hurdy-gurdy girls can get rich real fast!"

"I really don't want to dance," Elizabeth protested, half yelling above the whooping men and loud piano playing. "It hurts my shoulder."

"Just one little dance, lady?" her partner begged.

"Really, I…"

Suddenly a big fist rammed into her partner's jaw, sending the man flying across two tables. He landed against a bar stool and everyone backed away from Elizabeth. She turned to see Mitch Brady standing there with a dark look of rage in his eyes. "The lady said she didn't want to dance!" He scanned the room. "Everybody here understand that?"

The man Mitch had clobbered rolled to his knees, groaning.

"Stu was only wantin' a dance, Mitch," another man spoke up. "Ain't no harm in that."

"There is when the woman was dragged in here against her will and never agreed to the dance!"

Everyone backed farther away, and Elizabeth could see no one in the room was about to give Mitch any more trouble.

"You broke my goddamn nose!" Mitch's victim grumbled. Two other men helped him to his feet. He held a hand to his nose, but blood was running from under his hand and dripping onto his shirt.

"Oh, Mitch, you didn't have to hit him that hard," Elizabeth protested, feeling sorry for the man.

Mitch looked down at her with a scowl. "Believe me, I *did* have to hit him that hard, or he and some of the other drunks in here would have danced you till you collapsed. After that things would have gotten worse." He took hold of Elizabeth's arm and led her toward the swinging doors at the saloon entrance. "Let's go," he said.

Elizabeth followed him out. "I could have handled that."

"For God's sake, woman, you underestimate most

of these men. I told you that you shouldn't walk these
streets alone before they get to know you better and
understand you're a proper lady. Where were you
going anyway? First you go see Sarah, which doesn't
look good for you, then you walk past two saloons—"

Elizabeth jerked her arm away, wincing with
renewed pain. "Where I go and why is my business!"

Mitch sighed. "Come here." He led her across an
alley and pointed to a wooden bench on the boardwalk. "Sit down."

"Please stop giving me orders!"

"Sit down!"

Taking a deep breath, Elizabeth sat down on the
bench. Mitch sat down beside her, stretching his long
legs out in front of him. Elizabeth noticed his leather
boots were worn.

"Now, answer my questions," he told her.

Elizabeth wanted to hit him. "I went to see Sarah
because I need some practical dresses to wear in this
uncivilized town and Ma Kelly told me Sarah was
pretty much the only seamstress around here...her
second job, I'm told."

"Second job is right. You go in there and men who
don't know you will think you're asking her about
joining her in her other occupation."

"That's ridiculous. They know she makes clothing...by day. Besides, I feel kind of sorry for her after
learning how she ended up here doing what she does.
I actually like her. She's very nice."

"She *is* nice, but the fact remains men here have
a certain opinion of women like her. Don't think
I'm not sorry for them myself. I've defended some

of them who were used like a punching bag, but the fact remains they are what they are, and in a place like this, a proper lady doesn't want to be seen with any of them, at least not when she's new in town."

"She told me you practically beat a man to death once when he abused her."

Mitch didn't answer right away. He leaned forward, resting his elbows on his knees. "No woman deserves that." He spoke the words as though he was thinking of someone special when he said them.

Elizabeth thought how different his attitude was from the attitude of Alan Radcliffe. A woman didn't have to be a whore for Alan to beat on her. All she needed was to own something he wanted.

"What's a hurdy-gurdy girl? One of those men said I should be a hurdy-gurdy girl and I'd get rich."

Mitch's mood lightened a little and he leaned back again. "A hurdy-gurdy girl makes her money being paid to dance with men. It's only one step up from doing more than that. And yes, a woman can make a lot of money just dancing with the men, but most of them consider it hardly any more respectable than what the women above the saloons do."

"And I suspect you think just like the rest of them. After all, you must have already been in that saloon, probably drinking and carousing with the painted women. And practically the first thing you asked me when we first met was if I was a…you know. I hate the word. Be that as it may, you were disappointed to find out I was respectable."

He cast her an unnervingly handsome grin. "I was disappointed, but once I realized you really weren't one of them, I knew you'd need defending and that I'd need to keep an eye on you."

"No, you really don't. You're a busy man who lives a dangerous life. You have too many other things to handle in this territory."

He looked her over in a way that should have made her angry, but deep inside she continued to feel an odd attraction to the man. "Well, when I'm in town, I intend to make sure people here understand you're not to be disrespected," he told her. "And you didn't answer me. Where were you headed when they pulled you into that saloon?"

Elizabeth raised her chin. "I was going to see Carl Jackson. Sarah told me he would have paper and pens I could use. I want to put up some notices that I am available for teaching, and I am thinking about perhaps starting a newspaper or something like that."

Mitch sighed, rubbing his eyes. "I'll take you to Jackson, but keep in mind that although he claims to be an educated lawyer, he's shady and underhanded at times. He'll cheat you any way he can."

"I have nothing over which he *can* cheat me. All I want is some paper. Maybe after that, you can take me to whoever sells guns in this town and help me pick one out, since you're so bent on me owning one. Sarah advised the same."

"So, you'll do it for someone like Sarah, but not for me."

"She's another woman trying to survive in this town. I figure if she says you're right about getting a gun, then I should get one."

Mitch nodded. "Well, then I'm grateful to her."

They shared a moment of silence as horses and wagons clopped and rumbled through the street. Elizabeth watched a young boy shovel horse dung and put it into a wheelbarrow. She wondered if he was the child of a married couple, or perhaps some prostitute's child, or an orphan.

"Sarah said besides helping her once, you've stood up for a couple other women, too, at different times. Now you're following me around like some kind of watchdog. Why? You don't even know me. Maybe I'm not the proper lady you think I am."

"You don't fool me one bit. Don't tell me you aren't feeling scared and lost and alone, because I've seen the look. You don't need to put on an act of bravery for me, and you don't need to try to convince me you're anything less than a proper young woman who I suspect is well educated—maybe even from a wealthy family."

Elizabeth wished he weren't always so right about everything. She felt a sudden urge to cry but fought it, managing to keep her eyes averted. "Fine," she answered. "I'm feeling lost and scared and alone and I'm trying to figure out if there is one person in this town I can trust."

He touched her arm. "Look at me, Elizabeth."

She wanted to pull away, but every time he touched her it made her feel calmer, safer. It was the same feeling she'd sensed when he touched her arm that night at Ma's place. She dared to meet those blue eyes again.

"You can trust *me*, and Ma Kelly and Doc…and actually, you can even trust Sarah."

Elizabeth smiled away unwanted tears. "That's

exactly what Sarah said. I just wish you weren't a man, because I have a lot of trouble trusting your gender."

Mitch rose and helped her to her feet. "That's too bad. Some of us really *can* be trusted, Elizabeth." He pointed down the street, where men were building the framework for something. "That's the gallows they are building for tomorrow's hanging. Things will get a bit wild around here tonight, and I'll need to watch my back for Sam Wiley and anybody else who might decide to spring our two prisoners from jail. That's why you need to stay at Ma's and lay low."

Elizabeth felt a chill at the sight of the gallows. Hanging had to be a horrible way to die. "I have no plans to step outside the door later tonight or tomorrow."

"Good." Mitch led her one building down to where a sign hung from a post that read Carl Jackson, Lawyer. "How old are you, anyway?" he again asked Elizabeth. "All of eighteen or so?"

"I told you. I'm twenty-two," she lied.

Mitch just sighed. "Someday you're going to tell me the truth about your age and why you're here, because there is something about you that has a hold on me, Miss Elizabeth Wainright—if indeed that's your name." He led her into Jackson's log cabin, which was smoky from the fat cigar the man puffed on as they walked in. Elizabeth nearly choked on it.

Jackson's dark eyes lit up and he quickly smashed out his cigar when he saw Elizabeth. He rose and bowed slightly. "Well, to what do I owe the pleasure of your presence, Miss Wainright?" he asked with his strong Southern drawl.

"Cut the gentlemanly act, Jackson," Mitch told

him. "Do you have any writing paper you can sell to this young lady?"

Jackson looked her over, smoothing back his hair in a gesture that reminded Elizabeth of another man...a man she hated.

"Certainly. Plain paper or a tablet?"

"Either one will do," Elizabeth answered. "And I need a pen and some ink, if you can spare any."

Jackson pulled a handful of plain paper from one drawer and some lined paper from another, handing them to Elizabeth. "No charge for a beautiful lady like you."

"I can pay you."

"I'm sure you can," he answered with a smile, "but I won't hear of it." He turned to his desk and picked up a pen and a bottle of ink. "Glad to oblige, Miss Wainright," he added, handing her the items. "Just be sure to come and see me if you should need any legal services."

"She won't," Mitch answered before Elizabeth could. "Thanks for the paper." He quickly led Elizabeth out of the cabin before Jackson could continue their conversation.

"That was rude," Elizabeth told him, putting the pen and ink into her handbag.

"Believe me, it doesn't matter with a man like Jackson." Mitch led her across the street to a gunsmith's tent. "Now we're getting you a gun."

"If you insist."

"I do."

They walked into the tent, where a big, middle-aged blond man sat taking apart a rifle. Gun parts lay all over the table in front of him, as well as an array of tools. He looked up at Mitch and Elizabeth, his eyes lingering on Elizabeth. He nodded. "How do you do, ma'am?"

Elizabeth recognized a Swedish accent. "Fine, thank you."

"This is David Carlson," Mitch told Elizabeth. "Everybody calls him Swede." He turned his attention to the gunsmith. "We're here to find a small pistol for Miss Wainright's protection—something she can carry in her handbag. I'll teach her how to use it."

Swede nodded, getting up and walking over to a trunk that contained several compartments and shelves that rose separately as the lid was opened. The trunk held an array of small guns, whereas the entire tent was lined with wooden shelves holding numerous larger six-guns. Several rifles were laid out on another table, with long boxes underneath that Elizabeth supposed held more rifles. Swede turned back and laid a very small pistol into Mitch's hand. It fit in his big hand with room left over, and Elizabeth surmised the tiny gun was no more than six inches long from its polished wooden grip to the end of the barrel.

"This is a C. Sharps pepperbox, shoots four .32 rimfires—nice and small and light," Swede told Mitch.

Mitch nodded, studying the small gun.

"Barrel is stationary," Swede told him. "Square, with four chambers."

Swede's accent was so strong that Elizabeth had to concentrate to understand everything he said. The man was even taller than Mitch and stood slightly bent under the low tent ceiling. He took the gun from Mitch and removed the barrel. "You can take it off and reattach it." He cocked back the hammer. "Instead of the firing chamber rotating like your six-gun, the firing pin itself rotates to hit each of the four chambers every time you pull back the hammer. See?" He pulled back the hammer, showing Mitch how the firing pin moved in a circle. "Different, huh?"

"Very different, I'll say, but looks easy to use. Is it reliable? Well built?"

"It's a derringer—good, dependable little pistol, light to hold and small enough for a handbag. The little woman should have no trouble using it. I have plenty of rimfire shot for it and I can order more on my next trip to Virginia City."

"Good." Mitch took the supply of paper from Elizabeth's hands and laid it on Swede's desk. He handed Elizabeth the pistol. "Get the feel of it."

Elizabeth took the gun, surprised at how light it was. "I've never held a gun in my life."

"Soon as the hanging and all that is over with, we'll go practice using it."

Elizabeth sighed. "I'm not happy about this, but from all that's happened since I got here, I suppose I'll have to give in and carry the thing."

"Good idea," Swede told her.

"Pack it up with some shot," Mitch told Swede. "I'll pay for it myself."

"I can pay," Elizabeth told him.

"This one is on me," Mitch insisted.

Elizabeth sighed. "If you insist."

Swede packed the gun and bullets into a box and tied it with string, handing it to Elizabeth.

"Thank you." She faced Mitch. "I will likely never use this thing."

"I hope you don't find reason to." Mitch held the paper for her and led her back outside and toward Ma Kelly's. "I'll be pretty busy between now and tomorrow night, so I can't show you how to use that pistol right away, but at least you have it now. I can't say how much I'll be at Ma's tonight and tomorrow—probably not at all. Knowing you're there and safe will help me do my job and keep my attention on the right things."

Maybe you'll stay at Hildy's, or Sarah's, Elizabeth thought, a tiny part of her actually feeling jealous at the thought and then feeling ridiculously silly for caring. "Staying in my room sounds welcome anyway," she answered. "I still get tired easily after all that's happened, and my shoulder is giving me a lot of trouble. Being jerked into that saloon and forced to dance with those men didn't help."

"I'll get some laudanum from Doc and bring it to you," Mitch told her. "It will help you sleep, and you still need plenty more of that." They headed for Ma Kelly's, past a number of saloons and businesses, men glancing their way but none giving Elizabeth any trouble. She knew it was because of Mitch. Part of her resented it, but common sense made her grateful. When they reached the entrance to the boarding-house, she stopped and looked up at him.

"I guess I should thank you for getting me out of that saloon."

"I guess you should."

"And since you are so bent on looking after me, perhaps after all the turmoil over the hanging is over you can rent a buggy or accompany me on a stagecoach back to Virginia City so I can buy a few books that I'll need for teaching. I'll also need a few more personal supplies. Maybe I can even find a couple more dresses. I didn't have time to look around on the way here, because the stagecoach connection allowed me only a few minutes."

"And something tells me you packed up pretty fast to head out here—too fast to bring everything you would have liked to bring."

Elizabeth looked away. "That doesn't matter now."

Mitch put a hand out and braced himself against the doorjamb, his tall presence making Elizabeth feel tiny and vulnerable. "Sure, I can take you to Virginia City."

"And then maybe you could accompany me out into the hills where the miners are so I can talk to some of the wives about teaching—at least those who have children along."

Mitch frowned. "Going out there might be a little dangerous."

"With *you* along?" Elizabeth quipped, meeting his intensely blue eyes again.

Mitch grinned, a rare sight. Elizabeth was struck by how he looked even more handsome when he smiled. She wasn't used to actually liking a man, certainly not used to trusting one, especially one built like Mitch Brady. She'd known the bad side of that kind of strength, so how she felt in Mitch's presence confused her. Was it foolish to allow him to take her places where they would be alone at times? The man could break her in half, if he wanted.

Afraid he would read her thoughts, she turned

and went inside the boardinghouse. Mitch followed behind, his big frame filling the doorway. He actually had to duck a little when he came inside.

"Be careful with that gun," he told her. "Don't try anything with it until I have a chance to teach you how to use it. A lot of people in these parts get hurt or killed because they buy guns to protect themselves but don't know how to use them."

Elizabeth looked up at him. "I'll be careful."

What was that she saw in his eyes? Why did she suddenly want him to hold her? She backed away. "Be careful out there. That brother you mentioned seemed very intent on making good on his promise to get you for bringing Hugh Wiley in to hang."

Mitch shrugged. "I'm used to threats."

"I've heard stories about vigilantes…at least a couple I read about in newspapers back East. It's not all good."

Mitch put his hat back on. "No, it's *not* all good. But a lot of men come out here thinking they can live just as lawless as they want, and that can't be allowed. Most of the really bad stuff goes on outside of Alder—murders, cattle rustling, stage robberies, and such. Quite a few men came here after bad experiences in the war, some carrying big grudges because they lost everything—their farms, their businesses, family members. It's mostly a rough and angry bunch of men who've come West over the last couple of years, but I can handle myself. I learned how years ago when I was an orphaned kid running the back alleys of New York City."

Elizabeth quickly averted her eyes. "That's too bad," she told him. "I'm sorry."

Mitch grasped the door handle. "Couldn't be helped, but that's why I know how you're feeling right now, except that it's worse because you're a woman in a place where she sure as hell doesn't belong."

Elizabeth swallowed back her secret terror. "Well, like with you, it couldn't be helped."

"Couldn't it?"

Again he was trying to get more out of her. She refused to comply. "I'm very tired. I'm going to my room to lie down." She met his eyes again. "Thank you for accompanying me and helping me find the right pistol. I'm sorry when I seem ungrateful. It's just that I hardly know you, and like I said earlier, that makes it hard to trust you or anyone else."

"The trust will come, in time."

Mitch turned and left, and Elizabeth wilted onto a settee in Ma Kelly's parlor. She'd never felt so confused about her decisions and her feelings in her life. Everything was twisted and turned upside down. Nothing was as it should be, and it had been that way since the night of her mother's terrible and untimely death.

"God, help me," she whispered. She didn't want Mitch to leave. She wanted him to stay right here beside her. What was happening? It couldn't be love, because she barely knew the man, and she suspected his own life was one big mess like her own. Yet she found herself caring what happened to him. The thought of him being out there in the streets the next couple of days where men who hated him lurked in the shadows was unnerving. She wanted to scream at him to come back and stay in hiding with her.

She went to the door and opened it, looking out. He was nowhere in sight. The man kept appearing just when she needed him most, then disappearing again, and she had no idea how to find him.

She turned away and closed the door, feeling better remembering he'd promised to take her to Virginia City and maybe even out to the mines. She went upstairs to her room, leaving her pistol in the box and slipping it under some clothes in a dresser drawer.

Twelve

"WHAT SHOULD I DO, CLAIRE?" MITCH DOWNED A shot of whiskey.

Claire McGuinnes smiled through painted lips. "I think that for tonight you should forget about that girl and concentrate on matters at hand. Sam Wiley could be out there anywhere. In fact, you should probably get over to the jail and help Randy out. He doesn't have the skills you have, if somebody should try to get the lowdown on him and break into that jail."

"I know." Mitch sighed. "I'm headed over, but for now Len is there. Not many men would try a jailbreak with that mean skunk around."

Claire grinned. "That's true enough."

Mitch drank down one more shot of whiskey. "I just had to tell somebody how I'm feeling, and you're always easy to talk to."

Claire stroked his arm. "I'd rather be helping you in other ways, you big lug."

Mitch studied the lines around her eyes, the scar on her cheek left by a man who'd told her that older whores weren't worth paying and that he'd fix it so no man would want her again. Mitch had beat the man to death.

"I'd gladly oblige," he told Claire, "but that woman over at Ma Kelly's has a hold on me, Claire. I've never wanted just one woman before."

Claire leaned against the bar, putting one hand on her hip, her bosom spilling over the top of her dress. "Then go charm her into your bed. You're damn good at that."

Mitch just grinned. "She's not easily charmed." He frowned then, growing more serious. "Something happened to her, Claire. She's afraid of everything and everybody, especially men."

"Well, then, it's up to you to find out just what it is that's got her so scared. And while you're at it, ask yourself how you managed to fall in love with a complete stranger in just three days. I thought you had more common sense than that."

Mitch downed yet another shot of whiskey. "Lord, Claire, I didn't say I was in *love* with her."

"Really? Why else would you suddenly not want any other woman?" Claire tapped his chest. "You'd better be careful, young man. You don't know a thing about her."

"I know enough." Mitch began rolling a cigarette. "I know she's hiding something, and I think she's running from someone. Whatever it is, I know she's a victim."

"You see all women as victims. It's your one big weakness. And don't confuse feeling sorry for her with being in love."

Mitch shrugged, licking the cigarette paper and

sealing it. "I've felt sorry for plenty of women without wanting them in other ways—and I've never been in love with one, nor do I intend to let that happen." He shoved his shot glass aside.

"You just might not be able to fight this one, young man. Just be on guard. See what you can find out about her."

"I know when a woman is no good just the same as when I can pick out the no-good men." Mitch walked over to an oil lamp at the end of the bar and used it to light his cigarette, taking a deep drag. He returned to Claire, frowning. "I don't know a damn thing about love, Claire. I've never felt it before, and Lord knows I've never *been* loved, so it's all new to me and I don't know how to tell for sure."

Claire re-pinned a curl that was coming loose from her graying hair. "You loved your mother, didn't you?"

An old pain stabbed at him at the words. "All kids love their mothers. Mine died so long ago, I hardly remember how it felt. Besides, this is different. Something about her makes me want to follow her around and keep her safe. Eventually I'm going to break that wall she's built around herself and find out why in hell she came to a place like Alder."

Claire walked closer and stood on her tiptoes to kiss his cheek. "Promise me that for tonight you will forget about her and stay alert."

Mitch kept the cigarette between his lips as he smiled wryly. "I will." He laid money on the bar to pay for his drinks and left the Saddleback Saloon, heading for the jail. Night had fallen, and every saloon was alive with drinking and gambling and dancing

and talk of tomorrow's hanging. Several miners had
come in from the gulch for the big event. Mitch had
seen neither hide nor hair of Sam Wiley or Bobby
Spence, Hugh Wiley's friend who'd also threatened
him the day of the trial. He wore two six-guns and
carried a rifle in one hand, ready for whatever might
come, forcing himself to stop thinking about Elizabeth
Wainright and keep all senses alert for any wrong
movement or odd shadow.

His deputy, Randy Olson, was at the jail with two
volunteers who'd agreed to stand guard over Hugh
Wiley and Jake Snyder. Mitch headed over there,
keeping to the shadows himself and stopping to eye
each alley he came to before crossing it. He stayed
under overhangs whenever he could to help protect
him if someone was on a rooftop figuring to ambush
him. Luckily there were more tents than buildings in
this town, making it difficult for a man to find many
rooftop angles.

When he reached the jail, which was made of
cemented stones and barred windows, he finished
his cigarette and stepped it out, tapping on the door.
"Randy? Let me in."

The door opened and Mitch stepped inside. "Where
have you been, Mitch?" Randy Olson asked. The
young man walked to peer out a window, fingering
his rifle nervously.

"With that new gal, I bet," Len Gray answered
wryly. The older, graying man cast a sly grin at
Mitch. A drifter all his life, Len feared nothing and
was dependable in a pinch. He was known for his
expertise with a rifle. The man constantly needed a

shave yet never actually grew a full beard. He wore a plaid shirt with a cowhide vest that he seemed to wear constantly. Sometimes Mitch wondered if he slept in it. The dark-eyed, gray-haired man had the angled, weatherworn face of someone who'd lived outside more than inside most of his life, spending most of his years helping ranchers herd cattle.

Randy, on the other hand, still had the taut skin of an eighteen-year-old. He was a kid from somewhere back East, come to get away from an abusive, alcoholic father. Randy always wore clean clothes whenever possible, kept his hair cut, and was usually clean-shaven. The green-eyed kid was a real hit with the whores because of his youthful good looks. He landed in Alder one day just as Mitch was cleaning out a saloon full of drunks, helped Mitch, and decided to stay on as a deputy just for the excitement and because he had no particular place to go.

Mitch laid his own rifle on the wooden table that served as a desk in the tiny jail entrance. "If you want the truth," he answered Randy, "I was with Claire over at the Saddleback."

"Whooee!" The jab came from a third man there to help guard the prisoners, Benny Carson—thirty, a farmer from Missouri who'd lost everything, including his wife, in the Civil War, which had affected thousands of men who then headed West to start life over. Benny was medium in every way—age, build, looks—and was a quiet man who never talked about himself but who'd done a lot of hunting in his life, so was handy with a rifle.

"Let it be, Benny," Mitch answered with a frown. "We were standing at the bar talking, that's all."

"Well, I hope you didn't drink too much," Len told him, walking to the other window to look outside. "You need to be at your best tonight."

"I had three shots of whiskey. That's like drinking a glass of water to most folks."

"What the heck does a man talk about with a whore?" Benny asked. "I don't generally waste my time with talk."

"It's that new girl in town," Len repeated. "What's wrong, son? Need a woman's advice on what to do about her?"

"One more word about Miss Wainright and I'll open that door and throw all of you out in the street," Mitch answered.

"By God, Len, I think he means it," Randy joked.

"Getting nervous, Mitch?" The goading came from Hugh Wiley, who leaned against the bars of his cell. "You do know that my brother and some friends will make sure me and Jake here don't hang tomorrow, right?"

"You'll hang, all right. You'd better think about making things right with the Almighty tonight. If you don't, after we stretch your neck tomorrow, you'll be someplace where it's damn hot."

Hugh chuckled, but Mitch could see the terror behind the man's fake confidence.

"Men like you enjoy watching a man kick and gag, don't you?" Hugh sneered. "Vigilantes love stringin' men up, and that's what all four of you are—vigilantes. Vigilantes ain't no better than outlaws and murderers." He grinned. "What does that new little gal you rescued think of you, Mitch? Does she think you're a murderin' vigilante, or have you already charmed her into bein' your own personal whore?"

Mitch stepped close to where Hugh stood gripping the cell bars. Without warning he slammed the butt of his rifle against Hugh's fingers. Hugh screamed out and went to his knees, cussing a blue streak and calling Mitch names that would make even the lowest man in a saloon cringe. "Shut your damn mouth, Wiley, or I'll come in there and beat you till you can't stand up," Mitch fumed.

More curses flowed from Hugh's mouth, but they were mumbled as he curled up against the wall. Jake Snyder sat on his cot in the same cell, watching everything and saying nothing. He looked truly scared. Mitch threw him a warning glance and turned away.

"It's going to be a long night," he told the others. "If one of you wants to go lie down on the cot in the corner there, we'll take turns getting an hour or so of shut-eye through the night so we aren't all four of us so damn tired by morning that we aren't alert. I'll be glad when this shit is over with."

"You're not the only one," Benny answered.

"I get first dibs on the cot," Randy stated. "I've been here watching those two worthless bums the longest."

"Hell, you're the youngest among us, kid. You shouldn't need any sleep at all," Len teased.

Randy shook his head and walked over to the cot, setting his rifle aside and lying down, leaving on boots and guns and putting his hat over his eyes.

"You sure you're up to this?" Len asked Mitch. "Only a couple days ago you were lyin' over there at Doc's place passed out from loss of blood."

"I'm fine," Mitch argued, not wanting to admit that his side ached fiercely and he still had a strong desire to go back to bed. "I'll get some more rest after the hanging."

"Suit yourself. I—"

Len's words were interrupted by a shout from outside.

"Mitch Brady! Come on out here and have them friends of yours release my brother!"

Mitch recognized Sam Wiley's gruff voice. Randy jumped up and grabbed his rifle. Benny doused the oil lamps to darken the jail.

"I *told* you Sam would come for me!" Hugh Wiley groaned.

"Shut up!" Mitch ordered.

Hugh rose from where he was curled up on the floor. Holding his smashed right hand, he joined Jake Snyder as the two outlaws pressed themselves against the bars to hear what was going on.

Mitch went to a window, pressing his back against the wall beside it and turning his head just enough to look outside. By the dim light of an evening not quite all the way dark yet he saw Sam Wiley standing in the street surrounded by four other men. Beside him, forced to stand there by Sam's arm crooked around her neck, stood Elizabeth, looking terrified.

"I'm ready to trade, Brady," Wiley told him. "My brother for this pretty little gal here."

"Sweet Jesus," Mitch muttered. "They have Elizabeth!"

Thirteen

MITCH RAGED INSIDE AT THE SIGHT OF SAM WILEY'S grip on Elizabeth's neck as he held a cocked six-gun to her head. Four other men with guns sat mounted on their horses, holding three more horses that were saddled and ready for a quick escape.

"Shoot me, and this gun goes off, taking this little gal down with me!" Wiley shouted gruffly. He was a big man, and Elizabeth looked so small and helpless in his grip. Mitch could see the terror in her eyes, and it reminded him of another woman helpless in a man's grip, her face pummeled until she was nearly unrecognizable. The memory of his mother's beating when he was too small to help her would live with him forever.

"Send my brother out, Brady, or I ride off with this little lady here!" Wiley yelled. "And you won't like what we do to her! Send Jake Snyder out, too! And you come out yourself—unarmed!"

"What do you want us to do, Mitch?" Randy asked, standing at the other window and gripping his rifle.

"Let them out."

"What?" Benny asked.

"You heard me," Mitch answered, still watching Sam Wiley. He wanted nothing more than to put a bullet in the man's head, but Wiley was right. If he was hit, his cocked pistol would go off and Elizabeth would be dead. *Damn* her! This would be a lot easier if he didn't care so much.

"That sonofabitch!" Len Gray grumbled. "He won't get away with this! I'd like to see him hang tomorrow right along with his brother."

"We'll make sure they *both* hang," Mitch answered. "Right now we'll just let him *think* he's getting away with this."

Benny unlocked Hugh Wiley's cell and Wiley walked out, Jake Snyder following close behind. Wiley grimaced at the pain in his hand. "I *told* you my brother would come for me," he sneered at Mitch. "And I'll pay you back for smashing my fingers. I'll smash every bone in your body!"

The look Mitch gave him caused Wiley to back away. "Enjoy your five minutes of freedom," Mitch told him, moving away from the window. He laid his rifle on a table and removed his six-gun from its holster. "Get your ass out that door."

"I want a gun."

"Let your brother give you one. You'll not get one from me."

Wiley spit at Mitch. "You're fixin' to make a mess of this, ain't you?"

"I'm just doing what your brother asked so he'll let the woman go."

Wiley smiled nervously. "You know damn well Sam won't let her go right away. If he did that, your men would shoot him and me both soon as she's free. He'll take her with us for a ways, for insurance."

"I don't doubt that. Now get going."

Hugh hesitated and Jake Snyder looked confused and afraid. "Go on, Hugh! This is our chance. Do you want to feel a rope around your neck tomorrow? I'd rather go down with a bullet than get my neck broke and my breath cut off. It's a hell of a way to die, Hugh!"

Wiley kept his eyes on Mitch. "I'm just tryin' to figure what this bastard vigilante has in mind."

"There's no time for that. Just go!"

"Shut up, Jake!"

"The hell with you!" Jake made for the door. "I'm comin' out, Sam!" he yelled. He opened the door and walked outside.

"Hurry it up!" Sam told him. "Go mount up!"

With the door open, Mitch could see Jake walk around Elizabeth and climb up on a horse. "You're next," Mitch told Hugh. "Let's get this over with."

Hugh stood there a moment, eyeing Mitch closely. "I don't trust you, you sonofabitch. Somethin' tells me you don't give a damn what happens to that little lady out there."

"It's up to you, Wiley. You can die today...or tomorrow. You know damn well that if I let you ride off right now, whether that woman is with you or not, I'll find you. And you and your brother will *both* hang."

Hugh Wiley looked around at the others. Randy just smiled. Benny Carson shrugged and Len Gray spit tobacco juice on Wiley's boots.

"A man ought not hide behind a woman's skirts," Len snarled. "You and your brother just keep diggin' the hole deeper and deeper."

Hugh swallowed, glancing outside.

"Get the hell out here, Hugh!" Sam shouted. "'Fore I choke this little lady to death!"

Hugh took a deep breath and headed out. Mitch glanced at Len. "You know what to do." He walked out unarmed, his hands in the air and his gaze fixed on Sam Wiley while Hugh ran over to climb up on one of the free horses. "My men are inside with guns leveled on you," he told Sam. "They won't shoot as long as you ride off without the woman."

Hugh grinned. "Come on, Mitch. I ain't that stupid. She's goin' with us. It's the only way there won't be no shootin'."

Mitch shook his head, refusing to look at Elizabeth because it tore at his heart to see her fear. "You take her, we start shooting," he told Sam. "She's better off dead than going with the likes of you. I mean it, Sam. I'll let her die first."

Elizabeth let out a whimper.

"The only reason I'm letting Hugh go is so you leave the woman behind," he told Sam. "That's it. You can shoot me dead now if you want, but half the town will witness it—you shooting down an unarmed man and kidnapping an innocent young woman. You didn't think this through very well, did you, Sam?"

Sam glanced at the jail to see a rifle leveled out of each front window.

"Let her go, Hugh," Mitch repeated. "If you want any hope of getting out of here alive, let her go."

"Damn it, Sam, you shouldn't have done it this way!" Hugh yelled at his brother. "It was damn stupid! You never did think with your head on straight!"

"I got you out of there, didn't I?" Sam growled, eyeing Mitch steadily.

"Sure, but you'd better let that woman go if you want to make it to the end of the street!"

Sam's breathing quickened. "I got your word you'll let us ride off?" he asked Mitch.

Mitch nodded. "My word as sheriff of Alder."

A crowd had gathered, a mixture of businessmen, miners, and saloon girls, all waiting with bated breath. The air hung completely silent for a moment. Sam Wiley finally let go of Elizabeth and gave her a shove so hard, she fell forward.

Mitch immediately dove to the ground to cover Elizabeth as bullets started flying. Women in the crowd screamed and everyone ran for cover. Sam and Hugh Wiley both went down, and three of the other four men ducked for cover. Jake Snyder tried to ride off while shooting back at Randy, Benny, and Len, who came running out of the jail with flames shooting from their gun barrels as they unleashed a round of bullets. Randy ducked and rolled toward Mitch.

"Here!" He tossed a six-gun to Mitch. Mitch stayed on top of Elizabeth as he took a last shot at Jake Snyder. The man yelled out and fell from his horse.

By then the crowd had corralled the other three men, who raised their arms and gave themselves up. Snyder lay dead in the street from Mitch's bullet.

Len, Benny, and Randy all proceeded to round up the living, including Sam and Hugh, who'd been wounded but not killed. Sam was screaming with the pain of a bullet in his gut. He was dragged to the jail while someone went to get Doc Wilson.

"Wounded or not, these two will hang tomorrow," Len shouted.

Mitch eased off of Elizabeth. She sat up and just stared at him wide-eyed, her face red from being half choked, tears leaving clean lines where they trickled through the dust on her face. Her ears rang from all the gunfire. Mitch scooped her into his arms as he rose and carried her down the middle of the street toward Ma Kelly's. People stared and mumbled to each other about the new woman in town and how Mitch Brady had risked his life to save her...yet again.

Elizabeth laid her head on Mitch's shoulder and sobbed. Mitch held her closer.

Fourteen

"MITCH, I'M SO SORRY!" MA KELLY APOLOGIZED AS she opened the front door and let Mitch carry Elizabeth inside. "They held me back and grabbed Elizabeth soon as you left. Is she all right?"

"She will be. She's just shaken up." Mitch carried Elizabeth down the hallway and up the back stairs to her room. Ma followed behind, opening the door to Elizabeth's room so Mitch could lay her on her bed.

"I'll get a rag and some cool water," Ma told Mitch.

Mitch stopped her. "What about you, Ma? You okay?"

"Oh, it takes a lot to bring down this old buzzard," she answered. "I'm all right." She patted Mitch's arm. "You tend to that little gal there."

Ma left, and Elizabeth rolled away from Mitch, lying on her side. "I hate this town! Why did I come here?"

Mitch leaned over and gently smoothed back her hair where it had fallen from its pins. "That's what I'd like to know, Elizabeth. Why *did* you come here?"

"I can't tell you. And right now I don't know what to do," she sobbed. "Just go away."

Mitch pulled a chair close to the side of the bed. "I'm not going anywhere, and I don't blame you for hating this town, but there really are some good people here, Elizabeth. All that's happened—it's not the usual here—not this bad, I mean. I'm sorry you were introduced to Alder this way."

"I came here to be left alone, and all I've been is the center of everyone's attention." She managed to sit up straighter, wiping at her eyes with shaking fingers. "I'm sorry. I'm acting like a child."

"My God, Elizabeth, you have a right to cry. I'm so goddamn sorry about all of this. I should have seen it coming." He put his head in his hands.

Elizabeth moved to the edge of the bed, reaching into her pocket to find a handkerchief. "What about you? What about that wound?"

Mitch looked down at himself, realizing the site of his wound stung like crazy. He saw a spot of blood. "I guess diving to the ground with you opened things up again."

"Oh, Mitch, go see Doc Wilson, please!"

He sighed and leaned back in the chair, running a hand through his hair. "I will soon. I hope you know I didn't mean it when I said I'd let you die. I would have let Sam Wiley blow a hole right through my belly to get you away from him, if that's what it took."

Elizabeth sniffed and wiped at more tears. "I was hoping you were just bluffing."

Mitch wanted to smile at the smeared dirt and tears on her cheeks. Even when she was a mess, she was beautiful. "I feel like an ass. I should have realized Sam might pull something like this. I should have sent a man over here to keep an eye on you and Ma till the hanging was over."

Elizabeth looked him over. "Your arm is bleeding."

Mitch looked at his right forearm. "Just a scrape from tackling you to the ground. I hope I didn't hurt you. I'm not exactly a lightweight. You're lucky I didn't break something."

"My shoulder hurts, but that's all. It all happened so fast. When you pushed me down and covered me, I thought for sure you'd been shot and killed."

Mitch smiled sadly. "Does that mean you would have cared?"

"Of course I would have cared. You risked your life for me."

"Well it wasn't just me, you know. I had to rely on my men knowing what to do when I tackled you to the ground."

"You must really trust them."

"In what we do, you *have* to have men you can trust. The fact remains, none of it would have happened if I'd done my job right. I guess this wound and all the other things that happened distracted me. *You* distract me. Since you came to town, Elizabeth Wainright, I haven't been myself."

Elizabeth looked at her lap. "Then you need to stop following me around and worrying about me. I'm no one to you, Mitch. Three days ago, you didn't even know I existed. I chose to come here, and it's up to me to decide what to do now. It's not your worry."

"It *is* my worry. And it's not true that you're no one to me. There is something special about you that…"

He trailed off when Ma Kelly returned with a wet cloth and two cups of coffee on a small tray.

"You two had better get some hot coffee in you." She set the tray on a table beside the bed and used the cloth to gently wipe Elizabeth's face. Elizabeth took the cloth from her.

"I can do it, Ma. I'll be all right."

"You sure? You've been through an awful lot in the last three days, little lady."

"Believe me, I've been through worse."

Mitch came alert at the remark. He watched her carefully as he drank some of the coffee while Elizabeth wiped dirt from her face as best she could without a mirror.

"I really am not one to cry so easily," she told Mitch. "It's just that when you picked me up..." She reddened. "It just felt good to lean on someone." She set the cloth aside. "It doesn't mean I intend to lean on you or anyone else under normal conditions. And it doesn't mean I'm a helpless waif."

Mitch leaned closer. "I don't think of you that way one little bit. Whatever brought you here, Elizabeth, it took courage. I admire that. I just wish you would tell me what it is you're running from—how I can help you."

Elizabeth shook her head. "I can't. I still don't know you well enough to completely trust you." She raised her chin defiantly. "One thing you *can* do is teach me how to use that gun. I would have gladly shot Sam Wiley with it earlier if it had been loaded and ready."

Mitch grinned. "The day after tomorrow. Let things

calm down from the hanging." He drank some coffee. "And I intend to send a man over here to sit in Ma's parlor and keep an eye on things until then. With Sam and Hugh both wounded, it's not likely anything will happen now, but we can't be any too careful. Hugh Wiley's wife, Trudy, is more man than woman, and she can be as vengeful as her husband's brothers. She's a tough rancher's wife, who can use a gun and stand up to any man with it. I'll have to watch out for her the same as any of Wiley's brothers or ranch hands. I'm just embarrassed that this happened at all. I should have realized they might use you to get what they want."

Their gazes held. "Because they think you're sweet on me, I suppose. It's a little embarrassing to be talked about that way when no one even really knows me yet. And for heaven's sake, how can they think such things when we still barely know each other?"

Mitch noticed a small cut on her lip. He dearly wanted to beat the hell out of Sam Wiley. He leaned back in the chair. "Folks around here are just hungry for gossip and news," he answered. "A pretty young girl with a mysterious past and no escort comes to town…not just in an ordinary way, but the victim of a stagecoach robbery, riding into town with a vigilante, the extra horses carrying two dead bodies… All this has made you the center of attention, and because you're young and beautiful and unattached, you're a woman wanted by practically every man in town, most of them still trying to figure out if you're a lady or…something less than a lady."

Elizabeth pushed back a strand of hair. "And what do *you* think I am?"

"You already know what I think."

"Well, you might think I'm a proper lady, but I'm still trying to decide if you're a proper gentleman," she answered. "Other than Ma Kelly, I've reasoned that your only female friends are *not* ladies, and I've seen how rough and unfeeling you can be."

Mitch shrugged. "It's pretty hard to find female friends out here who *are* ladies. A man doesn't have a whole lot of choice. And as far as being rough and unfeeling, I grew up *having* to be that way." Damn if this young woman didn't have a way of making him open up about himself.

"How did you end up out here?" she asked.

Mitch shifted in his chair. "I drifted south, fought in the war for a while, then headed west just to see what it was like. I ended up defending a few people, wound up in a gunfight, and got named the local lawman without even saying I wanted to do it. I rode with vigilantes for a while in an attempt to end a range war and cattle rustling, and now here I am, just doing my job." He looked her over. "I was really worried you'd get hurt bad out there, and it would have been my fault. It won't happen again, I promise."

She shook her head. "You don't need to promise me anything. I'm not your responsibility, Mitch. You shouldn't let it get so personal, if it means endangering yourself."

Mitch rose and walked to the door. "I don't have any choice. Feelings have a way of shoving themselves unwanted into a person." He studied her lovely green eyes and saw the frightened girl behind them. "I'm real sorry about what happened today."

She looked away. "Thank you." She folded her arms, appearing nervous and embarrassed. "Please go see Doc Wilson. I have to admit that I'm not sure what I would have done if you were killed today. I guess I would have moved on to another town."

"Does that mean you're definitely staying? You said you hated it here."

She faced him. "You have to teach me how to use that gun, don't you? I guess that's reason enough to stay for now. Besides, I really do think I could make my way here by teaching and writing. What those men did isn't the fault of the rest of the town. I at least have a friend in Ma Kelly...and you, I guess."

They stood there frozen in the moment, both wanting to say things it was too soon to say.

"I...it's just difficult for me to trust anyone, Mitch, let alone someone I've known such a short time. After my father died, my mother turned to someone she thought she could trust, someone she'd known for years, and it ended in tragedy."

Mitch frowned. "Elizabeth, whatever happened to your mother shouldn't mean you have to live the rest of your life all alone, never trusting anyone and never asking for help."

She held his gaze. "Isn't that what *you've* done most of your life?"

Mitch put his hat back on, smiling softly. "You've got me there." He nodded to her. "Get some rest. Someone will be here tonight and tomorrow to keep watch until the hanging is over." He hesitated. "You sure you're okay?"

"I'm sure. I guess it's kind of like with you...I've been through some things that toughened me up."

He ached to hold her. "I wish you'd share those things with me, Elizabeth."

She turned away. "You'd better go. It doesn't look good, you being alone with me here in my room. Heaven knows we're both providing food enough for gossip. We don't need to add fuel to the fire."

"Sure." Mitch forced himself to turn and go out the door. It was the hardest thing he'd done in years.

Fifteen

ELIZABETH SAT IN MA KELLY'S PARLOR READING *The Mill on the Floss*, a strangely fascinating story of a young girl's survival over poverty and her confused love life. It was one of several books Ma kept on a shelf against the wall for her patrons' entertainment, and Elizabeth relished the distraction from her own woes and the perils of her own predicament.

Ma's three other boarders, all men, had gone out to watch the hanging. Elizabeth didn't know much about them, other than one intended to leave soon and go looking for gold. He roomed with a drifter traveling the West, and one was waiting for supplies to arrive because he meant to open a hardware store. The gold seeker and hardware-store owner both had wives who would follow as soon as they determined if they were going to stay in Alder.

She laid the book in her lap, thinking how she didn't care much one way or the other about the boarders, or about any of the people outside, except for one...Mitch Brady. He was out there somewhere in the streets handling things, his life always at risk simply because he was a lawman. She hardly knew what to make of a man who seemed such a contrast of good and bad, caring and cold. Could he turn on her the way her stepfather had turned on her mother? Was he like all other men, wanting only one thing from a woman? Was he the type to marry just to be able to possess anything of value that woman owned?

Randy Olson walked past the window, stopping to peer inside for a moment to make sure Elizabeth was still sitting unscathed and unthreatened in a rocker beside the fireplace. Elizabeth looked at him and smiled. Randy nodded and walked to stand beside the front door.

She'd also read bits and pieces from *The Vigilantes of Montana*, written by an Englishman who was living in Virginia City and had made detailed observations of life in the West. Some of what she'd read seemed a stark contrast to the caring side she'd seen in Mitch, and even in Randy and the other men who worked with him. Young Randy was affable and good-looking and seemed trustworthy.

But it was Mitch who fascinated her the most. From the first day they met, the man had been either rescuing or defending her, risking his life more than once to do so. It seemed such a strange way to meet a person, and she couldn't help wondering if the conditions under which they met were what had attracted her to him and made her want to be near him—because he made her feel safe. She hadn't felt safe for a long, long time, and the conditions under which she'd left New York made her wary of trusting a man to help her now, especially one who could be violent. She'd had enough of violence.

She heard singing then—a hymn! She set her book aside. "Ma, come here," she yelled down the hall to the kitchen.

Old Ma Kelly came down the hallway, wiping her hands on her apron. "What is it?"

"Singing! I think the people out there are actually singing a hymn. It just seems so strange, to hear hymns in such a wild, lawless town."

Ma Kelly smiled with a bit of sadness in her eyes. "They always sing hymns before a hanging," she told Elizabeth. The two women walked to the door and Ma Kelly opened it and began humming. Randy turned and put his arm out. "Best if you stayed inside," he told Elizabeth. "Them's Mitch's orders."

"I was just surprised to hear them singing a hymn."

Randy shrugged. "That always happens at a formal hanging. They ask each man if he has anything to say or wants to pray and make things right with the Almighty. Then the whole crowd sings a couple of hymns for the men about to die."

Elizabeth shivered at the sight of men standing on the scaffold down at the end of the street. She was glad it was far enough away that she couldn't see their eyes. She wondered how it felt to stand on a scaffold staring at a noose and knowing for certain that in the next minute you would be dead. The entire hanging ceremony seemed ludicrous.

"Where is Mitch?" she asked Randy.

"Oh, he'd be up close to oversee it all. Doc Wilson will be there to verify the men are dead after the hanging. One has to hope the nooses are tied just right. The guy who prepared them claims he's done it before. It's not always easy to find a proper hangman. There ain't a whole lot of them around."

Elizabeth frowned. "What happens if the noose isn't tied just right?"

Randy glanced at her, shaking his head. "You don't want to know." He looked down the street. "Let's just say it ain't a pleasant way to die, if there *is* a pleasant way."

"They aren't hanging Sam Wiley, too, are they? He didn't kill anyone."

"No, ma'am. Mitch wanted him to hang for what he done to you, but you're right. He didn't kill anybody. He's layin' back at the jail bad wounded. If he lives, Mitch will take him to Virginia City, where a judge will decide how much jail time he ought to spend for kidnappin' and for tryin' to spring his murderin' brother from jail and for shootin' at the law. I expect he'll spend some time in prison, probably farther east. There ain't much out here yet in the way of real, secure prisons."

The singing stopped and the crowd quieted.

"I expect Preacher Greene is prayin' now," Randy told Elizabeth, his voice lowered.

"Alder has a preacher?"

"Yes, ma'am. No church, though. Just a travelin' preacher. He happened to come to town yesterday, so that's good timing. He's kinda old, but he still manages to make his rounds."

Elizabeth thought about the abundance of churches in New York and in most towns back East. The incredible contrast in lifestyle and amenities out here would take a lot of getting used to. She wasn't sure she ever would. Everything she'd left behind seemed so far away and unreal now. She missed her mother so much. Life would never be the same for her again.

She could see someone putting the nooses around the necks of the two men standing on the scaffold. Hugh Wiley and Jake Snyder had both been wounded yesterday, and it looked like someone was helping one of them stay on his feet. Elizabeth turned away, not wanting to watch what would happen next. She walked back inside and down the hallway, going upstairs to her room. She opened her small trunk, feeling for her mother's necklace hidden in the lining. She pulled it out, thinking how she, too, might go to prison or be shot or maybe even hanged because of one man's lies...one very powerful man.

Even though she was upstairs and at the back of Ma's house, she heard the crowd gasp in unison. The deed was done. In spite of how Hugh Wiley and Jake Snyder had treated her, she prayed their nooses had been properly tied and that they'd died quickly.

Sixteen

DARKNESS SET IN, BUT THE SALOONS REMAINED ALIVE with music and drinking and dancing. Elizabeth still sat in the parlor reading, trying not to think about the hanging…or about Mitch Brady. That effort failed when she heard a key turn in the front door and she looked up to see Mitch Brady walk inside, dressed in a clean shirt, a leather vest, and dark pants—and of all things, wearing no guns. He held out a bouquet of roses.

"These are for you," he told her. "The blacksmith lives outside of town and his wife has a green thumb for roses. I asked her if I could have some."

Elizabeth was dumbfounded. She rose, quick instincts telling her not to laugh. Indeed, she suspected this was a gesture that actually took courage for a man like Mitch. Not only was this unlike anything she'd expect from such a man, it was a kindness she'd never seen in *any* man except once when she was little and her real father had brought flowers to her mother.

"Mitch, they're beautiful." She took the roses from him. "Wait here." She went to the kitchen and found a vase to put them in, adding water from a pitcher on the counter. Ma Kelly was tired and had gone to bed early. Elizabeth came back into the parlor and set the roses on a small table beside a chair. "They look lovely." She met his eyes. "Thank you for bringing them."

Mitch sat down in a stuffed chair, taking a thin cigar from a pocket inside his vest. "Mind if I smoke?"

"No."

He grasped an oil lamp from a table beside the chair and held the cigar over the chimney to light it. "I brought those flowers just to show you there are other normal women in this town, wives and mothers who cook and bake and grow roses. After all you've been through, I just wanted you to see there are a few good things here, and I thought maybe you'd like to see there is a normal man behind those guns I wear."

He smoked quietly as Elizabeth took a chair across from him. "I can't believe you thought to do this."

Mitch took another drag on the thin cigar and then set it in an ashtray nearby. He leaned forward and rested his elbows on his knees. "You sat through that hanging all alone, wondering what the hell you'll do next and if you even want to stay in this town. This is just a way of apologizing for all you've been through since you got here. It's also my way of showing you that I want you to stay in Alder. You don't have to tell me anything about why you're here. I just don't want you to run again. I want you here so I can keep you safe."

Elizabeth felt a catch in her heart. "Why do you care so much?"

He looked at the floor. "Because you…remind me of someone, that's all."

"Who? A wife? A sister? Did something bad happen to some woman you cared about? Sarah told me what you did to that man who hurt her, and she said you're always defending women and—"

"I can't talk about it. Not yet anyway. You keep telling me you don't know me well enough to tell me everything about yourself. I guess I feel the same way."

"Except to tell me you're a worthless, no-good, murdering vigilante?"

He grinned. "Except that. And don't forget that I don't lie, so that really is part of what I am."

Elizabeth studied him quietly. "I might believe the murdering vigilante part, because I witnessed as much But something tells me you aren't worthless and you aren't a no-good. You've certainly been good to me, and others tell me you're a good man. Of course, those others have been women. Why do I suspect every woman in this town is in love with you? Even Ma?"

He laughed then, actually looking embarrassed. "Hey, the men who work with me or for me are pretty good friends, too. Most of them would have my back anytime. And the women are all just—" He shrugged. "Good friends," he finished.

"I'll bet they are." Elizabeth smiled, while deep inside she felt an odd jealousy. Why? She knew in the worst way the horror of being with a man, but part of her also knew there was supposed to be something pleasurable about it. After all, her mother had seemed so happy with her father. But then he died…and then there was Alan Radcliffe. She sobered.

"You've lost your pretty smile," Mitch told her, smoking again. "What is it?"

Tell him! What if Alan finds you here? Mitch might be able to help. "It's just one of those things I'm not ready to tell you yet, if ever," she answered, "just like there are things you won't tell me."

"If I did, would it help you open up to me?"

She shook her head. "I don't think so." *He's a lawman,* she reminded herself. *By now you could be a wanted woman.* How she hated Alan Radcliffe! He'd ruined her chances of ever being really happy, made her come to this wild, reckless town where she could probably never lead a normal life. He'd taken away all her dreams of what love should be like, her dreams that a man could be gentle and caring.

"What happened at the hanging?" she asked Mitch, forcing back the ugly memories, wanting to change the subject by grasping at anything else. "Did it go right? I heard that if they don't tie the rope knot right—"

"It went like it should," he interrupted. "I'm glad you stayed away. If you've never seen a hanging, it's pretty hard to watch."

She shook her head. "I still can't believe people let their children watch."

"That's life in a Western gold town." Mitch set the cigar aside again. "I guess you get so used to it that you don't think much about it. As far as what I do, if you don't deal vigilante-type justice out here, Elizabeth, people don't survive. There's no other kind of law. Without it you'd have rapes and murders and stealing going on night and day. There's enough of that as it is, but striking fear into the hearts of most men helps stop a lot of it. I saw plenty of lawlessness in the back alleys of the poor neighborhoods of New York City. When I made my way out here, I decided I'd rather be on the side of the law. I already told you how I kind of fell into the rest."

Elizabeth nodded. "I see."

Mitch sighed. "You probably *don't* see, considering the kind of life I think you've likely led up to now. If you come from the right side of town, you can go your whole life without seeing a crime committed or the horrible things people can do to each other. I *have* seen the worst of it, so if I sometimes come off as uncaring, it's probably because in situations like that I *don't* care—not about the person committing the crime anyway. I guess I just need you to know that. It doesn't mean I'm a horrible person you can't trust. And because of how I figure you grew up, I know all the things you've witnessed and suffered the last few days must have been terrifying for you. When you talked about leaving Alder…" He shook his head. "Just don't leave, okay? Things wouldn't be any better in any other town out here, and at least now you've already made a couple of friends. I don't want to worry about you traveling someplace else all alone, maybe meeting up with something worse than what happened in that robbery."

Elizabeth met his gaze, eyes too blue to be real, a kind of sparkling blue that could hold kindness and yet blaze with ruthless anger when he was riled. That was what she wasn't quite sure of yet. She'd seen what a man could do when suddenly and unexpectedly angered.

"I'm not totally unfamiliar with violence, Mitch."

There came several long seconds of silence as their gazes held. "I wish you would tell me about it."

She finally tore away from his penetrating gaze. The man seemed to be able to read a person a bit too well. "Maybe—once I know you better. Right now I just want to get oriented here. I feel better, now that all those men are dead and gone. And I feel safe here at Ma's. And I *have* to stay a while yet, because Sarah owes me some dresses."

"She's a good seamstress. She's made me several shirts."

Elizabeth toyed with an embroidered flower on her own dress. "Is she… I mean…have you and Sarah—"

Mitch grinned again. "That's an unfair question for a single man in a town full of loose women. I guess that's my business, isn't it?"

Elizabeth reddened. "It wasn't an unfair question. It was a *stupid* question. I have no idea why I asked it."

Mitch crushed out his cheroot in the ashtray. "I'd like to think you asked it because you think you and I could be more than acquaintances. At least I'd like it that way. You know me—honest Mitch Brady. A person always knows what I'm thinking, and I'm thinking you're beautiful and alone and I would like nothing more than to court you. This is my feeble attempt at doing just that. I'm not real good at these things, not with a woman like you, anyway."

He rose, and Elizabeth followed, feeling flustered and embarrassed. How could she explain to him why a young, unattached woman wouldn't be interested? It certainly didn't have anything to do with Mitch Brady himself. He was just about the most handsome, virile man she'd ever met…and so far he'd been attentive and kind and...hell, he'd saved her life—twice! She couldn't bring herself to meet his eyes. "I guess you can call on me again," she told him. "I just need a few days to get my thoughts straight."

He grasped her arm gently, forcing her to look up at him. "Elizabeth, when it comes to women, I'm not the brute you've seen when I'm using my guns. And I'm not stupid enough to think you're ready to trust a near stranger. I'm just trying to make myself less of a stranger and more of a friend." He let go of her and walked to where he'd hung his hat near the door. "I'll be gone about a week. I'm taking Sam Wiley to Virginia City. That will give you time to think about a few things." He started for the door.

"Wait!" she called out.

Mitch hesitated, meeting her eyes again.

"Thank you...for the roses. That was nice of you. And—" She glanced at his hips, where she'd always seen him wear those guns. "Is it safe for you to be out there in the streets without your guns?"

He smiled again. Then he reached down, pulling up the cuff of his right pant leg and taking a six-gun from his boot. "I am never completely unarmed," he answered, holding up the six-gun. "Now you don't have to worry." He was still grinning as he shoved the pistol into his belt. "You take care of yourself and stick close to Ma while I'm gone. And a couple of my men will be keeping an eye on you."

He walked out the door. Elizabeth couldn't decide how she felt. She glanced at the vase of roses. The man could show stark contrasts of personality, and all of them confused her.

Seventeen

FIVE MORE DAYS PASSED. ELIZABETH SAW NOTHING OF Mitch, who sent Randy to her with a message that he'd left for Virginia City, where Sam Wiley would be jailed, sentenced by a judge there, and likely be sent to a prison farther east. Mitch had taken two men with him to testify as to what Sam did, adamant that Elizabeth herself would not have to go and testify. He wanted Sam Wiley jailed and out of the way, anxious for things to get back to normal, whatever normal was for a place like Alder.

Elizabeth worried about him the whole time he was gone. Hugh and Sam had other friends who now probably hated Mitch. She just hoped that if and when Sam Wiley ever got out of jail, he would stay away from Alder. The preacher who'd presided over the hanging had left town, and the last five days had been relatively quiet, other than the street noises Elizabeth was beginning to get used to. She'd enjoyed a more welcome rest than anything she'd experienced since her spectacular arrival here. She took advantage of the chance to let her shoulder heal more and to stay away from staring eyes. Since the excitement of the hanging died down, she hoped the curiosity over why she was here would also die down.

For these past five days there was only Ma Kelly to talk to. Even the other boarders were never around much, except at breakfast, and they were for the most part respectful toward her and didn't ask too many questions. In fact, all three of the original boarders had left, and two new men had moved in, both of them just looking for jobs in town. None stayed long enough to get well acquainted, and that was fine with Elizabeth.

For any who tried to pry into Elizabeth's business or gave a hint of wanting to take her out on the town, Ma Kelly promptly set them straight. Doc Wilson had supper with them one evening at Ma's invitation. Elizabeth enjoyed the visit, but she'd not asked much about Mitch, not wanting the doctor to think she cared one way or the other about the man. Her only other visitor had been the lawyer, Carl Jackson, who came calling one day unexpectedly. Ma turned him away, and after he left Ma warned her that Jackson was not a man she should encourage, voicing her opinion that the man was "as crooked as they come." Between that remark and Mitch's poor opinion of the man, Elizabeth was perfectly happy to see him turned away at the door.

It was Mitch Brady who gave her restless thoughts and attracted her in ways she'd rather not admit. She'd not come here to find a man, and after what she'd left behind, she doubted she'd ever allow a man to touch her anyway…not even Mitch Brady. Love and trust were two things she'd likely never experience again.

Still, Mitch stirred emotions she didn't think she'd ever feel. And he'd brought her those roses…

Again, unwanted memories slammed her heart and thoughts, always hitting her unexpectedly, always alarming, always depressing. In the nine days she'd been here in Alder, she'd managed more and more to push away the events that brought her here, push away the memory of Alan Radcliffe and his brutality, push away the memory of her mother's cruel death… and the fact that she'd not been able to say good-bye.

She blinked back tears and took a deep breath. *Not today. Not today.* An explosion from one of the bigger mines in the surrounding mountains helped bring her thoughts to the present. The sudden rumbles made the small boardinghouse shake, but they no longer startled Elizabeth. Each explosion was a signal that some mine owner was going deeper into the mountains. She'd learned a little about how it all worked, and now she was curious to see it for herself. She figured she'd do just that when Mitch took her through the various settlements scattered along Alder Gulch to see about teaching.

That day had come. Yesterday Randy delivered the message that Mitch was back and was coming today to take her outside of town for some shooting practice. They would also visit some of the settlements in the gulch, and she'd prepared some handwritten flyers to give out to families, telling them where to find her if they wanted their child to get some schooling.

She studied herself in the mirror, wearing the first dress Sarah had managed to finish for her. It was made of the brown cotton material with tiny yellow flowers in the pattern. Elizabeth was impressed with Sarah's abilities as a seamstress. The dress fit well; it was a one-piece princess style with buttons from the top of the slightly scooped neck all the way down the front to the very bottom of the hemline. Dropped shoulders led to long sleeves that fit loosely, the neckline and sleeves designed for the hot July days. Because of the heat, Elizabeth wore only one petticoat, which left the skirt hanging almost straight.

Following Elizabeth's instructions, there were no embellishments on the dress. Here in Alder it just wasn't practical to dress in lace and ruffles and a pile of petticoats and jewelry. She'd twisted her hair into a large round bun at the back of her head, held with plain combs, and she wore tiny drop earrings, just a touch of rouge, and nothing more in the way of extra jewelry or makeup.

She pinned on a small straw hat, glad to have unexpectedly discovered hats in a general store. She'd gone out shopping only once, accompanied by Ma Kelly, Randy Olson always hanging nearby, according to Mitch's instructions. Elizabeth appreciated the fact that his presence, as well as Ma Kelly's, helped keep strangers away, but part of her still hated being followed.

She heard the front door open, then heard voices. It irked her that she was actually excited to see Mitch again, but she couldn't stop the emotions he stirred in her. She smoothed her dress and picked up the derringer from where she'd laid it on the bed. She put it into her drawstring handbag, picked up one box of ammunition and a few of her flyers, and walked out and down the back stairs, where she nearly ran into Ma Kelly.

"Mitch is here, dear," she told Elizabeth, looking her over. "You look lovely, Elizabeth." She gave Elizabeth a sly smile.

"Ma, don't be making something out of nothing."

"Oh, I don't think I'm doing that at all." Ma chuckled and walked into the kitchen, and Elizabeth went down the hall into the parlor. Mitch Brady's tall, broad presence seemed to fill up the room, and there was no way Elizabeth could miss the pleased look in his blue eyes when she came closer. Part of her was happy to see him, and part of her wished she'd not taken so much care about how she looked today.

"I...Sarah made this dress for me. Is it plain enough? I mean...I don't want to be out of place when we're going out to shoot guns and visit mining camps."

Mitch grinned. "You look perfect."

She felt naked under his gaze.

"But then how could you *not* look perfect?"

Damn, if he didn't look more handsome than ever himself. He wore dark pants with a blue shirt that matched his eyes, a leather vest with a badge on it, a small red cotton scarf around his neck, and, of course, the ever-present six-guns on crisscrossed gun belts. "You always look ready for a small war," she told him.

He flashed the handsome smile that only accented his full lips and his tanned, clean-shaven face. "If all I was going to do is sit in the parlor like last time, I would have left the guns off. But a lawman headed for Alder Gulch has to be ready for anything."

"I've already seen why you need them." Elizabeth struggled not to show her secret pleasure at seeing him again. She reminded herself of his size, and the fact that he was, after all, a man...and one who was no stranger to violence. When Alan Radcliffe married her mother, he'd seemed like a nice man, too. And he'd been tall and handsome and charming... and cunning. Could Mitch Brady be cunning? If he knew about the valuable necklace she owned, would he be attracted to her only because he wanted to get his hands on it? Knowing about the necklace could change him completely.

"I'm glad you made it back here fine and healthy. I was a little worried about you taking Sam Wiley to Virginia City."

"Well, it all worked out fine and he's likely already on his way to prison." He looked her over again in that way he had. "I hope you got plenty of rest while I was gone."

"I did. I've stayed right here, away from all the bustle out there in the streets. I did go shopping once with Ma Kelly, and your young friend followed us around like a puppy. I really don't need so much guarding now, Mitch. People in this town are getting used to me, and all the craziness over how I arrived has mostly gone away, from what I can tell."

Mitch put on a wide-brimmed hat. "Maybe so, but you're still going to be a curiosity for several weeks, and there will still be times when you might be glad you have that gun. Did you put it in your handbag?"

Elizabeth nodded. "Yes, sir." She handed over the box of bullets. "And I brought these. I also have a few flyers I'd like to hand out if I get the chance."

Mitch took the box of bullets and headed for the door. "Well, let's get going then. I borrowed a buggy from Doc Wilson. Couldn't find a sidesaddle, so I figured the buggy would be best, especially since that shoulder of yours is probably still hurting. I'm not much for riding in a buggy, but I'll put up with it today."

"I appreciate that."

Mitch opened the door and Elizabeth stepped outside, going down the steps and climbing into the buggy, which she was glad to see had a top on it that would shade them from the hot sun. She noticed Mitch had tied his own big roan gelding to the back of the carriage. Was he wanting to be prepared to go charging after some outlaw if need be? She decided not to ask. He came around and climbed into the buggy beside her, picking up the reins and slapping the rump of the big black mare hitched to the vehicle to get the horse into motion.

Elizabeth shoved her flyers into a leather pocket at one side of the buggy, then held on to a seat railing as Mitch drove the buggy out of town and past staring eyes. A few men whistled and a couple of them made remarks about Mitch Brady getting the prettiest girl in town.

"Ignore the remarks," he told Elizabeth.

"I'm trying my best."

He glanced sideways at her. "You *are* the prettiest girl in town, though."

Elizabeth stared straight ahead. "Thank you for the compliment, but this isn't a courting trip, I hope you know. You're going to show me how to use my gun and you're escorting me to some of the mining camps so I can hand out my flyers. That's it. Nothing more."

"Oh, I assure you, I don't consider this courting either. Just keeping a promise to teach you how to use that gun and introduce you to a few people in the gulch. Believe me, when I court you, you'll know that's what it is."

His closeness upset Elizabeth in ways it shouldn't. The buggy was so small, their legs couldn't help but touch. "This is a one-passenger buggy, isn't it?" she commented.

"It was all I could find. If you want to ride, we can go back and saddle a horse."

"No, thank you. This will do."

"Yes, ma'am."

Elizabeth caught the sarcasm in his answer. She wanted to hit him and make him take her back to Ma's place, but she needed to learn how to use her gun.

She had to keep her guard up. Most men wanted only two things—women and money. If both things were wrapped into one package, all the better. Love was not part of the equation. Such feelings meant nothing to a man. She must remember that. She stared straight ahead as Mitch drove the buggy out of town and toward the mountains.

Eighteen

On her journey West, Elizabeth had been so fearful of being found and dragged back to New York that she'd not paid a lot of attention to the landscape. Rather, she'd huddled inside trains and stagecoaches, trying her best not to draw attention to herself. Even when she rode horseback to Alder after the accident, she'd been so shaken and in so much pain that she did little more than just follow behind Mitch, in no mood to look around. After that, there had only been Alder.

Now that she had a chance to truly feel safe and feel free to notice her surroundings, she marveled at the immensity of the yellow-grass valley through which they rode, feeling tiny and insignificant compared to the endless horizon to the north and south of the little winding dirt road. An array of colorful wildflowers were sprinkled amid the yellow grass, creating a view that almost looked like a painting. Mitch headed the buggy into hillier country beyond which lay mountains that rose up in a looming wall that made her wonder at the bravery it took to go into them and try to settle.

"Do you like this valley?" Mitch asked her.

"Yes, it's beautiful. I like all the wildflowers. But it's so big! I feel swallowed up."

They passed a huge supply wagon coming down out of the gulch, and Mitch nodded to the driver.

"I love this place," he told her. "It's magnificent country, and a man can be as free as he wants out here, settle where he wants."

"Do you think much about settling?"

Mitch reached down and broke off a piece of tall grass, putting it between his lips to chew on it. "Sure I do. But I wasn't raised to know much about family life, so I'm not sure I'd be very good at it." He glanced at her. "A man needs just the right woman for that."

Elizabeth looked away. "I've heard Montana referred to as big-sky country," she commented.

"It certainly fits," Mitch answered. "It's only been an official territory for a couple of years, and right now Virginia City is the capital. You probably didn't pay much attention when you were on the stagecoach, but from Virginia City on north and west there are settlements scattered all over because of the gold mining. This is one of the few more open areas, but soon we'll head into the mining area where there is a streambed off the Ruby River and settlements that stretch for a good ten miles. If you wanted to see it all, we'd have to stay somewhere the next couple of nights. There are a couple of rooming places in small settlements throughout the gulch. The gulch runs for about fourteen miles, with little towns, if you want to call them that, situated all along the creek."

"I think if we go that far, it should be another time. I didn't come prepared to stay overnight."

Mitch nodded. "Miles of mining through the gulch is why I'm sometimes gone for days at a time. Vigilantes are pretty much the law in Montana Territory, and wherever there is gold, there are men willing to try to steal it, or steal someone else's claim, or rob the supply wagons that take the gold to and from Virginia City."

They passed more wagons and riders coming out of the gulch.

"If and when I settle, I figured I would take up ranching, maybe settle somewhere in this valley, but like I said, I wasn't raised to know how to do that, especially how to be a father."

Elizabeth wasn't sure what to say. The man was opening up a little more to her. Why?

"Do you have family back in St. Louis, or wherever you're really from?" he asked then.

I'm from New York, just like you. Elizabeth thought about the normal, happy family life she'd once known. "I have no family—never had siblings, and both my parents are dead."

"How'd they die?"

"You're asking too many questions."

Mitch sighed. "Just trying to make conversation, that's all. My own pa was never around much before he drank himself to death. My mother was…" He paused. "Let's just say she had it rough. She was finally beat to death…right in front of me when I was too little to stop it."

The air suddenly hung too silent. Elizabeth was

stunned at what he'd just told her. They had both watched their mothers die right before their eyes. She felt a new connection to the man. Part of her wanted to tell him about her own experience. Surely Mitch Brady would understand… But there was always the fear of Alan Radcliffe finding her and painting a very different picture. "I…I'm so sorry," she told him.

He reined the horse to a halt. "So am I. I didn't mean to tell you something so ugly and so soon." He sighed, staring at the landscape ahead. "Being around you makes me want to talk, and I have no idea why. At any rate, I shouldn't have told you that, but the fact remains that life was never very normal for me when my mother was alive, and then after she died, I just grew up a homeless kid fighting his way through life. So like I said, I know next to nothing about a normal family life other than what I've seen at times in other families…and what I sometimes daydream about. I guess all men at some time in their lives think about settling, taking a wife and all."

Elizabeth was beginning to realize that the way his mother died was something that deeply affected Mitch Brady, leading to his apparent need to defend women. It began to dawn on her then that whatever else Mitch Brady might be, he was not a man who would ever beat on a woman. After living with the likes of Alan Radcliffe and seeing the bruises on her mother, terror over the possibility of marrying such a man herself had made Elizabeth vow to never marry at all. She never saw the beatings. It always happened when she wasn't around…until that one fateful night.

"I think every man has a right to settle and marry,"

she told Mitch. "Maybe, because of how you grew up, you'd make a better father than most men, because you know how you would like that kind of life to be."

Mitch nodded. "Maybe." He turned to meet her eyes for a moment…close, so close, still sitting side by side in the buggy. For one quick moment she thought the man was going to lean in and kiss her, but he turned away again and snapped the reins. "Up ahead there is an area where there is plenty of loose rock, just before we head into the deeper part of Alder Gulch. We'll stop there and do some practice shooting."

They passed a sagging sod house beside a stream a couple hundred yards to their right.

"That's Moss Hillinbert," Mitch told her. "Pans for gold all day long beside that stream. He's alone there. He left a wife back East somewhere, like most men who live all along the gulch. Most of those living here are poor people hoping to strike it rich, a lot of them people who lost everything in the war. Some have already struck it rich and sold their claims to even richer men who have the means to actually mine it the right way. Of course, those rich men don't live around here. They just do the investing from someplace back East and pay men to come out here and oversee everything, hire men to go into the mountains and hack their way through veins of gold and run it through stamp mills and such. It gets pretty complicated. Most of the richest miners live in Virginia City, getting richer from supplying the miners up here in the gulch."

An explosion in the mountains ahead rumbled through the air like thunder. "Most men who come out here looking for their dreams don't realize how much is involved in actually extracting enough gold to make big money," Mitch continued.

"You're not interested in looking for gold?"

Mitch shrugged. "Not really. Being rich doesn't mean much to me. Just being happy is all that matters, and having enough to eat and a place to sleep."

Being rich doesn't mean much to me. How unlike the man Elizabeth was hiding from. Were there really men in this world who actually married for love, who didn't rule over their wives like prison wardens, and who really wanted a happy family life and children?

She shook away the questions that raced through her mind as Mitch approached an area of huge boulders, below which lay scattered rocks. The horse pulling the buggy shied a little when another explosion rumbled in the mountains.

"Settle down, boy," Mitch soothed. He climbed out of the buggy and tied the animal to a lonely pine tree that had somehow managed to find life beneath the rocky landscape. Elizabeth had to wonder how anything grew from such hard ground, yet for most of their ride from Alder she'd noticed thick shrubbery and even large groves of trees along the gulch.

"What kind of trees are those tall ones I've seen?"

"Alder trees. That's how this area got its name. The short, bushy kind are what mostly grows all through here, but gray alder grows all over these hills, too. In the spring the leaves look more purple—a pretty sight against the blue skies and greener grass."

Elizabeth was surprised that the big, tall, rugged Mitch Brady noticed such things.

"Climb down and get your gun out. I'll show you how to load and shoot it," Mitch told her. He looked around. "Won't be more than six weeks or so when cold weather will start moving in. You'll have to practice closer in to town then. I brought you out here so you wouldn't draw so much attention for now." He came closer, towering over her in that way he had, making her feel both protected and intimidated. She was never quite sure which way she should take being alone with Mitch Brady. "You should know that Montana winters can be pretty rough."

"I've known some pretty bad winters," she answered, reaching back to the buggy seat for her handbag and the small box of bullets.

"In St. Louis?"

There he was again, trying to pry information out of her. Elizabeth realized she'd almost given something away with her remark, and she was angry with herself. It was New York winters she'd known. "It gets plenty cold in St. Louis," she answered.

Mitch led her over to a spot where there were some flat rocks. "You haven't known snow and cold until you've spent a winter in Montana, believe me. The settlements all along the gulch get snowed in, and some people nearly starve to death because supplies can't get through. The price of food supplies go up so high, people can't afford it. Last winter there were some raids on some of the stores and men like me were busy trying to keep the peace." He left her side to pick up some medium-sized rocks and set them on top of the flat rocks.

"I'll survive," Elizabeth answered, secretly hoping they *would* get snowed in. Being buried here for the winter meant it was even less likely the wrong people would ever find her. They at least wouldn't be able to get through to her.

Mitch came back to her side, looking around again in a watchful way. "Sometimes Indians will wander this way. That's another danger here, but mostly down along the Bozeman Trail. The Sioux are not at all happy that we've come into their land to look for gold. There has been a lot of trouble, but not so much around here. We also have to keep an eye out for bears, mainly grizzlies."

"Are you trying to scare me, Mitch Brady?"

Mitch grinned. That smile was full of such bold handsomeness that Elizabeth had to look away in an effort to control the attraction she felt toward him. "I'm only trying to make sure you know what you've gotten yourself into," he told her. "That way you can't say I didn't warn you."

"I learned what I was getting myself into the day my stage was attacked."

Mitch put his hand out. "Give me that gun and let's get to work learning how to shoot it then."

Elizabeth put the gun into his hand.

"I do have to tell you that the only way this thing will put a man down is if he's really close. Don't try firing at him if he's several feet away. You won't do much damage, and this thing won't be very accurate at any kind of distance. And believe me, it sure as hell won't bring down a grizzly."

"Well then I'll be sure to stay away from bears, and

I'll make sure to let a man get really close before I put a hole in his belly."

Mitch frowned, meeting her gaze again. "Why do I feel like that remark was meant for me?"

Now Elizabeth had to smile. "Maybe because it *was*… you and any other man who gets wrong ideas about me."

"Well then, I'll make sure I have your permission before I get too close." He gave her a sly grin. "Hand me some of those bullets and I'll show you how to load this thing."

Elizabeth obeyed, watching carefully as he demonstrated how to detach the short barrel and put a .32 rimfire into each of the barrel's four chambers. He reattached the barrel.

"Most handguns have a revolving chamber," he explained. He removed one of his own revolvers and spun the chamber to show her, explaining the mechanics of his .44 Colt. Elizabeth jumped slightly when he shot at some of the rocks he'd set up, blowing them to pieces in quick succession and seemingly without even needing to aim. Elizabeth wondered, between spending time in the war and then as a lawman and vigilante, how many men he'd actually killed.

Mitch handed her his own gun and took her derringer. "Get a feel of it. If the day ever comes you need to grab a gun like mine and use it, you'll know what to expect as far as its weight. There is one bullet left in it, if you want to try shooting it."

"If you say so." Elizabeth used both hands to raise the revolver. "It *is* heavy! How on earth do you draw and shoot this thing with one hand?"

"Takes practice."

"And a lot more strength."

Elizabeth held out the gun and Mitch wrapped a big hand around her own two hands. "Don't just pull the trigger quick. Squeeze it. And keep your arms out straight."

He let go, and Elizabeth squinted and tried her best to take aim, but it was hard to hold the heavy gun steady. She envisioned one of the rocks as Alan Radcliffe and she pulled the trigger. The gun kicked much harder than she expected. "Ouch!" she exclaimed. "That actually hurt my hand. And it's so loud," she told Mitch, her ears still ringing from his own first shots. She gladly handed his bigger gun back to him. "Here. I'll stick to my little pepperbox."

Mitch traded with her, grinning. "I just want you to get a feel of how different guns can be. A rifle will kick pretty good. A shotgun would probably knock a woman your size on your—" He hesitated. "It would probably knock you down." He reloaded his revolver and put it back into its holster. "You'll feel a big difference when you shoot that little derringer, but at least you will have some protection, which makes me feel better."

"As long as it doesn't kick. My shoulder hurts again."

"It won't kick. At first you might still want to use both hands, though. Let's walk up closer. You need to practice with that thing at a closer range or you're just wasting your time and ammunition." He led her much closer to the rocks. "Do you remember what Swede showed us? That little gun doesn't have a revolving chamber like mine does. The firing pin rotates every time you pull back the hammer, so it hits on each of the four chambers. Those bullets are .32 rimfire. They won't do as much damage as my .44s, but they'll serve the purpose if a man is close enough. Go ahead and get a feel of how it fires."

Elizabeth held the small pistol out and pulled back the hammer, then pulled the trigger, very pleased with how much easier it was to shoot than Mitch's revolver. "This I can handle," she told Mitch.

More wagons and men on horses rode back and forth along the nearby road while for another half hour or so Elizabeth practiced loading and shooting the derringer. Each time she finished shooting it, she had to wait a few minutes for the barrel to cool off before she could remove it and reload. Mitch finally had her load it one last time and put it into her handbag.

"You are now armed and probably dangerous," he told her. "Be careful with that thing."

"Yes, sir. And thank you for showing me how to use it."

"Yeah, well, just don't use it on me."

"Make sure you don't give me *cause* to use it," she quipped.

Mitch chuckled and led her back to the buggy, then pulled a thin cheroot from his vest pocket and stopped to strike a match against his boot heel. He lit the cheroot and drew on the smoke, then took Elizabeth's arm and helped her climb back into the buggy. "We'll visit a couple of homes now, if you can call them homes. From here on you'll see tents, houses made of trees and brush, sod houses, log houses, you name it. For the next ten or twelve miles all sorts of so-called homes are scattered everywhere along the creek." He walked around and climbed in beside her, picking up the reins. "You need water for placer mining, so pretty much every place there is mining, there is also a river or a creek. Farther up in the mountains some men even live in little caves. You won't find many women out here, Elizabeth. I only know of two close enough to visit and get back to Alder in one day, and only one of them has a child, a boy about six. The others are a lot farther up the gulch. It's impossible for them to come all the way into Alder for school, and you'd have to make circuit trips like a preacher to reach all of them where they live, and that would be very unwise...and in winter that, too, would be impossible."

Elizabeth frowned. "So you're saying I probably won't be able to do any teaching?"

"There are a few kids in Alder," Mitch answered with a shrug. "So you still might be able to do some teaching. Just don't ever try coming up here alone. That gun won't do you much good if you're taken by surprise and there's no time to reach into that handbag." Mitch turned the buggy in order to head farther into the gulch. But he suddenly pulled the horse to a halt again when he spotted riders heading toward them from the direction of Alder.

"Damn!" he swore, slamming on the brake again. "Get out of the buggy!"

Alarmed, Elizabeth looked in the direction Mitch was watching. "What's wrong?"

"Those riders coming toward us—they're from Hugh Wiley's ranch. Do like I said. Get out of the buggy and stay down on the other side of it."

Elizabeth pulled her gun from her handbag.

"No!" Mitch told her. "Keep that thing hidden and just stay out of the way. That little pistol won't be much good in this situation."

Her heart pounding, Elizabeth climbed down and moved behind the buggy, wondering if violence and danger was all anyone knew in this country. In spite of what Mitch told her, she slipped her pistol into a pocket in her skirt so it would be easier to reach if necessary. "How do you know they even mean any harm?" she called to Mitch.

"Because I've been doing this long enough to know, that's all. Wiley's brother and his wife are still damn unhappy about that hanging." Mitch climbed down from the buggy, reaching inside on the floor to take hold of his repeating rifle. "Good thing I spotted them before they could ride up behind us," he told Elizabeth. "I have no doubt they meant to get the drop on me." He cocked the rifle as four men and one woman drew closer.

Nineteen

ELIZABETH STUDIED THE APPROACHING RIDERS, THE four men ranging widely in ages and sizes, all needing shaves. She recognized one of them as Bobby Spence, Hugh Wiley's friend who'd threatened Mitch the day Hugh Wiley and Jake Snyder were first brought into town. All four men were well armed, and Elizabeth was terrified for Mitch. He couldn't possibly take all of them, could he? The woman with them wore a man's cotton pants that fit her because she was as big as a man herself. There was nothing soft or pretty about her. Her dark hair hung in an uncombed mess beneath a wide-brimmed hat, and Elizabeth had no doubt it was Trudy Wiley. The way Mitch had described her, she was likely as adept with a gun as the men who rode with her.

Mitch cocked his rifle. "Don't say a word," he told Elizabeth without turning around. "They don't give a damn about you. They're here for me." He raised the rifle. "That's close enough, Trudy," he yelled out.

The woman reined her horse to a halt and put up her hand, signaling those with her to stop. She lowered her hand. "We ain't here to kill you, Mitch Brady—not right now."

"What do you want, then?"

"Just to warn you. I want you to worry, you bastard. I want you to have to keep lookin' behind you."

"Trudy, your husband dug his own grave when he attacked that stagecoach and killed those men. I'm not responsible for that. You know that out here a man pays for his crimes."

"Yes, and you vigilantes make sure even some *innocent* men die."

One of Wiley's men went for his gun. Elizabeth jumped when Mitch's rifle boomed and the man's gun and its holster went flying right off his gun belt. As it tore through the gun belt, the bullet also ripped through the man's hand, and the force of it made him lose his balance. He cried out and fell from his horse, then rolled to his knees, shaking and holding his wrist, staring at his bloody hand. The whole thing took a mere half second, and in the other half second Mitch had cocked his rifle again and aimed it steadily at the rest of them.

"Anybody else want to even *think* about going for his gun? He'll get the same thing. That includes you, Trudy."

"Mitch Brady wouldn't shoot a woman," Trudy sneered.

"Don't bet on it, Trudy."

"You can't get all of us, Brady, and you're riskin' that little lady hiding behind the buggy getting killed, too," another man answered.

"Seems to me Hugh Wiley and those who ride

with him like hiding behind a woman's skirts," Mitch answered. "Hugh tried attacking this woman when he robbed the stage, and then he tried to use her for cover when he got out of jail. It didn't work either time, so if you think having this lady along can slow me down, think again. Do you want to end up like Hugh did? Or that friend of yours on the ground? You start shooting and vigilantes will hunt you down to the last man…and woman, if need be. All of you had better pick that man up and ride out of here."

Elizabeth noticed two riders in the distance riding hard toward them. Were they more of Trudy Wiley's men?

"Killin' you might be worth a hanging," Trudy told Mitch. "You vigilantes think you can just run your own courts and make your own judgments and hang men at random. You stole my husband from me."

"He made sure of his own death when he robbed that stage. You know damn well he deserved to hang."

"He was my husband."

"And I once considered him a friend until he decided to take the easy way of making money. I'm sorry you lost nearly all your cattle last winter, Trudy, but that's no excuse to kill for money."

The other two riders came closer, and Trudy and her men turned to see who it was. "Bastards!" Trudy spouted once she recognized them.

"You got a problem here, Mitch?" one of the riders asked.

Elizabeth breathed a sigh of relief. They apparently knew Mitch and were here to help.

"You might say that," Mitch answered.

"We was in Alder to see you when a couple of miners from the gulch rode up and told us they'd seen Wiley's men ridin' out toward the gulch—said you'd come out this way with the lady there. We figured we'd best come and see what this bunch was up to."

Mitch had still not lowered his rifle. "I have to say I'm glad to see you, Hal," he answered.

The two well-armed men moved their horses closer and faced Trudy Wiley and the men with her. "You'd best be on your way," the one called Hal told them. "It doesn't take much to get hung in these parts, so if you don't want to feel a rope around your necks, ride off."

Trudy's men looked at her as though asking what she wanted them to do. Trudy squinted her eyes, glaring at Hal. "We'll leave. We didn't come here to kill nobody just yet. You boys, on the other hand, don't seem to need much excuse to kill."

"Your man went for his gun, and when it's five against one, I don't take chances," Mitch told her. "Pick that man up and get going."

Mitch still had not lowered the rifle.

"Your time is comin', Mitch Brady," Trudy told him.

"If it does, there will be another hanging in Alder, maybe more than one."

"Sure. You vigilantes wouldn't think nothin' of hangin' a woman. Even so, I'd go down knowin' you're dead."

"Whatever suits you."

The other two vigilantes sat with guns drawn. "Pick that man up and get out of here before we hang you just for your threats," Hal warned. "There's an innocent woman here and you took a chance on her getting hurt. Get the hell out of here!"

One of Trudy's men dismounted and helped the injured man to his horse. The injured one cursed a blue streak as he managed to remount. The second man also mounted up and they turned to leave.

Trudy backed her horse. "Have a pleasant day," she sneered at Mitch. "And if you're sweet on that dainty little woman with you, you'd better marry her soon, because you don't have much time left to bed her." She turned her horse. "Come on, boys."

All five rode off and Mitch lowered his rifle. A shaken Elizabeth, embarrassed and angry over Trudy's last remark, put her pistol back into her handbag. She came from behind the buggy, not sure what to do or say.

"You two were almost too late," Mitch told the men who'd come to their rescue.

The one called Hal grinned. "I have a feeling you would have found a way to get out from under that bunch," he told Mitch. "We didn't ride out here to save your hide. We were just worried about that pretty little lady with you."

Mitch grinned, and Elizabeth was surprised that all three men could brush off coming so near to death as though it was an everyday experience.

"The lady's name is Elizabeth Wainright," Mitch told them, extending a hand to urge Elizabeth to come stand beside him. "She's new in Alder. I brought her out here to teach her how to use a gun."

"Good idea," Hal answered.

"I reckon' she'll be needin' her own gun in a

place like this," the second man remarked, studying Elizabeth. "What on earth brings you to a hellhole like Alder?" he asked. "Surely you don't intend to try to mine the creek."

"Now, David, you know anybody who comes here has a right to privacy," Mitch reminded the man before Elizabeth could answer. He turned to her then. "The nosy one there is David Meeks. The other one is Hal Wallace. Both of these men have wives in Virginia City. In fact, Hal has a small ranch just south of there."

Elizabeth nodded. Both men were a bit older than Mitch. They were clean-shaven but looked as though they needed baths and a change of clothes. She turned to Mitch. "Vigilantes?"

Mitch nodded. "Good men, both of them."

Hal winked. "Ma'am, we thought maybe you'd need more protection from Mitch here than from Trudy and her bunch."

"We were at the hanging last week," David told Elizabeth. "I'd heard about you but never got to meet you." He grinned. "It figures Mitch would end up bein' your escort. He's a real ladies' man, Mitch is."

"And you like to stir up trouble," Mitch answered. "You're quite the ladies' man yourself when your wife isn't around."

"Whooee!" Hal shouted. All three men laughed. Elizabeth frowned, wondering how much of that was true…especially about Mitch Brady. And something about the other two made her uncomfortable. They were armed as though going to war, and she couldn't dismiss the stories Ma Kelly had told her about vigilantes, let alone what she'd read. The power they held in these parts made her shiver. She'd seen the ruthless side of Mitch, and she remembered Ma's warning that certain vigilantes stretched the law a bit too far, hanging men who barely had a chance to prove their innocence. Ma claimed Mitch wasn't that way, but Elizabeth had seen his violent side. Was he worse when he was with men like Hal and David? Were they the type who were a bit too eager to hang a man? They'd already hinted at doing just that to Trudy Wiley's men, just for threatening Mitch. Were they also capable of hanging a woman? Mitch even said he'd shoot her if he had to.

Ruthless or not, she couldn't help being grateful these two men had come along when they did. "Thank you for coming out to help," she told them.

Hal tipped his hat. "It was worth it just to get a look at you, ma'am. You take care now, and don't trust Mitch any farther than you can throw him." He and David Meeks both laughed as they rode off.

"Don't listen to those two," Mitch commented. He turned and put his rifle back behind the buggy seat, then offered a hand to help Elizabeth climb back up.

She hesitated. "How can you treat all that so lightly?" she asked, still shaking.

"You do what I do long enough and you just get used to it."

"And you apparently have a lot of enemies."

"It comes with the job," he answered, his hand still out.

Elizabeth turned away, taking his hand and climbing back into the buggy. Mitch climbed up beside her and snapped the reins, heading toward the gulch.

He waved and nodded to more riders and wagon drivers as they made their way deeper into the wide, rocky gulch. Elizabeth said nothing, trying to fathom how a man could be taking a pleasant buggy ride one minute and then find himself in a shoot-out the next—then go right back to the pleasant buggy ride afterward. She wanted to go back to town, shaken by the confrontation with Trudy and her men, but she didn't want to seem weak and childish.

They rounded a corner, and the vast, wide gulch opened before them, littered with sluices, all sorts of mining equipment, and ruggedly built homes—some made of logs, others out of sod or rocks, and some just tents. They were spread out all over the gulch for as far as the eye could see. It was like riding into a wide tunnel, with high rocky walls on either side that jutted into the sky as though forbidding anyone to try to get past them.

"I can't imagine living like some of these men are living," she commented, overwhelmed.

"Men will put up with anything they have to in order to get rich," Mitch answered. "From here on, the gulch is dotted with little towns and homes and mines all along the way, kind of like one big city that stretches for about twelve more miles. That's what keeps us vigilantes busy—lots of thieving, fighting, and even murdering over gold, food, women, you name it. There's a special code among miners and they don't put up with much. They'll hang a man faster and for less reason than my men and I would."

Elizabeth could do nothing but stare as they drove past cabins and tents and all sorts of crude shelters. Some were supply tents and makeshift saloons. Roughly dressed men with long hair and beards worked stooped over the stream with pans and sluices. She turned to look behind them. "Are you sure Trudy and her men won't come back for us?"

Mitch shook his head. "You can bet Hal and David are scouting around behind us, making sure that bunch goes back home. Don't worry about it."

"But Trudy wants to kill you."

Mitch held his cigar at the corner of his mouth as he talked. "She's not the only one. A lot of people talk big, Elizabeth, but they don't follow through." He slowed the buggy and took the cheroot from his lips, pointing.

"Those wooden troughs you see going way up into the mountains are flumes built to bring water down to keep it flowing through the sluices," Mitch told her. "The miner shovels gravel into the sluice from the streambed and is able to wash away most of the dirt. Gold is heavier than dirt, so it is usually left behind—mostly tiny nuggets, sometimes bigger scads that can be worth four to five dollars, sometimes more. Some miners go higher up into the hillsides and the mountains in the distance and blow their way into them looking for heavier veins of gold."

Men dug ditches. Some were up higher, chipping away at the rock walls with picks. Another explosion even higher made the ground shake.

"Some of these miners have four and five men working for them. Some find ways to pocket some of the nuggets and dust, which leads to trouble. Then there are the road agents, like Hugh Wiley, who decide to rob a payload headed for Virginia City, or rob one of the wagons coming out of here carrying gold."

Elizabeth struggled to concentrate on what he told her, still upset over the shooting. Mitch apparently thought nothing of wounding a man. She realized he'd done what he had to do, but it seemed so easy for him.

The wild and noisy activity in the gulch helped steer her attention to things Mitch was showing her. "They're tearing up the earth, destroying the natural beauty of this place," she observed.

"It's like I told you, men will do anything to get rich. There used to be a lot of alder bushes and trees all along this creek, but most of them have been cut down for building cabins and burned for heating and cooking." Mitch snapped the reins again and drove the buggy over a crude wooden bridge to the other side of the stream and toward a cabin made of wood slats. "The woman with a little boy that I told you about back in town lives up there in that cabin. We'll go talk to her about schooling."

Men glanced at Elizabeth and whistled. Some stood up straight and just stared at her. A couple of them nodded to Mitch.

"Stop for a minute," Elizabeth told Mitch.

Mitch halted the buggy and looked at her. "What is it?"

"How can you… I mean, aren't you worried about what just happened back there?"

Mitch sobered. "Elizabeth, it's like I told you. People like Trudy and those men talk big and make threats. Trudy is probably angrier at Hugh for what he did than she is at me. She's just angry at the whole world right now."

"But they seemed to truly mean it. They want to kill you."

Mitch pushed his hat back. "A *lot* of men want to kill me."

Elizabeth frowned, still wary. "I heard about Sheriff Henry Plummer and his bunch, and the shootings and hangings that went on," she told Mitch. "If you were a part of all that, it makes me wonder…"

"Wonder what?"

Elizabeth looked away, refusing to meet his blue eyes because whenever she did, she felt things she shouldn't, and she was having a lot of trouble trusting anything Mitch told her. "It makes me wonder how you would treat someone you cared about if you knew they had broken the law. I have a feeling the law comes first with you and feelings second."

Mitch sighed, resting his elbows on his knees and staring at the activity that stretched all up the gulch. "It would depend on a lot of things, Elizabeth, and if it involved a woman, I'd no more hang a woman than I'd hang myself. I know Hal and David and I threatened we'd even hang Trudy Wiley, but we wouldn't."

Elizabeth looked at her lap as he leaned closer…too close in the small buggy.

"Elizabeth, if you're talking about yourself," he continued, "I can tell you right now that if you've done something you're afraid to tell me about, don't be." He sighed. "I'm your friend and I'll protect you with my life if need be. And right now, I know you're upset over what just happened, but that's just how life is out here. It's survival of the fittest, and there is nothing wrong with admitting you're scared or that you need help sometimes." He put a hand on her arm. "You okay? We can go back to town right now if you want."

"No." Elizabeth raised her chin. "We've come this far. I just have to get used to all of this. Let's go meet that little boy."

Elizabeth felt torn between a desire to let him hold her and distrust of all men. Mitch pulled the buggy closer to the cabin, then put on the brake and handed her the reins before climbing down. "I'll go see if she's there."

Elizabeth watched him walk up to the cabin and knock on the door. The door opened and a very thin, haggard, and sad-looking woman greeted Mitch. They talked a moment, and then the woman shook her head and broke into tears. Mitch said something more to her, then touched her arm before turning to walk back to the buggy. The woman glanced at Elizabeth, then closed the door.

Mitch returned and climbed into the buggy. He just sat there a minute, not speaking.

"What's wrong?" Elizabeth asked. "That woman was crying. Is her little boy sick?"

Mitch shook his head. "He died a few days ago— run over by a supply wagon. She's in a pretty bad way."

"Oh, no, that poor woman!" Elizabeth felt like crying herself. "Should I go talk to her?"

Mitch pulled off the brake. "No. I offered, but she doesn't want to talk to anyone right now. Life is hell out here for the few women who choose to come to these mining camps with their husbands."

"But she *needs* to talk to someone. The women out here need each other's company."

"The few up here in the gulch find ways to get together. And there's a dance and picnic coming up in Alder in a couple of weeks. You'll meet some of them then. That's probably the best time to hand out some of your flyers." He faced her before getting under way. "Now you see how hard life is here. Between that thing with Trudy and her men, and seeing how the people live up here in the gulch, maybe you understand why I want to look out for you and why I wanted you to get that gun. More than that, I've got feelings for you I've never felt for another woman. I want you to know you can trust me, Elizabeth. Please just trust me, and help me know whether or not I should do anything about these feelings I have for you. I know this isn't a courting trip. God knows the way things turned out it would have spoiled all that anyway. But I don't want you to keep judging me by these guns."

Close again. So close in the small buggy seat. He had a way of drawing her to him without touching her. Elizabeth found herself leaning closer, wondering what it felt like to be gently kissed by a man, truly loved by a man instead of...

The sharp memory of Alan Radcliffe's cold lips and rough hands made her stiffen and pull away. No! She could not allow this!

Mitch grasped her hand. "What is it, Elizabeth? What are you afraid of?"

She pulled her hand away. "Nothing. I mean...

everything. My whole life has been turned upside down, and all this—" She waved her hand to indicate the gulch and the mining and the people there. "All *this*. I hardly know where I am or *who* I am. I don't really know you. You're telling me you have feelings for me, yet you don't know me any better than I know you…and…all this violence and—"

"Stop," Mitch told her. "Look at me."

"I can't."

"Why? Because you know damn well you *do* have feelings for me? It isn't this place or what you've been through or me voicing my feelings that has you confused and afraid, Elizabeth. It's something else. Someone, somewhere, has terrified you. You've been through something as bad or worse than what you've experienced here, back wherever you came from— and don't tell me it's St. Louis, because I don't believe it. *Look* at me, Elizabeth."

She finally obeyed, angrily wiping at a tear.

"You say you don't know me, but you do, because I don't hide anything and I'm not a liar. I'm Mitch Brady from New York City. I'm a man whose alcoholic father abandoned him. My mother turned to sleeping with men for money in order to feed me, and one of them beat her to death right in front of me when I was too little to stop him."

Elizabeth closed her eyes and shook her head. "That's so sad."

"She did what she had to do." He turned away for a moment. "When she died, I ran the streets and did whatever I needed to survive. I ended up in the war and then wandered out here and fell into vigilante work, and that's all there is to know about me, except that you don't ever have to be afraid of me or what I do—or think that just because I'm a lawman, I'd somehow turn on you if you told me the truth about yourself." He met her gaze again. "I'm an open book, Elizabeth, and you're the first woman who's come into my life who has wrapped herself right around my heart and made me think she's supposed to be there. You might even say I'm in love with you "

He turned again and snapped the reins, heading the buggy out of the gulch and back toward Alder. "Admitting that is damn hard for a man like me," he continued. "A minute ago, you almost let me kiss you, but something pulled you back like whiplash. That something has to do with why you came out here. Don't deny it."

Elizabeth swallowed against more tears. "I *don't* deny it. I just… I can't allow myself to have feelings for you until I know for sure what you'll think of me when I tell you why I'm here."

"You've got time. I'm taking you back to Alder because that run-in with Trudy and her bunch set us back, and I can tell you're still pretty upset over it. I'll bring you back here and show you about mining and introduce you to more of the wives another time. Once we get back, I'll be leaving for a couple of weeks, so you'll have plenty of time to do your thinking."

They rode on silently for several minutes. "I'm sorry about your mother. That's an awful thing for a little boy to see." *I saw my own mother murdered.* If only she could share that. "And I'm sorry for what life must have been like for you after that."

Mitch sighed. "Well, somehow I survived, and ever since then I've hated seeing a woman abused."

More silence.

"Where will you go?" Elizabeth finally asked. "You said you'd be gone for a couple of weeks."

"I'll make my rounds like I always do. I'll come back up here and see what needs doing, visit some of the ranchers, scour the road to Virginia City, meet up with Hal and the others—general patrolling for trouble."

Elizabeth was surprised to realize she'd miss him. She didn't want him to go away, but maybe that was best for now. "I'll worry about you."

"Good. That means you care, at least a little."

"Of course I care. I've told you that more than once."

He slowed the horse. "How will you get by?" he asked her.

"Get by?"

"I mean, you still don't have any kind of job yet."

"Thank you for asking, but…I have money. Enough to get me through the winter." Elizabeth knew he was wondering where she got it. "I…inherited it."

He closed his eyes and shook his head. "Well, however you got the money, at least I know you'll be all right while I'm gone. I want your promise to stick close to Ma Kelly's when I'm gone, and if you have to go out, do it when she can go with you—or get a message to Randy or Benny or Len. They'll all be around and they'll keep an eye on you. And I'd like your promise that I can take you to the dance and picnic when I get back."

Elizabeth nodded. "All right." She finally faced him. "But I really will worry about you. You have so many enemies."

"I'll be fine. You know I can handle myself."

"Not against back shooters."

He brought the buggy to a halt again and gave her a reassuring smile. "You just lay low and keep that gun of yours handy when you're out in the streets. We'll see more of each other when I get back."

Again, so close. This time she didn't pull away when he leaned closer and kissed her softly on the lips.

"There. That wasn't so bad, was it?" he teased.

Elizabeth studied the honesty in his eyes. Could a man really be sincere and capable of love and gentleness? "No," she answered, blushing. "It was nice."

Mitch grinned. "Tell me just one truth. How old are you—*really*?"

Elizabeth gave in. "I'm eighteen."

"Truth?"

"Truth."

"Well, that's a relief. I was afraid you were even younger than that. If you were, I'd feel like a brute for wanting you."

A brute did want me, back in New York. I ran from him.

Mitch snapped the reins again. "I don't ever need to know anything more about you if you choose not to tell me, Elizabeth. It won't change how I feel, but knowing more would make helping you a lot easier. And I'd do that much even if I *didn't* have feelings for you."

Elizabeth wished she could believe that. She dearly wanted to. She looked around the side of the buggy toward the now-distant poorly built little cabin where a woman sat alone crying over her dead little boy. Things she had experienced made her want to run away from this place. She could try it while Mitch was gone, but running again could mean risking being found by Alan Radcliffe. Worse, it might mean never seeing Mitch again. She settled back into the buggy seat, her hip touching Mitch's, his presence emanating strength and making her feel protected.

She'd stay in Alder. She'd stay because of Mitch Brady. She'd stay because part of her already knew that if she left, she'd never forget him. She'd stay because she already knew she was daring to fall in love with him.

Twenty

ELIZABETH OPENED THE PARLOR DOOR AFTER SEEING through the curtained window that a woman and young girl stood outside. "Yes?"

"I'm Anne Henderson," the woman greeted Elizabeth with a very strong Southern accent. "My husband, Charlie, runs a general store up the street. I saw your poster about teaching, and I wondered if you'd teach my girl here. Her name is Tilly. She's seven."

Elizabeth welcomed the chance to finally have a purpose here in Alder. "Yes, come in!" she told Anne, stepping aside.

The woman and her daughter entered hesitantly. Anne Henderson was very thin, with ash blond hair and pale brown eyes. Her hair was drawn tightly back into a bun and her dress was a plain dark blue. Tilly stared at Elizabeth wide-eyed, but smiled when Elizabeth said hello to her.

"Are you a trained schoolteacher?" Anne asked Elizabeth after they sat down.

"Well, not as far as having a specific certificate to teach, but I…" She told herself to be careful about her background. "I went to a women's finishing school in St. Louis, and I am quite well educated—enough to help teach reading and basic math to youngsters. When I arrived here I thought it might be a way to make a little money. I thought ten cents a day for each child would be fair. I would of course furnish the books. Do you think that's reasonable?"

Anne smoothed the back of her daughter's hair. "In a gold town, suppliers like my husband do well enough to afford that. We came out here from Alabama. We lost our home and farm in the war. Luckily my husband had saved some money nobody knew about. We used it to buy a wagon full of supplies and headed west. We didn't know what else to do." A sadness came into her eyes. "I miss our home, but a man has to do what he can to feed his family, so here we are."

"I understand. I miss my home, too."

Anne nodded. "You do seem well-bred, so some of us can't help wondering what brings a fine young lady like yourself to a place like Alder. After all, a lot of people come here with questionable pasts, and we will be entrusting our children to your care."

Elizabeth wondered how much longer she could avoid the truth. "It's a long story, and I prefer not to share it for now. I assure you that I am reputable and well educated. I just thought I could use that in places like Alder, where there are no schools yet."

Anne scrutinized her warily. "Well, I suppose that's good enough for now. At least you live here at Ma's and not above one of the saloons."

"I assure you, I am not of that sort," Elizabeth answered. She was growing tired of the constant reference to the town prostitutes, but she supposed it was a natural curiosity in a place like Alder. "You said earlier 'we will be entrusting our children to your care.' Are there other children you think might be able to take advantage of my teaching?"

Anne nodded. "In a gold town, there are very few children or wives and mothers, of course, but there are four or five others who might want to take advantage of some schooling for their children. Up the street is a blacksmith who has a wife and little boy. The blacksmith's name is Barney Deets. His boy is named Andy, and I think he's about eight years old. And a lady named Ethel Green, a miner's widow, runs a little restaurant in town called Eats. She's awful busy trying to make ends meet and her daughter, Lucinda, helps her, so she wouldn't be able to come every day. I think she's about ten. I expect she'd only be able to come maybe once a week."

Elizabeth nodded. "That's fine. I was thinking only two days a week anyway. I have a feeling that in a place like this, the children are needed to help with chores and such. I have to travel to Virginia City first to pick up some books and supplies, so I can't get started right away. I'll get word to everyone when I'm ready. I'm afraid I can't get the supplies for several days yet. I have to wait for Mitch Brady to accompany me. After what I went through coming here, I'm not quite ready to make that trip back along the road to Virginia City by myself."

Anne nodded, frowning. "You do know that Mr. Brady is a vigilante?"

"Yes, and I am indebted to the man for what he did

when my stagecoach was attacked. He's been kind and respectful since then, and…a good friend."

A wry smile crossed Anne's lips. "Mr. Brady does seem to be a good man, but he can also be quite violent. Have you read any of Professor Thomas Dimsdale's articles on the vigilantes in the *Montana Post*?"

"Yes, I have over these past several days. I am interested in starting a newspaper here in Alder. I have learned a lot about life out here just reading those articles."

"Well, Professor Dimsdale came here from Canada for his health, but I have heard he is failing fast. He did manage to get his articles compiled into book form. It's called *The Vigilantes of Montana*. You might want to read it. Perhaps you will meet the professor when you go to Virginia City. Things are so much more civil there. It's the capital of Montana Territory, you know. Maybe if you visit the *Post*, you could come up with some ideas for our newspaper here. The professor had his printing press shipped all the way up here from St. Louis. You say that's where you are from?"

Elizabeth suspected Anne Henderson was quite the town gossip. "Yes," she lied, hating the hole she was digging for herself every time she lied about her background.

"Some people are not fond of some of the tactics of the vigilantes," Anne went on, "but then, they are all we have to keep order in these parts, and it's no easy job. I just don't want my daughter exposed to any violence, mind you."

Elizabeth frowned. "Mrs. Henderson, I assure you Mr. Brady will not be a part of my teaching. He does also live in this boardinghouse, but he is gone far more than he is here. I have seen neither hide nor hair of him for nearly two weeks now. Ma Kelly has told me I can use her parlor for teaching, and it's quite safe here. I hope I can convince the townspeople to build a small schoolhouse for us. Perhaps you could convince your husband and others to see that gets done."

Anne nodded. "I will try." She cleared her throat. "I am afraid I have to tell you, though, that…well… Henrietta Deets, the blacksmith's wife, is hesitant to send her son here for school because… Well, gentleman or not, town gossip has it that Mr. Brady is sweet on you…and after all, you both live under the same roof. The other mothers and I feel either you or he should perhaps find other quarters."

Elizabeth struggled with a quiet anger at the insinuation. She'd been wanting to form a women's club, a way to get together with the other women here, but now she wasn't so sure that she wanted to know *any* of them. At the moment, she marveled at the fact that a lady of the evening like Sarah Cooper could be easier to talk to and a more understanding friend than the "proper" Anne Henderson. If she and the other women found out why she really came to Alder, they would probably run her out of town before she could explain.

Still, Anne and the other women were entrusting their young children to her, and she needed the work. She tried to look at the situation from their point of view. "I can understand your concern," she told Anne. "Please consider that our both living here was just how circumstances left things. I needed a safe place to stay and I knew no one, so Mr. Brady thought this would be the safest place for me for now. I have already given thought to moving out, but I am so new here, I have no idea where I would go. I went through a bad experience and am not ready to live alone. Ma Kelly has been very good to me, and my room is on the second floor in back, not near Mr. Brady's. And like I said, he is gone far more than he is here. When he returns, I will bring up the matter."

"Perhaps Mr. Brady is the one who should move out. He obviously is one who would be just fine living alone, and Ma's place is about the best quarters you will find in Alder, so you should stay. Heaven knows it's a rough town. Please don't take offense. I am just telling you how it looks to others. You seem to be a very nice young lady. I'm sure you want to keep your reputation intact, since you will be teaching."

"Yes, of course. Thank you."

Anne rose. "Just get a message to me when you are ready to start classes and I will tell Mrs. Deets and Ethel Green. Will you be at the picnic?"

"Yes. And you should know Mr. Brady has asked me to go with him. I am not prepared to be walking around alone in this town. I hope you understand."

"Certainly. I am sure Mr. Brady will be quite the gentleman. As a guard, of course, a person couldn't ask for better than Mitch Brady, especially a woman. He's known to staunchly defend the female person, even the…well…the ladies of the night. You should realize, though, that he also frequents those same ladies for pleasure."

Elizabeth felt an unexpected stab of jealousy, combined with a great desire to hit Anne Henderson.

"That matters little to me," she lied. "As I said, Mr. Brady is simply an acquaintance who helped me out of a bad situation. He is also a single man who has a right to visit anyone he wants, including the women to whom you refer. I have no control over that."

They finally said their good-byes and Anne Henderson left with her daughter. Elizabeth turned away with a sigh. Where she or Mitch lived was none of the woman's business, but she could see where it might lead to gossip.

Ma Kelly came into the room then, wearing an apron. "I was preparing bread dough, but I heard some of your conversation," she told Elizabeth. "Don't let the so-called proper women of Alder get to you, dear. They obviously don't think anything wrong is going on here—yet. But she's right that if you or Mitch don't move out soon, the talk will get worse. I'm sure Mitch will be the one to move, and he won't mind."

Elizabeth thought about Anne's remarks about the prostitutes. "Where would he go? To live with one of the whores?"

Ma Kelly snickered. "Does that bother you?"

Elizabeth faced her. "I have to admit that it does."

Ma folded her arms and raised her chin. "Elizabeth, I have a feeling that the man hasn't visited any of those women for a while now—not since meeting you. I've come to know him pretty good, and I expect he's the type who would step away from such things if he found a special woman he cared about. I know from the few things he's said to me that he thinks of you as special."

"Actually, he has expressed feelings for me. He

wants to court me, although I'm not sure what his idea of courting is. He did bring me those roses."

Ma smiled. "Well, for that man to admit to feelings means he cares a great deal. I'd give some weight to it."

Elizabeth walked over to a stuffed chair and sat down. "But he's violent, Ma, and lives a dangerous life. He's made a lot of enemies. I'm afraid to let myself care about him. Besides that, there are things about me… I mean, part of the reason I left was to get away from a big, strong man who was abusive. I am having a hard time letting myself trust any man, let alone one built like Mitch Brady, with that violent side."

"Big and strong matters little." Ma Kelly sat down across from her. "Honey, when it comes to women, there is nothing abusive about that man. He'd never harm a hair on your head."

"He doesn't know the whole truth about me. No one here does."

"Well, there's no truth that would cause Mitch Brady to be mean to a woman. I watched him drag a man out in the street once and beat him near half to death for taking his fist to one of the whores. He kicked him out of Alder and said if he ever came back, he'd kill him outright. He'd do it, too. And throwing men out of town for hurting a woman has happened more than once."

Elizabeth stared at a frayed spot on the chair. "Well, the fact remains, one of us can't remain here. It's only right that I move. Mitch has lived here a lot longer."

"I'd like to see you stay, and I suspect Mitch would never make you move instead of him. This would be a much safer place to meet with the children than a place where you're alone. Besides, I enjoy your company and appreciate your help in the kitchen. Well-bred as you seem, I am surprised you have so many domestic talents."

My mother was once a servant. There was so much she needed to talk about but was afraid to bring up. "My mother taught me how to cook and clean and such so that I could always take care of myself. She used to say that you never know when you might end up alone and poor. She was so right."

"Well, the dance and picnic are only a couple of days away, so I reckon Mitch will be back any time now. I guess your living situation is something you'll have to discuss with him."

"Yes, I suppose," Elizabeth answered. *Among other things.* The thought of Mitch with other women stirred far more anger and jealousy than she cared to admit. She rose and walked to a window. "Right now I just hope he *does* make it back and that he hasn't been hurt."

"There is another solution to the housing problem," Ma Kelly told her.

Elizabeth faced her. "Oh?"

Ma nodded. "You two could get married."

Elizabeth gasped. "*Married!*" She laughed. "That's ridiculous! I hardly know the man!"

"Oh, you know him pretty darn good already. And out here, men and women usually marry quick. I've known perfect strangers to marry just for convenience. Usually both widowed, the man needing a wife to cook for him and care for kids left behind and the woman needing a man's help and protection as well as help with her own brood of kids."

"Well, neither of us is in that situation. Honestly, Ma, how can you talk about marriage? That is the last thing I want. I've seen the worst that can happen when a man takes over a woman's name and possessions."

"Mitch Brady isn't that kind of man."

"You don't know that for certain."

"Well sometimes you can know a person just a few days and know him damn good," Ma retorted. "Others you can know for years and find out you never knew them at all. Mitch Brady is the kind you get to know real fast. The man is an open book."

Elizabeth faced the woman. "And I knew the other kind of man back East. He destroyed my trust in men."

"Suit yourself, but I guarantee Mitch is thinking marriage." Ma patted her shoulder and walked back into the kitchen.

Elizabeth stared after her. *Marriage!* What a ridiculous thought. No man was going to own her the way her stepfather had owned her mother…and no man was going to get his hands on her precious heirloom necklace. Nor was any man going to touch her intimately again. Besides, men like Mitch Brady weren't the marrying type. He'd more than likely love to get his hands on her *without* the trappings of marriage. He might have feelings for her, but he sure never mentioned getting married.

Still, there was that little part of her that liked being close to him. She hated admitting it, but with Mitch gone for nearly two weeks, she was scared to death he was hurt or dead. She'd be very happy to see him walk through the door unscathed, yet seeing him again wou'd mean having to make a lot of decisions she hadn't expected to have to face when she first came to this place.

She touched her lips, unable to forget how gently he'd kissed her the day they went to Alder Gulch. She'd had no idea a kiss could feel that nice, or that a man like Mitch Brady could have a gentle bone in his body.

Twenty-one

ELIZABETH ANSWERED THE DOOR OFF THE KITCHEN TO see Sarah Cooper standing there holding two brown-wrapped packages. "I have your other two dresses here."

"Oh, come in!" Elizabeth stepped back to let her inside.

"Are you sure?"

"Of course. Why on earth shouldn't you come in? In fact, what are you doing at the back door? There is more mud in the alley back there."

Sarah smiled a bit sadly. "You don't want people to see me coming in the front door, honey, especially now that I hear you're going to be teaching soon. A teacher has to watch her reputation and who she's seen with."

"Well, then I'm not so sure I want to teach," Elizabeth joked. "Now come inside. It's actually a bit chilly this morning. Ma has some coffee on the stove."

Sarah looked around before stepping inside. "I see you're wearing the brown flowered dress."

"Yes. I just got it back from Lee Wong's, cleaned and pressed. It fits really well. You're a good seam-stress, Sarah."

Sarah set the two packages on the table. "Well, here are your other two dresses. They should fit just as well. Sorry it took a little longer than I thought. I wanted to do an extra nice job, considering you're probably used to the finer things in life."

Elizabeth poured two cups of coffee. "That was nice of you, but I am fast learning that out here it doesn't make much difference how perfect something is."

Sarah snickered. "In more ways than one."

Elizabeth smiled, urging Sarah to sit down to the kitchen table. "Ma went shopping. And as far as you thinking you shouldn't come in, I'll not stand for people dictating whom I can and cannot be seen with. I like you and I'm glad to have someone I can visit with. How have you been?"

"Oh, life is the same as always. Work all day... sometimes half the night, if you know what I mean. More men have been pouring in, headed up into Alder Gulch."

Elizabeth was already learning to ignore why Sarah had been up *half the night.* "Yes, and I don't like how they are blowing and hacking that gulch to pieces. This is such beautiful country, and miners are destroying it."

Sarah raised her eyebrows. "So you're already growing to appreciate this wild country?"

"For its natural beauty, yes. But it's a bit too wild in other ways."

Sarah chuckled. "That's a fact."

"Mitch took me up into the gulch about two weeks ago," Elizabeth told her. "He ended up in a shooting confrontation with Trudy Wiley and some of her men and then went on into the gulch like the shooting was nothing. Then we went to see a woman whose son I thought I might be able to teach, but he'd been killed in an accident with a supply wagon. I felt so sorry for the mother. I can't imagine living up there under such sad conditions and lacking so many amenities. It's bad enough here in Alder, let alone in the gulch. And then to lose a child…" She sighed. "That and the shooting—it all just made me see how lawless and hard this place is."

"And winter is coming on. It hits here earlier than in places at lower elevations, and believe me, you haven't seen winter till you've spent one in Montana."

"So people keep telling me."

Sarah sipped some coffee. "Speaking of our wild vigilante, Mitch Brady, I am supposed to tell you he's back, and he's fine. Had a few troubles but nothing he couldn't take care of."

Elizabeth frowned. "Back? He hasn't been here."

"Well, he wanted me to tell you he's staying in a room above the Antelope Saloon. He'll send Randy over to get his things from here."

Elizabeth felt a keen disappointment. "Don't… certain women also live above the saloon?"

Sarah smiled wryly. "Yes, but one of them has left for Virginia City. Mitch took her room." She leaned closer. "Mitch isn't using their services, if that's what bothers you."

Elizabeth folded her arms. "I find that hard to believe—and no, it *doesn't* bother me."

"Of course it does. I'm no fool, Elizabeth Wainright. I've been around way too long for that. You love this country because Mitch is here, and the 'wildness' you speak of refers to Mitch Brady. He's become your hero."

"Nonsense."

"I don't think so. I saw the fallen look on your face when I told you where he is. And if you're wondering why he hasn't been over here to see you, it's because he only got back late yesterday and he was in bad need of a bath and a shave and some sleep. He didn't want you to see him that way. I ran into Ma Kelly yesterday morning at the dry-goods store and she told me what Anne Henderson said about you and Mitch living under the same roof. Mitch stopped by my place with some material he got in Virginia City and asked me to make him a couple of shirts. I told him what Ma said, and he decided right then and there not to come here last night. He doesn't want to spoil your chance to teach. That big galoot really cares about you."

Elizabeth drank some of her own coffee, her feelings mixed. She'd tried so hard not to care, but knowing Mitch was back made her want to see him right away. "He should have asked me about it first. I hate for him to have to live someplace else. Ma cooks for him and keeps his room straightened. Who will do that for him now?"

Sarah gave her a knowing look. "Honey, he won't lack for such attention over at the Antelope." She grinned. "I assure you, though, he's not seeing any of those women in any other way. When he dropped off that material, he admitted to me that he missed you a lot, and he wanted to know if you're all right."

If he knew the truth, he wouldn't be so worried about my reputation. Elizabeth felt herself falling into a deeper and deeper mess. She was beginning to care too much about a man who had the ability to legally send her back to New York, where she was probably now wanted…for murder and theft. She had no doubt that Alan Radcliffe had done a grand job by now of setting her up for judgment and sentencing. She found herself blinking back tears.

Sarah sobered. "Elizabeth, what is it?"

Elizabeth waved her off. "Oh, a lot of things."

"Honey, I'm serious about Mitch staying away from the women over there. Don't be upset by it. Oh, he'll talk with them and drink with them and be the man that he is, but he's got a real thing for you and he knows you wouldn't give him the time of day if he was doing anything more than that."

Elizabeth shook her head. "It's not that, Sarah."

"Then what is it?"

Elizabeth hesitated. The other roomers were gone, and she could hear the grandfather clock ticking in the parlor. "Mitch doesn't know everything about me, that's all. And I'm afraid to tell him, afraid to trust him."

Sarah folded her arms matter-of-factly. "Elizabeth, you can trust that man with your very life. Has anybody ever told you why he's so protective of women?"

"Because of how his mother died. He told me himself."

"Is that so?" Sarah shook her head. "If he admitted that to you, it means he really trusts you and cares about you. Did he tell you how his mother made her living?"

Elizabeth nodded.

"Well, he's never blamed her for what she did to help support them. I think that's why he doesn't look down on women like me. That man has a real forgiving heart, Elizabeth—maybe not with law-breaking men, but he won't put up with a woman being abused, so you'll never have to worry that he'd blame you for whatever it is you're hiding. And if you're worried about his violent side, he'd never take a rough hand to you. Never! Not Mitch Brady."

Elizabeth closed her eyes, thinking about her own mother's murder. "I've had experience with a violent man, Sarah." She took a deep breath, then met Sarah's gaze. She was longing to talk to someone about it. Ma was always too busy with her chores and Elizabeth thought her a bit too old to understand. But someone like Sarah would.

"I'm not a virgin, Sarah. I think Mitch believes that I am. I'm not the proper lady he believes me to be." She quickly wiped at a tear that escaped down her cheek. "There. I've said it."

Sarah just nodded and thought a moment. "Honey, I'm no mother and never have been one, but I can sense when somebody your age needs someone to talk to. In the short time I've known you, I've never doubted your respectability. If you think telling me something like that would shock me, think again. You weren't willing, were you?"

Elizabeth shook her head, wishing she could kill Alan Radcliffe. "Most certainly not!"

"And you think a man like Mitch couldn't understand and forgive something like that?"

Elizabeth rose and turned away. "Maybe he could. It's just that I think he has this vision of me being something I'm not."

"Hey, Mitch has seen and done it all. Nothing would shock that man. Is the person who abused you the one you're running from?"

Elizabeth realized she'd said too much, but Sarah was so easy to talk to. She ached for the days when her mother was alive and they could talk to each other and share things. "Yes, but please don't say anything to Mitch about this. I'll know when the time is right."

"I won't say anything, but don't put it off too long, Elizabeth. Be honest with the man. If anybody can help you, it's Mitch Brady. He'll face down any man on any level, and he needs to be aware of what's going on in case this sonofabitch comes here for you."

"He's rich and powerful. He has ways of getting what he wants, and I have something he wants, something…valuable. And he'll find a way to get around vigilante law if he finds me here."

"Oh, Elizabeth, you totally underestimate Mitch Brady—and vigilante law as well. If Mitch is sweet on you, God himself couldn't take you out of here against your will."

Elizabeth faced Sarah. "I came here because this is the last place this person would think to look for me. He'd think I couldn't survive in a place like this."

Sarah smiled. "Honey, you're far stronger and braver than you think. Just coming out here alone shows that. But in places like this, even the strongest women need the backup of a strong, able man, and they don't come any better than Mitch."

Elizabeth sighed. "I've been reading a little about Montana's vigilantes. Some of it is pretty ugly."

"So are some of the things robbers and murderers

do. We don't have much help out here, Elizabeth. Somebody has to do the dirty work."

"I suppose. But what if I let myself…care…about Mitch, and then he gets hurt or killed? I'm afraid to care for so many reasons. It's hard to stop natural feelings, Sarah, but just as hard to fight our natural fears. Besides, I'm not sure I can stand to have a man get close to me again."

"If he's the right man, it won't matter."

Elizabeth managed a smile. She took a handkerchief from a pocket on her dress and wiped at her nose and eyes. "An awful lot of people in this town are trying to get me and Mitch together."

"That should tell you something. It means that all those people care about Mitch. There must be something special about the man, if that's so."

"I never thought of it that way."

Sarah rose, walked over, and embraced her. "You can talk to me about anything, Elizabeth."

Elizabeth put her arms around the woman. "Thank you. My mother died in my arms, Sarah, only about seven weeks ago, yet sometimes it seems like years already. I've been so scared and alone since then."

"I damn well know the feeling, honey." Sarah pulled away and grasped her arms. "Mitch will likely be coming around tomorrow to make sure you're going with him to the dance. You should seriously think about telling him everything, Elizabeth."

Elizabeth shivered, pulling away. "I don't know. I'll think about it." She moved around and picked up the packages. "Thank you for these, and—oh, wait! I have to pay you."

"You can send the money over."

"No. Wait right there." Elizabeth hurried up the back stairs, feeling like a silly young girl at how her heart pounded over knowing Mitch would likely come and see her tomorrow. The thought of it took away her sorrow and fears. She went to her room and opened her trunk, taking some money from where it was hidden in the lining.

She sobered then, reminding herself that Alan Radcliffe would consider it stolen money. If he found her here, he'd call her a thief and a murderer. Maybe she *should* tell Mitch everything, before he heard it the wrong way from someone else.

She fished through the lining and felt for the necklace. Yes, it was still there, reminding her that no matter what she did with her life, no matter if she might be falling in love, there was always the dark shadow of Alan Radcliffe hanging over her, stealing away in the corners of her mind and the back doors of her memory.

She counted out enough money to pay Sarah, then closed the trunk and rose. The thought of telling a lawman—a vigilante, no less—about what happened in New York terrified her. If Mitch Brady turned on her, there was no one left on whom she could depend.

Twenty-two

Elizabeth winced against the dust that rolled in from the street when she opened the parlor door. A west wind was stirring up the dry earth after nearly three weeks of no rain.

There stood Mitch Brady.

"Come in quick before Ma's parlor ends up a dusty mess!"

Mitch stepped inside and removed his hat. His thick sandy hair nearly touched his shoulders, but it looked clean. The man himself wore dark cotton pants, a clean white shirt with a black leather vest, and a blue checkered kerchief tied around his neck. He wore the ever-present six-guns on his hips but not the extra cartridge belts he usually wore on the job. He looked wonderful but also intimidating. "I'm glad to see you back. I missed you, Mitch." She fought an urge to hug him in joy at seeing he was back safe and sound.

He flashed the wide, handsome grin that made her want to throw aside all caution. "Really?"

Elizabeth couldn't help her own smile. "Yes, really."

"I missed you, too." He looked her over. "You look…beautiful, as always."

Elizabeth felt a bit embarrassed, hoping she hadn't made it too obvious that she wanted to look nice in case he came to call. She knew he'd likely show up today, so she'd taken care to wear one of her better dresses and curl her hair. She'd pulled it back at the sides but left it long in back, and she wore tiny earrings and had applied a touch of rouge to her cheeks. She'd told herself she shouldn't care how she looked, but the part of her that wanted to please Mitch Brady won out.

"Thank you. Come sit in the kitchen. Ma went to do some shopping, but she left some coffee on. The boarders are gone, too." Elizabeth turned to go down the hallway, feeling Mitch's eyes on her as he followed behind. As usual, his presence filled all the space in the small house. His heavy footsteps and the clink of spurs said a big man was in the house, and she felt enveloped in him without even touching him.

"I just came to get more of my things," he told Elizabeth.

"Yes. I saw Sarah yesterday. She told me you were moving out." She faced him when they reached the kitchen. "You don't have to do that, Mitch."

Hat still in hand, he nodded. "Yeah, I do. With little to do to pass the time in this town besides hangings and whores, one of the prime forms of entertainment is gossip." He sighed and sat down to the table. "Soon as I got back, Sarah told me rumors are already starting about you and me living under the same roof."

Elizabeth poured them some coffee. "I appreciate

what you're doing, but I feel responsible for putting you out." She set a mug of coffee in front of him. "Besides, I'm not terribly happy about your new living quarters," she added.

Mitch met her gaze and laughed lightly. "Does it bother you that I'm around those women? Maybe you're even a little jealous."

Elizabeth sat down across from him. "Don't be silly."

"I don't think it's silly. I think it matters to you."

Elizabeth stared at the checkered tablecloth. "Maybe a little, but it's really none of my business where you live."

Mitch leaned back, looking too big for the chair he sat in. "There is nothing going on over there other than me having a room to sleep in," he told her. "And it's just temporary. I'm having a little room added onto the back of the jail. That's where I'll be living soon. I always meant to do that anyway, but Ma made it so easy here, cleaned up after me, cooked for me, and such."

Elizabeth smiled sadly. "I'm sorry, Mitch. I feel so responsible."

"Well, maybe I can talk Ma into bringing me some of her fresh bread once in a while."

"I'm sure she'd love to," Elizabeth replied. She sobered then. "I really am glad you're okay," she told him. "After that incident up in the gulch with Trudy Wiley—"

Mitch waved her off. "She knows that was wrong and that she's lucky she didn't go to jail for it. I still think that's where she belongs. I let her off way too easy."

"I don't like the thought of a woman in jail,

especially one freshly widowed, but she did seem awfully serious about killing you. After all, she already tried."

"And failed. She'll calm down now—too afraid of prison. A lot of people like to talk tough, Elizabeth, but most don't follow through on their threats. She's lost yet another of her men from that mess before I left. She's no threat anymore."

A moment of awkward silence followed as they both drank more coffee. Elizabeth suspected that just as she was, he was remembering their kiss during their ride to Alder Gulch. He took a cigarette paper from his shirt pocket and a small pouch of tobacco from an inside pocket of his vest. "Mind if I smoke?"

"Not at all. You never have to ask me that. My grandfather smoked. My father smoked, and my—" *My stepfather smoked.* Elizabeth felt naked and vulnerable under his gaze. The man had a way of undoing all her good intentions to remain formal and detached, her resolve to keep everything about her past secret. "I have to admit…knowing you were here in the house made me feel safer. I kind of hate to see you go."

He tamped some tobacco onto the paper, then picked it up and licked and sealed it. "There is one way to solve that little matter," he told her. He put the cigarette to his lips and got up, going to the cookstove and removing the coffeepot and the grate it sat on. He leaned down to light the cigarette from the burning wood under the grate, then replaced the grate and the coffeepot. He came back to sit down, taking a pull on the cigarette. "We could get married and live together legally. Then you'd feel safe all the time."

"*What?* You can't be serious!"

There was a shadow of sadness behind his smile. "I've been gone nearly two weeks, Elizabeth, and I've never missed anyone like I missed you while I was away. Not only that, but I worried about you—if you were safe, if you were sad or happy, if you might decide to run off while I was gone and I'd come back to find you gone and never be able to find you. If you *had* run off, I'm ashamed to admit I would have hunted you down like the worst outlaw, and when I found you I'd wrap you up in my arms and beg you to never leave again."

Elizabeth felt her cheeks growing hot and her breath growing short. She couldn't bring herself to meet his gaze. Her mouth felt too dry to talk, but she managed to get the words out. "I...can't believe what you're saying."

"Neither can I, but I've never been one to avoid the truth. You saw that the day I set your shoulder and asked if you were a whore. I don't mince my words then and I'm not going to now. I'm tired of being a lonely man who's never settled anywhere and never had a real family. It all just kind of hit me after I met you, and the idea just kept growing. It got bigger while I was away and realized how much I care about you. And out here, people sometimes get married after knowing each other only a few days. It's not unusual."

Elizabeth felt dizzy with indecision and disbelief. "I... Mitch, there is so much you don't know, and I'm just getting settled here and still trying to figure out for sure what to do with my life. I mean...I don't want to fall into something out of desperation."

"Is that how you feel? Desperate?"

Elizabeth swallowed before answering, feeling ridiculous and embarrassed and weak because of a sudden need to cry. "I have felt desperate since before I left home."

"And where is home, Elizabeth? I have a strong feeling it's not St. Louis."

She turned away. "I can't tell you."

"Why not?"

"Stop pressing me, Mitch."

He sighed, and a strained silence hung in the air while he smoked quietly, watching her.

Elizabeth rose and carried her cup to the kitchen cabinet, where Ma kept a pan for washing dishes. "I am starting to feel like a criminal being interrogated."

Mitch drank more coffee. Elizabeth heard him draw deeply on the cigarette, heard a shuffling sound, then felt him standing close behind her.

"I'm sorry I made you feel that way," he told her. "I didn't mean to." He grasped her shoulders and forced her to turn toward him. "Look up here, Elizabeth."

Reluctantly, she raised her eyes and met his gaze.

"I meant every word I said," he told her, sincerity in his unnerving blue eyes. "But I didn't mean it should happen tomorrow or a week from now or a month from now. I'm simply saying that I'd like you to be my wife, and that no matter what's in your past, I don't care. I'm asking you to trust me and let me help you. I can't stand the desperate fear I see in your eyes sometimes, and I know it's not just a fear of your new surroundings. It's something else. Proper young educated women don't come alone to a place like

Alder unless they're damn scared and trying to hide. I know the feeling, Elizabeth. I went through it as a young kid, and it's hell."

All the running and worry and the things she'd been through and the horror of losing her mother the way she did caught up with her then, and Elizabeth collapsed against him, relishing the feel of his strong arms when they came around her reassuringly. It felt so good to feel that safety and protection, to be able to lean on someone. She wept, and Mitch didn't say a word. He just let her cry against his chest until her tears were spent. He started to pull away, but she grasped the front of his shirt in her fists and clung to him. "Don't let go yet."

He moved his arms back around her and rested his chin on the top of her head. "Who's after you, Elizabeth? And why?"

"My stepfather."

"Why?"

"I can't tell you why. Give me some time."

"What's his name? I can at least keep an eye out for him."

She breathed in the smell of man and leather. "All I'll tell you for now is that he's wealthy and powerful, the kind of man who always gets what he wants." She pulled away and wiped at her eyes. "He won't find me here. A place like Alder is the last place he would look."

"If you're this afraid of him, then he's smart enough and has enough money to pay people to find you no matter *where* you've gone. At least tell me where you're really from. That gives me a little something to go on."

Elizabeth hesitated. Was he just using this vulnerable moment to get something out of her? She took a handkerchief out of her pocket and pressed it to her nose and eyes before facing him.

Yes. Something about those too-blue eyes told her he was being honest. "Believe it or not, I'm from the same place you came from—New York City."

He frowned and nodded. "I suspected all along."

"What made you think so?"

"Just something about the way you dress and talk. People from St. Louis have a hint of a Southern drawl. I know a New York accent when I hear it. Hell, *I'm* from New York, remember?" He stepped closer and grinned. "Besides, if you want to hide where you are from, you should remove all signs of it on your baggage. I took a quick look for any identifying marks on your trunk and found a metal tab screwed to one side that showed a New York City address. I don't remember the street address—I was wounded and pretty damn busy that day and had no way of writing it down, but I do remember it said New York."

Elizabeth closed her eyes in dismay. "I was in such a hurry the day I left that I never thought to check for something like that. My mother had that trunk tagged for travel."

Mitch stepped closer again. "Is Elizabeth Wainright your real name?"

Elizabeth was beginning to see why Mitch Brady was a good lawman. He didn't miss a clue and was smarter and more insightful than he let on. She looked around, worried someone would hear her, seeing Alan Radcliffe around every corner.

"Elizabeth, the man who is after you is not here, and if he should happen to come here, he'll never get near you. Do you believe me?"

She met Mitch's steady gaze again. His whole countenance was indeed intimidating. If Alan Radcliffe did come to Alder, he'd have a time going up against someone like Mitch...unless Mitch decided to hand her over, if he ended up believing what Alan told him.

She put a hand to her head and turned away again. "Can we talk more tomorrow? I mean, do you still want to take me to the picnic and the dance?"

"Of course I do."

"Then maybe at the picnic we'll have a chance to sit alone somewhere. I need time to think about this. It's a long story, and I'm still not sure I should tell you or anyone else."

He let out a long sigh. "You can't keep putting this off, Elizabeth, and I meant what I said. No matter what you've done or not done or why you came here, I think you're beautiful and special and I want to protect you and keep you safe and...I just plain want you for my wife."

Mitch Brady's wife. The words stirred odd desires she'd never thought she would feel, after what Alan Radcliffe did to her.

"Elizabeth, stop looking away from me."

She turned, meeting his intense gaze, those handsome blue eyes that spoke of trust and protection. His next words seemed stunningly foreign coming from a big man who wore guns and grew up with prostitutes and shot men in the back or watched them hang as though it was all in a day's work.

"I think for the first time in my life that I'm in love with a woman," he told her openly. "If a man like me even knows what love is. I've wanted a lot of women, bedded a lot of women, but I've never been in love, Elizabeth. In a place like Alder, and the kind of job I have, there isn't much time or opportunity to court someone. Life is rough and people need each other, so don't be so shocked that I talk about wanting to marry you."

His bold honesty was both flattering and confusing...and strangely comforting. *But you don't know! I'm not the innocent you think I am.*

"It's hard for me to trust those words, Mitch," she answered. "For a long time before coming here, I only knew lies and deception and cruelty, all from a man I'd known for years, not just three weeks or so, a man whose background and upbringing I knew all about."

"You know all about me, too. I've already told you everything. There are no secrets in my past, just the hard truth, and that's all I want from you—the hard truth."

Elizabeth stepped farther away. "The hard truth might bring out the lawman in you. As I've said, I've been reading Thomas Dimsdale's articles on the vigilantes of Montana. I know they're a rough bunch."

"With outlaws, not with women."

"You already said Trudy Wiley should be in jail. How do I know you won't put *me* in jail?"

"Jesus, Elizabeth!" Mitch sighed and ran a hand through his hair. "You didn't try to *kill* me! You can't compare yourself to someone like Trudy. How many ways can I say it? I'm not going to harm a hair on your head. I *love* you, Elizabeth Wainright, or whatever your name is. And as far as the vigilante work, I'd give it all up for you, if you asked me."

Elizabeth shook her head. "Something tells me that what you're doing runs in your blood. You grew up fighting your way through life and you're still doing it."

"Because my life had no purpose. Now it does!"

She folded her arms, finally facing him again. "You won't give up trying to win me over, will you?"

"No, ma'am. And it's not easy for a man like me to admit to loving someone. That should tell you something." Mitch gave her a rather sad smile, and the air hung silent for a moment as they just watched each other. A shot rang out somewhere outside and another distant explosion disrupted the moment. Mitch's gentle gaze and masculine presence drew her to him. Mitch in turn stepped closer to her. He touched her face so very gently, moved his hand down her arm to take hold of her hand and squeezed it. "Damn it, woman, let me *help* you."

Elizabeth enjoyed the feeling of being totally loved and protected, something she'd not felt for so very long. She lifted his hand and put it to her face again, brushing his palm with her lips. "Do you mean it? You'll still care about me no matter what I tell you?"

"You know by now that I don't dance around my words, Elizabeth. I told you the first day we met that I don't lie and I don't leave anything out, but you're leaving out plenty, and I can't help you if I don't know it all."

She closed her eyes, still holding his hand to her face. "What if…what if I told you I'm not… not…untouched?"

He squeezed her hand but didn't answer right away. "I'm no fool, Elizabeth," he finally said. "If you think that news shocks me, it doesn't. It's been obvious by the way you've reacted to any advance I ever made toward you. It wasn't bashful innocence. It was terror, and it only makes me want to kill the man who touched you, because I damn well know it couldn't have been something you wanted. And if it wasn't, then you haven't been touched at all."

Elizabeth collapsed against him. To her, those were the most beautiful words she'd ever heard. Mitch moved his other arm around her and pulled her against him. He moved a thumb under her chin, making her look up at him. "I'll say it again, Elizabeth. I love you. There's a reason you ended up here, lady, and I'm it."

He leaned closer, and Elizabeth did not resist when his full lips met her mouth in a gentle kiss that made her head spin. To her surprise, she returned the kiss, enjoying the taste of his mouth, the scent of leather and tobacco and the fresh Montana outdoors. He was a man as big as the territory he roamed in search of thieves and murderers and rustlers. The thought of the dangers he faced made her move her arms around his neck and let the kiss linger and deepen. She wanted him right here, where he was safe and sound. The feelings he stirred in her were almost startling. Was she actually falling in love, too?

Mitch moved both arms around her and lifted her off her feet. She buried her face against his neck. "Part of me wants you in every way, Mitch," she told him softly, "but I'm scared I'll lose you afterward, and I'm scared of…"

Memories. Bad memories. She suddenly wiggled out of his arms and pulled away. She put a hand over her eyes, turning away again. Unwittingly, the words came spilling out then. "It was awful, Mitch. I can't go through that again. He forced me."

"Who? Your *stepfather*?"

Elizabeth shivered, unable to face him. "He threatened me with prison, and he has the power and the means to put me there."

"For what?"

"For…for theft…and what he'll say was murder."

Elizabeth heard him mutter a profanity, followed by a deep sigh.

"And you really think I'd believe that?"

"I don't know. You're a vigilante. They don't need a lot of reason to hang someone out here."

"Not for something someone did fifteen hundred miles away! And I sure as hell wouldn't believe something like that anyway. For God's sake, Elizabeth, tell me what's going on! How many ways can I ask you to let me *help* you?"

Elizabeth jerked in a sob. "But what if I…tell you…and you turn on me?" She finally faced him again. "More than anything on this earth I want to trust you, Mitch. I can't do this by myself. I thought I could, but so much has happened—"

Before she finished, he whisked her up into his arms. Just then the back door opened and in walked Ma Kelly. She stopped short, raising her eyebrows.

"Well now, seems I've interrupted something," she said, setting some packages on the table. "Should I leave again?" She smiled wryly.

Elizabeth curled up tighter in Mitch's arms, keeping her face buried against his shoulder.

"No," Mitch answered her. "You can stay, but this woman and I have some talking to do. I'm taking her up to her room, and nobody will ever know. Right, Ma?"

Ma Kelly folded her arms. "You know me better, Mitch Brady, than to think I'd tell a soul. I've figured all along that that little gal needs a solid man like you to help her out with whatever she's needing help with. Go on upstairs. I'll get rid of that cigarette butt and any other sign that you're here." She picked his hat up from where it hung on the corner of his chair, then reached up and put it on his head. "Go on with you, before one of the tenants comes back."

"Thanks." Mitch carried Elizabeth up the back stairs to her room, laid her on the bed, and closed the door.

Twenty-three

MITCH REMOVED HIS WEAPONS AND DROPPED THEM TO the floor. He then sat down on the bed and pulled off his boots.

"What are you doing?" Elizabeth asked, becoming alarmed.

"Don't worry about what I'm doing. Lie down and relax."

"Relax? You're undressing!"

He grinned as he stood up and took off his leather vest. "I'm only taking off what could get in the way."

"In the way of what?" Elizabeth remained sitting and scooted up to lean against the iron rails of her bed.

Mitch untied his neck scarf and tossed it. "Didn't I tell you to trust me?"

Elizabeth nodded.

"Then lie down like I asked you to do."

She just stared at him.

"Jesus, Elizabeth, I'm not asking you to take your clothes off." He held out his arms. "Look. I'm still dressed myself. Not another article of clothing is coming off."

Elizabeth warily scooted down, remaining on top of the bedcovers. She lay flat on her back, staring up at him.

Mitch chuckled, moving onto the bed and straddling her in order to get on the other side of her. "For God's sake, woman, you're lying there like a corpse." He moved beside her, forced her to turn facing away from him, then moved his arms around her from behind and put one leg over her skirts. He pulled her close against him, his head above hers on the pillow so that she nestled nicely against his chest. "There. Now talk."

She lay there quietly for a moment.

"Elizabeth, I'm showing you that you don't have to be afraid of me. I want you to get used to being held without there being anything more to it than someone caring about you. We are going to lie here like this and you're going to tell me the truth about why you're here. What's your real name?"

"Elizabeth."

"No, it isn't. What's your *real* name?"

She sighed, astonished he could lie on a bed with her without trying to do more. The last time she was on a bed with a man, he'd beaten her first. She had to admit, feeling Mitch's arms around her almost made her feel like a child in her father's embrace, something she hadn't experienced in years. The day her father died was the last day she felt safe. "Emma," she answered.

"Emma what?"

"Radcliffe."

He kissed her hair. "I remember something about the

Radcliffe Company when I was a little boy, running the streets of New York. Rich family. Same Radcliffes?"

"Yes."

"And what could make you leave all of that?"

"It's a long, long story."

"I'm not going anywhere."

Emma thought about the necklace. Did she dare tell him about it? "I'll tell you right now that I'll never get any of the Radcliffe money, in case you think marrying me would make you a rich man."

"You already know how I feel about that. Wealth means nothing to me. Besides, didn't I tell you I loved you before you even mentioned any of this?"

She sighed. "That's true."

"So tell me the story," he repeated.

Emma relished the protection of being wrapped into him. Alan Radcliffe could never get to her here. "Back in the 1820s, in England, my grandmother was forced into marriage to a cousin who had distant ties to the royal family," she answered. "Her family was dependent on the cousin for survival. They had lost their fortune and were living on his estate, so my grandmother married him so her family could continue living comfortably. But my grandmother was so unhappy that she ended up having an affair with a commoner. Her cousin—I guess I should say her husband—found out, and he divorced her, keeping everything of any value except…"

"Except what?"

"I'm afraid to tell you. It's why my mother died."

"That means maybe you could die too for possessing something valuable?"

She hesitated. "I want so bad to trust you, Mitch."

"Have I done one thing to cause you *not* to trust me?"

"No."

"Then keep talking."

Emma swallowed. "Her husband let her keep a valuable necklace, a piece of jewelry he'd inherited that was once worn by Princess Caroline of Brunswick, King George the Fourth's wife. No one is sure how my grandmother's cousin ended up with the necklace, but he did, and he gave it to my grandmother. The older it gets, the more valuable it becomes. My grandmother never told her lover about it, afraid he'd try to steal it from her, because he turned out to be no good. He never married her and in fact deserted her after learning she was with child...*his* child. The rest of my grandmother's family turned her away in humiliation, so she came to America. She worked as a maid and cook for the Radcliffe family. They let her keep her baby and raise her to also be a servant for the family. That baby was my mother. Her name was Mary Benedict—my grandmother's maiden name."

Emma grasped Mitch's muscled forearm, feeling more comfortable in his embrace. "My grandmother died, but not before telling my mother about the necklace and urging her to keep it and never sell it unless she became so destitute that she had no choice. Eventually one of the Radcliffe sons, John, fell in love with my mother and married her. She was very beautiful."

He kissed her hair again. "Seeing you, I can believe that."

Emma smiled. "Thank you."

"Keep talking."

"My mother said people talked at first, a Radcliffe marrying one of the maids and all, but my father and his parents were wonderful, kind people, and since Mary literally grew up in their house, they didn't really see her as a lowly servant. They loved and respected her, and they approved of the marriage. I am the result of that marriage."

"So you stand to inherit the Radcliffe fortune."

She closed her eyes. "I suppose, what's left of it, but after what I've been through, I really don't want any of it. Besides, Alan Radcliffe will make sure I never get a dime of it. Alan was my father's brother, and we seldom saw him. He'd branched out into his own businesses and was always traveling to Europe and such, so we never really got to know him well, but he was friendly enough to me and my mother when he came for the holidays. Apparently my father told him once about the necklace, because he asked my mother if he could see it. She refused, said she'd rather keep it hidden and not let too many know that it even existed." She drew even closer to Mitch. "I'll always remember the flash of dark anger I saw in Alan's eyes when my mother refused his request. I guess she didn't notice it, but I did, and from that day on I didn't like him. But then my father died, and Alan started coming around, at first to console my mother, then to befriend her and pretend to want to help her because she was his sister-in-law. He seemed to be just as good a man as my father had been, but I suspected different. Still, he was raised the same as my father and his parents were such good people, we really had no reason to believe he wasn't as good a man as my father was.

And my mother seemed so happy that I didn't want to spoil it for her.

"Then my paternal grandparents died, and I think my mother felt she needed help handling all that she'd inherited, so she accepted Alan's offer of marriage. He explained that it would benefit her and me both, because my mother would remain in the Radcliffe family and inherit not only his parents' fortune, but the extra fortune Alan had built... I should say, the fortune he pretended to have."

"Pretended?"

"Alan turned out to be a heavy gambler. He lost nearly all of his parents' fortune after they died, and before I left New York he'd lost quite a bit more. He was getting desperate for money, so he began badgering my mother about the necklace. He said, since she was his wife, the necklace belonged to him to do with as he pleased. My mother refused, saying the necklace was to be handed down to me. Things got worse and worse, and Alan began showing his true colors. He began beating my mother, and once I...matured...he began eyeing me in ways I didn't like. Then one night he came into my bedroom and planted his hand over my mouth before I could scream."

Emma curled her knees up closer to her chest. Mitch held her even tighter and kissed her hair. "I hate having to tell you this," Emma told him in a near whisper.

"You don't need to if you don't want to. I have a pretty damn good idea what happened."

Emma gripped his arm tighter. She felt his own tension, knew his anger toward Alan Radcliffe was building. "He...told me I'd better let him have his way, or he'd beat my mother again…and then he'd tell her he didn't love her anymore because I had been coming to his bed and it was me he loved and wanted—that I was after his fortune and wanted her out of the picture."

"For God's sake, he was your *uncle*!"

"He was an animal with an obsession for young women and money, or so I soon learned. He said if I screamed, he'd claim I'd lured him into my bedroom…and the maids and everyone would hear and the gossip would spread and I'd be disgraced and so would my mother. I'd just turned seventeen and had never…" She shuddered at the memory.

Mitch kept a firm grip on her. "It's all right, Emma. I'm going to call you Emma from now on, because that's your name and you should be using it. And don't be ashamed of what happened. That bastard should die for it. It's bad enough that he was older and stronger and violated you to begin with, but to have it be his own brother's daughter…the man deserves something *worse* than death."

"Don't let go of me."

"I wouldn't think of it. I'll hang on to you as long as you want me to."

Emma closed her eyes. "I couldn't tell my mother about it. I was afraid she wouldn't believe how it happened—that she would believe Alan's version of it. I didn't want her to hate me. Then Alan sent me to a finishing school for six months. I think he wanted to get rid of me for fear I'd have the courage to tell. I'm sure while I was gone he made life hell for my mother. When I came home she seemed so…broken and unhappy. She gave me a key to a safe-deposit box and told me the necklace was in it and to never tell anyone—that it was mine forever. I think she was afraid by then that Alan would kill her. Not long after, he got drunk and they had another big fight. He pushed my mother down the wide staircase the led up to the bedrooms. She broke her neck in the fall."

She stopped, the tears coming then. "I started to pick her up," she managed to choke out, "and her head fell back grotesquely. It was horrible…my own mother…dead in my arms."

"Damn." Mitch sighed. "I know the feeling."

"And you were just a little boy. I'm so sorry, Mitch. You have your own horrible memories. When you first told me about your mother, I was struck by the fact that we've both watched our mothers die violently."

"At least in my case, I didn't have to deal with someone like Alan Radcliffe afterward. Tell me the rest of it, Emma."

She took several deep breaths first to control her tears. "Alan told me I'd better go along with his story that it was an accident. He said he'd tell people I pushed her myself, that I had been after his affections and was jealous of my mother and wanted her out of the picture. He said he had connections, that he could have me sent to prison, that if I tried to tell the truth, no one would believe my story. He's such a powerful man, Mitch…and he does have connections in the right places. I believed I really could go to prison. He said I would, if I didn't tell him where the necklace was. He was getting desperate for money. I refused to tell him. He grabbed me and dragged me upstairs and threw me on his bed and forced himself on me again, saying he'd have me every night if I didn't tell…and there was my mother, still lying dead at the bottom of the stairs."

"My God, I'd like to get my hands on that man." Mitch crushed her closer.

"The next two days were busy with reporting my mother's death and holding her funeral. Alan put on a great show as the mourning husband, and every time the prosecutor came around, Alan gave me that dark, menacing look that said I'd better not tell the truth or he would turn it all against me. I knew he could, so I decided to run away. I felt I had no other choice. I was afraid he'd have me arrested anyway, because he was so angry that I wouldn't tell him where the necklace was.

"The night of the funeral, I looked through the newspaper, trying to figure out where I could go, looking for a job. I just wanted to get out of that house, but then I realized that if I went anywhere in New York, he would easily find me. It had to be some-place far away. Then I saw a little article about how women were needed out West as cooks, laundresses, waitresses, wives… 'Come to Alder, Montana,' it said. And then I realized some little mining town way out West was the last place someone like Alan would ever dream of looking for me, so as soon as he left on business the next day, I packed as fast as I could. I found some money in one of Alan's drawers, and I took it because I knew I'd need it. I took the key for the safe-deposit box and went and got the necklace. I discovered my mother had put a lot of money in the safe-deposit box along with the necklace. I think she knew for a long time that I might end up needing it, so I took that money, too, along with the necklace, and I headed west and never looked back."

Emma finally turned onto her back, looking into Mitch's eyes, seeing he truly understood and cared. "By now Alan is probably so angry that he's told a huge lie to the prosecutor in New York. They're good friends. He might even have a warrant for my arrest if I ever come back to New York State, for murder and what he'll probably call theft of his money—and of the necklace, which he'll consider his, because it belonged to my mother and now she's dead."

Mitch leaned down to kiss her gently. "Did you honestly think I would believe you killed your own mother?"

"I couldn't be sure. You're a man. Maybe you'd believe I really did throw myself at my uncle."

He pulled her into his arms. "Emma, I've known you all of three weeks, and I'd never believe a thing like that. I'm betting no one back in New York would believe it either. Alan Radcliffe took advantage of your youth and your ignorance of men. He used brutality and threats to make you believe whatever he wanted you to believe."

Emma was surprised that she didn't mind him holding her the way he did. "But he's rich and powerful, Mitch. He knows all the right people and he always gets his way, and I was so scared you'd send me back to New York or that he'd follow me here. I'm *still* scared he'll find me."

Mitch rested on his elbows, kissing her eyes, her cheeks. "I hope he *does* follow you here. This isn't New York, Emma. This is Montana, *my* jurisdiction.

Here *I'm* the one with the power. He'll have me to deal with if he shows up here!"

She studied his eyes, wondering why it didn't frighten her to have him over her the way he was. "You truly believe me?"

"Of course I believe you. I *love* you."

He kissed her again, this time on the lips...so gently...and she wasn't afraid. She felt joy and relief and love. Yes, she loved him. She moved her arms around his neck. "Don't let him ever touch me again, Mitch."

"He'll never touch you again."

"Say it again."

"He'll never touch you, and in a way, he never did. You've only been touched that way when *you* want to be touched that way. And from now on, I'm the man who will be doing the touching, and it will be because I love you and not because I want to hurt you."

She felt lost in him then as he kissed her again, this kiss much deeper. He moved his lips to her neck. "It doesn't have to be a terrible thing, Emma, not if you're in love." He kissed her again. "Marry me, Emma. I'll love and protect you forever, and I'll settle this thing with Alan Radcliffe once and for all."

He kissed her again, a long, delicious kiss that made her wonder what it would be like to take a man she really wanted. "Marry me," he repeated. "I want to make you mine, Emma." A deeper kiss, gentle touches. He had a way of taking away all the fear and ugliness.

"Will you truly marry me?" she whispered.

"I'll marry you today...right now."

"But I don't want to stop," she whispered. "I don't want this feeling to end."

"Then I'll stay right here and show you what it will be like to be Mitch Brady's wife…and tomorrow at the picnic we'll make it legal. By this time tomorrow you'll *be* Mitch Brady's wife, and I'll protect you with my life, Emma."

"Please don't be lying."

"You already know I don't lie."

Another kiss. He had a way of taking command, not through violence but through kisses and the way he touched her. He moved a hand under her skirt and along her thigh in a way that brought out a need she'd never felt before.

Emma closed her eyes. "I want it to be nice, Mitch."

"It will be, but if you want me to stop, I'll stop." More kisses. "It won't be easy, but I never want you to feel like I'm forcing you to do something."

"No. Don't stop." She kept her eyes closed as he pushed up her skirt and slipped her bloomers down her legs, over her ankles. He moved back over her, kissing her neck. She met his gaze and realized he'd really stop if she didn't want this. She knew by the honesty in those mesmerizing blue eyes that he was sincere and determined and filled with desire. He wanted her in a way that went beyond just having his way with her. It was nothing like what Alan Radcliffe had done to her.

"I never thought I could feel that way about a man." She sucked in her breath when he touched her in that place Alan Radcliffe had so rudely and violently hurt her. It wasn't like that this time. Mitch smothered her with the most gentle, delicious kisses while at the same time touching forbidden places with an exquisite expertise that made her want more. In moments she felt the most pleasant, exotic explosion deep inside that made her gasp with want for him.

Mitch moved between her legs, his powerful frame making her feel small and at his mercy, yet she didn't mind. He reached down and loosened his cotton pants, and the next thing Emma knew, Mitch Brady was inside her. His first thrust startled her and she dug her fingers into his arms.

"Don't be afraid of it, Emma," he whispered into her ear.

Their lips met, and Emma felt as though they were one body. Something rippled through her, an intense longing to please him, a hungry desire to be filled with him. He buried himself deep and she welcomed his fullness, amazed at her own eager desires as he moved with a perfect rhythm that took away all her inhibitions. She wanted to pull him deeper, as though taking him into her soul.

She felt Mitch's life surging into her then, but it was beautiful and sweet, not ugly and unwanted.

He relaxed beside her, and they lay there quietly for a moment.

"Are you all right?" Mitch asked.

"Yes." She couldn't get over the fact that he'd actually asked. She kissed his neck. "Please stay, Mitch," she whispered, shocked at her own words. It felt so good to actually want a man, to feel loved, to be held and protected.

"I'll stay as long as you want me to."

"I want to undress and be under the covers with you."

"You sure?"

"I'm sure. I just want you to hold me."

Mitch sat up and removed his shirt, pants, and underwear, taking his time. Emma sensed that he feared that if he moved too fast, the spell would be broken. He told her to sit up then and she obeyed, letting him unbutton her dress and slip it down to her waist. He removed her camisole, so carefully, as though she were made of china. She lay down and let him pull everything down over her hips, then over her legs and all the way off. He pulled off her stockings, and she blushed at her nakedness, closing her eyes and feeling an unexpected excitement at letting him see her this way. The next thing she knew, they were both moving under the covers and Mitch was gently fondling her breasts. She let him kiss her there, amazed at the passion he awakened in her—daring desires she never thought any man could bring out of her after her earlier terrible experiences. That hell had been replaced by pure heaven. Mitch moved on top of her again, and again she let him inside, wishing they could stay right here the rest of the day and all night and forever.

Twenty-four

ALAN RADCLIFFE MOVED OFF HIS BED AND PULLED ON a silk robe, glancing at the naked beauty lying in his bed. He smiled with satisfaction at the memory of what he'd enjoyed last night with the young Andrea Tate. The girl rubbed at her eyes in groggy confusion, then blinked as she looked at Alan.

"What happened?" she asked. "I feel terrible, and I hurt."

"You're fine, dear. You should be happy that you're a woman now."

The girl looked down at herself and gasped at the sight of blood on the sheets, then yanked the blankets up to her neck. "What did you do?" She looked around the bedroom. "How did I get here? All I remember is you telling my father you'd see that I'd get home safely after the cotillion last night."

"And you *are* safe. And thanks to you, your father has paid me for a gambling debt."

Andrea blinked against tears that started trickling down her cheeks. "What do you mean?"

Alan's countenance darkened as he walked closer

and grasped a bedpost, leaning close to the girl's face. "I mean, my dear, that your father owed me enough money to bankrupt himself if he had to pay it. That debt is now paid, so you can go on living in luxury and you can marry any young man of your choosing and go on with life as though this never happened. But if you tell anyone about this—your mother, a friend, whoever—I'll still come after your father for what he owes me."

"I *will* tell!" Andrea screamed. "I *will*! I *will*! You... you've raped me!"

Alan grabbed a fistful of her blond hair and jerked her head back. "You won't tell a goddamn soul," he snarled. "Do you want to end up a *whore* in the streets? Do you want to end up someone's *maid*?"

Andrea winced with pain. "You bastard! You've ruined me! You filthy old man!"

Alan kept hold of her hair and also grabbed her forearm with his other arm, jerking her closer and then bending her arm up behind her back with a painful twist. "You aren't ruined, you little bitch! You're just a woman now. In fact, when you marry, you'll be able to show your husband a good time on your wedding night, because I've already taken care of the uncomfortable part. Now *listen*! You aren't dead. You aren't even hurt. And you've done your father a great favor in keeping the family from poverty! By the time you bathe and dress and go home, you'll be over this and you'll realize none of this was all that bad."

He let go of her, roughly tossing her backward. "Be glad I drugged you so you didn't have to be awake when I made a woman of you. I would much rather have had you fight me and writhe underneath me and know what it's like to have a man master your body and soul. But your father and I are good friends, and I decided to spare you that part. Be grateful!"

He drew in a breath to calm himself. He walked over to his closet while Andrea curled into a pillow and sobbed. He pulled on some underwear and pants but left his silk robe on, then walked to a mirror to smooth back his hair. "Clean yourself up and get dressed," he ordered, heading for the door. "I'll have a carriage made ready, and my driver will take you home."

He walked out the door, closing it behind him and wishing he could keep the girl there another night or two, but her father had agreed to only one night, and Alan had accepted that as payment. He headed down the wide, winding staircase that led to the lower rooms of the mansion and into the kitchen, where he asked the cook for coffee and breakfast in his office.

"Yes, sir."

"Matilda."

The heavy-set, plain-faced widow turned to meet his gaze, obvious disgust in her tired eyes. "Yes?"

"You do know I spent the night here alone, right?"

Her eyes narrowed. "I need my job, Mr. Radcliffe. Yes, you spent the night here alone."

Alan grinned and went to his office, sitting down in his large, leather chair. He took a cigar from a silver box and lit it, taking a couple of puffs before going through some bills. He would rather have had John Tate's money, because he was getting low again, but his taste for young women had overtaken that problem and made him settle for a night with Tate's daughter.

That left him with the eternal problem of paying his bills and still being able to gamble heavily, which he dearly loved doing.

If he could have found his dead wife's valuable necklace, it would have been a tremendous help. Not only that, but that damn daughter of hers had stolen some of his money. When Mary died, everything should have gone to him…including her daughter.

Damn Emma Radcliffe! Where in hell was that little bitch? Weeks of searching had turned up nothing. Not only had she stolen the necklace and money, but she'd ruined his plans for keeping her there and giving her everything she might want, as long as he could have her in his bed. How could she turn down the life of a wealthy, privileged woman and run off to who knew where and surely live the life of a commoner?

She was bound to run out of money eventually. Then what? She'd have to work as a maid or a cook… or perhaps sell her body. After all, she was no longer a virgin, so what difference did it make? And if she thought she was going to marry for survival, she'd damn well lose her husband once the man found out she was wanted in New York for murder and theft.

Emma Radcliffe was doomed. That was his only comfort. It might take him a while to find her, but find her he would!

He pulled a cord that rang a bell in the maid's quarters. He picked up a newspaper and began reading as he smoked his cigar, waiting for Bess to come see what he wanted. He was down to just her, a stableman, and a cook now, which was embarrassing. All his friends had several house servants. He'd given the excuse that

with his wife dead and his daughter absent, he didn't
need as much help because he was the only one living
in the house. Truth was, he couldn't afford more than
what he had.

Bess finally arrived, bowing slightly. "Yes, sir?"

"There is a young lady upstairs in my bedroom.
Help her get cleaned up and do her hair for her. I want
her looking perfectly neat and clean by the time she
leaves here. I'll have Pete out in the stables get a buggy
ready so he can drive her home."

"Yes, sir," Bess answered with a nod. As always,
the obedient woman showed no sign of disgust or
criticism. She'd even seen Andrea Tate completely
passed out in his arms when he carried the girl upstairs
to his room, and she'd said nothing. It wasn't the first
time she'd seen such things, but she knew better than
to tell a soul.

Bess went upstairs to find a naked Andrea Tate shaking
and crying in the bathing room off of Alan Radcliffe's
bedroom. Blood ran down the inside of her legs and
dripped onto the tile floor. Bess well knew the horror
the girl was suffering. She hurriedly found her some
clean towels. "Let me help you, Miss Tate."

"Don't look at me!"

"It's all right. I've been through this before."

"*Before?* What does that mean? Does Mr. Radcliffe
make a habit of bringing young virgins up here and
drugging them and then disgracing them?"

"I can't say, ma'am."

Andrea angrily washed herself and pulled on her

bloomers, stuffing a small towel inside them because she was still bleeding. Bess picked her clothes up from the bedroom floor and laid them out on a large stuffed chair, then began removing the bedding.

"Stop!" Andrea ordered, with the tone of a rich young woman accustomed to giving orders to maids.

Bess turned. "Ma'am?"

"Don't put that in the laundry. I want it."

Bess was surprised at the dark, determined look in the eyes of a young girl who before now Bess had known to be only sweet and innocent and even kind to the servants. This was a different Andrea. The girl walked over to the chair and began dressing. "I'm keeping that sheet for proof."

"Proof?"

"I'm going to the prosecutor and I'm telling him what Alan Radcliffe did to me." She straightened. "Come cinch my camisole for me."

Bess obeyed.

"I'll bet that bastard has raped you, too, hasn't he, Bess?"

"No, ma'am."

Andrea whirled. "Don't you lie to me! He *has*, hasn't he?"

Bess's eyes teared. "I could lose my job. That might not mean much to somebody like you, but it's everything to me. Mr. Radcliffe has ways of—"

"He's a brute and a *rapist*! I don't care if my father *does* end up broke for what I'm going to do! I'll hate my father forever for what he allowed Alan Radcliffe to do to me last night! Alan told me he'd make sure my father lost everything if I told, but I don't care now." She grasped Bess's arms. "*Help* me, Bess. I promise you, it will be worth it. Whatever happens to my father, my mother has a fortune of her own and we'll be all right. I promise you that if you help me get Alan Radcliffe arrested, you'll always have a home and a job with me and my mother. You have an old grandmother you help take care of, don't you?"

"Yes, ma'am."

"Then we'll take her in, too, and make sure she gets medical help."

"I… How can I believe you?"

"Look at me, Bess. *Look* at me! Can't you see I mean it?"

Bess took strength in the girl's determination. "Yes, ma'am, I believe you do."

"Tell me, Bess. Has he raped you, too?"

Bess's eyes teared as she slowly nodded.

"More than once, I'll bet. What happened to Emma Radcliffe? Why isn't she around anymore?"

"She ran off."

"Why? Did he rape her, too?"

Bess slowly nodded.

"And what about Emma's mother? Everybody is wondering what really happened to her and why Emma ran off."

"I… He pushed her down the stairs. I saw it. He told Emma he'd say she did it out of jealousy, that she wanted him for herself, wanted to be sure of Radcliffe money for life."

Andrea turned around so Bess could continue lacing her up. "Emma would never hurt her mother. And Alan thinks he's irresistible to women—that when he rapes them, they *like* it! He thinks nothing of it. He told me he hadn't hurt me at all, that all he did was break me in, so when I marry I can show my husband a good time." She broke into tears. "I was... saving myself. No decent man will want me now."

Bess finished lacing up Andrea's camisole, and the girl stepped into her slips, then raised her arms so Bess could put her dress over her head. Bess pulled it down and began buttoning it for Andrea.

"Go with me to the prosecutor," Andrea pleaded. "My mother will support us. I know she will. When she finds out what happened here last night, she'll divorce my father and she'll make sure Alan Radcliffe gets what's coming to him. He thinks I'm just another simpering, frightened young girl who's worried about what people will think, but I'm not like that. I don't care what people say! I want Alan Radcliffe to *pay* for this, and I want people to know what he did to his wife!"

"They might not believe me," Bess objected. "I'm just a maid."

"I'll back you up. I'll save that sheet for evidence. If we could find Emma, I'll bet she could put the final nail in Alan Radcliffe's coffin. She must be running scared somewhere. Do you have any idea where she might have gone?"

Bess swallowed. Could she really trust Andrea Tate? She'd never considered that someone of her class could actually team up with a lowly street girl to go after a man like Alan Radcliffe. The thought of exposing the man's evils was a pleasant one indeed. "I...I think I might know where."

Andrea's eyes lit up. "Where, Bess? We have to find her! Maybe the prosecutor can have someone go after her and bring her back."

Bess looked toward the door. "Wait here. I have to get something from my room." She hurried out, looking over the railing downstairs to make sure Alan was nowhere around. She ran up the narrow stairs to her attic room, then grabbed the folded newspaper and brought it back to Alan's room, where Andrea was re-pinning her hair. "Here." She handed the newspaper to Andrea. "I found this in Emma's bedroom closet, and when I saw where it was folded to, I thought maybe that's where she went. I don't even know for sure why I saved it. I just thought it might be important someday, but I didn't want Mr. Radcliffe to see it."

Andrea took the paper and scanned it. "What am I supposed to be looking for?"

Bess pointed to a small ad. "Right there. I'm sure Miss Emma meant to take it with her but forgot."

Andrea read the ad Bess had pointed out.

Wives, cooks, laundresses, and help maids wanted. Payment in gold nuggets! Young ladies, widows, women of any age and proficiency are welcome to come to Alder Gulch and get rich! Come to beautiful Montana and enjoy wealth and freedom!

She looked at Bess. "Do you really think this is where Emma went?"

"She could have. She's smart. I think she figured she'd be safe there because Mr. Radcliffe would never think to look for her in a place like that."

"So he doesn't know about this?"

"No, ma'am."

Andrea raised her chin. "We'll take it to the prosecutor and we'll tell him everything."

"But Mr. Radcliffe will beat me to death if I do that!"

"No he won't, because you'll be with us. I promise, Bess, with all my heart, that nothing will happen to you."

Bess thought about Prosecutor Hayes's own promise to protect her if she told him the truth about what had happened to Mary Radcliffe. She thought how wonderful it would be to escape the clutches of Alan Radcliffe, even more wonderful to see the man go to prison. "I…I think Matilda can also testify. She has seen and heard a lot of things, too."

"Then I'll have my mother send for her secretly and we'll find out what she knows."

"She hates Mr. Radcliffe. I know that for certain."

Andrea glared at a painting of Alan Radcliffe that hung over the bed. "He'll not get away with any of this," she nearly growled through gritted teeth. "I'm not going to become one of his victims. Not *me*! I told him I'd get him for this, and I will!" She turned to Bess. "You just go on like nothing happened and wait till I send for you. Put that sheet in a laundry bag and save it in a closet somewhere. Promise me, Bess."

"I promise." Bess couldn't help a sudden urge to reach out and hug Andrea. "Thank you. I'd like nothing more than to be out of this house for good."

Andrea hugged her in return. "And you will be, Bess. I promise."

Twenty-five

THE STREETS OF ALDER WERE PACKED WITH MINERS, business owners, prostitutes, ranchers, wives, and the few children who lived there. The saloons were overflowing with people dancing both inside and outside to fiddles and piano music, and crude tables made out of barrels and boards were set up in the street and covered with all kinds of food, cookies, cakes, pies, and assorted goodies made by the women in town, some even cooked by the prostitutes. The air was filled with the aroma of beef and pork roasting over open fires, and the mood was joyous and excited, because in addition to the planned picnic, the whole town would witness today the marriage of Mitch Brady and Emma Radcliffe.

Word had spread like wildfire about the wedding, and about the fact that Elizabeth Wainright's real name was Emma Radcliffe and that she'd come to Alder to get away from an abusive uncle. That was all Mitch wanted anyone to know, and he'd made sure Randy, Len, and Benny said nothing more as they walked around town letting people know about the wedding.

Sarah helped a nervous Emma put on the only really good dress she'd brought with her, an evening dress in pale yellow. The bodice was cut low and off the shoulders, trimmed with white lace that draped downward to the elbows, and tiny white bows trimmed the upper edging. The upper skirt was made of white lacy tulle draped over an underskirt of yellow silk puffings tied with deeper yellow velvet ribbon.

Ma Kelly's parlor was filled with prostitutes who were dressed to the hilt, some of their dresses surprisingly tasteful. They'd all come over to help Emma with her hair and a touch of makeup and were excited to make Mitch Brady's fiancée as beautiful as possible.

Emma would have found the entire situation comical if not for the fact that she suspected a good number of these women had slept with her soon-to-be husband. She could tell they were being very careful not to joke about it, but once in a while a comment would slip about the fact that Emma was getting "quite a man, in more ways than one." Claire McGuinnes lamented over never getting another visit from "that man," and another younger woman started to reply, when Sarah reminded them to "shut up."

"He's marrying now, and that's that, and I'm happy for him. The man is truly in love, and just look at Emma, here. Isn't she the most beautiful young lady who ever stepped foot in Alder?"

They all gushed over the results of their primping when Emma rose and turned in a circle for them. "How do I look?"

"Lord, girl, Mitch will carry you off so fast your head will spin," one of the women joked.

They all howled in laughter and Emma blushed, but deep inside she couldn't wait for tonight, to truly be Mrs. Mitch Brady and be able to sleep with Mitch without having to hide it. She intended to please him in every way he wanted, so much so that he'd never need the services of any of these women again. Giving herself to Mitch Brady had been the most pleasurable, erotic, deeply satisfying thing she'd ever done, and he'd taken away all her inhibitions and fears, had turned into beauty the ugliness Alan Radcliffe had instilled in her.

Soon she would be Emma Brady, Mitch's wife, and with Mitch Brady to protect her, Alan Radcliffe could never touch her again or bring her harm. What pleased her most was that when she offered to show Mitch the necklace, he'd refused. "I don't even want to see the thing," he'd told her. "It's yours. I never want one dime of any money that might come of it. I'm marrying you, not that damn necklace."

"I've never seen Mitch look so happy as when he came to me yesterday afternoon, asking me to help you get ready for a wedding today," Sarah told Emma, interrupting her thoughts. "That man is beside himself." She shook a finger at Emma. "And don't try to tell any of us that something besides just a kiss didn't happen between the two of you yesterday morning," she teased. "That man left to go see you, and we all know he didn't come back to his room until very late last night."

"And he looked damn happy," Hildy added. "When he said he was marrying you today, we had a pretty good idea what went on over here."

Emma blushed, realizing there was no pulling the wool over the eyes of these women. She covered her face with her hands. "Don't forget that I am supposed to teach here. If word gets out—"

The room erupted in shrieks of laughter.

"We'll never tell," Sarah told her.

"Do you think we don't know how Mitch can talk a woman under the covers?" Hildy joked.

"Hell, with a build like that and that gorgeous face and those damnable blue eyes, he doesn't have to do *any* talking!" another put in amid more laughter.

"Now, now!" Sarah put her hands up to stop all the talk. "The fact remains that after today, you'll have to forget about Mitch Brady. That man is as honest as a dollar, and once he pledges to Emma here, we all know as sure as the sun rises every day that there won't be another woman for him."

Ma Kelly came into the room then, carrying a mixture of roses and wildflowers. "I managed to find some flowers for you," she told Emma. "The blacksmith's wife brought over these roses, and I have some wildflowers growing out by the horse shed behind the house. I trimmed off the rose thorns so you can carry them without harm." She handed the flowers to Emma.

"Oh, thank you, Ma." Emma hugged the woman.

"Let's put a couple of those wildflowers in Emma's hair!" Hildy exclaimed.

They proceeded to make Emma sit back down while they placed flowers into the mass of curls they'd assembled earlier. Emma took one last look in the mirror, surprised at how perfectly the women had fixed her hair and at the delicate pink of her cheeks and soft rose color on her lips. Considering the way most of these women painted themselves up, she was surprised at how tastefully they'd fixed her own face, following Sarah's orders that they not make her look "anything less than a true lady."

"Thank you all so much," she told the women.

"Well, we can't exactly thank you for taming that man down so fast," Hildy answered, "but we're glad he's happy."

Laughter filled the room again, and Emma was amazed at how she now considered some of these women friends. When she first arrived in Alder, she'd not only looked down on them but had even been afraid of some of them.

"Come on, honey, it's time!" Hildy told her. "I bet Mitch is already standing on that platform they built for the ceremony."

"Good thing Judge Brody happened to still be in town," another put in. "Who knows where the preacher is right now, he travels so far for his work."

"This town could use a school *and* a church," Emma put in. "If I'm going to start raising a family here, I intend to see we get both."

"Hey, don't go putting us out of business!" one of them joked.

"In a *mining* town?" Sarah answered. "Not likely!"

They all howled with laughter again as they rushed Emma out the front door, where Randy and Len waited, armed as always.

"Whooee!" Randy yelped. "Ain't you the prettiest thing that ever walked. That damn Mitch is the luckiest man in town."

Emma barely had time to think. The crowd around her grew as she walked toward the wedding platform. She wanted to laugh at the fact that she was accompanied by prostitutes and vigilantes as she headed toward a platform that not long ago was used for a double hanging. The hanging posts had been removed, and now the platform would be used for a wedding between a man and woman who'd known each other all of three weeks! Only in a place like Alder could something like this happen.

A few men shot their guns into the air and Randy ordered them to stop.

"No gunplay today, boys. This is a wedding! We don't want anybody gettin' hurt."

The few children in town sat on their fathers' shoulders so they could see better, and rooftops were lined with more onlookers. They reached the platform and Randy helped Emma up the steps while someone somewhere nearby played the wedding march on a piano. When Emma reached the platform, Mitch was indeed already standing there waiting.

"Oh, my gawd, look at him!" one of the prostitutes commented.

"Don't he clean up just damn fine!" Hildy added with a sigh.

"Never a more handsome man walked the earth," Sarah added.

"His pa might have been a drunken bum, but I'll bet he was one good-looking man," someone else added.

Emma just stared a moment. Mitch stood there in a fine black suit with a white shirt and black string tie, his sandy hair clean and pulled into a short tail at the back of his neck. Today he wore no guns. His tanned face was clean-shaven, and his blue eyes shone with nothing but love and an appreciation of how beautiful she looked. He smiled the smile that turned her heart into a melted mess.

"I already thought you were beautiful, Emma, but not *this* beautiful."

Emma felt warm from the memory of the hours they'd spent quietly making love at Ma's place the day before. "And you look…" She shook her head. "You look wonderful." She forced back tears. "Put an arm around me, will you? I'm a nervous wreck and scared to death!"

He leaned closer, pulling her against him while the huge crowd whooped and howled.

"What are you scared of?"

"I don't know… Scared that this is too good to be true, I guess. Scared of losing you. Scared someone will come for me."

"You already know there isn't a man alive who can get close to you once you're mine, Emma Radcliffe. So be happy. Look around you at all these people, and Randy and Len and Benny—they're all out there keeping watch. Even Hal Wallace and his wife are here all the way from Virginia City. His wife is mad at him for making the breakneck trip to get here in time. David Meeks is here, too—plenty of lawmen and vigilantes." He leaned down and kissed her lightly, and the crowd went wild. "Let's get this over with," Mitch told her. "I can't wait to spend the whole night with you in my bed."

Emma smiled, sniffing back a few tears and turning crimson. "I can't wait either."

Mitch kept an arm around her and faced the judge. "Hitch us quick, Brody."

The judge nodded and proceeded with the ceremony. Emma was amazed at how the rowdy crowd quieted. She and Mitch spoke the usual wedding vows, and Mitch placed a plain gold band on her finger.

"I'll get you something fancier in Virginia City," he told her.

"I don't want anything fancier," she answered. "I'll treasure this one the rest of my life."

"I now pronounce you—"

"Wait," Mitch interrupted the judge, studying Emma intently. "I have one more vow to make."

The crowd quieted to the extent that Emma was sure she could have heard a piece of straw fall to the ground.

"I promise you, Emma Brady, that I will never bring you harm, to your body or your feelings—ever. I promise you will never have to be afraid of anything or anyone again. I promise that I will never betray your trust."

Emma couldn't stop her tears then. She reached up and threw her arms around his neck and they shared a passionate kiss that brought thunderous applause from the crowd while the judge yelled as loud as he could, "I now pronounce you man and wife!"

Piano and fiddle music poured from saloons, and the prostitutes began to mingle among the miners, some carried off in men's arms, screaming and laughing. People surrounded Mitch and Emma as they descended the platform steps arm in arm.

The afternoon was filled with wild celebrations, more food than Emma could possibly eat, and men downing buckets of beer, while gift after gift was presented to Mitch and Emma. There were quilts, kettles, pans, and other kitchen goods, a set of china in a box of straw, candles, lanterns, feather pillows, and an array of items to set up house. Emma wondered how on earth everyone had come up with so many gifts so quickly. They even received two crates of canned goods, and one rancher promised ten pounds of smoked beef.

Len told Mitch that men were already building a one-room house at the end of town so Mitch and Emma would have a place to call their own until they decided where they would live and what kind of home they wanted. Emma realized they hadn't even discussed those things.

"Ma Kelly has shooed her boarders out for the night," Randy told them. "You'll have the whole place to yourselves. Ma will stay with Sarah and we'll take all your gifts there, too, till you have a place to put it all."

Music, dancing, eating, and more dancing… Emma had never felt so special, not just because of Mitch's love for her, but because of the surprising generosity from a horde of people who barely knew her…but they knew Mitch, and their joy for him only told her she'd made the right choice—that Mitch Brady was every bit the honest, trustworthy man she'd already judged him to be.

Day turned to dusk, and everyone paraded Mitch and Emma to Ma Kelly's. Ma opened the front door and

Mitch carried Emma inside to hoots and whistles and laughter. Mitch kicked the door shut and kept Emma in his arms, carrying her to his old room, where Ma had put clean bedding on the iron bed, as well as setting out clean towels and a washbowl and pitcher.

"Well, Mrs. Brady, how does it feel to be married?" Mitch laid her on the bed.

"It feels wonderful."

Mitch removed his hat, boots, and string tie, opening his shirt partway. He spied a bottle of wine and two glasses someone had left for them on the dresser. He uncorked the wine and poured a little into each glass, bringing them over to the bed. Emma sat up and took the wine, and Mitch sat down beside her.

"I hope you noticed I didn't drink today," he told her. "I dearly wanted to get stupid drunk, I'm so damn happy, but I didn't want to ruin tonight."

He faced her, and Emma studied him lovingly. "Thank you."

"But we can have this one drink." He raised his glass. "To us."

Emma raised her own, and they touched wine glasses. "To us," she answered.

They each sipped some wine. Mitch stood up then and removed his shirt. Emma noticed the scar at his side where he'd taken a bullet the day he saved her from Hugh Wiley and his men. It reminded her that the man still lived a dangerous life.

"Mitch, will you continue being a lawman? I'm scared for you."

He set his glass aside and removed his pants, then crawled onto the bed. "I don't know yet. We'll decide together what to do next. Right now I just want to spend the rest of the night making love to my new wife." He took her glass from her and pulled her off-shoulder dress farther down, pushing it and her camisole past her breasts and grasping them gently in his big hands.

Emma closed her eyes and drank in the joy of his lips gently parting hers as he laid her back on the bed.

Mitch rolled her onto her side, unbuttoning her dress. Emma enjoyed the ecstasy of letting him undress her, the keen pleasure of lying naked beneath him then, letting Mitch Brady taste every inch of her, touch all the secret places that brought fire to her blood. His kisses were delicious, a taste of wine on his lips, fire on his tongue. She had no idea when he'd managed to remove the rest of his own clothes. She only knew he was touching and exploring her body more intimately than the day before, perhaps because yesterday he didn't want to do too much too soon—another sign of how much he loved her.

This time he moved his fingers inside of her in a way that made her cry out with want for him, and in the next moment he was filling her almost painfully, but it was a glorious pain, not a frightening one. She hoped it wouldn't take long for these moments to lead to a pregnancy, for she dearly wanted to give Mitch Brady a child, couldn't wait to set up a real home and give him the family life he'd never known and so much wanted.

They mated...and explored, and mated...and slept...and mated. Tasting, touching, sometimes gently, sometimes in wild passion. Emma felt as though she couldn't get enough of him, and Mitch voiced the same. By dawn they were exhausted. Mitch pulled her close then, her back to him. He wrapped his arms around her and moved one leg over hers, just as he'd done the morning before when he professed his love for her and made her tell him the truth of why she'd come to Alder.

"Mitch," she said softly.

"Hmm?" He sounded sleepy now.

"What about…what if he finds me?"

"How many times do I have to tell you not to worry about that man? I'm not even going to say his name, Emma, and I don't want you to say it either. Your own name is changed now, so you never even have to use his last name yourself." He pulled her closer. "You're Mrs. Mitch Brady now, and not only do you have a husband who will never allow that man to touch you and never allow you to be taken from here…you have a whole town behind you, as well as the Montana vigilantes. There are no *what-ifs*, Emma. It's simply not going to happen."

Emma studied the hard muscle of the arm that enveloped her. "I just still have to get used to not being afraid," she told him, "and used to being loved and protected."

Mitch kissed her neck, then pulled the covers over them against the cold morning air. Both of them were too tired to get up and make a fire in the little wood burner in the corner of the room. Emma thought how, no matter how hot the days were, it was always chilly in the Montana mountains at night, and by morning a small fire was usually necessary.

Outside there came two distant booms. The mining continued in Alder Gulch, and by now most of yesterday's crowd had gone home, returned to their mining, or were sleeping off a good drunk. She never dreamed coming to this place would lead to love and marriage and a whole new life, or that the man who charged into the stage robbery, guns blazing, would end up sharing her bed.

"I love you, Mitch, more than anything or anyone on the face of the earth."

His reply was deep, rhythmic breathing. Emma closed her eyes and enjoyed the first true peace and joy and feeling of safety she'd known in a long, long time.

Twenty-six

ALAN RADCLIFFE QUICKLY SPLASHED WATER ON HIS face and ran wet hands through his hair to smooth it back. He rubbed a towel over his face to dry it and took a quick look in the mirror to make sure he looked halfway decent. Being awakened at 2:00 a.m. angered him but also alarmed him. His stableman had come in through the back door and up to his room to let him know Terence Giles was at the back door.

That was not good news. Giles was Alan's snitch. He was a man who seemed to have a knack for being in the right place at the right time to hear the right gossip. For Giles to come here at two o'clock in the morning meant an emergency of some sort.

Alan pulled on his silk robe, irritated at the pile of clothes on the floor in the corner of his room. Bess and Matilda had both up and quit on him, and he'd asked Giles to find out why. He'd had trouble finding someone new—his laundry was piling up and there was a mess in the kitchen—and was embarrassed at having no help. On top of that, he'd lost considerably more money gambling. He blamed everything on

Emma. When she ran off, she'd taken his hope of new riches and stirred up a lot of talk about her mother's death. Gerald Hayes had never shown up with the warrant for Emma's arrest, another thing he'd asked Giles to check into.

He grumbled profanities as he grabbed some money from the top drawer of a large oak dresser, shoving it into a pocket in his robe and hurrying down the stairs and into the kitchen, where Giles sat at the table, smoking a thin cigar. Alan hated the pip-squeak of a man but had to admit he was good at his job. "What on earth are you doing here this hour of the morning?" he asked, going to a cupboard and taking down a bottle of whiskey and two small glasses. He brought them to the table and poured some of the liquor into each glass.

"You're gonna need that stuff, that's sure," Giles told him, picking up one of the glasses and downing the alcohol.

Alan only sipped his, still standing. "What's going on?"

Giles grinned, putting out his hand. "Ten dollars might save your ass, Radcliffe."

Scowling, Alan took the bills from his pocket and grudgingly handed ten dollars to the man. "Out with it."

"Well, sir…" He shoved his glass over, indicating he wanted more whiskey.

Alan refilled the glass while Terence Giles talked.

"Seems Bess and Matilda quitting is all tied up with why you haven't gotten that warrant yet from Gerald Hayes." He slugged down the second dose of whiskey.

Alan drank more himself, eyeing Giles darkly. "Go on."

"Seems as though *you're* the one who's to be arrested."

Alan slowly set down his glass. "*What?*"

Giles pursed his lips, then licked off the whiskey that still lingered there. "Seems that the little vixen you raped several nights ago went to the prosecutor—took the bloody sheet and took your maid Bess with her. Bess said as how she saw you drug the girl and carry her to your room passed out. The girl and her ma dragged her pa down to testify he'd paid a gambling debt off to you by letting you have his daughter for a night. He's in jail on charges they haven't even come up with yet, and you're gonna be arrested for rape."

Alan's hands balled into fists. Giles reached over and poured himself yet more whiskey. "It gets worse," he added.

Alan thought he might explode with hatred and anger. If Bess were here right now, he'd choke her to death and throw her into the sewer along with little Miss Andrea Tate. "That little bitch!" he snarled. He stood up and threw his whiskey glass against the iron cookstove, shattering it. "What do you mean by worse?"

"I mean that Gerald Hayes also intends to charge you with murder. Seems Miss Bess also saw what happened the night your wife died, and saw you drag Miss Emma to your bedroom, most likely to be raped. Seems Miss Bess is pretty sure where she ran off to, and Hayes is gonna send somebody for her so she can testify as to what really happened that night."

Alan paced, enraged, wanting…needing…to slam his fist into something. "They know where Emma is?"

Giles nodded, picking up the whiskey bottle and drinking more whiskey straight from the bottle. "Seems Miss Bess found a newspaper article with an ad

in it inviting women to come to a place called Alder
Gulch in Montana. They all think Miss Emma went
there, thinking you'd never look for her in a place like
that. Guess she was right."

Alan closed his eyes, so angry he feared he might
have a heart attack. *Alder Gulch in Montana!* The little
bitch knew damn well he never would have considered she might go West. Maybe she hadn't even
survived the trip. The land west of Chicago was full
of Indians and outlaws and miners hungry for women.
A pampered Eastern girl couldn't possibly survive in a
place like that! He turned his gaze to Giles. "When are
they coming for me?"

Giles shrugged. "Tomorrow, I expect."

Alan took another ten dollars from his pocket and
handed it to the man. "Take this and that whiskey and
get out of here! And don't you dare tell anyone you
told me any of this!"

"I won't tell. My job is to tell you what I know and
nothing more." Giles took the money and the bottle
and sneaked out the back door.

Alan went to the window to see a light on in the
room off the stables where the stableman slept. Good.
He'd gone back to the stables and hadn't heard any
of his conversation with Terence Giles. Alan hurried
back up to his room. If Gerald Hayes was coming for
him tomorrow, he'd find no one home. He ached with
a desire to beat Bess to death, and that damn spoiled
bitch Andrea Tate! There was always the chance no
one would believe what she told everyone, and Bess
was nothing more than a waif off the streets who
would do or say anything to have a job and a place to

stay. That's probably what Andrea had offered. The only person who could truly seal the accusation of murder was one Emma Radcliffe, and now he knew where to find her!

Montana. What a godforsaken place for someone like Emma to go. The little trollop was more clever than he'd given her credit for, and a lot braver than he'd expected. But the fact remained that she'd run off, one strike against her when it came to his own testimony. *She ran because she was guilty!* That's still what he'd use against her, but the fact remained he had to find her before Hayes came for him. He damn well was not going to prison! And if he could find Emma and beat her into telling him what she'd done with that necklace, he could take it and head for San Francisco. He'd have to kill Emma then—shut her up so she couldn't testify against him. He could always say she'd been murdered by Indians or ruthless outlaws. Then he could sell the necklace and get on a ship to South America or the Orient, someplace where a wealthy American could start over.

No matter what happened, this all boiled down to Emma and her mother refusing to give him the damn necklace. He'd by God take possession of it this time, even if he had to kill Emma Radcliffe to get it. She'd have no protection in a wild mining town. He could go there and accuse her of murdering her own mother. Maybe he could even get her hanged. What a sight that would be! Emma Radcliffe hanging by the neck.

Twenty-seven

Mitch and Emma headed for the dry-goods store, where Emma intended to pick out material for curtains for their new home. It didn't matter that it was only a twenty-by-fifteen-foot room for now. It had a wood-burning stove that would keep them plenty warm in the upcoming Montana winter: three windows; a real pinewood floor; a brass bed that Sarah and the girls had shipped in from Virginia City, with a real down-stuffed mattress and real bedsprings; a cupboard for their china; a rocker made for them by Sparky Thomas, the feed-store owner, who was also a good carpenter; and a table and two chairs from George Calus, the supply-store owner, and his wife, Mary.

Emma had almost everything she needed to set up house, and they had moved their personal belongings into it this morning. The house was even close to the town's ground well, which was fed by water that seeped in from farther up in the mountains. Emma would have close access to the well, but Mitch had already insisted he'd be the one to carry the water. He didn't want Emma having to do it.

Sometimes Emma felt almost guilty for having found so much happiness from something that had started out with such tragedy and horror. She decided that God himself had led her to Alder just so she'd find Mitch Brady. Tomorrow they planned to travel to Virginia City for more supplies and a cookstove. In the spring they would decide if Mitch would continue as a lawman or if they would move farther out into the valley and start a ranch and build a bigger house. For now Emma was happy to stay in Alder, where everyone had been so good to both of them, and where she and Mitch could live cozily in their tiny house.

"I hope you realize I have a lot to learn about cooking Western-style," she told Mitch, "with big steaks, fried bacon, and potatoes." They strolled together toward the supply store. "I grew up knowing how to cook fancy dishes you probably wouldn't even like."

Mitch waved her off. "You've already learned a lot from Ma Kelly, and you make the best biscuits in town. And at the rate people keep bringing us beef and baked goods, you don't have to worry about cooking for a while yet anyway." Mitch patted his stomach. "You don't want a fat husband, do you?"

"I'll always want you, whether you're fat or skinny," Emma answered. She hung on to his arm. "What about me? What if *I'm* the one who gets fat?"

Mitch pulled her into an alley and moved a hand to the middle of her back, pressing her close. "If you get fat it means you're carrying, and I couldn't care less how big you get when it's my kid in your belly." He leaned down and kissed her gently.

"Well, at the rate we're going, that's bound to happen sooner rather than later," she told him. They started for the boardwalk when someone farther back in the alley called out.

"Mitch Brady!"

Mitch turned.

"Today you die!"

Mitch ducked and shoved Emma to the ground. To her dying day she would not know how he moved fast enough to get her to the ground and pull his own six-gun while the man who'd threatened Mitch stood there with his gun already drawn, but somehow Mitch got off a shot just as the intruder fired at him. The intruder cried out and fell, and it took Emma a moment to realize Mitch had also been shot. He just lay there on top of her for a moment, then wilted beside her, blood pouring from his head.

Emma stared in horror, at first unable to find her voice. *Mitch! Mitch!* He looked dead.

"No!" she finally screamed, ignoring her own scrapes and bruises. She managed to sit up and raise Mitch's head. She put it in her lap and blood immediately soaked the skirt of her dress as she screamed his name.

In the next moment Randy was there, followed by a growing crowd of onlookers.

"He killed him!" Emma screamed. "He killed Mitch. He killed Mitch!"

"Jesus!" Randy exclaimed. He knelt down beside Mitch. "Holy God, he's been shot in the head." He stood up. "Somebody get Len and Benny!" he screamed. "And get Doc Wilson!" He touched Emma's shoulder. "We'll get him to the doc," he told her.

"He's already dead! He's already dead!" Emma mourned, rocking back and forth.

Randy ran farther back in the alley and more people moved closer.

"Oh, my God, it's Mitch!" a woman exclaimed. "It's Mitch!"

Suddenly Sarah was there. She leaned down and pressed her head against Mitch's chest.

Randy came walking toward them then, supporting a stumbling man who was bleeding badly from his middle. Emma looked up at him, recognizing he was one of the men who'd ridden with Trudy Wiley the day Trudy threatened Mitch at Alder Gulch.

"Murderer!" she screamed at him. "Murderer!" She picked up Mitch's gun where it still lay beside him and made ready to shoot the man a second time, but Len grabbed her arm.

"Give me the gun, Emma! We'll take care of this!"

"He killed Mitch! He didn't even give him a chance," she screamed.

"Somebody get Doc Wilson!" someone yelled.

"Emma, his heart is still beating," Sarah told Emma.

Len took the gun from Emma's hand and began prying her away from Mitch.

"No!"

"Emma, we have to get him over to Doc's place. If you want Mitch to live, it's important to move fast. Come on now, move back."

Emma watched as men hurriedly picked up Mitch's body and made off with it. It took four men to carry him. She watched in stunned confusion. Randy walked past them, half dragging the man who'd shot Mitch. He was begging for water and for a doctor.

"It's Pete Bailey!" someone yelled.

"String him up!" another yelled. "The sonofabitch killed Mitch Brady!"

"Hang him!" shouted another.

"Back off!" Len told them, waving a gun. "Bailey will get treated and get a trial." He moved away from Emma and kicked Bailey in the back, sending him sprawling. "*Then* we'll hang him!" Len added.

The crowd erupted in cheers and angry shouts. They herded Bailey toward the jail while the man screamed for water and for help. Emma stared after him, Sarah standing beside her. She looked at Sarah, bewildered. "I…Mitch and I…we were going to buy some material. I was going to…bring it to you…for curtains."

"Emma, you're in shock. Come on. Let's get over to Doc's place. Mitch needs you."

"I bet Trudy Wiley paid Bailey to kill Mitch!" someone shouted in the distance.

"Bailey shot him in the head." someone else yelled. "Nobody can survive that."

Some woman screamed Mitch's name. *Probably one of his favorite prostitutes,* Emma thought absently, still unable to absorb what had just happened.

Sarah put an arm around her then. "Come with me, honey."

"Oh, my God, Sarah, what will I do without Mitch? What will I do without Mitch?" Emma felt dizzy and lost in some kind of vacuum of horror.

"Let's not jump to conclusions," Sarah answered,

urging Emma toward Doc's office. "Wait and see what Doc Wilson says."

In moments they were surrounded by a bevy of prostitutes, and behind them half the town's occupants, who all followed Emma and Sarah to Doc's office. Emma could hear some of the women crying.

"Poor Mitch! Why did God let this happen?"

Why indeed? Emma thought. All her joy, all the beauty of the past ten days of marriage, was gone, dumped into the black hole of death.

"What will I do, Sarah? I can't live without Mitch."

"You won't have to. He'll be all right, honey, you'll see."

Emma heard the slight break in the woman's voice, and she knew Sarah was only trying to make her feel better.

"He's shot in the head, Sarah! No one lives through that!"

"It can depend on a lot of things, Emma. And Mitch Brady is tough as nails. He'll get over this, and God help Pete Bailey and anyone else who had anything to do with this, once Mitch is better. If Pete Bailey lives, you can bet Len and the others will beat the truth of why he did this out of him, and they will by God save Pete's hanging for when Mitch is better and he can watch."

"I knew it! I knew something would happen to him. I saw the look in Trudy Wiley's eyes, Sarah. I knew she'd kill him or hire someone to do it. I wanted him to stop what he was doing. I wanted him to quit vigilante work and raise horses and cattle—anything— anything besides risking his life like he does."

"I expect when he gets well he'll give a lot of thought to that, honey, but what he does is in his blood and it will be hard to give it up. I'm betting he'll do it for you, though. He'd do *anything* for you."

Emma hesitated at the door to Doc Wilson's place. She took a deep breath. "Sarah, what if he's dead? The last thing he did was kiss me and tell me he...couldn't wait for me to be fat with his baby."

"Emma, you have to think positive. I've known men who were shot in the head and lived."

"Don't lie to me, Sarah."

Sarah sighed deeply, and Hildy moved up to stand on the other side of Emma. "Honey, Mitch is such a strong man, and he loves you so much. He'll live for you. I just know he will."

Emma's legs felt like rubber and her whole midsection—stomach, lungs, heart—hurt with dread and tension as she clung to Sarah and managed to walk inside. She thought about how violently and suddenly her own mother had died, how alone and terrified she'd been ever since then...until Mitch Brady came along. He was her lover, her protector, her friend. He'd promised her she never had to fear that anyone would ever hurt her again. If only she could have promised the same thing in return. Now there he lay, motionless, blood covering his head and face. She stumbled to his side, melting down beside the cot, realizing only then that her own dress was wet with her husband's blood.

Twenty-eight

"Doc!" Emma whimpered. "Please tell me he's not dead."

Doc Wilson sighed. "He's not dead, and it's good you're here. Just hold his hand. He might sense your presence, and that's important."

Doc leaned over to try washing away the blood, then glanced at Sarah. "I'm glad you're here, Sarah. Keep some water hot at all times, will you?"

"Sure, Doc."

"Benny, make sure nobody out there in that crowd tries to come in. See if you can quiet things down out there some."

Benny walked out and Emma grasped Mitch's hand, which was usually strong and firm and comforting but now simply hung limp. She kissed the back of it before pressing it to her face.

"Mitch? Mitch, hang on. You have to hang on. I can't go on without you, Mitch Brady."

She broke into sobs, clinging to his hand.

"Make her some tea, Sarah," Doc told the woman. "I have something I can put in it to calm Emma down."

"Don't put me to sleep, Doc," Emma told him. "I have to be here for Mitch…talk to him. I don't want to sleep. What if he dies while I'm asleep?"

"I won't put you to sleep. I just want you to relax. Mitch will need you the next few days. You don't want to wear yourself down to where you get sick."

"The next few days? Does that mean you think he'll live?"

"I'm afraid it's hard to say, Emma. You never know with a head injury. These things can turn out fine, or he could end up paralyzed or a vegetable or…worse."

Mitch groaned, moving his head slightly.

"Mitch?" Emma squeezed his hand. "Mitch, it's me—Emma. Please wake up, Mitch! Please hang on."

Doc leaned closer, checking Mitch's pupils. "Sometimes a person can seem unconscious but they can hear and understand everything people are saying," he told Emma. He looked over then at one of the miners who'd helped carry Mitch inside. He stood aside waiting for some kind of orders, unsure what to do next. "Get Emma a chair, will you?"

"Yes, sir." The man hurriedly brought a wooden chair over next to the cot. "Sit down in this, ma'am. You shouldn't be on the floor there," the miner told Emma. He took Emma's arm and helped her up. "I'm right sorry about this, ma'am."

Emma never let go of Mitch's hand as she sat down into the chair. Doc Wilson managed to wash away most of the blood. "Looks like more of a crease," he told Emma. "It's deep, though. Real deep."

"Don't let him die, Doc. Please don't let him die."

Doc studied the wound. "This kind of injury can

affect the brain in a hundred different ways. He could have a concussion, or maybe a cracked skull—it's hard to say. It knocked him out the same as if somebody had clobbered him with a hammer. Blows like that can do a lot of things to the brain. I just can't tell till he wakes up...*if* he wakes up."

Emma drew in her breath. "You mean...he might always be like this?"

The doctor bent closer and opened Mitch's shirt, listening to Mitch's heart with a stethoscope. After a few seconds he straightened. "It's like I said, Emma," he answered sadly. "I don't like to make promises or predictions. I'd rather give you the worst scenario than to promise something that might never be. His heart is strong and he's plenty healthy, so he could recover. It's a good sign that he moaned a minute ago, a sign he's struggling to regain consciousness, but he could come and go like that for days, maybe even weeks."

"We were going to buy material for Sarah to make us some curtains," she said softly, never taking her eyes off of Mitch. "And out of nowhere Pete stepped from the shadows in an alley and said, 'Mitch Brady—today you die.' Everything happened so fast then. Mitch drew his gun and pushed me down at the same time. They both seemed to fire at once, and Pete Bailey went down first. Then Mitch just laid there a minute. I didn't even know he'd been hit till he rolled away from me. Bailey just shot Mitch...like an execution."

"That sonofabitch," Sarah grumbled, filling a tea strainer with tea leaves. "I hope he dies a horrible death over there in that jail. Doc, don't you dare leave Mitch to go help that bastard Bailey."

"I don't intend to."

"I hope he *does* live, so we can watch him hang," the miner added.

Emma broke into tears again, putting Mitch's hand to her cheek. "Mitch, I'm here. I'm here. Please wake up. Please!"

It was too much. Her mother's death, Alan Radcliffe's attack and his threats to have her sent to prison, her flight into a land totally foreign to her, the attack on the stagecoach and ensuing violence, being stuck in a wild, unruly town full of threatening strangers, a whirlwind romance with a wild, sometimes violent man who'd won her heart in three short weeks. Everything closed in on her, and she broke into deep sobs.

Sarah brought her some tea, touching her shoulder. "Here, honey, drink this. And maybe you *should* let Doc give you something to help you sleep."

"No! I have to be here for Mitch, in case he wakes up." She reluctantly let go of Mitch's hand and took a handkerchief from a skirt pocket to blow her nose and wipe her eyes. She took the tea from Sarah. "Thank you." She sipped the hot brew, taking strength from the strong beverage and the warmth of the steam. She looked at Doc Wilson. "There is nothing to do now but wait, right?"

Doc nodded. "I'll shave the hair around the crease and clean it out the best I can, then stitch it up. After that, yes, there is nothing more I can do. He'll either wake up and be fine, or maybe wake up and have amnesia or be otherwise mentally affected, or he won't wake up at all. We have to pray for the first outcome."

Emma rose. "Then when you're finished with him, I want him taken over to our place. I'll take care of him myself."

"Emma, I don't know if you're strong enough," Doc objected.

"I am far stronger than you think." She looked at Sarah. "You can help on occasion, can't you?"

Sarah smiled softly. "You know I will. And so will the other girls. We'll all take turns."

Emma turned back to Doc. "You're a busy man, Doc, and you might need the room here. And sometimes you're out riding circuit for days at a time. You said yourself there is nothing more you can do, so like I said, I'll take care of him. Just tell me what to do, what to watch for, how to get some nourishment into him."

Doc ordered Sarah to bring a bowl of water over, told her where he kept a razor, then turned back to Emma. "All right, Emma, I'll have some men take him to your place soon as I'm done here. I have to be blunt with you, though, it might not be as easy as you think. He could have fits of vomiting. Head injuries can sometimes cause that. You'll have to make a special point of watching for that, because if he's lying on his back and unconscious, he'll choke to death on his own vomit. I hate to talk about the raw parts of this, but you need to know. And you'll have to stuff some towels under him. His bodily functions will keep working, which means he'll urinate but can't be moved. You'll just have to keep cleaning him up."

Emma raised her chin. "I am not the wilting flower you might think I am," she answered. "I'll do whatever it takes. I love Mitch more than anything on this earth, and I took a vow to stand by him for better or worse, in sickness and in health, and I intend to do just that."

Doc Wilson nodded. "All right—but you promise me you'll let others help out and get some decent sleep. It takes strength to care for somebody in this shape, and that means eating and sleeping. Lord knows Sarah and Ma Kelly and sometimes Randy and Len and Benny can help, and most of the whores in Alder will gladly help you out, too. Promise me you'll let them help."

Emma closed her eyes. "I promise." She sat back down, grasping Mitch's hand again while Sarah helped Doc Wilson shave the area around the ugly crease in his scalp. Doc poured whiskey into the wound and Mitch groaned again.

"Good. He's feeling some pain," Doc commented. "That means something somewhere is working." More groans tore at Emma's insides as Doc sewed up the open wound with a large needle and catgut. Outside, a commotion arose.

"Go see what's going on, Cletus," Doc told the miner. "And make sure no one comes in here, except maybe Randy."

"Sure, Doc." Cletus went outside, then returned after a few minutes, looking a bit nervous.

"What is it?" Sarah asked him.

Cletus glanced at Emma. "He died, ma'am. Pete Bailey. He's dead. They're, uh, they're dragging his body out to the graveyard clear up the hill past town— gonna bury him right now with no ceremony."

Emma closed her eyes and rested her forehead against Mitch's hand. "So much violence."

"Emma, this is Alder, Montana," Sarah reminded her, "and you married a lawman. Out here it's survival that matters. Mitch knows that. That's why he does what he does, but I know he never wanted any of the violence to visit you like this."

"None of it will matter if Mitch dies." She kissed his hand and watched as Doc Wilson finished sewing up the wound. Mitch's forehead was turning purple. She couldn't imagine how he would survive this, or how she would herself survive if Mitch Brady died.

Twenty-nine

FOR EIGHT DAYS, EMMA SAT BY MITCH'S SIDE, TERRI-fied he would die or simply never wake up. She bathed him, shaved him, and forced food and water down his throat to keep him alive. Mostly she gave him only broth. He instinctively swallowed but gave no sign that he was aware of being fed or touched in any way. He didn't speak, didn't open his eyes, barely moved. The few times he did shift slightly, Emma rejoiced that he was moving at all. That meant he wasn't paralyzed. She talked to him constantly, deciding to have pretend conversations just to keep her own sanity and in hopes that one day he would open his eyes and answer her, or at least indicate that he heard what she was saying and understood.

People brought food, so much that Emma had to send it back with others. She had little appetite of her own and was almost too tired to eat anyway. Sarah set up volunteers who came to relieve her for three hours out of every eight so that Emma could sleep, and when she slept it was right beside Mitch, hoping he would sense she was there. Most of the time there was someone else there, too, not wanting Emma to be alone even when it was her turn to do the caring. Doc Wilson visited as often as possible, but always with the same prognosis, which was that he had no idea if or when Mitch would wake up, or what condition he would be in when he did.

Len, Benny, and Randy took turns sitting with Mitch, and the traveling preacher came and prayed over him whenever he was in town. Judge Brody visited, as well as Sparky Thomas, the feed-store owner, and his wife, Dora. Vigilantes Emma had never even met paid their respects. Some of them paid a visit to Trudy Wiley, telling her that if she ever stepped foot in Alder, they couldn't guarantee a crowd of angry men wouldn't hang her, woman or not. Some of them wanted to hang her, but Judge Brody warned there was no hard evidence that the woman had actually hired Pete Bailey to kill Mitch, and because she was a woman, hanging her could worsen their violent reputation. Trudy finally sold all her stock and left for parts unknown, which was fine with the vigilantes and everyone in Alder.

Bandages were removed, stitches were removed, and Mitch's hair was so thick that it easily covered the scar on his scalp. Still, Mitch just lay there. Emma ached to hear his voice, to feel him hold her again. Sarah made the curtains Emma had been wanting for her windows, and Hal Wallace and David Meeks brought Emma an iron cookstove from Virginia City, taking out the potbelly heating stove and hooking up the cookstove instead. George Calus brought braided rugs for the floor and another rocking chair to set outside on the little front porch some of the men had built for Emma. Miners brought a huge supply of wood down from the mountains, and people talked about how early winter made its appearance in the Montana mountains.

"You'll need this wood sooner than you think," one man told her. "One more month and we'll be in the season where it could be seventy degrees one day and blizzarding the next. That's how it is in Montana."

Emma thanked him and closed the door. *That's how it is in Montana.* Yes life out here was certainly different from anything an Easterner could imagine. But what surprised her the most now was how warm and caring a lot of these rugged, drunken, brawling complete strangers could be in a pinch. In places like this, people had to look out for each other, because this place and each other was all they had. In spite of how unbearable life would be if Mitch didn't pull through, Emma knew that most everyone here would watch out for her and help her until she decided what to do next. And if Mitch remained a vegetable for life, they'd help her with him, too. She'd spoken her wedding vows not quite three weeks ago, and one of them was to stay by her husband's side in sickness and in health. She'd stay through his sickness, no matter how long it lasted, even if it was months or years.

Dear God, don't let that happen to a man like Mitch! So big and strong and brave and blustery and sometimes just plain mean...lying here lifeless. She wondered how she would get through a long, dark winter without going crazy if Mitch didn't wake up. She looked around their little house. All the gifts and work of others had made the one-room cabin a home in every way...except one. It needed to be lived in, in the normal way, with a man and woman settling in, eating meals together, sleeping together at night...making love and babies.

She walked to a calendar on the wall and marked off another day...number nine. Nine days with no sign of Mitch coming around. She looked at a mantel clock sitting on a table beside her rocker, then walked over to wind it before lying down, thinking how Mitch had promised that someday they would have a bigger house with a real fireplace and mantel where she could set the clock. She could hear his voice, see his handsome smile, taste his lips, envision the look of love in those captivating blue eyes.

Another day...another night of utter despair and loneliness. She changed into her nightgown. She'd told Sarah not to come tonight, feeling guilty for taking so much of the woman's time and more able now to do everything that needed doing herself. She was touched by how much Sarah and some of the town prostitutes had done for her and smiled at how sometimes they argued over who got to help take care of Mitch next.

She left a lantern dimly lit on the table, hating total darkness. After all, this was still a wild mining town. Mitch's intimidating six-guns hung on the wall beside the door, and she knew Randy and Len took turns watching the cabin at night, just as a safety measure. After all, Alder still teemed with new arrivals and strangers. With Mitch unable to perform the role of protective husband, she was truly a woman living alone. The thought always made her want to cry, remembering the luxury of lying in Mitch Brady's arms at night, always feeling so safe and protected.

She crawled into the bed beside him as she'd done every night since he was shot. She constantly hoped he would sense her presence. She moved under the covers and was soon asleep from exhaustion. She woke up once, remembered hearing the clock chime two notes…2:00 a.m. She fell back to sleep, unsure of how much longer she slept before Mitch's movement woke her. He'd turned on his side and had moved an arm and a leg around her in the way he'd always done when they slept together.

Emma's heart pounded harder. She turned to look at him, but his eyes were closed. Was he just sleeping normally? His breathing seemed more rhythmic, different from the shallow breathing of an unconscious man. All this time she and others had constantly lifted him to a sitting position for hours at a time while he was unconscious, heeding Doc Wilson's warning that if they left him constantly flat, he could get pneumonia.

Emma swallowed, daring to touch his face. "Mitch?" She spoke his name softly.

"Hmm?" he answered sleepily.

Emma gasped, putting her hand to her mouth.

Mitch opened his eyes. "What's wrong?"

Emma sat up. "You don't know?"

"All I know is that you woke me up. Is something wrong?" He sat up and looked around. "When did we get curtains? Last I knew we were going to look for material so Sarah could make them for us."

Emma burst into tears of joy. "Mitch!" She threw

her arms around him. "Thank God! Thank God!" His own strong arms came around her in that familiar embrace that enveloped her in safety and love.

"I don't know what the heck is wrong with you, woman, but I have a headache from hell," he told her.

He was back! Emma smothered him with kisses. "Just lie back, Mitch. Don't get up yet!" she told him.

Mitch watched her in confusion as she literally hopped off the bed and went to the door. She opened it and hollered out to Randy.

"Randy, go get Doc Wilson! Mitch is awake and talking!"

Mitch glanced at the clock on the table: 3:00 a.m. The door opened more, and Randy stepped inside to see for himself as Emma turned up the oil lamp, then quickly pulled on her robe.

"What the hell are you doing, standing outside my door at three in the morning?" Mitch asked him.

Randy broke into a wide grin. "Hell, I was hopin' you wouldn't wake up so's I could steal your wife, you sonofabitch."

He let out a whoop and left, and Mitch stared at the door in complete confusion. He sat up again, throwing his legs over the side of the bed. "What in God's name is going on?" he asked Emma. He looked down at himself. "Why am I naked with a bunch of towels around me?"

Emma walked over and knelt in front of him. She ran her hands over his face, down his arms, still hardly able to believe he was awake and talking. She grasped his wrists. "You were shot, Mitch, nine days ago. The bullet creased your skull and you've been unconscious ever since. Doc Wilson wasn't sure you'd ever come out of it, or what shape you'd be in when you did."

Mitch scowled, running a hand through his hair. He frowned when he felt the deep crease. "Who the hell shot me?"

"One of Trudy's men, Pete Bailey. You actually managed to get off a shot yourself and you killed him." She kissed his hand. "Mitch, when you went down, I thought I'd die."

Mitch just sat there a minute. "You were *with* me?"

"Yes."

"My God, the bullet could have strayed and hit you instead! I could have lost you!"

"But you didn't, and you're back in the land of the living, Mitch. That's all that matters."

"Not if you're in danger every time we walk out the door together."

"Don't think about that right now. And please don't get up or move around right away," she asked again. "I'm scared this won't last. Wait till Doc has a look at you. You have to be careful for a while, Mitch, till we're sure this is going to last."

Mitch touched her tangled hair. "My God, Emma, what have I put you through?"

"I'm fine. Mitch, I had so much help. So many people in this town care about you. And Len and Randy and Benny all made sure I was always all right."

They heard shouts and running footsteps then, and Doc Wilson barged in along with Randy and Len. They all stopped short, just staring as though they were looking at a ghost. Emma rose and stood aside.

"He's awake, Doc, and he's talking normally. His memory and everything seem to be fine."

Mitch sat there stark naked with only a towel to hide what needed hiding, still looking confused. Doc Wilson, Len, and Randy all burst out laughing, both with relief and at the comical situation.

"Now, ain't you a sight?" Len joked.

"Last time I saw you caught naked like this was when we had that shooting a few months back and I had to come and get you at Hildy's," Randy teased.

They all howled until Mitch reminded them with a scowl that Emma was in the room. They quickly sobered and Randy glanced at Emma. "I'm sorry, Emma. That was a mean remark to say in front of you, but you gotta admit, Mitch looks pretty funny sittin' there naked as a jaybird."

"Randy, I'm so happy to see him back in the land of the living that I wouldn't have cared if he *did* wake up in Hildy's bed," Emma answered. She glanced at Mitch. "Except I would have killed him all over again."

They all broke into laughter again and Mitch pulled the blankets around himself. "All right, you bunch of no-goods, you've had your fun. Now get the hell out of my house."

"You gonna jump up from that bed and *make* us leave?" Len joked. "I'd sorely like to see that."

They all laughed again, including Emma, who sat down to the table while Doc Wilson walked up to Mitch, putting out his hand. "Welcome back, Mitch."

Mitch's scowl at the laughter softened some as he shook Doc's hand. "What the hell happened, Doc?"

Doc took out his stethoscope. "Well, like Emma

probably already told you, you were shot. The bullet slammed across your skull, kind of like if somebody had knocked you out with a rock or a hammer." He stopped to listen to Mitch's heart. "Head wounds are a funny thing, Mitch. It's next to impossible to predict the outcome. We had no idea if you'd ever wake up at all, or what shape you'd be in when you did. Everybody has been taking turns helping Emma take care of you, and we've all just been waiting it out, hoping for the best."

"Mitch, look around," Emma told him. "Everybody has been wonderful. We have curtains and a real cook-stove and a porch with a rocking chair and…" She stopped, tears of joy choking her voice.

Mitch turned back to Doc Wilson. "I don't remember a damn thing about how I got here."

"That's normal, but for you to remember every-thing else, remember all these people and all, that's a real good sign, Mitch. You should be damn grateful to be sitting here alive and well. I would suggest, how-ever, that you take things really slow, Mitch. Really slow." He looked over at Emma. "Not too much physical exertion for a while."

They all laughed again and Emma put her hands over her face, hating them all for the embarrassment and loving them all for their fierce loyalty to Mitch.

Randy ran outside and yelled to someone that Mitch Brady was awake and okay. Emma heard shouts and people yelling and even some celebratory shoot-ing. She thought how only in Alder would there be people still up and carousing at three o'clock in the morning. Men and women alike came running, and

Mitch scowled at Doc and Len and the others. "For God's sake, everybody get out of here and close the damn door!"

Len chuckled, nodding at Emma before stepping outside. "He's back, all right," he told her with a wink. "I just hope that head injury hasn't made him even meaner than he already was."

Len and Randy walked out and closed the door.

Mitch rubbed at his eyes. "I have one hell of a headache, Doc."

"Let's hope that gradually goes away." Doc rose, putting his stethoscope back into the small leather bag he seemed always to have with him. "I'll come back in a few minutes with a tonic that should help the headache. It's good to see you back to your old self, Mitch. You just remember what I said. Take it easy for a while." He looked at Emma and winked. "I'm counting on you to make sure he does."

"Oh, I will," she answered. "You can be sure of that."

Doc Wilson left, and Emma walked over to the bed. "Lie down, Mitch."

"Get me some damn clothes, woman."

Emma grinned, going to their one and only chest of drawers and taking out some long underwear. She knelt down to help him put them on, but Mitch grabbed them out of her hands. "For God's sake, Emma, I can put my own clothes on!"

Emma blinked, looking at him as though he'd hit her. Mitch threw aside the blankets and leaned forward, wrapping her into his arms as she burst into tears.

"I'm sorry, Emma. I'm just confused and I'm damn embarrassed you've had to take care of me like this."

"You're my husband. I would have taken care of you for years if I'd had to."

"Don't you think I know that?" He kissed her hair and Emma pulled away.

"Doc is coming back," she reminded him.

Mitch wrapped himself into the blankets again. "Emma, I'm just upset that something could have happened to you when I was shot, or afterward."

She wiped at her tears, sitting down in a chair beside the bed. "Mitch, we have to think of right now. I'm fine and you are recovering. That makes both of us very blessed. And if you never came back to me, so many people in this town would have made sure I was all right. People can say what they want about Montana's vigilantes, but I know any of them would have done anything for me if I needed it. You should rest easy knowing that."

He nodded. "I'm just not used to depending on anybody else for anything. I've been fending for myself since I was six years old, Emma, and *I'll* be the one to look after you."

Emma folded her arms. "Mitch Brady, count your blessings. I know there isn't a better man in all of Montana, but sometimes even the best of them needs help, and there is nothing wrong with that. You make sure to thank Len and Randy for all they did—and Sarah and Hildy and a lot of those other women. If not for the humor they used around me when helping take care of you, I would have gone crazy. It's time for you to come to realize you're not alone in this world, Mitch, not just because of me but because of a lot of people out there beyond the door."

He moved a hand from under the covers and Emma took it. Mitch squeezed her hand. "Help me get these damn long johns on, will you? I have such a damn headache, I'm afraid I'll fall over when I stand up."

Emma smiled. "And you really think I could hold up a man your size if you started going down?"

He thought a moment. "Let's wait for Doc Wilson to come back."

Emma kept hold of his hand. "Don't let go yet."

Mitch finally smiled in the way that always melted her. "Oh, I won't let go, Emma Brady. I'll *never* let go."

Thirty

EMMA WELCOMED HER HUSBAND INSIDE HER SOUL, taking in his rich, deep kisses, offering herself to him in sheer ecstasy and in the joy of realizing Mitch Brady had not lost any of his ability to please a woman in every way.

"Am I back in working order?" he asked softly, moving inside her for a second time.

Emma breathed deeply, grasping his hard-muscled arms. "What do you think?" she whispered, arching up to meet each deep thrust.

Mitch reached under her hips, thinking how he could grasp most of her small bottom in both his hands, relishing every curve, every soft place, the look of pure pleasure in her eyes, and the feel of her spasms of climax that made him penetrate her with a gentle rhythm that led to that moment when he could no longer hold back. His life spilled into her again, both of them hoping that soon it would take hold and Emma would have the baby they both wanted.

He relaxed then, pulling her close. Emma snuggled against him, neither of them wanting to get up and wash just yet. She kissed his neck. "These last five days of more bed rest that Doc ordered were worth the wait, Mitch," she teased. "Are you okay?"

"Oh, lady, I am just fine." Mitch ran a hand over her breasts, leaning down to kiss them tenderly.

Emma pushed at him playfully. "Time for a break, Mr. Brady. You shouldn't exert yourself too much at once."

"Oh, but this kind of exertion is good for a man." He kissed her lightly as Emma smiled with the sheer joy of knowing her husband was back in every way.

"Mitch, I was thinking today as I looked around our little home what a contrast it is to the kind of home I grew up in…a mansion with maids and a butler and fine china and silver, all the beautiful clothes a young girl could want…and that I've never been happier than right here in this uncivilized little town in my hastily built little cabin made of fresh pine—just one room and three windows."

"I wish I *could* give you all those other things, Emma."

"I'm trying to tell you that I don't *want* them. I just want you beside me at night, making me feel safe and loved. Whatever we do from here on, wherever we go, how we live, none of it matters as long as we have each other."

He sighed. "I've been thinking about that…about the vigilante work. I have some money saved up, Emma. I could start a business as a gunsmith. David Carlson told me a couple of weeks ago that he's thinking of moving on to California, so Alder will need a gunsmith, and one thing I know is guns. If I work with something like that, I wouldn't feel quite so far removed from being a lawman. I worry about you getting hurt because of what I do. It still bothers me that you were with me the day I was shot."

Emma traced her fingers along a vein in his arm. "I'll never ask you to go against whatever you really want to do, Mitch. I know it's kind of in your blood, and heaven knows you're good at what you do. What you do has to be your choice, Mitch."

He stretched. "We might end up moving to Virginia City. We have a lot of friends here, but gold towns can become ghost towns overnight once the gold runs out and the inhabitants move on to the next discovery."

Emma leaned up and kissed his cheek. "Well, wherever we end up and whatever we do, my offer still stands. If you want to go into your own business or build a ranch and buy cattle and horses and such, I can sell the necklace."

"No," he answered emphatically. "It's yours to hand down to a daughter of your own, or to keep for a true emergency if something did happen to me. I have some money saved, and you can still teach. We'll manage just fine. Some day you will have a bigger house and some of the finer things a woman wants and needs, and it will be because of *me*, not because of that necklace."

"Well, I mean it, Mitch. I know in my heart you didn't marry me for anything I own, and so selling it is fine with me if we ever need to." She kissed him again. "You still have never seen the necklace. Do you want me to show it to you?"

He grinned. "You're dying to, so go ahead. I really don't care one way or the other."

Emma crawled out of bed, commanding that he not look at her while she quickly washed. Mitch had to laugh at the fact that he'd seen and touched and tasted every inch of her, but she didn't want him to see her up naked and washing herself. He turned away and took a cheroot from a little stand on his side of the bed. He scooted up and removed the chimney from a nearby oil lamp, lighting the cheroot from its flame. He replaced the chimney and put a pillow behind him, relaxing against the headboard of the bed, smoking quietly while Emma pulled on a robe and went to her trunk in the corner.

"*That's* where you keep a valuable necklace?" he asked.

"I had no place else to hide it. The day of the robbery I had it inside my camisole. I was so scared those men would rip my clothes off and find it."

Mitch chuckled. "I would think you'd be more afraid of what they would have done with you once they got your clothes off," he teased.

"Well, that, too."

Mitch laughed harder, enjoying the look of her after lovemaking, her hair a mess, her beautiful skin natural, no paint, nothing fake or false about her. She wrapped something into her robe and came back to the bed, moving up against the headboard to sit beside him. She took the necklace from under her robe and held it up. "This is it," she told him.

Mitch took the cheroot from his lips, gawking at a spectacular necklace. "Jesus," he muttered, losing his smile. He stared at the delicate, lacy-looking cascade of gold embedded with more jewels than he'd ever seen in his life—more jewels than pretty much *any* human being had ever seen. "For God's sake, Emma, that thing should be in a bank safe in Virginia City! Maybe it should even be in a vault in some bigger city that has more law and order. It must be worth thousands!"

"I'm sure it is. It's pure gold, and all the jewels are real—sapphires, rubies, diamonds, garnets, pearls, emeralds, amethyst. Besides the value of the jewels themselves, the fact that it belonged to a member of the royal family makes it even more valuable." She handed it out to him, but Mitch put out his hand defensively.

"No thanks! I'm not sure I even want to *touch* it." He frowned. "No wonder Alan Radcliffe kept trying to get his hands on that thing. If he was losing money like you say he was, that necklace could have kept him going for a long time."

The mention of Alan brought a quick pain to Emma's chest. She lost her smile. "I'd almost forgotten about Alan," she told Mitch, staring at the necklace.

Mitch laid the cheroot in an ashtray on the nightstand. "We'll figure out what to do about Alan Radcliffe," he told her. "I'll see if I can find a way to learn if he's actually put out a warrant for you back in New York. Hal Wallace and David Meeks can maybe find the right person to send a telegram to."

Emma clutched the necklace. "But if you do that, they'll know I'm here. They'll come after me!"

"In Montana? There isn't a man alive, including the president himself, who'd come out here and go up against the vigilantes. No one is going to lay a hand on you, Emma. I don't want you to worry about it." He leaned closer and kissed her lightly, finally taking the necklace from her. "Turn around. I didn't want to touch this thing, but I can't resist seeing how it looks on a naked descendant of the royal family."

Emma laughed lightly, turning her back to him. "Mitch, my family is *not* descended from the royal family."

Mitch clasped the necklace around her neck. "I don't care. I now pronounce you queen of England," he teased.

Emma turned, and Mitch shook his head. "My God, you're beautiful! What the hell is a woman who grew up in a mansion and led a pampered and spoiled life and who went to finishing school and is the most beautiful creature on earth and the heiress of a necklace worth thousands doing married to a man like me?"

Emma ran a hand through his thick hair, carefully avoiding the still-healing wound that had nearly taken him from her for good. "She's married to you because there isn't a man anywhere, no matter how rich and sophisticated and educated, who can hold a candle to my rugged, handsome, brave, able lawman, or who could possibly make a woman feel the way you make me feel."

He frowned. "Even though I'm a worthless, no-good, murdering vigilante?"

Emma grinned. "Even that."

He touched the necklace again, studying it more closely. "We do have to decide what to do with this thing," he added. "Something this valuable shouldn't be lying around in a trunk in a one-room cabin in a lawless town full of gold-hungry men. We'll take it to Virginia City with us and find a safer place for it. And

you need to draw up a will or something that says if
something happens to you, the necklace goes to your
children, if you have any. Or you can designate it goes
to a museum or something."

"Not to you?"

"No, ma'am. That necklace is made for better
things than the saddlebags of a drunken saddle bum,
which is what I would be if anything ever happened
to you. Life wouldn't be worth living, rich or poor,
without you in it."

She touched his face. "You really mean that,
don't you?"

He kissed her hand. "I really mean it."

"And there is your answer as to why this woman
of royal blood who grew up in a mansion and led a
pampered and spoiled life married a man like you.
You are a good and unselfish man."

"I'm not so sure about the good part." He grinned,
moving a hand inside her robe to gently fondle her
breast. "Tell me something if you can." He pushed the
robe off her shoulders, exposing her breasts.

"What is it?" she asked.

He leaned close and kissed her. "If your grandmother's husband was so angry with her for her affair,
and if he banished her like you say he did"——he moved
his lips to her neck——"why on earth would he have
given her such a valuable necklace? He took everything else from her. Why not that?"

"Well, the answer is kind of embarrassing."

He stopped his kisses, meeting her gaze. "Tell me."

Emma scooted down, grinning as he moved on top
of her. "According to what my grandmother told my

mother, her husband, who like I said was actually her cousin…" She hesitated. "It's hard for me to say this."

"Oh?" He leaned down and kissed her throat.

"Yes. I mean…well, my mother told me that according to my grandmother he…he preferred men. He never even once made love to my grandmother."

"Preferred men?" He shook his head. "Not that I haven't heard of such things, but what's that got to do with the necklace?"

"According to what my grandmother told my mother, it was a payoff. He told her she could have one valuable thing to help her provide for herself and her baby if she never told anyone he'd never shared her bed. In return, he'd let her out of the marriage because she was so unhappy."

Mitch kissed her breasts, then moved between her legs again. "Well, I can assure you, Mrs. Brady, that *this* man definitely prefers women." He relished the feel of her as he invaded her yet again, unable to understand how any man wouldn't want what he had right now in his arms…in his bed…in his life.

He made love to her yet again, thinking how the necklace sparkled, even in the dim light of an oil lamp. He didn't want to tell her, but it worried him now that he'd seen what a treasure it was. It reminded him that he had to find a way to settle the problem of Alan Radcliffe so Emma could finally have total peace of mind.

Thirty-one

EMMA FINISHED DRESSING AND PUT JUST A LITTLE color on her cheeks. She pinned up the sides of her hair and left it long in back because Mitch liked it that way. She studied herself in a mirror that hung on the wall between the bed and the dresser. It was something Mitch had bought for her "because the most beautiful woman in town should have a mirror for dressing and pampering herself."

She smiled at the memory. She wasn't so sure she was "the most beautiful woman in town," but if he thought so, that was fine with her. Once she was with child and grew a big belly, he might change his mind, but he'd already told her she would be even more beautiful then. She wore a green ruffled dress Sarah had made for her, and she studied the tailored waistline. So far she still had a small waist. She tried to imagine what it would be like to be big with child and how happy she'd be to start a family for Mitch, to give him the home life he'd never known. She hoped that wouldn't be much longer, and she wondered if Sarah had ever made a dress with an overblouse that would hide a pregnant belly. It would be a little embarrassing going out in public that way, but she would also be proud it was Mitch's baby she was carrying.

Mitch had taken a change of clothes and left a half hour ago to visit Lee Wong's bathhouse and get a shave and haircut, leaving Randy outside to keep an eye on the house. Emma shook her head at the fact that he still thought she should be watched. The whole town had become their friends and Emma no longer feared any man in Alder. They all knew she was Mitch Brady's wife, and that was good enough to ensure her safety. Mitch argued that plenty of newcomers came and went daily in and out of Alder, which was reason enough to still be careful.

He would be back soon, and their bags were packed. They were going to Virginia City by stage today, which meant spending the night there before coming back to Alder. Emma looked forward to the trip. She wouldn't have to be afraid of an attack with Mitch Brady right by her side. They intended to pick up needed personal items, and some of the tools Mitch would need to start working as a gunsmith, at least in his spare time for now. He wanted to try it out and stay in town, continuing his work as a sheriff but stopping his work as a vigilante. He no longer intended to spend weeks at a time away from home. He wanted to be right here in Alder for her.

Life would be good. They would purchase books and tablets and other supplies for her teaching, and Mitch wanted to see about a safer place to keep her necklace, which was tucked away in her carpetbag for the trip. They would even see a lawyer about the will

Mitch wanted her to have drawn up. He refused to use Carl Jackson, because he didn't trust the man and didn't want him to know about the necklace. In fact, he'd told no one in Alder about it, not even Randy or any of his men.

She made ready to pin on a hat when someone tapped on the door. She unbolted it to see Randy standing there. He tipped his hat.

"Ma'am, there's some kind of ruckus going on at the saloon across the street and down a ways. I can hear shouting and arguing. Len and Benny are out on the trail, and Mitch isn't back yet. I'm going over to see what the problem is, so just keep your door bolted till Mitch comes back."

"That's fine, Randy."

"Do like I say and stay inside. You know Mitch. To him you're like a flower—blow a little wind on it and the petals come off. He's the most god-awful protective man I ever knew."

Emma laughed. "Go on, Randy. There isn't a person left in Alder I need to worry about. Mitch needs to start understanding that."

"If you say so."

Emma watched him walk across the street, then closed and bolted the door. She finished pinning on her hat, then heard another knock at the door. Sure it was either Randy or Mitch, she opened the door again, then gasped in horror when Alan Radcliffe quickly and viciously shoved the door wider, knocking her down. He closed and re-bolted the door as Emma scrambled to her feet, standing there speechless with astonishment.

"You never thought I'd find you, did you, you little *bitch*!"

Emma made for a rifle Mitch kept in a rack on the opposite wall, but Radcliffe grasped her hair and yanked, clamping a big hand over her mouth so she couldn't scream. "That two-bit, gun-toting kid who was outside fell for the little ruckus I paid a man to start, so he's not around to protect you, you little whore! Neither is that excuse of a lawman you've been sharing your bed with! It's just you and *me*, my sweet!"

He bent one arm up behind her back, keeping her mouth covered. "When you ran off, you shouldn't have left behind that newspaper article giving away your destination," he growled.

The article! Emma remembered losing it. She'd been in such a hurry, she forgot to bring the newspaper with her! Alan bent her arm more, reawakening the pain in her still-tender shoulder.

"Where is it, Emma! Where's the goddamn necklace! That's all I want! Give me the necklace and I'll leave you to your stinking little excuse of a house and your cowboy husband!"

How did he know about Mitch and where they lived? And how did he know Mitch wasn't here? Alan whirled her around and backhanded her before she could cry out. She landed against the table, and she tasted blood as he jerked her up and dragged her to the bed, pushing her onto it and holding her arms down. He pressed a knee into her stomach so she could barely breathe.

"You stupid little slut!" he growled, his dark eyes blazing. "If you had willingly come to my bed and let me have the necklace, you'd be living the life of a wealthy woman right now! I wouldn't have gone to the prosecutor and told him you killed your own mother and stole from me! But things have changed, Emma, and I need that necklace!"

She shook her head and spit at him. "The...vigilantes...will hang you...for this!"

Alan pressed his knee harder. "Give me the necklace or I'll snap every rib in your body! I'm headed for California! Give me the necklace and I'll go and you'll never see me again!"

Emma cried out with pain, but it was more of a squeal because she could barely take a breath. "Why... California?" she managed to grunt.

"I've lost everything, thanks to you, you little thief! If I had that necklace, I could have saved my home and what was left of my businesses! You and that damn stubborn bitch of a mother of yours ruined my *life*!"

Emma gritted her teeth. "*Gambling*...did...that."

Alan pressed again and Emma heard a crack and nearly fainted from the pain. "Where is it!" he demanded.

His eyes were wild. He looked truly desperate, and Emma wondered what had gone wrong back home. This seemed to be something worse than just losing money to gambling debts. It was as though he was running from something. One thing was certain, he really meant business this time, and she didn't want to die. The necklace wasn't worth that. The stubborn part of her said to keep defying him, but the part of her that wanted to live for Mitch made her talk. "Carpet...bag..." She moved her eyes to where her packed bag sat on the floor.

Alan glanced at it, then eased off, but he back-handed the other side of her face to stun her into silence before going over to the bag. He tore it open and flung everything out of it, then tore at the lining to find the necklace.

All the while Emma struggled to get up, but the pain in her left side was excruciating. Her handbag lay nearby on the bed. She tried reaching for it while Alan shoved the necklace into an inside pocket of his fancy waistcoat. He turned back then, noticing her trying to get up.

Furious with her for all he imagined she'd done to him, he came back to the bed and wrapped his big hands around her throat, pushing her onto her back again.

"I said I'd leave when I got the necklace," he told her, "but I didn't say I'd leave without *killing* you! I wouldn't want you telling people who did this, now, would I?" He began squeezing, and Emma's eyes grew wide with terror as he choked off her air.

Randy! Mitch! She managed to get hold of her drawstring handbag and reached inside it. How she was able to keep from passing out, she wasn't sure, just as she wasn't sure how she managed to find her little derringer and cock it. She put it against Alan's side and pulled the trigger.

Alan jerked, his eyes wide with shock. He let go of her and straightened, looking down at himself, then reached under his waistcoat and felt his side. When he pulled his hand out, it was covered with blood. He gawked at her then, astounded, noticing the small handgun still in her left hand.

"You fucking little bitch!" he exclaimed. "You shot me!"

She still couldn't get her breath and was sure he'd crushed something in her throat so that she'd never breathe again. Alan backed away as she tried to point her gun at him again, but she'd lost too much oxygen to have any strength left. The last thing she saw before passing out was Alan Radcliffe turning and going out the door.

Thirty-two

RANDY CAME OUT OF THE SALOON AND LOOKED FAR-ther down the street at Mitch's place. The door was standing open. Figuring Mitch must be there, he walked over to check and let him know about the ruckus Boot Tully had started in the Saddleback Saloon—it was something very unusual for Boot, who was known as the town drunk but never as a troublemaker. Randy frowned in puzzlement over why Boot would have suddenly started a row with Bart Hillandale, one of the biggest brawlers and brag-gers in Alder. While Randy tried to settle things, Boot had begun waving around twenty dollars, offering to buy drinks.

"Where in hell did Boot get that much money?" Randy wondered. He reached Mitch's place and went inside, stopping cold when he saw Emma lying on the bed, her face pummeled, her derringer in her hand, and a carpetbag opened with clothes scattered everywhere!

"Jesus, oh Jesus!" Randy groaned. He ran over to Emma, feeling her neck for a pulse. It was then he noticed the horrible purple color there. Someone had choked her nearly to death! "Emma? Emma, can you talk?"

She made an odd choking sound. "Emma? Oh, Jesus God, Mitch is gonna string me up for this, and I deserve it!" He scooped Emma up in his arms and carried her out the door, running down the street with her toward Doc Wilson's. "Please be there, Doc! Please be there!"

What the hell happened? Who in Alder would do this to Mitch Brady's wife?

People began following Randy. "Get Mitch!" he yelled to someone. "He's at the bathhouse!"

Randy could barely see for the tears in his eyes. If Emma Brady died, it would be his fault, and he'd rather shoot himself than see the look in Mitch's eyes if he had to put his wife in the ground. People everywhere were shouting now.

"Get Mitch!"

"Somethin' happened to Emma Brady!"

"Looks like she might be dead!"

Randy wondered if this could have something to do with Trudy Wiley and her bunch. Maybe one of them was still out to get Mitch and chose to hurt him by beating up his wife. No matter the reason. The fact remained that Randy had allowed himself to become distracted and take his attention away from keeping an eye on things. As soon as he delivered Emma to Doc Wilson, he intended to have a talk with Boot Tully.

Others arrived at Doc's ahead of Randy, and Doc Wilson was already standing ready at the door when Randy got there. Farther down the street he could see Mitch running from the bathhouse, his shirt open, no hat or vest, his hair still wet, and both of his gun belts in one hand. Doc Wilson stepped aside and told Randy to lay Emma on a cot inside. He ordered onlookers to step back and he closed the door, but he'd no sooner bent over Emma to take a look when the door burst open then and the room was filled with Mitch Brady and the fury that came with him.

"What the hell happened!" he asked, hurrying to Emma's side.

Randy stepped back. "I…I don't know. I found her this way at your place!"

"Oh, my God, look at her throat!" Mitch shoved Doc out of the way and bent over Emma. "Emma! Emma, who did this?"

Her eyes fluttered and she made a horrible gagging sound.

"Jesus, Doc, she can't breathe! She can't breathe!"

"Then get out of my way and let me help her!" Doc told him. He quickly took a scalpel from a tray nearby.

"What are you doing?"

"I'm going to cut a hole in her trachea so she can breathe. If she goes much longer like this, she'll have brain damage."

"I won't let you cut into her!" Mitch roared.

"Do you want her to *die*?"

Mitch turned away, obvious tears in his eyes, a sight none of them had ever seen.

"You go find out who did this, Mitch!" the doctor told him. "You do *your* job and let me do *mine*!"

Mitch ran a hand through his still-wet hair. "I can't leave her."

"Then go around the other side of the cot and help

me!" Doc told him, looking scared himself. "Let's sit her up a little and help her breathe. Maybe I can avoid a tracheotomy."

Mitch wiped at his eyes and knelt down on the other side of the bed.

"Randy, go get Sarah!" Doc ordered.

Mitch looked up at Randy.

"Jesus, I'm so sorry, Mitch. I only left for a few minutes. It's like somebody planned this. There's no other way he could have been there right at that time."

"Go get Sarah." Doc ordered again.

Randy hurried out.

Emma made an odd gulping sound, and Mitch smoothed back her hair from her bloodied face.

"I can't stand for her to hurt, Doc."

Both men helped her sit up more as Emma struggled to get air to her lungs. "Someone choked her so hard it nearly collapsed the trachea, but it might be open enough that she can breathe without me having to cut into her."

Mitch gently touched her bruised face. "Emma, nod or something. Do you think you can breathe on your own?"

She managed to nod, grasping his wrist in terror. She tried to talk, but nothing would come out. Doc Wilson gently felt her face and jawline. "I don't feel any broken bones." He moved his hands down her body, and Emma jerked back from pain when he touched one spot on her left side. "Lay her back and get her dress off!" Doc ordered Mitch.

Sarah came inside then. "Oh, my God, what happened!"

"Some bastard beat the hell out of her!" Mitch seethed. He helped the doctor remove Emma's dress and camisole. Sarah gasped at how purple Emma's whole midsection was, and Mitch groaned with pity and a need to kill someone. Doc felt around Emma's ribs. "She has at least one broken rib, probably more," he told Mitch. "From the look of this center bruise, someone either punched her a good one right in the middle, or maybe he pressed her down with a knee, something like that."

Mitch wilted into a chair beside the cot, putting his head in his hands. Randy came inside then and Doc covered Emma.

"I don't understand this," Sarah exclaimed, her eyes wide with confusion and horror.

"I failed her," Mitch answered, his voice raspy with fury and regret. "I failed to keep the one extra promise I made her when we got married. I said no one would ever hurt her again."

Sarah tried to soothe him. "Mitch, this isn't your fault."

"Isn't it?" He looked up at her with tear-filled eyes, but along with the tears was something else, a rage worse than anything Sarah had ever seen. "It's just like what happened with my mother! When she needed me most, I couldn't help her!"

"And you were a helpless little boy then! You're a *man* now, Mitch Brady, and you sure as hell *can* help! You can go out there and find out who did this!"

Mitch got to his feet, bending over as though in pain. "Look at her! When I left, she was happy and packing our things for Virginia City and—" He stopped, angrily wiping at his eyes. He turned to

Randy. "What else happened over there? Did some-one go through our bags?"

A devastated Randy nodded. "There were clothes strewn all over the place."

"Shit!" Mitch threw the chair against the wall. "I know who did this! And he's got the necklace! He's got the necklace, and he decided to make her suffer for keeping it from him!"

"Mitch, calm down or get out of my office!" Doc ordered him. "And don't forget you aren't completely well yourself yet. You could pass out if you let your anger get the better of you. Your blood will rise to your head and could cause a stroke. Your brain and the inside of your skull are still healing, so calm down and think this through! Emma will need you, but she doesn't need a roaring grizzly bear at her side. She needs her *husband* in a calm, reassuring state. And she doesn't need to come out of this to find out you're *dead*!"

"Mitch, what are you talking about? Who has what necklace?" Sarah asked. "You aren't making sense."

Mitch turned in circles, putting his hands to his head. "How did he get to her?" he asked himself aloud. "How did he know where we were—where we lived?"

"Who?" Sarah asked.

Mitch looked at Randy. "Tell me everything that led up to this! Why did you leave your post?"

Randy swallowed. "You can beat the hell out of me and string me up, Mitch. I deserve it."

Mitch closed his eyes. "No, you don't. This is no one's fault but my own. I wasn't as watchful as I should have been. I didn't tell any of you that uncle of hers might come here looking for her. You had no idea or you might have been more aware. I thought I could handle it myself, because Emma didn't want anybody to know about…all the facts behind why she came here." He looked at Randy again. "I'll explain later. Just tell me what distracted you."

Randy explained, looking ashamed and devastated.

Mitch began buttoning his shirt and tucked it into his pants. "Boot Tully never causes trouble, and he never has money on him. That was a setup, Randy. Someone paid him to start a ruckus and get you over there…someone who'd been watching our movements. He probably saw me go to Lee Wong's and figured I'd be there a while." He walked over to pick up his guns from where he'd thrown them onto the floor. He began strapping them on.

"Who, Mitch?" Randy asked.

Mitch finished buckling his gun belts while Sarah and Doc Wilson helped soothe Emma, urging her to relax and get as much air into her lungs as possible. Mitch tied the ends of his holsters around his thighs. "His name is Alan Radcliffe," he seethed. "Emma and I both knew he might come here looking for Emma. I figured he'd stand out in a crowd here because he's a businessman from New York City who wouldn't fit in out here. I should have realized strangers, even fancy ones like Radcliffe, come and go in this town every day and wouldn't draw that much attention. He must have managed to get information out of people who didn't realize why he was really here…enough information to figure out where Emma and I lived and how to catch Emma alone."

"Why would he do this to Emma?" Sarah asked.

Mitch straightened, pain in his eyes when he glanced at Emma again. "Because she had something he wanted, something very valuable. It's a necklace, unlike anything you've ever set eyes on, believe me. When we have more time, I'll explain what makes it so valuable." He looked at Sarah. "I didn't tell anyone about it because I didn't want people knowing Emma possessed anything of value. We were going to Virginia City to find a safer place to keep it, but Radcliffe got here before we could do that."

"And who is Radcliffe?" Randy asked.

Mitch felt he might explode with fury. "Her stepfather, who also happens to be her blood uncle. He murdered Emma's mother and…" He took several deep breaths to keep from ramming his fists into a wall. He told himself not to be angry with Randy. The kid didn't know the whole of it. "Never mind the rest," he added. "The point is, Emma is scared to death of him and I let him get to her after promising that would never happen!" His hands balled into fists. "Somehow the sonofabitch figured out where she was and managed to slip into town like some fancy trader or something and avoided running into any of us. I don't even know myself what he looks like. I only have Emma's description of him—tall and dark, built a lot like me, but older. We have to find him and show him how in Montana a man *pays* for something like this!"

"Mitch, when I found her, her derringer was in her hand and there was blood on the floor," Randy told him. "I think maybe she managed to shoot and at least wound him. That will slow him down—maybe even leave us a blood trail."

Mitch's jaw twitched with his furious need for revenge. "Then I guess she's got a bit of vigilante blood in her, doesn't she?" he tried to joke, but his voice broke as he spoke. He turned away.

"Mitch, she's going to be okay," Doc reassured him. "None of this is life threatening. I'll take good care of her. You go find this man and hang the sonofabitch!"

Mitch cleared his throat before turning around. "He'll head back to New York. That's where he's from. He's got the necklace now and he'll sell it as fast as he can. He'll get more money for it from a museum or something like that in a big city."

Emma made an odd choking sound then and they all turned. Her eyes were open, and she was trying to say something. Mitch and Doc Wilson went to her side, leaning close.

"I'm so damn sorry, Emma!" Mitch told her, touching her hair again and leaning closer to kiss her bruised cheeks. "This is all my fault."

She shook her head, taking a deep, raspy breath. She opened her mouth, whispering something. Mitch leaned closer and she managed one raggedly whispered word. "California."

Mitch frowned, meeting her eyes. "California?"

Emma managed a nod.

"Radcliffe is headed for California?"

She nodded again.

"Why in hell would he—"

Emma grasped his forearm and squeezed, signaling

she needed to say more. "Running," she rasped. "He's…in…trouble…headed…west…not east."

Mitch started to rise, but she squeezed his arm again, and he leaned close. "I…shot him," she managed to say. "Felt…good."

Mitch managed a smile. "I bet it did."

Emma managed a smile through tears. "Don't… blame yourself…Mitch."

He took her hand and kissed her palm. "I can't help that part, but I can promise I'll make up for this, Emma. When we're done with him, that man won't be alive to ever bother you again."

Emma took several deep, desperate breaths. "Scared…for you. You're…not well."

"Don't you worry about me," Mitch told her, fire in his eyes. "I'm well enough for this!" He straightened. "He's heading west. Emma says he's in some kind of trouble, and we know he's wounded. Let's go! I have to go to the bathhouse and get my hat and vest. Randy, you go get our horses ready and go back to my house and get my carbine. We'll pick up his trail from there."

Both men headed out the door and hurried off in two different directions. Sarah looked at Doc Wilson. "Oh, Doc, pity the man who dared to lay a hand on Emma Brady. It was bad enough what Mitch did to that man who beat me up. I can't imagine what it will be like for a man who beat on the woman he loves."

Doc Wilson scowled "I don't pity the man at all. I *am* a little worried about Mitch, though. He's beside himself with anger and sorrow. That's not good for him right now." He walked over to give Emma a better examination for injuries.

Moments later, someone knocked at the door. "Doc? It's Len Gray."

Doc opened the door and let the man inside.

"I just rode in and somebody told me something happened to Mitch's wife." Len glanced over at the cot. "God Almighty, what happened?"

"Mitch can explain," Sarah told him. "He's gone to get some things he left at Lee Wong's, and Randy is saddling their horses at the stables. They're supposed to meet over at Mitch's place. They're going after the man who did this to Emma. I would explain more but I don't understand all of it myself. You should go with them, Len. Doc says he's worried about Mitch—the mood he's in and all. He's awfully worked up, and that's not good with that fresh head injury. If you go now you can join them before they leave."

Len looked at Emma again. "Yeah, I'll damn well go along." He made for the door and Emma managed to reach up with one hand.

"Len," she said weakly.

"Emma wants you," Sarah called out to him.

Len walked over to the cot, wincing with fury at the sight of Emma's battered face and neck.

Emma struggled to speak. "Watch out…for… Mitch." A tear slipped down the side of her face. "He's so…angry. He shouldn't…get into a…fight. He's not…completely healed."

"Oh, I know what Mitch is like, Emma. Don't you worry about it. I'll keep him reined in as best I can, but I have to say, after seeing what's happened to you, it will be hard for even me and Randy to hold him back." He took her hand. "You just lay real still and get better. I'll get Mitch back here safe and sound."

She squeezed his hand. "Man...they are after...a good hunter...big game...hunting trips...powerful rifle. He might have...that rifle. Warn Mitch."

"I will, sweetheart, I will." Len patted her hand and turned to go out.

"Be careful..." Sarah told him.

"Always am." He put on his hat, stopping near Sarah as he headed out. "When was the last time this old boy paid you a visit, Sarah?"

Sarah grinned. "Too long ago."

"Well, now, I reckon I'll have to fix that when I get back." He looked her over. "Thanks for everything you've done, Sarah—for Emma there, and for Mitch when he was hurt."

Sarah shrugged. "Some people deserve help and some don't."

He nodded. "That's a fact." Len went out and Doc Wilson grinned.

"Well, now there are *three* vigilantes after that man," he commented. "He doesn't have a chance in hell of making it five miles out of Alder."

Thirty-three

"I SURE AM SORRY, MITCH," RANDY SPOKE UP. "I LET you down real bad. I wouldn't blame you if you found a way to accidentally shoot me while we're out here."

Mitch dismounted and studied the tracks they were following. "You're too good a man, Randy," he answered, rising. "I've thought of beating you within an inch of your life, but you're too valuable to the vigilantes to outright shoot you." He glanced at the young man who sat astride his pinto horse. Randy looked truly worried. "Randy, I'm not serious. I hope you know that."

Randy shrugged. "I wasn't sure. Soon as I saw poor Emma layin' there all beat up..." He shook his head. "Man, I figured I was done for, and right then I wouldn't have cared, cuz I never felt so bad in my whole life, and that's a fact."

Mitch took a cheroot from his saddlebag, along with a match. He lit the cheroot and smoked a minute, studying the vast Montana landscape ahead of them. "It's my fault anyway for not telling you everything you should have been watching for," he told

Randy. He climbed back onto his horse. "He's headed right through that valley ahead, and at a pretty good clip. He has to wear down pretty soon. That little gun of Emma's doesn't blow a big hole in a man, but he's hurting, I guarantee it, especially if she hit something important. I'm proud of her for managing to do what she did. A wounded man will be a lot easier to catch."

Len pushed back his hat, studying the valley and the mountains beyond. "She told me when I seen her at Doc's that this man we're after might have a high-powered rifle with him. Said he used to hunt big game with it."

Mitch drew on the cheroot. "Yeah, well he's not used to hunting *men*. Hank down at the stables told Randy he's riding that black gelding Hank used to enter in races. It's a good horse, but Radcliffe isn't used to him. It makes a big difference when you're riding your own animal. And Radcliffe is a city man. This country will get to him real fast. He doesn't have a clue as to what a man needs to take along when he's alone out here, and he likely doesn't even know for sure which way to go. He's heading west." He looked back at Len. "Right into Witch's Canyon."

Len grinned. "Lots of snakes there."

"Hell, no man in his right mind goes there," Randy added.

"Not unless he's a greenhorn like Alan Radcliffe, riding an unfamiliar horse and fighting a hole in his gut," Mitch added.

Randy nodded. "Ain't nobody knows Montana like the vigilantes," he answered.

"You're damn right," Mitch told him, kicking his

horse into a gentle trot. "And we don't have to be in a hurry, because this guy is going to be easy to follow. He doesn't have all that much of a head start on us. We'll give him time to lose some more blood, maybe so much that he's too weak to raise that fancy rifle of his." He studied the tracks again, then gave Randy a look that made the young man shiver. "Then I might have to reopen the wound and make him bleed a little more," Mitch added.

Randy glanced at Len, who just nodded. "Be glad you ain't the one he's after," Len told him.

"Oh, I am. I surely am."

They followed Mitch, all three men riding until it was too dark to keep going. They made it to the mouth of Witch's Canyon, where they made camp.

"Our man will hole up in there for the night," Mitch told them, rolling out his bedroll and using his saddle at the head of it for a pillow. "And when he wakes up in the morning and that sun shines onto the western rim of the canyon, he'll realize he's ridden right into a place he can't ride out of. He'll wake up to the fact that he has to backtrack right through here to get out of there and find a different trail. If a snake doesn't get him, and he doesn't die from that bullet Emma put in him, our dumb sonofabitch of a city man will ride right into our camp." He stood at the campfire drinking some of the strong coffee Len had made. "Alan Radcliffe might be a powerful man where he comes from, but out here he's nothing more than a scared little rabbit."

Len thought how, in the firelight, Mitch's eyes looked like the eyes of Satan. "Mitch, Doc said you have to be careful not to get too physical. That wound could still mean you blacking out if that head gets banged around too much."

Mitch tossed out what was left of his coffee and stooped down to stretch out on his bedroll. "Oh, I don't intend to manhandle the man too much. I'll just open that wound a little, maybe break a rib or two, considering how he broke Emma's rib—maybe more than one."

"That so?" Len asked.

Mitch put a hand to his head. "He hurt her bad, Len, real bad."

"I saw her face and her throat. I'm real sorry about that, Mitch."

Mitch glanced at Randy. "When you found her, she was just beat up, right?"

"What do you mean?"

"I mean…all her clothes were on, just like she was still completely dressed when I got to Doc's office. You didn't do anything to try to hide something worse?"

"Something worse?" Randy crouched by the fire to pour his own cup of coffee. "Shit, no, Mitch. If you're meanin' what I think you're meanin', there wasn't no sign of somethin' like that. Besides, the guy is her *uncle*, right? He married her ma, who you said was his brother's wife. I mean, a guy doesn't do somethin' like that to his own niece."

Mitch put his hands behind his head and stared at the flickering fire. "Doesn't he?"

Everything got quiet for a moment.

"Jesus," Randy muttered. "This guy is worse than I thought."

"He is," Mitch answered. "She had damn good reason for running from this guy, and it was more than just to keep him from getting hold of that necklace. She was hardly more than a scared little girl. He'd murdered her mother and then told her he'd accuse her of killing the woman out of jealousy because she wanted him for herself—said he'd accuse her of coming to his bed and trying to seduce him. He threatened her in every way he could to get that necklace from her, but she'd promised her ma that would never happen, so she just took the necklace and ran off, figuring a man like Alan Radcliffe would never dream she'd come to a place like Alder. I don't know how in God's name he figured it out, but he did. Once we take care of him, I need to find out if Emma is wanted in New York. I intend to straighten that out for her so she can finally have some peace of mind."

Len sighed. "I can't believe a man would do that to his own brother's child. He must be pretty desperate."

"Yeah, well, Emma said something similar—about him being desperate, I mean. I think his gambling led to maybe losing everything back in New York. She made it sound like he was out here for more than just the necklace and revenge. I have a feeling he's already running from something. Now he's got Montana vigilantes on his ass, so he's done for, one way or another."

"All the more reason why you can't let what he did make you do somethin' stupid, Mitch—somethin' that could mean Emma losin' you all over again. I've seen what you do to a man who beats up on a woman, but you think about Emma this time, not your ma and not your need for revenge. Your ma was dead and didn't need you anymore, so even if avenging her meant you gettin' hurt bad, it wouldn't have mattered. This time it *does* matter. to *Emma*. You keep that in mind. This guy is gonna get his due without you havin' to exert yourself beatin' him half to death. He ain't never gonna make it back to New York or out to California or any place else. You damn well know that."

Mitch sighed. "Yeah, I expect so."

"I'm willin' to bet there's a lynch mob formin' right now back in Alder. A lot of folks are gonna be wantin' revenge just as much as you, cuz they like that little gal you married," Len added.

Mitch smiled sadly. "True."

"And it's likely that mob will be so big and so determined that you and me and Randy and all the vigilantes in Montana won't be able to stop them. Know what I mean?'

Mitch met Len's all-knowing eyes. Len Gray was an older, wiser man whose past Mitch knew nothing about but who was hardened and tough and dependable. Mitch knew he was trying to keep his rage in check—not just for Mitch's sake, but for Emma's. "I know what you mean."

All three men quietly watched the fire. Mitch settled against his saddle. "Emma said something to you before you left, didn't she?" Mitch asked Len.

"Just a word or two."

"Told you to watch out for me."

"Kind of."

"You know damn well I don't need watching out for when I'm after someone."

"I know that, you stubborn ass. It ain't the other guy she's worried about. It's *you* gettin' in your own way. She's scared cuz of that wound that's still a bit too fresh to risk getting bashed in the head all over again. She knows you can handle yourself, and I sure as hell do, too. But sometimes you need somebody to slow you down some. I'll lasso you to a tree if I have to—for *her*—not because I give a damn about you. Got that?"

Mitch reached behind him and pulled a small flask of whiskey from his saddlebag. He uncorked it and took a swallow. "I got that just fine." He handed the flask out to Len, who walked over and knelt down to his own bedroll nearby.

Len reached out and took the whiskey, taking a swig of it and handing it back. Their gazes locked and held in silent understanding. Len nodded as he handed back the whiskey.

"Me and Randy love her, too," he told Mitch. "If you hadn't moved in on her so fast, we sure as hell would have tried, especially young Randy there. He don't feel like shit about what happened just because he was afraid you'd skin him alive for fallin' down on the job. He feels like shit cuz Emma is such a fine young lady and he let *her* down, too."

Randy waved them off and turned his back to Mitch, settling under his blanket.

Mitch took another swallow of whiskey. "Guess I didn't think of it that way."

"Yeah, well, you just keep yourself healthy for that woman, cuz if somethin' happens to you, she'll be somebody *else's* wife. I don't think you want that."

Mitch grinned, realizing Len Gray was using every sly trick he could think of to keep Mitch from going over the edge. "No, I sure don't want that," he answered, putting the cork back in the flask and setting it beside his saddle. "I surely don't want anybody but me calling that woman his wife."

He stared at millions of stars in a black Montana sky, listening to the crackle of the fire as it began burning down to embers. He wondered how one man could know so little about another man and yet be sure without a doubt that he could totally trust that same man.

"I have a question for you two," he said before they fell asleep.

"Ask away," Randy answered, still turned away.

"What if I bought some land and started ranching? I'd need some ranch hands to help with all the chores that come with that, help with roundups, guard against cattle thieves, watch out for Indian raids, build fences, and the like. Would you two be interested in something like that?"

Neither man answered right away.

"Hell, why not?" Len finally spoke up. "I've worked ranches before. There isn't much I *haven't* done, and if any man can make it ranchin', you can."

"I expect I don't have anything better to do," Randy put in. "Not much difference between ridin' the range herdin' cattle and watchin' out for thieves and Indians as a ranch hand and ridin' half of Montana lookin' for troublemakers as a vigilante. I don't see much difference, and there ain't nobody I'd rather work for than you, Mitch. You and Len are like...I don't know…like the pa I never had, I guess. Fact is, the reason I figured you'd beat my ass is because that's what my pa would have done for failin' him…and Lord knows he found plenty of ways to accuse me of lettin' him down so's he'd have an excuse to whale on me."

"The only thing that would make me want to beat the hell out of you is if you tried to make a move on my wife," Mitch answered.

"Shoot, Mitch, I ain't educated, but I ain't *that* stupid, either," Randy shot back.

All three men laughed, and Mitch felt some of his fury ease up. "You know, boys, I'm thinking we won't go any farther. We'll get us a good night's sleep and then we'll wait right here come morning. We'll let Mr. Alan Radcliffe come to us instead of us going after him. Maybe he thinks no one is even after him yet. Maybe he's cocky enough to think he's gotten away with this, like he got away with everything back in New York. Either way, he's gonna come right back through here when he figures out he can't get out of that canyon."

"Sounds good to me," Len answered.

"I can't wait," Randy put in.

All three men settled in for the night, but Mitch knew he wouldn't really sleep much. For the rest of his life, he wouldn't sleep well without Emma lying right next to him. He wanted desperately to be with her tonight, to comfort her in any way he could. The vision of her battered face, her purple ribs—the idea of a man his size pummeling a hundred-pound woman—it all kept slamming at his guts. It wouldn't be easy taking this calmly the way Len was warning him to do. That hundred-pound woman was his Emma, the very woman he'd promised would never suffer again at the hands of Alan Radcliffe.

No, he wouldn't sleep easy tonight.

Thirty-four

"Sit still, boys. He's coming," Mitch said softly.

All three men had packed up and moved their horses behind some of the masses of huge boulders that lay strewn over the vast flatland that led to the entrance to Witch's Canyon. They hunkered down behind more rocks and waited as a fine black gelding made its way through the canyon entrance. A tall man wearing an expensive but obviously soiled and dusty suit coat sat astride the horse. He wore a black felt hat and held a fancy hunting rifle in his right hand.

At the entrance he spotted the remains of Mitch's campfire and reined his horse to a halt, looking around like a wild animal that sensed danger.

"Morning, Mr. Radcliffe," Mitch spoke up.

Radcliffe whirled, his rifle instantly raised and ready to shoot. Mitch fired his own carbine. Radcliffe cried out when a bullet ripped through his hand and tore the rifle from it. The rifle went flying, slamming against a rock, the butt of the gun breaking away from the barrel.

Mitch, Len, and Randy all moved out from behind the rocks.

"We were kind of wonderin' how long it would take you to figure out you couldn't get out of that canyon," Len spoke up, his own rifle leveled at Radcliffe.

"You're lucky a rattler didn't crawl into your blankets to warm itself last night," Randy added, also leveling a rifle at the man. "That canyon is full of 'em."

"He probably wouldn't have been bit," Mitch said, moving into a position where Radcliffe could better see him. "Snakes don't bite each other, and I'll bet this man was the biggest, meanest snake in the canyon."

Radcliffe held out his bloody hand, his eyes wide, his body trembling. "I'm bleeding! And I've—" He opened his coat to show a huge bloodstain on his satin vest. "I've been...shot!"

"Oh, that's too bad," Mitch told him. "Ain't it, boys?"

"Sure is," Len answered

Radcliffe swallowed, studying Mitch closely as his face began turning whiter before their eyes. "You're the ignorant, murdering...low-life vigilante Emma's been...sleeping with, aren't you?" he sneered. "I saw you...a couple of times from a...distance. Someone... pointed you out to me...thought I was a reporter."

"Yeah, I'm the ignorant, murdering, low-life vigilante Emma's been sleeping with, and I could blow your head off right here and now and get away with it. Out here in Montana, we vigilantes have a way of doing whatever the hell we want with murdering, thieving rapists. Ain't I right again, boys?"

"Right again," Len answered.

"I suggest you get down off that horse," Mitch told Radcliffe.

Radcliffe just stared at him. "No."

"Mister, you either get down, or I'll shoot you off that horse. I'll start with one ear, then the other, then an elbow, then the other, and once you fall, I'll finish off both knees! Don't try my very short patience. Get off your goddamn *horse*!"

Radcliffe winced as he slowly dismounted. He stumbled then, his knees buckling. He ended up sitting on the ground and grabbing his side with his good hand. "I've lost a lot of blood," he told Mitch. "I... need a doctor."

Mitch motioned for Randy to grab the man's horse. Randy walked over and took the animal's bridle and led it aside. "Go get our horses, too," Mitch told the boy.

Randy hurried over to where their own horses were tied, and Mitch stepped closer to Radcliffe, Len staying close behind.

"Too bad about you needing a doctor," Mitch told Radcliffe. "Seems Alder's doctor is occupied with someone else right now, a tiny, hundred-pound woman you choked until she couldn't *breathe*!" He handed his rifle out sideways to Len, who took it from him.

"Mitch, be careful. Remember what I told you."

Mitch walked up to Radcliffe, his hands balled into fists. "Get up, you worthless piece of shit!"

Radcliffe hung his head. "Give me a minute."

Mitch grabbed him by his jacket and jerked him to his feet. "I said to get up!" he growled.

"Mitch, watch yourself!" Len warned, stepping closer.

"I'm *being* careful!" Mitch shot back. "You have no idea *how* careful!" He looked Radcliffe straight in the eyes. "So, you *are* my size." He gave Radcliffe a shove, and the man fell back to the ground. "Tell me, Radcliffe, how does a man your size live with the knowledge that he's the most worthless, cowardly, yellow cow shit of a man who ever walked?" On the word *walked*, he kicked Radcliffe in the side where he'd been wounded.

Radcliffe screamed with the pain and rolled away.

"God, how I wish you weren't wounded at all," Mitch told him, "so I could take pleasure in beating the hell out of you man-to-man! I guess I won't get that enjoyment, *will* I?" On the word *will*, he slammed a booted foot upward under Radcliffe's chin, sending him sprawling once more.

"Mitch, let's get him back to town," Randy yelled.

Mitch watched Radcliffe struggle to a sitting position. He bent over, fresh blood coming from his wound. "Call this your medical treatment," Mitch told him, "because this is as close as you'll get to doctoring!"

"Please...no more," Radcliffe panted.

"Did my *wife* say the same thing to you when you were beating her?" Mitch knelt down and jerked Radcliffe's head back by the hair. "Or maybe she never got the chance, since you were also trying to *choke* her to death!" He backhanded Radcliffe, then stood up, walking to his horse. He grasped the saddle horn and just stood there a minute, hanging his head. "God, I need to kill him so bad, Len."

"All three of us would like that, but this has to eventually be explained back in New York, Mitch, and vigilantes have a bad enough reputation in other parts of the country. We don't want to be called all-out murderers. Whatever happens to him in town, that's somethin' else. That's not the doin's of the vigilantes."

Mitch threw his head back, taking a deep breath. "Randy, see if you can get him back up on his horse."

Randy led Radcliffe's horse back to the man. "Get on up there," he ordered. "You're damn lucky I'm not the one who decides what to do with you right here and now, mister, after the way you got me away from Emma's place so's you could beat the living shit out of her. All three of us would like to string you up on the closest tree!"

Radcliffe just sat there, panting.

"Get up!" Randy shouted.

"Wait a minute." Mitch walked over to the man's horse, untying a small carpetbag. He tossed clothes out of it, felt around inside it, then threw it down. "Where is the necklace, Radcliffe!" he growled.

Radcliffe just sat there and shook his head. Mitch tore through every single item of the man's supplies without finding the necklace. Then he walked up to Radcliffe and jerked off the man's waistcoat while Radcliffe screamed with more pain. Mitch felt inside the coat and found an inside pocket in the silk lining. He reached into it and pulled out the delicate gold lace necklace. He held it up to Randy and Len. "This is what he killed Emma's mother and then came after Emma for."

"Holy shit!" Randy exclaimed. "I ain't never seen nothin' like that!"

Mitch carried the necklace over to his horse and dropped it into one of his saddlebags. "This necklace belonged to a member of the royal English family," he told Len. "How about that?"

Len shook his head. "I think you're right in finding a safer place than Alder for that thing."

Mitch nodded. He removed his saddlebags and walked up to Len's horse, throwing them over Len's saddle. "And now you know how much I trust you. Keep an eye on the necklace for a while. When we get back to Alder, things will be pretty wild and I might have a lot of distractions. You ride on over to the bank and have Jim Powers put my saddlebags in his safe till I come for them. Don't tell him what's inside."

Len nodded, mounting up. Mitch walked closer to Radcliffe again and jerked him to his feet. Radcliffe glared at him with dark eyes that spoke of evil, and Mitch could see how the man so easily terrorized Emma.

"Do you...realize who I am?" Radcliffe sneered at Mitch.

"Do you realize who *I* am? I'm a vigilante, Radcliffe, and you're the stinking rat-snake sonofa-bitch who was stupid enough to come to Montana to beat on a helpless young woman, your own *niece*, to boot! You gambled away your fortune, and you gambled with your life by coming here to try to steal the necklace!"

"I am a...wealthy...respected businessman...from New York...City," Radcliffe panted, "where the law...is handled professionally...by proper lawyers... and civilized...policemen...and fair judges. You can't...touch me...here. The government will...send out...investigators if something...happens to me!"

Mitch grinned. "Mister, you're in Montana now. There isn't a man alive, no matter how important he might be back East, who can help you out here. You tried to choke my wife to death, and before this day is out, you'll feel a rope around your own neck! A lot of people in Alder love Emma, and you'll likely face a mob when we get back. When a man is hung by a mob, he doesn't die right away by getting his neck snapped, because ordinary angry townspeople don't know a damn thing about the proper way to tie a noose. They won't wait for a trial or a gallows to be built either. They'll just string you up like a deer that's being gutted, and you'll slowly feel the air being choked out of you, and your face will turn purple, and you'll kick till everything finally goes black. I've *seen* that kind of hanging, and I'm going to enjoy watching *you* hang that way."

Radcliffe trembled with pain and terror. "You're a *lawman*! You can't legally let that happen!"

"I'm a *vigilante*. And out here, there is a very thin line between vigilantes and *outlaws*, Radcliffe." Mitch grabbed Radcliffe, and in spite of the man's size, Mitch literally threw him over his horse. Radcliffe screamed with pain. "Throw me a rope, Randy!" Mitch told the boy.

Randy quickly obeyed, and before Radcliffe could try to turn his body and sit up in his saddle, Mitch grasped his wrists and tied a loop around them, then brought the rope under the horse's belly and looped the rope around Radcliffe's ankles, jerking tight so that Radcliffe was hog-tied to his horse facedown.

"Let me up!" Radcliffe screamed.

"This is how a rancher brings in stray calves, Radcliffe—but then, you wouldn't know much about ranching or any other way of life out here in Montana, would you?" He leaned close to where Radcliffe's head hung down. "I'd like to take credit for bringing you in, but I can't. Seems that one little bullet from one little woman is what did you in, Radcliffe. It drained the energy out of you." He looked over at Len and Randy. "We'll chalk this one up to Emma," he told them. "Don't you think she deserves that?"

"Sure enough does," Len answered.

Randy nodded, grinning.

"I guess showing her how to use that little pepperbox paid off," Mitch added. "I told her it worked best up close, and by God, it sure does." He walked over to his own horse and mounted up, wincing and rubbing his eyes.

"You okay, Mitch?" Len asked "You just lifted a man who must weigh a good two hundred pounds or more."

"I'll be all right." Mitch glared at Radcliffe. "Let's get that bastard to Alder and let the people there decide what to do with him. I have to get back to Emma, plus I have to see if Doc has something for this headache."

Len looked over at Randy. "Pick up the reins to Radcliffe's horse and let's get back to Alder."

"Sure enough." Randy took hold of the reins and headed back east. Mitch followed, enjoying the groans and screams that came from Radcliffe's lips as his body was jostled with every step his horse took.

Len followed behind, nervous over the responsibility of taking care of what was in Mitch's saddlebags. He shook his head at the realization that Mitch had married someone who came from money and could probably buy half of Montana for him. *And I'll bet he never lets her*, he thought. Radcliffe had murdered and risked prison and a hanging for that necklace, while Mitch wouldn't want anything to do with it. *And that's why little Miss Emma loves him.*

Thirty-five

WORD SPREAD FAST THAT MITCH AND HIS MEN WERE returning with the mysterious stranger who'd beat Mitch Brady's wife and left her for dead. Most weren't quite sure of the whole story behind it. They only knew what happened, and most were itching for revenge.

A crowd gathered as soon as the men arrived with their half-dead culprit, and immediately the questions flew.

"Who is he, Mitch?"

"Why'd he beat on your wife?"

"Is he dead?"

"We're gonna hang him!"

As soon as Randy saw Boot Tully, he jumped down from his horse and started whaling on the town drunk. The crowd circled around them, and Len dismounted and walked over to pull Randy off the poor drunken and older Boot.

"He didn't know!" Len warned Randy. "People here like Boot!"

"What'd I do?" Boot asked, rubbing at a bleeding

lip with one hand and holding a flask of whiskey in the other.

"You took money from a stranger to start a fight and lure me away from Mitch's place!" Randy answered, enraged. "Didn't you wonder why that man paid you to do that?"

Boot shrugged. "Heck, no. He gave me whiskey money."

"And he walked over and nearly killed Emma Brady, you stupid drunk!"

Boot blinked, turning to look at the man Mitch brought in draped over his saddle. His eyes widened, and he looked up at Mitch. "I didn't know, Mitch! You gonna hang me?"

Mitch rubbed his aching head. "Not today, Boot. Just stay out of trouble, and don't offer information to complete strangers. Send them to me or Len or Randy with their questions."

Len remounted, and he and Mitch continued down the street, a growing crowd following them. Randy shoved Boot aside. "You let that man make a fool of both of us!" he spat at Boot. He remounted and rode to catch up with Mitch and Len. After Randy's row with Boot, the crowd was getting more worked up as Mitch and Len headed for the jail. A couple of men raised ropes in the air.

"Hang him now, Mitch! He nearly killed your wife!"

"No man oughta do what he done!"

Mitch turned his horse when they reached the jail. He put up his hand to quiet the crowd as best he could as Len and Randy untied Alan Radcliffe and pulled him off his horse. The man collapsed to the ground, his shirt and vest covered with blood. "Need…a doctor," he groaned weakly.

"This man murdered his wife back in New York," Mitch shouted. "She was Emma's mother! I'm not going to explain all of why Emma fled this man and came to Alder, or why he came here and tried to kill Emma. I can only tell you she had good reason to fear for her life, and that it's a fact Alan Radcliffe murdered her mother and tried to kill Emma. Where's Judge Brody? Is he back from his circuit yet?"

"Right here!" The bearded and aging Judge Leonard Brody moved through the crowd to stand closer to Mitch. He frowned at the sight of a groaning, bleeding Alan Radcliffe lying in the street. "Who shot him?" he asked Mitch.

"Emma did when he attacked her yesterday. It was obviously self-defense."

"What about his hand?"

"I shot his rifle out of that hand when he intended to use it on me," Mitch answered.

"And Emma testified to you that he murdered her mother?"

"She did. He pushed her down the stairs and she broke her neck."

Judge Brody scratched at his beard, then stepped up onto the boardwalk in front of the jail. With his deep barrel of a voice, he made the pronouncement. "I find this man guilty of murdering his wife and attempting to murder Emma Brady. I sentence him to be hanged!"

"Wait a minute!" someone shouted. It was lawyer Carl Jackson. "The man deserves some kind of defense!"

"Who's gonna defend him, Jackson?" A man from the crowd stepped forward, holding a shotgun. "You?"

Jackson looked around. "Well, it's…it's just how things are done."

"You go take a look at Mitch's wife and then tell us he needs defendin'," another spoke up. "And how about her ma—layin' dead in her grave cuz of this sonofabitch!"

"Maybe we should hang you, too, Jackson!" another shouted. "Everybody in town knows what a shyster you are!"

Jackson backed away and waved them off. "Do what you're going to do," he grumbled, walking away.

The crowd went wild and pounced on Alan Radcliffe. Neither Mitch nor Len tried to stop them. Randy actually joined them as they dragged a screaming Radcliffe away. Radcliffe begged them to stop, cursed Mitch for not properly conducting his arrest, cursed the judge for his hoax of a trial, cursed the vigilantes as nothing better than murdering outlaws.

Mitch looked at Len. "Are you a murdering outlaw?"

Len grinned. "Fact is, I used to be one."

Mitch shook his head. "Damn. I always suspected as much."

"I just decided to use my gun for good instead of bad. Can I stay on as a vigilante?"

"Depends. I offered you a different kind of job last night, if you will remember."

Len shrugged. "When you're ready to take that badge off your shirt, I'll consider working a ranch for you."

Mitch glanced at Doc Wilson's office. "Right now

I have to get my wife well. I also still need something for this blasted headache."

"You'd better get over to Doc's then—and stop slinging two-hundred-pound men around like babies."

They could hear more screaming up the street. Mitch saw a rope being flung over a post in front of the livery. "Seems they took Radcliffe's horse back to the livery for him." He watched men hoist Radcliffe back up onto the horse. "Look, he's even still riding it," Mitch commented.

Someone put a noose over Radcliffe's head and tightened it while another man tied his hands behind his back. Someone smacked the horse's rump and the animal took off.

"He's not riding the horse anymore," Len added.

Both men watched Radcliffe swing, his legs kicking in a desperate attempt to keep breathing.

Mitch shook his head. "That kind of hanging is pretty ugly, isn't it?"

"Yup." Len sighed deeply. "I'm going to the bank with these saddlebags. Then I'm going over to the Saddleback Saloon and have a drink. Then I'm gonna look up Sarah."

Mitch nodded. "Have yourself a good time." He remounted and trotted his horse over to Doc's. When he got there, Doc walked out to greet him.

"Glad you're back, Mitch. Emma's doing pretty darn good and wanted to go home. She's there now with Hildy. I sent Sarah home. She was pretty worn out."

Mitch nodded. "You sure she was well enough to go home?"

"I wouldn't have let her go if she wasn't."

Mitch breathed a sigh of relief as he rubbed the back of his neck. "You got more of that tonic for a headache?"

The doctor nodded. "Give me a minute." He stepped inside and returned a moment later with a small brown bottle. He handed it up to Mitch. "Drink some of this and go lie down with your wife. You both need rest and you need to be together."

Mitch took a swig of the tonic.

"Not too much, or you'll get a worse headache from the damn tonic!" Doc warned.

Mitch grinned and slammed the cork back into the bottle. "You sure this isn't just whiskey?"

"It's not, but I'd advise not drinking any whiskey after you've taken that stuff."

Mitch nodded. "I'll keep that in mind." He turned his horse and headed for the other end of town—to the little cabin he and Emma called home. He dismounted and walked inside.

"Mitch!" Hildy rose from the rocker to greet him. "She's doing good, Mitch."

Mitch removed his hat and guns. "Thanks, Hildy. You can go now. Take my horse to the stables for me, will you?"

"Sure, Mitch." Hildy pressed his arm. "We're all real sorry, Mitch. I hope she gets completely well real soon."

Mitch patted her hand. "Thanks, Hildy. We both just need some peace and quiet now for a while."

Hildy left, and Mitch watched the look of relief on Emma's face as he walked over to the bed. He sat down on the edge of it and pulled off his boots and unbuckled his guns, hanging them over the bedpost. Nothing was said until he climbed, fully dressed, into bed, collapsing beside Emma and pulling her close but being careful not to hold her too tightly because of her ribs. "I wanted to die when I saw what that man did to you yesterday. I'm so goddamn sorry, Emma. I broke my promise."

"You didn't know," she whispered, unable to fully use her voice yet. "Nobody knew." She grasped his forearm, kissing it. "I'm glad…you're home safe."

Mitch held her in that way he had of making her feel totally safe and loved.

"It didn't take much. You're the one who caught him, Emma. That bullet in his side slowed him down and sapped his strength. You dealt your own justice this time."

Emma shivered in a choking sob. "When I saw those eyes again…"

Mitch wished he could hold her tighter but was afraid of hurting her. "It's over, Emma. He's out of your life forever."

Emma winced with pain.

"We could have stopped the hanging," he told her, kissing her hair again. "Len and I declared what he did and Judge Brody went along with it, convicted him and sentenced him…and the town took him away… and Len and I just sat and watched."

Emma lay there a moment to catch her breath, then put her fingers to his lips. "You look so tired," she said in an ugly, raspy whisper that tore at Mitch's gut. "Just sleep, Mitch. It's all right…what you did. I don't… blame you…for what happened to me…or for how that man died. I just want to lie here…and enjoy the wonderful peace…of knowing he's gone."

Mitch kissed her gently. "I can't stand those bruises, the pain in your eyes."

Emma closed her eyes. "You have to stop blaming yourself…for your mother…for me. Please just sleep, Mitch."

He let her settle into his shoulder. Before they fell asleep, they heard Randy and Len outside the door.

"Len, I thought you were goin' to see Sarah," Randy said.

"I am. I came over here to make sure everything was okay."

"I seen Mitch go in there and we ain't gonna bother them. I'm gonna stand right here and make sure nobody else does either. I don't need you to help out."

"If Mitch is in there, even *you* don't need to be out here either. Besides, there isn't a soul left in this town who'd want to bring either one of them any harm. Why don't you go visit Hildy or something? She's done a lot for Mitch and Emma. Go thank her in her favorite way."

"You're an ass, Len Gray, a damn whorin' outlaw."

"And I'm enjoyin' life to the fullest."

Mitch quietly grinned as the two kept exchanging barbs as they walked away, their voices fading.

"Oh, my…God," Emma whispered. "How did I… end up falling in with such men?"

Mitch closed his eyes, glad that Doc Wilson's tonic was finally taking effect. "Beats me," he answered. He just then realized that Emma hadn't even asked about the necklace. She was probably more relieved to know Alan Radcliffe was dead than worried about what had happened to it.

Thirty-six

TEN MORE DAYS PASSED, AND MITCH SPENT EVERY hour nursing Emma, feeding her, helping her to the privy out back, carrying the water, cooking, bathing her, washing her hair, putting creams on her face and body, helping her change into clean nightgowns. She finally had to order him to let her dress and stay out of bed for the day.

"And shouldn't you be out there patrolling the streets or something?" she asked. Her voice was back but still hoarse.

"You trying to get rid of me, woman?"

"No." They sat at the table drinking coffee. "Never." Emma smiled at him. "But you have to be tired of this, Mitch."

"Not when it comes to taking care of you."

"Well, I'm not a helpless waif, and I want to get back to a normal life—maybe even plan that trip to Virginia City and get started teaching. We need to get on with life, Mitch, and you need to put your guns and badge back on and go out there and do what you do best. There are no threats to me here in Alder anymore. You have to stop treating me like I'm a piece of china."

"You are, to me."

"And I love you for that, but I'm also stronger than you give me credit for, and I have an independent streak, like my grandmother, I guess. I want to teach, Mitch, unless and until I become a mother. Then I'll devote my life to our children, but I intend to do all my own cooking and chores and whatever comes with being a wife out in this country. I can do it."

Mitch studied her lovingly. "I have no doubt about that."

"And for right now, I want to get dressed by myself."

He nodded and rose. "Okay, I will put on my guns and my badge and go out there and see what Len and Randy are up to—no good, I expect. They're probably both sacked out with Sarah and Hildy and nobody is keeping an eye on things."

Already dressed, he took his gun belts from where they hung near the door. He'd finished strapping one on when someone knocked at the door.

"Who is it?" Mitch asked.

"It's Len. I've got some New York City man here with me—came in on the morning stage, looking for Emma. Says his name is Cabel Brown from the New York City Police Department."

Emma gasped. "Mitch! They've come for me!" She backed away.

Mitch walked over to her and grasped her arms. "Emma, do you really think one person here would let that happen? Now go put on a robe."

"Mitch, I know who Cabel Brown is. I remember

him from social parties Alan used to have at the mansion. Alan used to bribe men like Cabel Brown. The man arrests people!"

"Emma! This is Montana, and I'm still the law here. Nobody is going to come here and arrest *anybody* without my say-so. Now put on your robe and sit down at the table. Don't you be worried or afraid for one second."

Emma's heart pounded as she walked to a hook on the wall and took down her robe. She quickly pulled it on, ignoring the pain of her still-healing rib. She walked over to the table, sitting down and folding her arms nervously, glad she'd already washed her face this morning. Mitch had combed out her hair for her and it was pinned back at the sides. She was reasonably presentable but wished she was dressed.

Len rapped on the door again. "Mitch, I already disarmed this guy. He says he's here with some news and not to arrest anybody."

Mitch went to the door and opened it. Cabel Brown looked Mitch up and down with obvious surprise. Hesitantly, he stepped inside, looking like a very small man as Mitch towered over him.

"I, uh, I'm not here to cause any trouble."

Mitch nodded. "That would be wise."

"You want me to stay?" Len asked.

"No. Thanks for checking him out first and coming here with him."

"Yeah, well, nobody from New York City is gonna get far in this town anymore, that's for sure." Len nodded to Brown. "When you're done here, you can come back to the sheriff's office and get your weapon."

Brown frowned with obvious irritation. "I am a

member of the New York City Police Department. I assure you I'm not here to shoot someone. You really have no right—"

"You're in Montana, mister," Mitch interrupted. "We have a right to ask whatever we want of strangers, even a policeman from New York. Like Len said, you'll get your weapon back when we're finished here." He turned to Len. "Go ahead. We're okay here."

"I see you're wearing your gun. You gonna get off your lazy ass and get back to work soon?"

Mitch gave him a shove. "I figured I'd just lie around and let you and Randy handle everything."

Len grinned and tipped his hat to Emma. "You're lookin' much better, sweetheart," he said, then walked off.

Mitch closed the door, coming around to offer Brown a chair. "Sit," he told him, taking a chair himself.

Brown cleared his throat and removed his black felt hat, looking at Emma. "Hello, Emma."

Emma nodded. "I certainly never expected to see you of all people here in Alder, Mr. Brown."

"Well, from what I know, I'm sure you *did* worry you might see me."

Emma glanced at Mitch, who kicked Brown's chair out a little farther. "Sit and say your piece," he told the man with a warning look. "And don't be saying anything to alarm my wife. She's been to hell and back because of Alan Radcliffe, who I'm sure has something to do with why you are here."

Brown glanced at Emma again. "I assure you, I'm not here to bring anyone any harm." He sat down, and started to reach into his frock coat.

"Hold it!" Mitch told him.

"It's just some papers," Brown told Mitch. "Your thug of a friend already disarmed me, remember?"

"Take the papers out slowly," Mitch told him. "And if it's any kind of an arrest warrant, you might as well stop right where you are and head back to New York."

Brown shook his head. "I've heard a lot about you vigilantes."

"And you probably heard right, which is all the more reason to heed what I say. And don't refer to Len Gray as a thug. He's a good man, as good as any man in the police department in New York City."

Brown slowly removed the papers. "Yes, well, your fellow law officer told me about what happened here ten days ago." He looked at Emma. "I'm sorry, Emma. Actually, it all might have been prevented if I could have gotten here sooner. Once we learned the truth, we had to get new warrants and permits and such, and by then Alan had a head start on us."

"A head start?" Mitch asked. "What warrants are you talking about?"

Brown shoved a piece of paper over to Mitch. "This is a warrant for Alan Radcliffe's arrest, not Emma's."

Mitch frowned, looking the paper over. He handed it to Emma. "He's telling the truth."

Emma studied it. "The day he…attacked me, he seemed desperate. He seemed to just want an expensive necklace I owned and said he was headed for California." She glanced at Mitch. "Now we know why."

"What was he wanted for?" Mitch asked.

"Rape and murder," said Brown. He frowned with concern. "I'm sorry to talk about these things in front of you, Emma, but it seems the man drugged and raped a young woman who came from a wealthy family. I can't tell you her name because she doesn't want too many people to know, but she was very brave about it and told the prosecutor. Her bravery came from one of Alan's maids, who confessed she'd seen Alan push your mother down those stairs and then…drag you off."

Emma closed her eyes against the horrible memory. "It must have been Bess who finally told you."

"Yes, well, this young girl's family promised her a job for life if she'd tell us the truth. She also saw Alan drug the girl and carry her to his room. We put a lot of facts together and figured out why you ran off. You should have come to us, Emma."

"Alan Radcliffe had all of you in his pocket," Emma answered. "And without a witness like Bess, I would have been arrested for killing my own mother. After I ran off, Alan probably also had you believing I stole from him."

Brown ran a hand through his hair. "Yes, well, be that as it may, Prosecutor Hayes said that he sends you his apologies and regrets. And the fact remains that I came out here searching for Alan Radcliffe to arrest him and take him back to New York." He turned to Mitch. "It is my understanding that you vigilantes already, uh, took care of the matter."

Mitch rose and walked over to a cupboard drawer where he kept prerolled cigarettes. "We took care of it, all right. You might say Emma took care of it. She managed to shoot Alan in the midst of him attacking her. The bullet slowed him down enough that he was an easy catch." He came to the table and removed the chimney from an oil lamp, lighting his cigarette and then replacing the chimney. "Once we got to town, the people here were riled up so much that we held a quick trial right then and there. Judge Brody sentenced Radcliffe to be hanged and the crowd carried out the sentence."

"And of course you couldn't stop them, even though vigilante law rules here and this whole town would probably stop in its tracks if you pulled that gun and told them to back off."

Mitch took a deep drag on the cigarette, sharing a knowing look with Brown. He exhaled. "They knew Radcliffe had murdered Emma's mother and he came real close to killing Emma. She still isn't fully recovered."

Brown glanced at Emma and nodded. "Well, considering that his crime of murder happened in New York, we would have appreciated it if you'd saved him for us, but then, you had no idea that we knew the truth and were after him ourselves."

"And I don't care how important the man was back in New York. Out here, he was of no importance at all," Mitch answered. "What are those other papers you brought?"

Brown cleared his throat again. "One is for Emma to sign verifying she witnessed Alan kill her mother. The other gives me permission to find an attorney to handle Alan Radcliffe's personal possessions, his businesses, home, valuable paintings, horses and carriages, any money in the bank and such, on behalf of Emma, so she gets her fair share. She'd have to come to New York—"

"No," Emma interrupted. "I'll never go back to New York, and I don't want anything that belonged to Alan Radcliffe. Give it to the poor or the state or whatever is done with unclaimed wealth. I highly doubt there was much left anyway, Mr. Brown, and I don't want anything to do with anything that represents that man. All I want is what was rightfully mine, and I brought that with me when I left—a necklace that belonged to my mother, and some money that was also hers. I admit I did take a little cash from one of Alan's dresser drawers. I can give it back if you wish."

Brown raised his eyebrows in surprise. "Considering what he did to you, I don't think a few dollars you took from him will matter. Are you sure you don't want to claim any of his remaining fortune?"

"There *is* no fortune, Mr Brown. And no, I don't want any of it." She looked at Mitch. "Is that all right with you?"

Mitch shrugged, taking another pull on the cigarette. "You know how I feel about it. What's yours is yours, to take or to refuse."

"Mr. Brady, it could be a lot of money," Brown explained.

"And I'm not stupid, Mr. Brown. I just don't want it. I didn't marry Emma for how rich she might be. Fact is, I didn't even know she *did* have anything of value when I decided I wanted to marry her. I married her because she's sweet and beautiful and was so alone I couldn't stand it. I was alone, too, and we both know about childhood tragedy. I promised her when I asked her to marry me that I didn't care about her past and didn't care if she could make me rich. I just plain love her. Is that anything you can understand?"

"It is, Mr. Brady." He looked Mitch over. "And it seems your feelings belie your size and rough exterior."

"Mitch is a good man, Mr. Brown," Emma put in. "Cross him and you'll wish you hadn't, but it's not that way with those he cares about. I'm happy, and I thank you for coming here and clearing things up. It must have been a long trip. If you need to rest up before you go back, you can stay at a boardinghouse called Ma Kelly's. She'll put you up."

"I'll do that." He moved a piece of paper in front of Emma. "That document gave your permission for me to choose an attorney to handle your affairs. If you would put something there in your own hand-writing stating you want nothing from the estate, I can use that to proceed with dispensing Alan's belongings and holdings."

"Gladly." Emma took the ink pen the man handed her. She dipped it into a small bottle of ink she kept on the table. Brown turned his attention to Mitch as she wrote.

"Police work out here must be vastly different from police work in New York."

Mitch grinned. "Vastly." He put out his hand then. "Sorry to be so rude, Brown, but we thought you might be here to try to arrest Emma."

Brown shook his hand. "I have a feeling I never would have gotten out of town with her."

Mitch squeezed his hand. "You're damn right."

Both men laughed lightly as Emma handed Brown the paper. He looked at Mitch. "May I draw something up to the effect that Alan committed crimes out here and was hanged? I need something official."

Mitch rose. "Tell Len back at the jail to take you to Judge Brody. He'll write something up for you."

"Good." Brown picked up his hat from the corner of his chair and put it on, glancing at Emma. "Again, Emma, I'm sorry for everything you've suffered at Alan Radcliffe's hands. Fact is, we are finding out a lot of people back in New York were relieved to know he was going to be arrested."

Emma smiled sadly. "I have no doubt of that, Mr. Brown. And please do thank the young girl who was brave enough to come forward and tell the prosecutor what he'd done to her. That took courage. If she wants to write me or something, I would welcome hearing from her. Sometimes it helps to share something like that with someone else who understands."

"I'll do that." Brown tipped his hat and Mitch followed him to the door, opening it.

"Ma Kelly's place is down to the left, toward the other end of town," Mitch told Brown.

Brown nodded and left. Mitch and Emma stood there watching for a moment, and Emma thought how Cabel Brown was taking all her fears and worries with him. Mitch moved behind her and wrapped her into his strong arms. "It's really over now, Emma."

She leaned against him. "Are you sure you're all right with me giving up whatever I might have inherited?"

"Do you really have to ask that?"

Emma turned to face him, moving her arms around his middle and taking joy in his gentle strength. She pressed her face against his chest and breathed in his manly scent. "I never want to go back there, Mitch. I want to stay right here in Montana. Home for me isn't a place. It's right here in your arms, no matter where we go or what we do." She looked up at him. "And I want to remind you once more that if we need money, I'll sell the necklace."

Mitch shook his head. "That necklace is your heritage—something to pass down to your own children someday."

"*Our* children."

Mitch leaned down and kissed her tenderly. He moved his lips to her neck. "I might remind you we don't *have* any children yet."

Emma caught his lips in another kiss. "Maybe we should get to work on that."

Mitch frowned. "I might hurt you. You aren't ready for that, Emma. Your rib isn't healed."

"And no man can be more gentle than you can. I have a feeling you can figure a way around it."

Mitch grinned and picked her up in his arms, kicking the door shut and letting the wooden latch fall into place on its own. "It's a damn good thing we have curtains," he told her, carrying her to the bed. He took his gun belt back off and hung it over a bedpost.

READ ON FOR AN EXCERPT FROM

Outlaw Hearts

COMING SOON FROM
SOURCEBOOKS CASABLANCA

From the author…

Outlaw Hearts is the story of wanted man Jake Harkner, who became an outlaw because of a traumatic childhood that led him to think there was no other way to live…until he met a woman who completely changed his life…and his hardened heart. Together they struggle through a life on the run while raising a family, until the law finally finds Jake. This story is about the power of love, a love that is strong enough to see through an outlaw's heart into the goodness that lies deep inside, a love that overcomes all obstacles to hold two people together against all odds. This book was so dear to me that when I finished it, I knew I had to write a sequel. Recently I did just that, and along with the reissue of *Outlaw Hearts* in 2015, the sequel, *Do Not Forsake Me*, will also be published, continuing the beautiful love story of Jake and Randy Harkner, and bringing the readers into the lives of their grown children, who possess the same qualities of strength and enduring love as their parents. I'd like to share with you an excerpt from *Outlaw Hearts*.

In chapter one, Miranda Hayes witnesses outlaw Jake Harkner shoot a man inside the Kansas City mercantile where Miranda is shopping. Startled and frightened, she pulls a small handgun from her purse and shoots Jake, thinking he might kill her, too. To her surprise, the dangerous-looking man just stares at her, seemingly dumbfounded, then stumbles out of the store and flees. Everyone in town praises Miranda's bravery in fending off a notorious wanted man, but secretly, Miranda can't help wondering if the man is perhaps not as bad as his reputation would dictate. He could have shot her, but he didn't, and now she feels guilty that the man has ridden off somewhere, wounded and in pain because of her.

In chapter two, Miranda, a widow living alone, goes home to her farm, where she finds a surprise waiting for her…

Two

SHE OPENED THE SHED DOOR, THEN GASPED WHEN she saw a strange horse inside the shed, nibbling away at fresh oats. The animal was still saddled, a rifle and a shotgun resting in boots on either side of the saddle.

Fear gripped Miranda in the form of real pain in her chest. Whose horse was this? She noticed a dark green slicker tossed over the side of the stall. It looked familiar. Hadn't Jake Harkner been wearing a slicker like that when she saw him in the store?

Every nerve end came alert as her gaze quickly darted around the shed, but she saw no sign of human life. She put her hand to the strange horse's flank and could feel that the animal was cool. Apparently it had been here for several hours. If so, where was the man who had ridden it?

She moved closer to study the animal, noticing dried blood on the saddle and stuck to the left side of the horse's coat. Whoever had ridden it was bleeding, which made it even more likely it was Jake Harkner! But why here? The man couldn't possibly know where she lived! And where was he? Waiting for her? Hiding somewhere, ready to shoot her down in revenge?

She put a hand to her head, which suddenly ached fiercely. Her heart pounded so hard she could feel it in her chest. She felt like a fool for not checking everything more thoroughly before Sheriff McCleave left. Now he was too far away to even hear a gunshot.

She moved past the draft horses to the wagon and reached under the seat to take out her father's Winchester that she always kept there. She cocked the rifle and looked around, holding the gun in a ready position.

"Wherever you are, come out now!" she said sternly, trying to sound unafraid. Her only reply was the soft quiet of the early evening. She checked around the shed once more, then walked back outside, her eyes glancing in every direction, her ears alert. She checked behind the shed, scanning the open land all around the cabin. Since the raid, there were really no buildings left but the shed and the cabin, and the land was so flat, except for the high hill to the west, that there really were no good hiding places outside. Even the hill itself was treeless. That left only the cabin.

The cabin! Surely whoever owned the horse wasn't inside the cabin! And to think that she and Sheriff McCleave had been inside there themselves!

She slowly approached her tiny log home, walking completely around it, seeing nothing. She approached the root cellar at the north wall of the building, swallowing back her fear as she reached down and flung open the door, then pointed her rifle into the cellar. "Come on out if you're in there!" she demanded. "Just get out and ride away and no one has to be hurt!"

Again her reply was only silence. She moved around to fling open the other heavy metal door, wishing it were brighter outside so she could see better down into the small dugout. "Did you hear me? Come out of there!" She reached down and picked up a couple of medium-sized rocks, flinging them into the dark hole, but all she heard were thuds as they hit the dirt floor. She knew from the size of the cellar and the small space in the middle of the surrounding shelves that if someone was down there, she could hardly have missed him with the rocks.

She backed away then, watching the cellar a moment longer, before turning and heading for the cabin's front door, her heart pounding even more wildly. Unless the owner of the horse had just wandered off, the cabin was the only place left where he could be. She looked down and saw a couple of spots of what could be blood on her porch. Why hadn't she or the sheriff noticed it before?

She cautiously pushed open the door with the barrel of her rifle, then stepped inside. Everything still appeared to be in order. Raising the rifle to a ready position, she headed for her curtained-off bedroom, hoping she wasn't so worked up with fright that she would pass out if confronted. She moved to the wall and pressed her back against it, then peered around just far enough to peek through a crack between the edge of the curtain and the door frame.

At that moment Miranda Hayes thought perhaps her heart would stop beating altogether, and she found it impossible to stifle a gasp. "My God!" she whispered. There on her own bed lay Jake Harkner, apparently unconscious, one of his infamous revolvers lying on his belly. He must have been there the whole time, even when Sheriff McCleave was inside the cabin! How had he ended up here, in her house? Did he know she lived here? Had he come to kill her but been overcome by his own wound?

She stepped inside the room, quickly raising her rifle again when he moaned. She studied him a moment, noticing that his forehead and the skin around his eyes looked sickly pale. Blood stained the cotton blankets beneath him, and his forehead and hair were bathed in sweat as well as more blood from where Luke Putnam had slammed his rifle across Jake's head. She had worked enough with her father to know this was not a man ready to rise up and shoot her. He looked more like a dying man.

She moved a little closer, her rifle still in her right hand as she reached out with her left hand to cautiously take hold of the revolver resting on his stomach. He made no move to stop her. She turned and laid the gun on a chair, and mustering more courage, she reached across him and pulled the second revolver from its holster. When he still made no move to stop her, she set her rifle in a corner and then took the two revolvers hurriedly into the main room, placing them into a potato basket under a curtained-off counter. If he did come around, she didn't want him to be able to find his guns right away.

She hurried back to the bedroom, wondering what she should do. If she went to town for help, he could die before she got back, and she was not sure she wanted to be responsible for that. Besides that, it was getting dark, and she couldn't be traveling to town at night. There was nothing to do for the moment but try to help him.

"Mr. Harkner? Jake Harkner?" She spoke up, leaning closer.

Her only reply was a moan. She breathed deeply for courage and began removing his clothing—first his boots, then his gun belt and his jacket. It was a burdensome project. The man was a good six feet tall and built rock-hard. On top of that, in his present state, he was deadweight. With a good deal of physical maneuvering, she pulled off his pants and shirt and managed to move his legs up farther onto the bed and straighten out his body. She hurriedly gathered some towels and stuffed them underneath him as best she could, then unbuttoned and pulled open the shirt of his long johns so she could see the wound, a tiny hole just below his left ribs.

She knew from working with her father and from his medical books that most vital organs were on the right side of a person's body, and she also knew that the small caliber of her pistol could mean no terribly dangerous damage had been done. The biggest problem was that the man had bled considerably, which was probably the reason he had passed out; or she supposed it could be from the vicious blow he had taken to the head. He could have a fractured skull.

She felt underneath him, pressing her hand at his back at the inside of his long johns, trying to see if perhaps the bullet had passed through him, but she already knew that for the size gun she had used, that was unlikely. She felt no wound at his back, and the sick feeling returned to her stomach. The bullet was still inside him and should come out, and there was no one but her to do it.

She knew that the first thing she had to do was to get him to drink some water to replace the body fluids he had lost from blood and perspiration. She worked quickly then, going to get a ladleful of water from the drinking bucket in the main room and bringing it back into the bedroom. She raised Jake's head and tried speaking to him again, asking him to drink the water. All she got was another groan. She managed to pour some of the water into his mouth, and she watched him swallow. More ran out of his mouth and down to the pillow. From the looks of her bed and the man in it, she knew both needed considerable cleaning up; but for the moment, her biggest concern was getting out the bullet.

She went into the main room to get her father's doctor bag. "Why are you doing this, Miranda?" she muttered to herself. "Just let him die." Wouldn't society be better off? That was what Sheriff McCleave had said. Still, her Christian upbringing had taught her that every man had value, and she reasoned there had to be a reason why this man had led the life he led. Why had he killed his own father, if indeed that was true? She could not forget the strange sadness in his voice when he had told the clerk this morning that it took more than a war to make a man lead a lawless life.

She set the doctor bag on the table and quickly built a fire in the stone fireplace at the kitchen end of the cabin. She hung a kettle of water on the pothook to heat, then grabbed more towels and the doctor bag and went back into the bedroom. She watched Jake Harkner while the water heated. Had God led him here deliberately? Was she supposed to help him? To her it seemed a kind of sign, that for some strange reason, he was supposed to be a part of her life, that there was some purpose for his being here.

She took a bottle of laudanum from the bag and uncorked it, again leaning over Jake and raising his head slightly. "Try to drink some of this," she said. "It will help kill the pain. I've got to try to get out the bullet, Mr. Harkner. I doubt that it went very deep. It was a small gun I used, and the bullet had to go through your woolen jacket first."

"San...tana," he muttered. "I tried...sorry...Pa. Pa!"

The word "Pa" was spoken with a hint of utter despair. Miranda found herself feeling a little sorry for him, then chastised herself for such feelings. *If the man wasn't in such a state, you'd probably be dead by now*, she told herself. Again she felt like a fool for wanting to help him, yet could not bring herself to let him just lie there in pain. She shoved the slim neck of the bottle into his mouth and poured. Jake swallowed, coughed, and sputtered. "No, Pa," he murmured. "Stay...away. Don't...make me drink it!" His eyes squinted up and he pressed his lips tight when Miranda took the bottle away. He let out a whimper then that sounded more like a child than a man.

Miranda stepped back in astonishment. His whole body shuddered, then he suddenly lay quiet again. He had mentioned his father twice, the first time with such utter pain, this time with an almost pitiful, childlike pleading. The laudanum would take effect quickly. She went back into the main room and rummaged through a supply cabinet until she found some rope. She went back into the bedroom and used the rope to tie Jake's wrists and ankles to the sturdy log bedposts, afraid that when she started cutting into him, he would thrash around and make her hurt him more—or perhaps he would come awake and try to grab her.

"As soon as this is over and I see you don't have a fever, I'll give you a bath and a shave," she said as she fastened the ropes tightly. "You'll feel a lot better then. I don't mean you any more harm, Mr. Harkner." She had no idea if he heard her. She only knew she had to keep talking to keep up her own courage. She had seen her father remove bullets a couple of times, but she had no real experience of her own. All she knew to do was to dig with a knife, or perhaps she would have to reach inside the wound with her fingers to find the bullet. Somehow it had to come out.

She went back to the fireplace to find the water was finally hot. She poured some into a pan and brought it back into the bedroom, setting it on a small table beside the bed. She then retrieved a bottle of whiskey from her pantry, something her father always kept around for medicinal purposes only, for he had not been a drinking man himself.

She doused Jake's wound with the whiskey. His body jerked, but his eyes did not open. She poured more whiskey over her own hands and her father's surgical knife. She drew a deep breath then and said a quick prayer. "Heavenly Father, if you meant for me to do this, then help me do it right."

Fighting to keep her hands steady, she began

digging. Jake's body stiffened and a pitiful groan exited his lips, but he did not thrash about. Miranda fought tears as she dug deeper and more sickening groans welled up from what seemed the very depths of the man. She swallowed, then reached inside the wound with her fingers, feeling around until she touched what she thought must be the bullet.

"Please let it be," she whispered. She got hold of the object between two fingers and pulled, breathing a sigh of relief when she retrieved the bullet and held it up to look at it. She smiled with great delight, an almost victorious feeling coming over her then as she dropped the bullet onto the small table beside the bed.

She wet a cloth with the hot water and began washing around the wound to get rid of as much fresh and dried blood as possible. She poured more whiskey over it, then threaded some catgut into her father's stitching needle. She soaked some gauze with whiskey and ran it over the catgut, then doused the wound again with the same whiskey before beginning to stitch up the hole.

Hoping she'd done the right thing, she untied Jake's wrists and ankles and managed to get his arms out of his long johns so she could pull the top of them down under his hips. Then she wrapped the wound, reaching under his hard, heavy body over and over to bring the gauze around and then tie it. She decided then that all his clothes needed washing and realized the man could have another kind of accident while lying there unconscious. She pulled the long johns all the way off him and tossed them to the floor, then wrapped a towel around his privates and between his legs, feeling a little embarrassed, but knowing it had to be done. Any nurse in a hospital would have done the same. When it came to medicine, there was no room for modesty.

"I'll give you a good bath when I'm sure you're all right otherwise," she told him. There came no response. She removed her prize quilt from the bed, glad to see he had gotten no blood on it. She replaced it with an older blanket and covered him, but his legs were so long that his feet hung over the end of the bed. As she drew the blanket up to his neck, she noticed another scar at his left shoulder, a sign of stitches at his right ribs, and as she drew the covers to his neck, a strange, wide scar at the right side of his neck.

She dipped some gauze into the hot water then and began washing the wound at the side of Jake's head, noting that the blow of Luke Putnam's rifle had left a deep gash from just in front of Jake's left ear across his left cheekbone. An ugly blue swelling surrounded the cut. She cleaned it as best as she could and dabbed at it with more whiskey. "I'm afraid you're going to have another scar here," she said.

She jumped back when Jake's eyes suddenly flew open. He stared at her a moment, his dark eyes looking glassy and blank. "Santana?" he muttered. His eyes closed again. Miranda put a hand to her chest and breathed deeply to stop her sudden shaking. Was she crazy to do what she had just done? She clenched her fists, forcing herself to stay calm. The man certainly couldn't do her any harm tonight, and he didn't even know where his guns were.

She went back into the bedroom to get her rifle.

The man still lay quietly resting. She hoped it was more of a sleep now than unconsciousness. She took the rifle and set it over near her father's cot in the main room. She stoked up the fire against what she knew would be a chilly night in spite of the warm day. She straightened, then rubbed her hands at her aching lower back. She longed to just lie down now, but she remembered the poor draft horses were still in harness. She lit one lantern and set it on the table, then lit another and carried it outside.

It was dark out now, which made everything seem more frightening. She hung the lantern in the shed and began the arduous task of removing the harness from the horses, a job difficult for most men and doubly difficult for her small arms, especially tonight, when her whole body screamed from a day of emotional upheaval and a tenseness that brought physical pain. She took care of the horses, then realized that in her concern for them, she had left her own rifle inside the house. She quickly took down the lantern and closed the shed door, then hurried back to the cabin to find everything the same. She went into the bedroom to check on Jake once more, only to find he had not moved. His breathing was deep and rhythmic, and she thought his forehead already felt a little cooler.

She picked up his clothes and carried them into the main room, where she took down a wooden laundry tub and set it near the fire. She threw his clothes into the tub, poured hot water over them, and added some lye soap. She would scrub them and hang them out in the morning. At least that would leave the man even more helpless for the time being—not only would he not have his guns, but he wouldn't even have any clothes to put on!

She closed her eyes and tried to make herself sleep, realizing the much-needed rest was not going to come easily. It had been a long day. It was going to be an even longer night.

❦

From the author…

Well, dear readers, wait till you see Jake's reaction when he wakes up naked and without his guns the next morning! He is going to be one angry outlaw facing a very determined woman who stands right up to him…and the sparks begin to fly, leading to a love story you will long remember!

Acknowledgments

I'd like to acknowledge *The Vigilantes of Montana* by Thomas Dimsdale, originally written in 1864 and reprinted in 1953 by the University of Oklahoma Press.

Do Not Forsake Me

The much-anticipated sequel
to *Outlaw Hearts*

by Rosanne Bittner

USA Today bestselling author

❧

1890, Oklahoma Territory

Jake Harkner spent the first thirty years of his life as a notorious outlaw, until the love of Miranda changed his ways. Now Jake's grown son, Lloyd, rides with his father as a Deputy U.S. Marshal.

Still reeling from the death of his wife, Lloyd seeks fulfillment in work and doesn't pay enough attention to his young son until tragedy strikes again in the form of vengeful outlaws. Now it's up to Jake and Lloyd to scour the West for the missing boy, with the help of a young Cheyenne woman, Dancing Wind, whose unexpected kindness promises to make Lloyd's heart whole once more.

❧

Praise for Rosanne Bittner:

"Bittner sweeps readers away to the days of early Western romance." —*RT Book Reviews*

"Ms. Bittner has a way of bringing the pages and characters to life…" —*Romancing the Book*

For more Rosanne Bittner, visit:

www.sourcebooks.com

Paradise Valley
by Rosanne Bittner

❦

Maggie Tucker has just gone through hell. Outlaws murdered her husband, looted their camp, and terrorized Maggie before leaving her lost and alone in the wilds of Wyoming. She isn't about to let another strange man get close enough to harm her.

Sage Lightfoot, owner of Paradise Valley ranch, is hunting for the men who killed his best ranch hand. But what he finds is a beautiful, bedraggled woman digging a grave. And pointing a pistol at his heart.

From that moment on, Sage will do anything to protect the strong-yet-vulnerable Maggie. Together, they'll embark on a life-changing journey along the dangerous Outlaw Trail, risking their lives…and their love.

❦

Thunder on the Plains
by Rosanne Bittner

— ❦ —

In a land of opportunity

Sunny Landers wanted a big life—as big and free as the untamed land that stretched before her. Land she would help her father conquer to achieve his dream of a transcontinental railroad. She wouldn't let a cold, creaky wagon, murderous bandits, or stampeding buffalo stand in her way. She wanted it all—including Colt Travis.

All the odds were against them

Like the land of his birth, half-Cherokee Colt Travis was wild, hard, and dangerous. He was a drifter, a wilderness scout with no land and no prospects hired to guide the Landers' wagon train. He knew Sunny was out of his league and her father would never approve, but beneath the endless starlit sky, anything seemed possible...

— ❦ —

"Bittner has a knack for writing strong, believable characters who truly seem to jump off the pages."
—*Historical Novel Review*

"I hated having to put it down for even one second."
—*Romancing the Book*

For more Rosanne Bittner, visit:

www.sourcebooks.com

Wildest Dreams
by Rosanne Bittner

———— ❧ ————

*With more than 7 million books in print,
RT Book Reviews Career Achievement Award–
winning author Rosanne Bittner is beloved by fans for
her powerful, epic historical romances.*

Lettie McBride knew that joining a wagon train heading
West was her chance to begin anew, far from the devastating
memories of the night that had changed her forever. She
didn't believe she could escape the pain of innocence lost,
or feel desire for any man…until she meets Luke Fontaine.

Haunted by his own secrets, Luke could never blame Lettie
for what had happened in the past. One glance at the pretty
red-haired lass was enough to fill the handsome, hard-
driving pioneer with a savage hunger.

Against relentless snows, murderous desperadoes, and raiding
Sioux, Luke and Lettie will face a heart-rending choice:
abandon a lawless land before it destroys them, or fight for
their…Wildest Dreams.

———— ❧ ————

"Extraordinary for the depth of emotion." —*Publishers
Weekly*

For more Rosanne Bittner, visit:

www.sourcebooks.com

To Have and to Hold

A Cactus Creek Cowboys Novel

by Leigh Greenwood

USA Today bestselling author

———— ❧ ————

A stranger to the rescue

Colby Blaine has been a loner his whole life. And he isn't about to change now. But that doesn't mean he can ignore people in trouble. When he rides up on an inexperienced wagon train under attack, he doesn't hesitate to jump into the fray. It's only after the raid that he really lands himself in hot water...

Naomi Kessling is certainly grateful to Colby for saving her family and agreeing to lead their train to safer territory. But the man has an infuriating way of knowing just how to get under her skin—he asks too many questions about a past she doesn't want to remember, and his touch makes her long for far more. Yet the more time they spend together, the more Naomi sees that perhaps it's Colby who needs rescuing the most...

———— ❧ ————

"Perfect pacing, intriguing characters, and an unpredictable plot...a thoroughly enjoyable escape into the world of romance and adventure." —*Historical Novel Review*

"A keeper to be enjoyed more than once." —*Long and Short Reviews*

For more Leigh Greenwood, visit:

www.sourcebooks.com

To Love and to Cherish

A Cactus Creek Cowboys Novel

by Leigh Greenwood

USA Today bestselling author

— ❧ —

Torn between a desire to be free…

When Laurie Spencer said "I do," she never realized she'd be trading one pair of shackles for another—until her husband's unexpected death leaves her with an opportunity to escape her controlling family for good. Determined to be independent, Laurie approaches sexy rancher Jared Smith with an offer she hopes he can't refuse…

Jared's determined to make it in Texas, but with the local banker turned against him, it looks like his dream may be slipping through his fingers. When Laurie offers a partnership, it looks like his luck may be changing…but when she throws herself in as part of the deal, Jared's not sure he'll be able to respect the terms of their agreement and keep his eyes—and his hands—to himself.

There's something about Laurie that awakens every protective instinct Jared has…and when all hell breaks loose, there's nothing and no one who'll be able to keep this cowboy from her side.

— ❧ —

"Greenwood is a master at Westerns!" —*RT Book Reviews*

For more Leigh Greenwood, visit:

www.sourcebooks.com

About the Author

Award-winning novelist Rosanne Bittner is highly acclaimed for her thrilling love stories and historical authenticity. Her epic romances span the West—from Canada to Mexico, Missouri to California—and are often based on personal visits to each setting. She lives in Michigan with her husband Larry and near her two sons Brock and Brian, and three grandsons, Brennan, Connor, and Blake. You can learn much more about Rosanne and her books through her website at www.rosannebittner.com and her blog at www.rosannebittner.blogspot.com. Be sure to visit Rosanne on Facebook and Twitter!